THE ENCHANTED BIRD

CALATINI TALES BOOK 1

KATHERINE DOTTERER

KatSpell Press

The Enchanted Bird

Cover by 100 Covers

Edited by Susan Bischoff, Lauralynn Elliott

A KatSpell Press Book

- ISBN 978-1-955614-03-0 (ebook)
- ISBN 978-1-955614-04-7 (trade paperback)

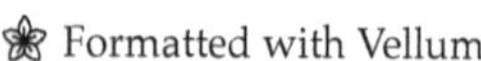 Formatted with Vellum

CONTENTS

ABOUT THE ENCHANTED BIRD

*C*alatini *is a kingdom suffused with magic. But strong spells come with high prices...*

Wren prefers a simple life of writing, reading, and volunteering at the orphanage to fashionable parties and balls at court. If she attends at all, it's because Hawke, the best friend she's secretly loved forever, convinces her. So when she learns his mother has arranged his marriage, she knows she must act. All she desires is a single night in Hawke's arms, so though she distrusts magic, Wren turns to a witch to create the perfect masquerade disguise infused in an enchanted bird.

Lord Beza—Hawke, to his friends—is a notorious rake, but he can't stop thinking about the mysterious lady who seduced him at the summer masquerade then disappeared. Fortunately, she left behind a clue: a small enchanted bird. And his clever best friend Wren will surely help him in his search—after all, wouldn't she want him to find love?

Never having dreamt Hawke would hunt for her, Wren is desperate to convince him to forget his "mysterious" lady—otherwise the enchanted bird will extract a growing price from them both. But their night of passion is impossible for either of them to forget...

THE ENCHANTED BIRD IS HEARTWARMING, **Regency-inspired fantasy romance at its finest, perfect for readers of Olivia Atwater's Regency Faerie Tales series,** *Miss Newbury's List,* **and Grace Burrowes' Rogues to Riches series of historical romance novels.**

CHAPTER 1

Wren nibbled her pen as she eyed her latest play for the orphanage. How could the talking cat and her bumbling master escape from the evil queen's slave pens? Not magic, since only magical creatures could generate magic, and the talking cat was no magical creature—they rarely ventured into human kingdoms since the catastrophic Stone Wars over a millennium ago. No, the talking cat was merely a house cat who'd tumbled into an enchanted pool and gained the ability to speak.

Wren shivered, her skin tightening. Besides, using magic might only worsen matters. Except for small spells with circumscribed influence, magic could be chancy to use. She'd learned that when she'd almost become addicted to a charmed pen eight years ago. After writing with it once, she'd burned to use the pen again and again, even after knowing it made her words true but twisted them. Why, she'd nearly killed that hapless troll the pen's magic had brought south in the middle of summer.

She sighed and returned to her play. Frowning, she tapped her pen against her lip as she reread the queen's abused handmaiden tending the new slaves' wounds. Instead of magic, perhaps the handmaiden could help them escape. But how?

Maybe by distracting everyone so the talking cat could concoct a plan...

Wren started at a knock on her door. Hawke, the best friend she'd loved forever, had probably come to visit. Since she rarely attended court events, few others bothered visiting when her parents were out. She grinned and swiveled from her desk. "Yes?"

Abby bustled inside Wren's chambers. "Lady Blaine is downstairs, Miss Wren."

Wren wilted with a grimace. Unlike Hawke, Kit wasn't a welcome visitor—the fashionable countess's calls were never pleasant. But she couldn't pretend she was out in order to avoid Kit. She trudged downstairs to the drawing room then paused at the threshold to brace herself before gliding inside. "Good morning, Kit. What brings you by?"

Her sable hair, smoky eyes, and porcelain skin as gorgeous as ever, Kit smirked at Wren from her seat. "We haven't seen each other often during my year of mourning for my dear husband, so I thought we should talk."

Wren forced a polite smile as she sat on the sofa across from Kit. She and Kit had never been close, even though they and Hawke were the same age and had grown up together on nearby country estates, along with Hawke's older brothers, Aragon and Mel. Plus, Kit loved needling her, whether by drawling sardonic innuendos, gifting her that wretched charmed pen, or stealing Hawke's first kiss. So Kit's visit today couldn't simply be to *talk*.

Kit's gaze flicked up and down Wren. "You appear as... well as ever."

Wren stiffened at the disdain shading Kit's drawl. Since they were girls, Kit had hinted Wren's ordinary beauty was lackluster. Yet being gorgeous wasn't enough to inspire love. Wren allowed her tone to sharpen as she replied, "And you appear dashing for a lady fresh from mourning."

Kit smoothed her sleek, burgundy gown. "Thank you. I purchased a new wardrobe from Celeste's yesterday. I was so weary of black." She gave Wren a sly glance. "While I was there, I saw your mother and the duchess."

Wren inclined her head. Mother had asked her to join them as she always did, but she'd refused so she could work on the orphanage play. Why did Kit appear so smug about Mother and her best friend dress shopping? "Celeste's *is* their favorite dress shop."

Kit's eyes glinted. "You should join them sometime. Celeste could do marvels with you—you might gain a suitor or two."

Except Wren despised dress shopping and cared nothing about gaining suitors. She was only interested in Hawke, but he'd never returned her interest, apart from a Longnight kiss when they were fifteen. A kiss he'd only attempted *after* kissing Kit the day before. So when he'd kissed Wren, she'd shoved him away and ordered him to stop. Despite loving him, she'd never be a dalliance to hone his rakish prowess. But that kiss was just the start; in the years since, he'd become a rakehell who found a new lover every few nights. And he told his best friend—her— all about them.

Her heart twisting, Wren thrust that aside and smiled at Kit. She mustn't show weakness. Kit would only use it as fodder to needle her. "I'll visit Celeste's one day."

Kit purred a chuckle. "Take care not to wait too long. You'll be a spinster soon, and not even being your elderly parents' only child and heir can atone for that."

Wren's lips tightened. Securing a husband wasn't the only aspiration in life, but she'd never convince Kit of that. Wealth and status had always preoccupied Kit, even when they were children, so she must end this pointless discussion. "If we're finished talking, I must return to writing my play for the orphanage."

Kit arched her brows and leaned forward. "But I haven't told you what I overheard at Celeste's yet. I promise you'll be interested."

Wren stilled at Kit's gloating tone. Kit was about to reveal her weapon at last. Finally. "Tell me then."

Kit nodded with a feline smile. "While waiting in the anteroom, I overheard the duchess tell your mother that she meant to see Hawke settled this season."

Wren's chest constricted. Settled? Settled with whom? Not Wren, or Kit wouldn't be here to gloat. She forced herself to nod. "I see."

Kit tossed her head. "The duchess didn't mention any ladies by name, but 'tis most interesting she spoke where I could overhear. And for her to wait until I came out of mourning..."

Wren paled. Surely the duchess wouldn't want *Kit* as a daughter-in-law. When just seventeen, Kit had beguiled the duchess's cousin into marrying her, even though his children were their age. She gulped a steadying breath. "The duchess has meant to see Hawke settled since Aragon asked Selena to marry him two years ago. Nothing has come of it so far."

Kit smirked at Wren. "I doubt the duchess devoted her full attention to settling Hawke before."

True. But Wren snorted and said, "Hawke is more intractable than a kelpie when he chooses." And the horse-like magical creatures were renowned for taking those attempting to capture them on wild rides in the depths of their watery homes. Such rides were often deadly to riders, although they were mere larks to kelpies.

Kit shrugged. "Perhaps, but even a kelpie must yield to an iron bridle eventually." In folk tales, iron was poisonous to magical creatures like the kelpie and could control them. "And the king's summer masquerade tomorrow shall be the perfect event to bridle him."

Wren's stomach knotted while she struggled to reply. Like Lord Blaine six years ago, Kit considered Hawke nothing more than a creature to capture, regardless of his or anyone else's feelings. If an iron bridle worked on humans, she'd have one on Hawke within moments of entering the masquerade.

Kit arched a brow then rose. "Now that I've shared my news, I'll let you return to your little play." She sashayed from the drawing room.

Wren retreated to her chambers but couldn't focus on the imaginary troubles in the orphanage play. Though she'd pretended to dismiss Kit's news, the duchess publicly discussing Hawke's betrothal was worrying. The duchess was a master meddler, and for her to discuss a private matter where she could be overheard meant she was determined this time. Hawke might end up betrothed before he realized what his mother was about.

She leapt to her feet. She must find Hawke and share his mother's plans. Abandoning her play, she rushed to his townhouse several streets over. Hopefully, he was at home and not attending a court event or dallying with yet another lover.

Her chest lightened when Hobb, Hawke's butler, told her Hawke was home and alone. She strode down the hall and burst into Hawke's study after a quick knock.

His inky-brown hair mussed as if he'd been teasing it like he did when upset, Hawke glanced up from his cluttered desk then grinned and leapt to his feet. "Afternoon, Wren."

She flung herself onto his sofa. He appeared pleased to see her, but 'twould change once she shared her news. "Afternoon. Kit just shared some worrying news."

Hawke's brows flew upward as he joined her on the sofa. "Oh?"

Her fingers itching to smooth his tousled hair, she nibbled her lip and studied his face. Speaking direct was best, even though her news would upset him. "She overheard your mother say she meant to see you settled this season."

Despite her warning, Hawke merely snorted. An impish glint flickered in his pale-blue eyes as he replied, "Mother has been saying that for years. Why such worry?"

Wren frowned at him. Hawke had yet to realize the implications of his mother's public disclosure. "Because the duchess spoke in public where Kit could overhear. I fear she's serious this time."

Hawke shrugged and shook his head. "So? No matter how serious, Mother's maneuverings shall accomplish nothing."

She pursed her lips. How could Hawke remain so nonchalant? Did he wish the duchess to see him settled? "Don't make light of your mother's maneuverings. She's the best meddler in all of Calatini. Look how she arranged Aragon's marriage."

Hawke snickered. "Aragon had rescued Selena from a black witch and a brothel. Anyone could see he was smitten and meant to marry her. Mother simply facilitated matters."

Wren slanted him a flat glance. How could she get him to see the danger? "I suspect she means to *facilitate* again."

Hawke waved a hand. "I shan't bring any ladies home from a brothel then."

Although she loved him, she ached to hit Hawke for being obtuse. But he'd heed her next words. "Kit assumes she'll be your chosen bride."

Hawke jerked back. "What?"

Wren nodded, her mouth crimping. "Why else would your mother wait until Kit was out of mourning? Summerday last month would have been ideal to see you settled." The summer festival of the Goddess celebrated fertility and courtship, so many couples married or handfasted then.

Hawke shuddered. "Mother can't want *Kit* as a daughter-in-law, and even if she did, I'd never marry Kit."

Wren tensed and narrowed her eyes at him. Hawke might not care to marry Kit, but he'd enjoyed kissing the sultry beauty before her marriage to Lord Blaine. If Kit pursued him, he'd kiss her again, and the duchess would see them betrothed within a week. She drawled, "Perhaps after years of rakehell behavior, your mother despairs of you ever marrying and shall settle for Kit."

Hawke snorted. "I doubt it. And why would Mother assume I'd be interested in Kit?" He shook his head. "Kit must be on the prowl for another husband and imagines marital plans where none exist."

A thrill darted through Wren when Hawke grasped her hands with a warm smile. Although they'd been best friends forever, Hawke rarely touched her unless escorting her somewhere. When he did, she yearned to lean in and kiss him.

Hawke squeezed her hands. "But to foil any plan Mother might have, I'll behave more scandalously than usual at the king's summer masquerade tomorrow."

Still struggling not to kiss him, Wren swallowed and licked her lips. "What could be more scandalous than your usual behavior? An orgy in the middle of the ballroom?"

CHAPTER 2

*H*awke suppressed a grimace. Wren was right. He'd have to be drastic to outdo his ordinary behavior and dissuade Mother. Perhaps Wren had a better idea. He squeezed her hands again. "What would you suggest instead?"

Wren's auburn hair shimmered as she tilted her head. "Perhaps if you pretended to pursue a suitable lady, your mother would relent."

He snorted. Mother was relentless once she decided to meddle. The only person who could get her to reconsider was Father, and he didn't always succeed. "Pursuing a marriageable miss would only encourage Mother."

Wren leaned forward. "I said you should *pretend* to pursue one."

Hawke snorted again and arched a brow. "Pretending would appear the same to Mother. Besides, I shan't trifle with any marriageable misses." 'Twould be cruel to raise their expectations when he'd no intention of marrying them.

Wren swallowed, her hazel eyes darting away. "You could pretend to pursue me. 'Twouldn't be trifling since I'd know 'twas counterfeit."

Hawke gaped at her, almost dropping her hands. Wren had been his best friend forever, and until eight years ago, he'd planned to marry her. He'd spent months plotting their first kiss on Longnight when they were fifteen. But she'd shoved him away then ordered him to *never* kiss her again. Her fury had shattered his childish dreams, and he'd never dared consider her in a romantic light after that. Instead, he'd begun pursuing various lovers since their come out, but none had captured his interest longer than a few weeks. Considering their lack of attraction and his many lovers, Mother would never believe he was pursuing Wren in truth.

Weight compressing his chest, he shook his head. "No one would believe that, but if Mother did for some reason, she'd see us married within a fortnight. You'd not want that."

Wren stilled as if turned to stone by a gorgon's gaze. "No, I suppose not." She gripped his hands. "But you can't allow your mother to marry you off. Don't you recall all those dreadful ladies she forced Aragon to meet before he found Selena?"

Hawke shuddered. His eldest brother had endured Mother's matchmaking with remarkable grace. He could never manage the same. Although he and his brothers all resembled Father except for Hawke's pale eyes, their temperaments were nothing alike. Hawke was far less patient than Father, Aragon, or Mel.

He grimaced. Fortunately, he'd managed to evade the worst of Mother's matchmaking by purchasing his own townhouse while Aragon was courting Selena. However, if Mother was serious about marrying him off, avoiding her would no longer be enough. Yet he'd find a way—marriage was a lifelong sentence. And he'd not marry unless he loved his bride, which seemed improbable given how swiftly he tired of his lovers.

He smiled at Wren. "Don't fret; I'll think of some way to foil Mother, starting at tomorrow's masquerade. Come and watch me."

Wren wrenched her hands free from his grasp. "Unlike *some*

people, I've better plans than a masquerade. I must finish my latest play for the orphanage."

He swallowed a sigh as memories of Wren's plays, rowdy larks, and childish giggles darted through him. He'd once been a frequent visitor at Waterstreet Orphanage, but tiresome court events had occupied his time for the past few years. "How are the orphans?"

Wren tilted her head. "Much the same. Some of the older boys ask after you every few months."

Hawke tensed and shifted in his seat. "I'll try to visit once the social season slows." Mother would notice otherwise and redouble her matchmaking. He couldn't risk that if she already meant to see him settled.

Wren nodded. "The orphans would like that. Especially if you bring your violin."

His fingers tingled as fiddle tunes echoed in his mind. The orphans so loved those, and playing for them was never dull. Unlike attending court events. "What's your latest play about?"

"A clever cat who rescues her bumbling master from an evil queen." Wren shrugged. "As usual, nothing deep, just something to amuse the children."

Hawke tsked. Wren never believed her clever plays were much, but the orphans adored them more than his fiddle tunes. "I'm certain they'll love it. As always."

A blush darkened Wren's cheeks. "Thank you, Hawke."

To distract her, he waggled his brows. "So you think I should start an orgy at the summer masquerade?"

Her blush fading, Wren blinked at him. "No..."

Hawke smiled. His distraction had worked—but he'd never actually start an orgy. Though his interest was fleeting, his affairs were exclusive while they lasted. Not that he'd bothered since last season. Pursuing lovers had become too tiresome. Yet he'd not admitted that to anyone, not even Wren. Shoving that aside, he flashed a crooked grin. "Too much perhaps?"

Wren's eyes narrowed. "Definitely."

He chuckled at her stern reply. "Well, how about a fast widow? But not one hunting a husband like Kit." The fashionable countess might be a sultry beauty, but she was even more manipulative than Mother. He'd witnessed her lure his cousins' father Lord Blaine into marriage, and he'd not become her next hapless victim.

Wren snorted. "You've been chasing them for the past five years. That shan't dissuade your mother."

Hawke sighed and shook his head. "True." Nothing so ordinary would dissuade Mother. But perhaps something magical could. "How about a spell repelling ladies who approach me?"

Wren wrinkled her nose. "You'd risk a potentially dangerous spell? Don't you remember my incident with the charmed pen? Magic is best avoided."

He arched his brows. Ever since using the charmed pen, Wren had been skittish about magic. "Surely a small charm wouldn't be dangerous." Such spells often had minimal magical costs, so most used them without hesitation. "Perhaps one making me reek like fish guts and sour milk left rotting in the summer sun."

Wren jerked back with a shudder. "That's vile." Then she shook her head. "But 'twouldn't succeed. You're the unwed son of a wealthy duke, so ladies would either ignore your stench or purchase a charm to destroy their sense of smell."

Hawke grimaced. She was right. So he must persist with dissuading Mother, but 'twould be wrong to use magic on *her*. He must make himself unsuitable for marriage instead. But how? He set his jaw. "Then my only option to foil Mother's meddling is to devise some scandal at tomorrow's masquerade."

Wren's lips tightened. "Do as you like. You always do." She rose. "I must return to the orphanage play. See you later."

He stared after Wren as she swept from his study. What else had Kit told her? Mother meaning to see him settled couldn't be all. Wren had been too perturbed for that. But Wren and Kit had never gotten along, even as children. Probably because Kit, the daughter of a gambling sot, had envied Wren's loving parents and comfortable fortune.

Hawke sighed and eyed the invitations he'd not bothered to sort for the past week. Unlike tangled female relationships, those he could handle. He grimaced at the heap on his desk without rising. Except he didn't want to handle them. Like pursuing lovers, court events had begun to pall during his first season years ago and had become unpalatable this summer. He'd only continued attending so Mother wouldn't notice his boredom and meddle. Yet she'd already decided to do so according to Wren.

He'd almost opened the first invitation when Hobb coughed and said, "The Duchess of Childes, my lord."

Hawke hid a wince when Mother entered. Goddess, what was she doing here just before luncheon? She was usually visiting Wren's mother Lady Keyes or attending court events. As Wren had said, Mother must be plotting his betrothal. He made himself to rise with a polite smile. "Good morning, Mother. What brings you by?"

Mother swept toward him as triumphant as the reborn Winter Queen in a Longnight play. "I'm here to invite you to luncheon. We've some news to share."

He tensed and narrowed his eyes. Their news had better not be about his betrothal. But he smiled and inclined his head. "How intriguing. I'd be delighted to come."

Mother's grin became even more blinding. "Excellent. Ride with me in my carriage."

Hawke sighed as he escorted Mother outside. She was definitely plotting something, and she adored nothing more than matchmaking. He must be vigilant to evade her. As he settled across from her on the backward seat, he asked, "So what's your news?"

"You'll hear soon enough." Mother's eyes gleamed as the carriage rumbled down the street. "Shall you attend Devon's masquerade tomorrow?"

He shrugged. "Most likely." After all, creating a scandal to foil her matchmaking should be simple at a masquerade.

Mother arched a brow. "What's your costume this year?"

Why did she wish to know? Hawke forced another shrug. "I've not decided yet." Or rather, he didn't have one. Until Wren had mentioned Mother's plans, he'd intended to miss the masquerade. Since everyone wore masks, no one would note his absence. "What are you and Father dressing as?"

Mother chuckled as the carriage slowed to a stop. "Your father and I aren't attending this year. Masquerades are for the young. The Keyes are coming over for a quiet evening instead."

He nodded and helped Mother alight. Although Wren's parents were a decade older, his parents had been their best friends long before he and Wren had been born. Their parents spent most of their time together; they had adjoining country estates, and only one neighbor separated their Ormas townhouses.

Hawke eyed Mother as he escorted her inside. But if his parents were spending a quiet evening with their best friends rather than attending the masquerade, why did Mother care what his costume was? What matchmaking scheme was she plotting?

Mother cocked her head. "Perhaps a horned man costume would suit."

He tensed. He'd not wear any costume she suggested while plotting his betrothal. "Perhaps."

His tension eased when they entered the family dining room. Not only was Father at the head of the table, but his brothers and Selena were seated as well. Joining them should distract Mother from tomorrow's masquerade. 'Twas rare for everyone to eat luncheon together. Although Aragon and Selena usually joined his parents, Mel often ate at the Great Temple where he lived and served, while Hawke preferred to eat luncheon at home or with Wren.

Hawke nodded at Father while escorting Mother to her seat.

Plus, Father would probably temper her meddling. Although he adored his wife, he always nurtured his sons' independence.

Father chuckled with a crooked grin. "From her prompt return, Caro must have found you at home. How unexpected. I thought she might miss luncheon entirely. But she was determined to fetch you."

Hawke shrugged as he sat between Father and Mel. Since lovers and court events bored him, he'd remained home most mornings this summer. But admitting that would shatter his rakish facade. To distract everyone, he winked at Selena across the table. Flirting with her never failed to rile Aragon.

As expected, Aragon's eyes narrowed. "I'm surprised Mother could drag you from your latest lover."

Hawke gritted a crooked grin as the servants brought the first course. "Mother insisted, and my lover shall wait." Indefinitely, considering she didn't exist. "I tied her to the bed to make sure."

Selena giggled while Aragon served her cucumber soup, then she said, "You did no such thing."

To sell his pretense, Hawke smirked then winked at her again over his wine glass. "Didn't I?"

As Aragon tensed and Selena touched his hand, Mel shook his head and said, "I hope you intend to bring back some food for the poor lady." Unsurprising his priest brother worried about a nameless woman.

"I had my servants feed her." Hawke waggled his brows over his roast lamb. "She'll require sustenance for what I have planned."

Father guffawed. "I imagine so if you tied her to the bed."

Mother pursed her lips at her husband. "Eldridge, don't encourage Hawke. He'll never secure a suitable wife if he continues acting the rakehell."

Hawke shuddered and quaffed his wine. No doubt Mother already had candidates in mind. He'd flee if 'twasn't the middle of luncheon. Plus, Mother hadn't revealed her news yet. "A suitable wife wouldn't suit me at all."

A smile curved the edges of Mother's lips. "Wouldn't she?"

Father arched his brows at her as the servants brought the second course. "I'll stop encouraging Hawke if you stop teasing him."

Mother chuckled as Mel served her grilled scallops. "Very well. Perhaps we should tell Mel and Hawke our news instead."

CHAPTER 3

As the carriage turned on a street leading to the docks, Wren sighed and gathered the canvas sack of golden-red starpeaches she'd brought for the orphans. After storming back from Hawke's, she'd headed straight to Waterstreet Orphanage to distract herself. Yet she'd spent the hour ride across Ormas brooding about Hawke.

Goddess, why had the stubborn fool ignored her warning? If he remained so nonchalant, the duchess would have him betrothed within a month. Her ribs seizing again, she clenched the canvas sack in her lap. Everything would change then. He'd belong to another, and she'd be left with nothing but her unrequited love. The closest she'd come to having a family would be the orphans.

Once the carriage halted, she quashed her brooding and leapt out with a bright smile. "Afternoon, Peter. Where's Kiera?" Kiera was the orphanage matron and Wren's best female friend. Talking to Kiera always grounded her, so hopefully, Kiera would ease the ache filling her chest at Hawke's imminent betrothal.

The burly porter shook his head. "She'd fetchin' the Bedsford twins for luncheon. They snuck out again."

Wren tsked, her tension lightening at the twin's antics. "Those scamps." She glanced past the worn rowhouses to spot her friend. "I see her and the twins now."

Kiera trailing behind them, John and Jacob Bedsford bounded up to Wren. "Afternoon, Miss Wren!"

A pang darted through her. They were just like Hawke as a boy, back when she'd not shared him with his various lovers. And soon she'd lose him forever to his wife. She shoved that aside again—she'd come to distract herself. She handed the twins her canvas sack with a stern glance. "Take these starpeaches to Mary on your way to luncheon." Mary was Peter's wife and the orphanage's cook.

John snatched the sack, and the twins scampered inside.

Kiera's dark-blonde curls jerked as she called after them, "I expect you two in my study after luncheon."

Wren pursed her lips, muffling a chuckle. "I doubt they heard you." Or ignored her if they had.

Peter grinned. "Never fear, Mistress Kiera. Mary and I'll make sure they find you."

"Thanks, Peter." Kiera waved for Wren to follow her. "We'd better head to the dining hall as well."

Wren nodded, and they strode inside. When they entered the noisy dining hall, children were crammed at the twelve trestle tables along the walls and chattering as they devoured luncheon. A few waved at Wren, but most were focused on their food and friends.

Once Wren and Kiera sat at the head table overlooking the orphans, Mary bustled over with black bread and bowls of fish stew. She beamed at Wren. "Thanks for the starpeaches, Miss Wren. The orphans love when you bring those. Almost as much as they love your plays."

Wren blushed but shrugged. Bringing simple treats like starpeaches was trivial when your family was wealthy. "I hope there's enough."

Mary chuckled. "There's enough for luncheon and dinner, don't you worry."

After the plump cook winked and left, Wren began eating then arched her brows at Kiera. "So where were the twins?" Those scamps could have been anywhere from the royal orchard to the docks.

"Visiting their father's old miscellany shop on Mountainglass Lane." Kiera flashed a wry smile over her fish stew. "They were unrepentant to be found wandering."

Not surprising. Hawke was never repentant of his escapades either, although as a child, Wren had often joined him, whereas now he simply told her every detail about his affairs. She dragged her mind to a happier time. "At least you didn't have to rescue them from the docks like some *other* twelve-year-olds all those years ago."

Kiera grinned at her. "Yes, but the Bedsford twins are Ormas born and bred—not rich cubs fresh from the country."

Which Wren and Hawke had been. They'd snuck out to visit the docks and never would have gotten home if Kiera, the head girl at Waterstreet Orphanage back then, hadn't rescued them.

Wren smiled as she nibbled her bread. "I'm glad we were such foolish cubs. Goddess knows I'd never have met you otherwise." And meeting Kiera and the other orphans had transformed her life. Once she'd seen how little they had, she'd dedicated herself to helping them. Even after her come out, she'd spent more time at the orphanage than at court.

Kiera chuckled and nodded. "True. A poor orphan has no reason to mix with children from the most influential families in Calatini."

Wren wrinkled her nose. Her parents weren't influential. They were merely neighbors and best friends with Hawke's parents, the Duke and Duchess of Childes, who *were* influential —they ruled one of Calatini's twelve duchies and were cousins to King Devon. "Well, 'tis fortunate we met. I can't imagine being idle like most of my peers. I'd have to attend more court events." And she despised those more than a firecat despised the sea.

Kiera tsked through pursed lips. "Court events can't be that hideous."

Wren grimaced, her throat tightening. "They're hideous enough." And they'd soon be more so with the duchess plotting Hawke's betrothal. Thrusting that aside again, she forced a bright smile. "I'd much rather be writing a play for here. I should complete the next one in a few days."

"Wonderful." Kiera beamed back then tapped her spoon against her lip. "We can start rehearsals in two weeks once the children finish copying *The Amun Prophecy*."

Wren shifted and stirred her stew. "Studying the foretold return of Rhiannon's Lost Grimoire trumps my little play."

Kiera leaned toward her. "Speaking of Rhiannon, I saw a witch shop beside the Bedsfords' old miscellany shop called Rhiannon's Veils. The twins said the owner can magic *anything*."

A chill skittering across her skin, Wren almost shuddered. She'd not purchased a spell or visited a witch shop since the incident with the charmed pen. Magic was too risky. "I'm not surprised. Only a powerful witch would dare name their shop after the founder of human magic."

Kiera's navy eyes darkened. "What spell would you purchase from a witch so powerful?"

Wren swallowed. "Nothing. I've all I need." Except for Hawke to love her as she loved him, but purchasing a love spell was wicked and wouldn't create the genuine love she craved. But what if another type of spell could grant her one night to express the love she'd bottled up for years? Warmth flooding her, she drove that from her mind. "What would you purchase?"

Kiera tilted her head as she finished her stew. "A spell allowing me to experience something new. Since I became the orphanage matron eight years ago, every day has been the same."

Wren blinked and set aside her empty bowl. When had Kiera become so restless? "Such a spell could be dangerous, not to mention expensive."

Kiera grimaced with a sigh. "I know."

To distract her, Wren said, "Guess what Abby unearthed this morning?" When Kiera arched her brows, she continued, "The masquerade costume Mother purchased during my first season." Which Hawke had never seen, so he'd not recognize her if she attended to watch his scandalous behavior.

Kiera frowned. "Why would your maid show you that?"

"Because the king's summer masquerade is tomorrow." Hawke kissing Kit and other ladies at the masquerade flashing before her eyes, Wren flushed and compressed her lips. "I've avoided attending all these years. Masquerades are just excuses for dalliances. They're even more tiresome than ordinary court events."

Kiera eyed her friend as Mary bustled over with sliced starpeaches. "Are you all right? You've been a bit off today."

Waving away her portion, Wren gritted a brilliant smile. "Of course, I'm fine." Except she was about to lose the man she'd loved forever.

Kiera pursed her lips as the cook left. "Wren..."

Wren winced. She'd not masked her distress enough. Distracting herself had failed, so perhaps she should tell Kiera. Maybe her friend would have advice that would help settle her. "The duchess is plotting Hawke's betrothal."

Kiera's eyes widened. "I see. To whom?"

Wren swallowed but shrugged. "I don't know." But please, Goddess, let it not be Kit.

Kiera cocked her head and began her starpeach. "The duchess shall probably pick you."

Wren snorted, her heart squeezing. "I doubt it." Although Hawke's mother treated her like a daughter, the duchess had never once pushed her at Hawke.

Kiera hummed then said, "Perhaps you should tell Hawke

how you feel. Then you could marry before the duchess betroths him to another."

Bile burned the back of Wren's throat. Except Hawke didn't return her love. He'd merely pity her, and she'd destroy their lifelong friendship. She lifted her chin. "I feel nothing for Hawke but friendship."

Kiera frowned at Wren, but the grinning Bedsford twins bounded over before she could reply. She slanted Wren a narrow glance then herded John and Jacob from the dining hall.

Her tension easing, Wren rose and began visiting with the orphans still in the dining hall. At the table by the door, a young girl with brown, loose curls leapt up and flung her arms around Wren's skirt.

"Thanks for the starpeaches, Miss Wren! They're my favorite." Amaranth swallowed, her brown eyes shimmering with tears. "I haven't eaten them since before Mama and Papa..."

As the young girl began sobbing, Wren knelt and embraced her. Amaranth and her teenage sister, Cassandra, had come to the orphanage a month ago when their parents had been killed. "I'm glad you like them. I'll bring them again soon."

Cassandra, who looked like her sister except ten years older and with mulberry eyes, darted around the table. "Sorry, Miss Wren. Amaranth hasn't learned to contain her grief yet."

Wren squeezed Amaranth. "'Tis fine. Losing beloved parents is hard for *anyone* to handle. Allow yourselves time."

Cassandra swallowed but nodded and coaxed Amaranth from Wren's arms.

Wren studied them as they followed the other orphans from the dining hall. If only she could do more for the grieving sisters. But nothing could soften grief but time. Wren sighed then left the orphanage.

Unable to resist, she ordered her carriage to stop by The Gold Griffin instead of heading straight home. The tavern was near Mountainglass Lane, so she could visit that witch shop with none the wiser. And she might find a spell that would grant her one night with Hawke.

When the carriage stopped, she leapt out and strode down the street then turned left at the first crossing. Rhiannon's Veils was the first door on the left. Her stomach tightening, she eyed the tiny witch shop. 'Twas unremarkable. A powerful witch really worked here?

She gulped a bracing breath and thrust open the witch shop's weathered red door.

CHAPTER 4

His fingers clenching his wine glass, Hawke straightened when Mother proposed telling him and Mel their news. At last. But from her words, Aragon and Selena must already know whatever she was about to share. Could they have helped Mother choose his suitable wife?

Father shook his head. "Aragon and Selena should tell them." He nodded at his eldest son. "Go on then."

Hawke relaxed as he began his scallops. Even if they'd helped find his suitable wife, Father wouldn't have Aragon and Selena reveal his betrothal.

Aragon grinned and threaded his fingers through Selena's. "Our healer just confirmed that Selena is with child."

Hawke's heart lightened. 'Twas wonderful news, much better than an unwanted betrothal. He chuckled and raised his wine glass. "Congratulations! Now the blasted duchy shan't fall to me. Thanks."

A dimple quivered in Selena's cheek. "We're pleased to have been of service, Lord Beza."

Hawke grimaced at his wretched given name. He'd always despised it, so he'd insisted on being called by the family name since he was five. Hawke suited him much better than *Beza*. Yet he was forced to hear it whenever anyone used his proper title, and he could never control his distaste. So unless in formal situations, his family and Wren only used it to tease him.

Ignoring Hawke's habitual grimace, Mel leaned toward Selena with a warm smile. "When are you due?"

"A month after Longnight." Selena gave Aragon a radiant glance. "Our baby might share their natalday with their father."

Aragon kissed her fingers. "'Twould be the best present I could receive."

His ribs squeezing, Hawke forced himself to finish his scallops. What would it be like to love a lady like Aragon loved Selena? And for her to be carrying his child? He'd probably never know. Wren was the closest he'd come to loving a lady, but she was nothing more than a friend, and she'd never want to be more. "We must go out to celebrate sometime soon."

Mother waved a hand. "I have the celebration handled. I'm planning a fete next month. The invitations shall be sent in a few days."

Hawke almost winced. The fuss she'd made to celebrate Aragon's betrothal and wedding had been excessive. And no doubt she'd be worse about her first grandchild. Although perhaps she'd be too focused on her fete to plot his betrothal. Yet he couldn't trust that. Mother was too sly.

Selena tilted her head. "But the fete shall be for all of court. A private celebration would be nice."

Hawke suppressed a chuckle. Meaning she and Aragon would be enduring rather than enjoying the fete. Not surprising. "Wren and I shall plan something then."

Selena smiled and sipped her water. "No, you boys should go alone. My energy wanes early, so I'd spoil the celebration."

Hawke nodded. If only he and his brothers were attending, they must visit The Gold Griffin. Despite being near the docks, Aragon had often visited the rowdy tavern until he'd met Selena. Yet the last time he'd visited had probably been when they'd celebrated his marriage last year.

Mother grimaced as the servants brought out the dessert course. "I remember those days. I love you boys, but thank the Goddess my childbearing years are past."

Shuddering, Father began his karamel nut sweetice. "I remember those days too."

Mother narrowed her eyes at Father. "Do you?"

Hawke almost laughed when Father flashed a crooked grin and drawled, "I certainly remember all the rampion you made me fetch, mostly in the dead of winter. I had to pay a witch a fortune to grow it. Can't look at rampion to this day."

His brow furrowing, Aragon eyed Selena. "Should I fetch you some rampion?"

Selena paled, her spoon halfway to her mouth. "No, the very thought is nauseating." She raised her spoon to her mouth then lowered it. "As is this karamel nut sweetice."

Aragon froze. "'Tis your favorite."

Hawke smiled as he ate his sweetice. Truly. She devoured karamel nut sweetice faster than a starving sprite. And she usually persuaded Aragon to give her at least half of his.

Selena took a bite then leapt to her feet. "Excuse me." She bolted from the room with Aragon close behind her.

Mother tsked and shook her head. "'Tis fortunate they aren't attending tomorrow's masquerade. Selena would never make it."

Hawke's skin prickled as he turned to Mel. Although 'twas unlikely, he asked, "Are you attending tomorrow?"

Mel arched a brow. "When have I ever attended Devon's summer masquerade? Such racy affairs aren't appropriate for priests."

Hawke grimaced. Great, he'd be the only Hawke attending tomorrow. All of court would be scrutinizing him. If not for his plan to dissuade Mother, he'd definitely miss the masquerade.

Mother finished her sweetice and beamed at Hawke. "Since you'll be representing the family, dance with genuine ladies. You might even meet your future wife."

Hawke leapt upright to forestall her lecture about marriage.

She could harp on that for ages. Why couldn't she let him handle his own affairs? "As fascinating as this discussion is about to become, I must be off."

Mel rose and clapped Hawke on the shoulder. "I must be off as well." Once they left the family dining room, Mel muttered, "I don't envy you. Praise the Goddess, Mother never lectured me about marriage."

Hawke snorted. "She'd no choice. Priests only marry with their god's permission. Even Mother's influence doesn't reach so high. So, with Aragon wed, she only has me to marry off." Unfortunately.

Mel straightened his priest robes with a smile. "I doubt you'll ever let that happen. You've always been the most stubborn. But perhaps Wren can help you elude Mother."

Hawke grimaced as he and Mel separated at the street. Except Wren's only idea had been for him to pretend to court her. His chest tightened. No, he must stage the perfect scandal at tomorrow's masquerade. But what?

His mind churning, he strode home, but no plans developed. Perhaps playing his violin would inspire one. He'd head straight to the music room and play until he'd a plan to foil Mother.

Yet when he returned, Hobb handed him a letter from Buford Leshane.

Hawke tore open the letter. Three years ago, he'd invested in Buford's first venture as a shipping merchant. Within a year, his small investment had returned a small fortune, so he could afford his own townhouse to escape Mother. And Buford's later ventures were just as profitable.

Hawke—

I've just received word about a find that should interest you.
Stop by sometime soon to discuss it.

Buford

Hawke grinned as he folded the letter. He'd visit Buford now.

Discussing an intriguing new find and potential profits were infinitely better than considering ways to foil Mother's matchmaking. He requested his gelding then strode upstairs to change.

Restraining himself to a trot, he rode to Buford's warehouse near the docks. He tossed his reins to an idle cabin boy and bounded up the mezzanine to Buford's office. He rapped on the door and entered. "Afternoon, Buford."

The merchant glanced up from his papers, his eyes bright in his weathered face. "Afternoon, Hawke. I see you got my note."

"Obviously." His senses alert, Hawke sprawled in the chair before the desk. He mustn't appear too eager. "What's this new find you mentioned?"

Buford leaned back in his chair and laced his fingers. "A magical fabric woven by the arachne on Mist Isle."

Hawke cocked his head. He'd never heard of that magical creature. Intriguing indeed. "Arachne?"

Buford nodded. "Giant, sentient spiders that only inhabit Mist Isle."

Hawke arched a brow with a frown. Giant spiders? That didn't sound promising. "How's their fabric magical?"

Buford smiled as he replied, "It changes color once bonded to someone."

The back of his neck tingling, Hawke straightened. Perhaps this find was promising, after all. "Bonded how?"

Buford shrugged. "Through a drop of blood. And the color can be reset with another drop of blood."

Hawke's pulse quickened. The possibilities for such fabric were endless. They'd earn a fortune. "Court shall need to see a sample first, but once they do..."

Buford chuckled. "My captain is sending an unbonded bolt ahead using his fae-albatross. That should arrive in two weeks."

Hawke blinked at him. Mist Isle must be across the Envel Ocean for it to take so long. No wonder 'twas new to Calatini. "When shall the full shipment arrive?"

"In a month or so if we finalize the deal now." Buford arched his brows. "Were you interested in investing?"

"Definitely. Once it arrives, I'll give the sample bolt to Mother for a new gown." Hawke grinned, almost rubbing his hands together. "The Duchess of Childes wearing our fabric shall make the rest of court need it as well. Especially if I spread word beforehand."

Buford's weathered face creased in an echoing grin. "I'll leave marketing the fabric at court to you. You understand them much better than I do."

Hawke shrugged. "Benefit of being the son of a duke, I suppose." Although he'd learned the art of finessing court by observing Mother, not Father. Mother could inspire almost anyone to do as she wished, and she usually convinced them 'twas their own idea too.

Buford chuckled. "Among other things."

True, and as a younger son with no estate duties or other responsibilities, Hawke had time to promote Buford's finds at court. He'd nothing else to do, other than avoid Mother's meddling, especially since he'd stopped pursuing meaningless lovers. "Send the sample bolt once it arrives. I'll let you return to work."

Energy surging through him, he rode home then forced himself to sort his stack of invitations to find court events to promote the arachne's magical fabric. Half his invitations were from acquaintances seeking to curry favor with an unwed son of a wealthy duke. Those he tossed after a glance. He could promote the fabric at such events, but they'd be painful to attend.

He saved the invitations from family or close friends, but he still had several events every day—more than he wished to attend, even to promote Buford's latest find. So he'd probably avoid some, like Kit's water party in a few days. Court might be excited for her first party since her husband died, but he'd only saved her invitation because she was family.

Sadly, the most interesting invitation he received wasn't an invitation at all, but an advertisement. The Nightingale was presenting another Lantos concert next week. A little-known bard from the previous century, Lantos had been his and Wren's favorite for years. He'd ask her to join him when he next saw her.

Hawke sighed as he eyed his sorted invitations. He must handle Mother's meddling before promoting the arachne's magical fabric. She might manage to entrap him if they kept attending the same events, and she'd not miss events hosted by family. So what scandal at the king's summer masquerade could foil her matchmaking?

He set his jaw then retreated to his music room. Playing his violin would allow him time to devise the perfect scandal. It must be bold but not reckless, and rakish but not heartless. Plus, it should involve a lady, but not so much that she was ruined or they became betrothed.

His ribs tightened as his fingers flew in a soaring sonata. He must devise something. He'd never allow Mother to marry him off. Considering his own lack of success, she'd never unearth a lady he could love. And he refused to settle for anything less.

CHAPTER 5

When Wren stepped inside Rhiannon's Veils, she almost sneezed at the pervasive incense. She clutched her reticule and glanced about the dim chamber. The shop was empty except for a wooden table with two chairs and cabinets holding spell ingredients, magical accoutrements, and other bizarre objects. Yet the air was heavy with magic, like humidity on a summer afternoon before a thunderstorm. She'd flee this uncanny shop, but only a spell could grant her one night with Hawke without destroying their friendship.

The tinkle of glass beads drew her gaze to the veiled woman entering from the back. Her hair and most of her face concealed by black veils, the witch performed a fluid bow then sank into the chair behind the wooden table. "How may I serve you today, my lady?"

Wren's heart throbbed in her throat as she perched on the chair before the table. "I require a spell, madam witch." But what type? Not a love or seduction spell. She'd never use either on anyone, much less Hawke.

The veiled witch flicked her fingers, jingling bracelets and tiny bells. "Clearly. A lady like yourself wouldn't enter an establishment like mine if you didn't."

Wren flushed and lowered her gaze. Perhaps a glamour spell would be enough. Then Hawke wouldn't recognize her and might finally see her as more than his best friend. And the king's summer masquerade would be the perfect opportunity to use such a spell. She looked up. "You know of tomorrow's masquerade at the palace?"

The veiled witch's exotically lined eyes studied her. "Yes. You want me to conjure an invitation?"

"I've an invitation. I require something else." Wren's stomach quivered. Could she actually use a glamour spell on Hawke? Although not as wicked as a love or seduction spell, a glamour spell was still deceitful.

An echoing silence stretched between her and the veiled witch until the witch leaned forward. "And that would be?"

Wren started then drew a deep breath. She must risk using a glamour spell. Without one, she'd never get one night with Hawke. "I require a glamour spell preventing me from being recognized at tonight's masquerade. My costume shan't be enough."

A sigh undulated the witch's black veils. "How many do you want to glamour, and for how long?"

"Just one gentleman, and only until dawn, but the glamour spell must also cloud his memories." When the veiled witch began shaking her head, Wren blurted, "Else he'll recognize me." And she'd lose their friendship forever.

Her dark eyes narrowing, the veiled witch hummed. "Are you certain you're prepared to pay the price such a glamour spell shall demand?"

A chill tingling through her, Wren withdrew a bag of gold coins from her reticule and tossed it on the table. "I've plenty of funds." And she'd pay more for one night with Hawke.

"I can see you do, although I wasn't referring to money." The veiled witch shook her head again. "I meant the price the magic itself shall demand. For those not born to magic, the price can be steep, especially for such an involved spell."

Wren's skin prickled. The price for the charmed pen had been twisted words and addiction. What would the price for a glamour spell be? She peered at the witch through her lashes. "Why would a glamour spell lasting one night be involved?"

"Since you want it to cloud his memories, I assume this gentleman is close to you." Once Wren nodded, the veiled witch continued, "So the glamour spell must be strong and shall demand a lot from you. And if he remembers your night often, it'll demand more from you each time."

Wren swallowed. Except Hawke would never bother to remember her. None of his lovers lasted long, so he'd not care if a mysterious lady seduced him then vanished. He'd simply find his next lover. So the price for the glamour spell would only be for their night together. She forced a shrug. "How bad could it be?"

The veiled witch snorted. "Bad. Magic demands equal payment and is more capricious than a cat in heat. It could extract its price from your fortune, your family, your life, or even all three."

Wren paled. So the price, whatever it was, would be steep. Yet if she didn't risk using the glamour spell, she'd never get to express her love for Hawke. Too soon he'd belong to another—perhaps even Kit. She lifted her chin. "I'm certain. What do you require for the glamour spell?"

The veiled witch's gaze bored into her. "Hair and blood from you and your gentleman as well as your names."

Swallowing again, Wren opened her reticule to withdraw the mementos she always carried and set them on the table. "This locket contains his hair, and this is our friendship stone." The lock of hair she'd filched as a lovesick teenager, and the heart-shaped friendship stone they'd created using their blood when they were seven.

The veiled witch pocketed Wren's money at last. She rose and gathered a glass bowl, several herbs, a vial of amber liquid, and a small wooden bird from the cabinets behind her. She returned to the table and sprinkled the inky-brown hair into the bowl. "I'll need your hair as well."

Her mouth drying, Wren plucked several strands and passed them to the witch.

The veiled witch added that hair then scraped the blood from the heart-shaped friendship stone into the glass bowl. "Your names?"

Wren's chest tightened as she tucked the empty locket and destroyed friendship stone back into her reticule. Goddess, let these be the steepest price for the glamour spell. "Mine is Renata Elise Keyes, and his is Beza Percival Hawke."

The veiled witch stilled. "The Duke of Childes's youngest son? You play a perilous game, even for a daughter of one of the oldest gentry families."

Wren hunched her shoulders. "I mean no harm." She simply needed one night with Hawke.

The veiled witch arched a brow. "On your head be it." She dropped the herbs into the glass bowl and drizzled the amber liquid on top. She waved her hand over the bowl and began murmuring a singsong chant.

Straining to comprehend the indistinct words, Wren shivered when the potion in the bowl started glowing like the sun through morning mist. So eerie.

The veiled witch snatched the small wooden bird and hurled it into the glass bowl. The glowing potion wicked into the bird, causing it to shimmer like an ocean pearl. She thrust the bowl toward Wren. "Hold out your hand."

Her heart galloping, Wren extended her hand and winced when the veiled witch poured the iridescent bird into her palm. She clutched her fingers about it and drew her fist to her chest.

"To activate the glamour spell, add a drop of blood." The veiled witch rose, her gaze intense. "To end the glamour spell, burn the bird to ash. And may I suggest you do so sooner rather than later. You know not what forces you've called into play."

Wren shivered again but slipped the enchanted bird into her

reticule. At least the veiled witch couldn't be a black witch. No black witch would deliver a warning like that. "My thanks, madam witch."

As the veiled witch sashayed behind the glass beads, Wren fled the tiny witch shop. Now that she had her glamour spell, she needed another spell—a contraceptive charm. She rushed to her carriage waiting near The Gold Griffin then ordered it to stop by her healer's.

Unlike the glamour spell, a contraceptive charm was minor magic and harmless. Hawke's father had given Hawke one on his sixteenth natalday, and he'd never experienced any ill effects. But two contraceptive charms would be safer than one, so Wren requested Healer Althea infuse her emerald earrings. Her mind already on tomorrow, she inclined an absent nod as the healer explained using the charm.

Wren hurried home and returned just in time to join her parents for dinner.

Over dessert, Mother cocked her head. "Are you certain you shan't attend the king's summer masquerade tomorrow? Hawke can ensure no unwanted gentlemen pester you."

If her glamour spell succeeded, he would, by pestering her himself. Wren gulped her wine to hide the blush heating her cheeks. "Hawke shall be too occupied to pay any attention to me. I'm staying home to work on my orphanage play. They're expecting it soon."

His eyes gleaming, Father chuckled. "Such sober dedication. You must have inherited that, along with your dainty looks, from your mother. I loved nothing more than a masquerade when I was your age."

Wren grimaced. "Dallying with masked strangers, no thank you." Except Hawke wasn't a stranger. But her parents couldn't suspect her scandalous plan.

So as soon as they left for the Hawkes the following evening, Wren summoned her maid. Her stomach roiling, she smiled when Abby bustled into the room. "Could you find that masquerade costume? I've decided to attend after all."

The maid beamed and extracted the costume with a flourish.

Wren eyed the leaf-patterned ballgown and its matching lace mask and summer cloak. The dryad costume was fancier than her normal gowns and would make her almost glamorous. Leaves painted on her skin would complete her transformation. Goddess, let that be enough to tempt Hawke. Even with her costume, she wasn't as glamorous as his usual lovers.

She dressed for the masquerade with Abby's help. Despite the late hour, she walked to the palace so only Abby knew she was attending. At the palace gates, she gulped a breath then activated the glamour spell. She must sneak inside and find Hawke before another lady captured his interest. Hopefully, she wasn't too late.

CHAPTER 6

*H*awke still hadn't devised a scandal to foil Mother's meddling when he strode into the king's summer masquerade. As he joined the throng, an arm slid through his.

"Hawke, there you are," Kit purred.

He stiffened and eyed the sable firecat beside him. "Good evening, Kit." How could he escape the husband-hunting widow without drawing unwelcome attention?

Kit slanted him a coy glance. "How bold of you to wear regular evening clothes and a black mask. What are you meant to be?"

Hawke shrugged. Finding an elaborate costume had been too much hassle. Plus, he'd be easily recognized during his scandal. "The youngest son of a wealthy duke."

"For shame, Hawke." The fashionable countess tilted her head. "Although I suppose your family is influential enough no one shall care you didn't wear a costume for the season's most exclusive masquerade."

He stepped back and managed to free his arm from Kit's grasp. Thank the Goddess. Now he just needed to divert her attention.

Kit moued. "Did you receive the invitation to my water party? I've yet to receive your reply."

Because he didn't plan to attend but couldn't admit that since she was family. Hawke arched his brows with a bland smile. "Really? How odd."

Kit's eyes narrowed. "Never say you've become as dull as Mel during the past year."

He snorted. "Do I appear a priest to you?" Although if the Goddess had called him like Mel, perhaps he'd not be suffering such boredom.

Kit grimaced and tossed her head. "Neither does your brother sometimes."

Hawke almost laughed at her sour tone. Kit and Mel were often at odds and had been since they were children. But their arguing was amusing, unlike her needling of Wren. That made him ache to shove Kit in the mud sometimes, yet Wren always remained gracious due to Kit's less fortunate childhood.

The opening strains of the first song drifted through the ballroom.

Kit flashed a coy grin and gestured toward the assembling dancers. "Shall we?"

He tensed. If he danced with her, she'd assume he'd be willing to marry her. He glanced about the ballroom, his gaze halting on a nearby lord adjusting the massive wings of his dragon costume. "I'm too thirsty to dance. Perhaps Lord Raven-stone might oblige you?"

Kit glared at him then whirled and sashayed over to the bearded count, who smiled and escorted her out onto the floor.

Hawke sighed as he headed to the refreshments table. He shouldn't have inflicted Kit on the genial Lord Ravenstone, but he had to escape.

Sipping a flute of sparkling wine, he strolled along the outskirts of the ballroom. His mouth twisted as he scanned the tumult. Despite the elaborate costumes, the masquerade was as tiresome as an ordinary ball. The same self-important people tittered over the same tedious gossip, like Devon escorting Lady Annalise Greysnowe.

His cousin had been escorting Lady Annalise for over three years, yet his dance with the lady, appropriately dressed as a siren, transfixed most of court. Not only because he was king and she the most beautiful lady in Calatini, but because the Greysnowe-Ravenstone feud would erupt if he chose her as his bride. Not that Devon had made any move to do so.

Hawke snorted and shook his head. If Lady Annalise wasn't a marriageable miss, he'd steal her from Devon's arms. *That* would certainly create a scandal to dissuade Mother. Until she managed to betroth him to Lady Annalise. He shuddered. Despite her extraordinary beauty, he'd never marry a lady called Lady Snow by most of court.

He drained his sparkling wine and handed his empty flute to a servant. He lounged against the wall and continued scanning the ballroom. He must stage a scandal before court became too inebriated to notice. But what?

A dryad slipping into the masquerade thrust staging a scandal from his mind. Her costume accentuating her auburn hair and dainty figure, she hovered beneath the doorway hunting for someone. She was exquisite and oddly familiar. Yet who was she?

Hunger consuming him for the first time in eight years, he thrust away from the wall to waylay her. His dryad was too delectable for him to permit other gentlemen to notice her. He swept a bow before her. "Your costume is more elaborate than most, my lady of the forest."

The dryad relaxed with a brilliant grin. "Unlike yours, Hawke. Does the duchess know you're wearing regular evening clothes?"

Hawke squinted at the dryad. How had she known to use his surname rather than his title and wretched given name? And she spoke like she knew his mother well. "Have we met?"

Her hazel eyes brilliant amidst her leaf mask, the dryad smiled. "I'm a member of court, so certainly. Don't you recall?"

"Would I ask if I did?" Tingling warmth filled him as he grasped her hand and kissed the leaf painted on the center of her palm. "What intriguing leaves. How far do they extend?"

The dryad cocked her head then chuckled and extracted her hand. "That's for me to know, and for you to fantasize about."

Hawke tautened as her body adorned only with leaf designs flashed before his eyes. "How cruel you are." He captured her hand again to pull her toward the ballroom floor. "In penance, you must dance with me."

"No," the dryad snapped. When he paused and arched his brows, she said in a softer tone, "But I'd enjoy a walk in the gardens."

"Even better." Heat surging in his veins, he whisked his dryad to his favorite corner at the far edge of the gardens. The night's balmy air was perfect for a garden tryst. Plus, she could focus solely on him, and no other gentlemen could notice her.

The full moon turning her vibrant hair brown and her green costume inky, the dryad giggled as she glanced at the profusion of flowerbeds, the swing beneath a honeysuckle arbor, and the small grotto with a marble bench. "So this garishly romantic place is where you seduce your lovers. I should have known."

A zing darted through his chest at her wry drawl. "You speak as if there have been hundreds."

"Haven't there been?" The dryad winked and slipped from his grasp.

Hawke placed a hand over his heart as she swished to the middle of the largest flowerbed. "Certainly not, my reputation is vastly exaggerated." And his past lovers hadn't enthralled him like she did.

Twirling in place, the dryad giggled again. "I doubt that. I know every detail of your exploits."

He seized her hand and pulled her toward him. "Who *are* you?" He must know her. But how? His head throbbed.

The dryad stilled a handbreadth away, a smile belying her lowered eyes. "Can't you guess?"

She must be laughing at him. Hawke set his jaw and dropped her hand. "No, I can't."

The dryad threaded her fingers through his hair. "Well, since you're so obsessed with my name, you may call me Rowan for tonight."

Why a false name? He narrowed his eyes. "If you think a false name shall prevent me from learning your identity..." When she shrugged, he grasped her hips and drew her against him. "You're quite mistaken."

Rowan linked her wrists behind his neck. "Must we quarrel? I'd rather dance."

Hawke stilled, his heart pounding. "You seemed opposed to the idea inside."

A faint smile curved Rowan's lips. "'Twas the location I despised, not the dancing."

"In that case." Heat consumed him as he began twirling her about the flowerbed with her molded against him.

Still smiling, Rowan echoed his movements. "A new style of dance, I see. When I was taught, arms were higher, and partners were a good foot apart."

Hawke winked and tightened his arms around her. "I thought you'd enjoy my style more." And he couldn't bear to release her.

"Oh, I do." Rowan laid her head on his shoulder, the delicate scent of violets wafting from her hair.

All they needed was music to make their dance perfect, so he began humming his favorite Lantos waltz.

A velvet alto joined him on the chorus,

"Love me under the sky,

Sparkling with stars and the moon so high,

And I'll be able to fly."

Hawke halted at the end of the chorus. "You know Lantos?" Not many appreciated her these days. Unfortunately.

"She's one of my favorite bards." Rowan's lips curved against his throat.

His and Wren's too. Tingling swept through him as he grasped her chin and tilted her head until her eyes met his. "Who *are* you? I *must* know you."

Her smile enigmatic as a shadowed forest, Rowan slid her hands from his neck to his chest. "Perhaps you do."

Hawke peered into her moon-darkened eyes but could read nothing. He'd taste her feelings instead. He lowered his head and brushed his mouth against hers.

Rowan's hands fisted in his coat as her lips parted with a sigh.

At her silent invitation, he deepened their kiss. He continued devouring her lips until his body throbbed. He wrested his head back and rasped, "Shall we take our conversation to a more private location, say, my chambers?"

An impish grin flitted across Rowan's face. "I'm relieved you finally asked. For a supposed rakehell, you took an age."

Another zing darted through Hawke, tempering his hunger. Only an intimate would tease him so. He began leading her from the gardens. "I apologize for my ineptitude."

Rowan licked her lips. "You should. 'Tis improper for a lady to ask."

Fire flashing through him again, he pulled her into a garden alcove and captured her mouth in another kiss. Goddess, she was perfect.

CHAPTER 7

*W*ren's blood fizzed through her veins as Hawke hauled her into the alcove by the garden door and kissed her again. 'Twas as if he couldn't bear to stop embracing her for more than a few moments. She suppressed a smile when he sighed and drew back. He definitely wanted her as she wanted him, and no spell had created that desire.

Hawke threaded his fingers through hers and led her inside. He scanned the hall before turning back to her, his pale-blue eyes gleaming in his black mask. "No one appears to be about. We'll leave through the kitchen to avoid being seen. Did you bring a cloak?" When she nodded, he pulled her close for another deep kiss then said, "Wait here."

Wren pressed against the wall, her skin prickling. If only she'd a place to hide. The hall was too exposed. Her glamour spell only prevented Hawke from recognizing her, and if rumors started, the duchess would meddle. Yet most wouldn't recognize the straightlaced Miss Keyes as a glamorous dryad at first, so she'd be fine if no one scrutinized her. Which was why she'd refused to dance in the ballroom.

Fortunately, no one walked by before Hawke returned. He winked and handed Wren her cloak. "Your cloak, my lady."

She flung the summer cloak over her shoulders and yanked up the hood. With her face and vibrant hair concealed, most of her tension eased. Now she was a nameless lady in a dryad costume.

Hawke chuckled and offered his hand. "Feeling shy?"

Wren shrugged as she accepted his outstretched hand. "You could name it that, I suppose." But wanting to preserve their friendship after tonight was more accurate.

Hawke kissed her palm then drew her down the hall. "You'll have to tell me why."

She tsked. "But 'twould destroy the mystery." Her mouth dried as they crept into the bustling kitchen. She checked her cloak still concealed her. Servants could recognize her too.

A crooked grin slashed across Hawke's face as he glanced down at her. "We'd never wish to destroy the mystery."

Once they slipped out the kitchen door, Wren relaxed and squeezed his hand. She flicked him a coy glance from beneath her cloak. "I'd be forced to vanish into the trees like a true dryad if we did."

"Not if I capture you first." With a faint laugh, Hawke pinned her against the palace wall then captured her lips.

Whimpering low in her throat, she fisted her hands in his inky-brown hair and returned his kiss with equal fervor. His kisses were addictive, even more than she'd ever dreamt. And she'd dreamt of them often since their Longnight kiss eight years ago.

Hawke yanked his head back and rubbed her tingling lips with his thumb. "We'd best stop if we're to reach my townhouse with our clothes intact."

Her pulse thundering beneath her skin, Wren grinned and nipped his thumb. "Cease kissing me along the way then. I can't help responding."

Hawke lowered his head until their lips almost touched. "Are you tempting me to misbehave again?"

Her breath stilled. She was. "Would I do that?"

Hawke laughed. "Yes, I believe you would." He stepped back and took her arm. "But I'll resist you. At least until we reach my chambers. Then I'll pounce like a satyr."

Yes, please. Heat flashing through her, Wren giggled. "Make haste. Dryads love satyrs."

Hawke shuddered and almost dragged her across the courtyard behind the palace.

She couldn't hide her grin. Thank the Goddess for her glamour spell. She could flirt as she'd always ached to do without destroying their friendship. Freely expressing her love and desire was glorious. If only she could do so as herself.

When they didn't head to the stables, Wren blinked. Although she'd walked to the palace to keep her attendance secret, Hawke surely hadn't. "Aren't we taking your carriage?"

"I thought you didn't wish to be seen?" Hawke wrapped an arm about her shoulders as they reached the back gate of the palace. "Now tuck your head against my neck and allow me handle the guards."

She pressed her face against his neck, her stomach hardening. No doubt his adroit plan was thanks to his many lovers. She gripped his evening coat. His other lovers didn't matter right now—tonight Hawke was *hers*.

While they strolled through the gate, Hawke nodded at the guards. "Evening."

"Evening, Lord Beza," the guards replied.

Her tension easing, Wren chuckled at Hawke's habitual grumble. Poor Hawke was doomed to hear his despised given name whenever anyone used his proper title.

Hawke shook her shoulder once the guards were out of earshot. "Are you laughing at me, Rowan?"

Still chuckling, she kissed his neck as they turned left onto Hawke's street. "I'd never do that." Except when he was being amusing.

Hawke tsked. "I think you would." He flashed a playful leer. "A kiss would stop your saucy mouth."

Warmth flooded Wren. She craved another kiss like a mermaid craved the sea. "Kiss me then."

Hawke bent and murmured against her lips, "Not until we reach my chambers. My next kiss won't stop at a kiss."

Her heart surged, and she almost whimpered as he straightened and escorted her down the street. He was cruel to tease her so.

Hawke waved toward his elegant townhouse when they reached his front steps. "My humble dwelling."

Wren arched a brow and drawled to repay his teasing, "Very humble for the son of a duke."

"I purchased it with my own funds." Even in the moonlight, Hawke's eyes gleamed. "I bet you didn't know that."

She hid a smile and lowered her gaze. Of course, she knew that—she'd helped him pick it after his small shipping investment had returned a small fortune. "I assume you've a plan to sneak inside your humble dwelling."

Hawke withdrew a key from his pocket with a flourish. "No need. I've a key, and the servants know not to wait up."

Tingling skittered across her skin as she slipped her arm through his and waved to the front door. "Lead on then."

Hawke escorted her up the front steps, unlocked the door, and ushered her inside.

As he locked the door, Wren glanced about the shadowed entrance hall. Although she visited Hawke almost every day, she'd never done so near midnight, and being in his home at this time of night transformed her tingling into prickling.

Hawke took her arm again and winked. "What do you think of my humble dwelling?"

Her heart racing, she tilted her head as he led her upstairs. What would a stranger say? Perhaps avoiding his question was safest. "'Tis dark."

Hawke grinned. "For some reason, that happens every night." He flung open the door to his chambers.

Wren swallowed. Goddess, she was about to make love for

the first time, with the man she'd loved forever, and she must conceal her inexperience from him. Yet making love with Hawke tonight would finally allow her to express her love. 'Twas her only chance.

She studied Hawke's chambers to distract herself. She'd last been here two years ago when they'd toured the townhouse before he'd purchased it. Then the walls had been a garish pink —no doubt chosen by a wife seeking to emasculate her husband. Now they were cream, and the furnishings were mahogany with hunter green fabric. Strong and masculine like Hawke.

"It must have taken forever to—" Wren snapped her mouth shut and flushed. Her nerves had caused her wits to vanish. Even though Hawke couldn't recognize her due to her glamour spell, she shouldn't flaunt her true identity. That might rouse his curiosity and make her memorable.

"What?" Having lit the candles around the room, Hawke turned toward her as he began disrobing.

"Nothing." She tossed aside her cloak, wincing at the enchanted bird's muffled thud. Her hands trembling, she untied her mask and dropped it on her cloak. She glanced at Hawke, who only wore trousers and was watching her with a half smile. She swallowed and managed an echoing smile. "You must undo my ballgown."

"My pleasure." Hawke strode across the room and unlaced her ballgown with fingers that displayed none of her trembling. "So how far do those leaves extend?"

"You're about to find out." Wren slid her ballgown off her shoulders then gulped a breath and stripped off her undergarments. She pulled free her hair pins and pivoted as hair cascaded down her shoulders. Would he still want her without her glamorous costume?

Hawke's eyes darkened as he caressed a leaf above her left breast. "All over, how bold. That must have taken hours. How did you do your back?"

"My maid." Her skin tingled at his touch, but her stomach

fluttered. She shrugged to feign indifference at her nakedness. "Do you intend to stare all night or do something instead?"

"How about I do both?" His hungry gaze never leaving her, Hawke dropped his trousers and drew her into his arms.

As their bare bodies touched, fire flared through Wren. Oh, Goddess. She clung to Hawke's shoulders and kissed his neck as he carried her across the room. After years of hiding her true feelings, she was about to express her love and experience passion.

Hawke laid her on his bed then slid beside her. His hands running along her body, he seized her mouth in a kiss.

Throbbing with emptiness, she kissed him back and drew him closer. She needed him—now. As Hawke made love to her, arousing caresses, ravenous kisses, and fiery hunger consumed her.

Afterward, as her senses returned and her pulse slowed, Wren trembled in Hawke's arms and inhaled his scent. Goddess, physically expressing her love had been glorious. Better than she'd ever dreamt. If only they could do it again, but he'd not want that.

She swallowed. And considering his complaints about past lovers, he'd also not want her nestling against him. So despite aching to remain entwined forever, she slid from his embrace and curled on her side. Now that she'd had her chance to express her love, she must leave. But how?

CHAPTER 8

*H*awke frowned when Rowan slid from his arms as soon as they finished making love. Her auburn hair hiding her face, she curled on her side with her back facing him and arm covering her chest. His ribs squeezed. Why had she withdrawn and feigned sleep? Previous lovers had enjoyed cuddling afterward. And why did her distance perturb him?

His eyes flicked to the red spot staining the sheet. Perhaps her distance was because she possessed no experience making love. Warmth spread through his chest. He'd never cared about that before. Why was Rowan different?

Pain bolting through his head, Hawke winced. Regardless, he'd stolen a gift meant for the man who loved her, or at least knew her true name. He sighed and strode to his washbasin for a cloth. Cleaning Rowan might help him atone.

When the damp cloth brushed the juncture of her thighs, Rowan stopped feigning sleep and winced away. Her voice shrill, she asked, "What are you doing?"

He continued wiping the faint smear of blood. "Washing you. Are you all right?" His stomach lurched. Goddess, what if he'd hurt her?

Rowan flashed a brittle smile. "Why wouldn't I be?"

His mouth tightened. She mustn't mean to reveal she'd been a virgin. So he couldn't ask if he'd hurt her when he breached her virginity. He tossed aside the cloth then slid back into bed. "Perhaps because you were pretending to sleep rather than cuddling?"

Still curled away from him, Rowan fingered a painted leaf on her neck and muttered, "I thought you wouldn't wish it."

Hawke eyed Rowan curled beside him. He never had with previous lovers, but he ached to cuddle with her. Why? Because she'd been his first virgin? He frowned. No, because he felt like he'd known her forever. Which was ridiculous—the only lady he'd known forever was Wren. Another sharp pain pierced his skull. He shook his head to clear it then rolled Rowan back into his arms.

Rowan splayed her hands against his chest. "What are you doing?"

He rested his chin on her head, his body stirring as he inhaled her violet scent. "Cuddling."

Rowan remained frozen in his arms. "Why?"

Tingling flashed across his skin as he held her. Despite her tension, 'twas as if Rowan was meant for his arms. "Because I wish to, and I think you do too."

Rowan sighed and melted against him at last.

Light suffusing his chest, Hawke traced a painted vine on her arm. Perhaps he could encourage further intimacy. "I wish you'd tell me your true name, Rowan."

She tensed in his embrace again. "Rowan is my true name tonight."

He sighed. From her adamant tone, she'd not elaborate, so he must stop asking for her to remain. And he needed her in his arms. But he still wanted to know more about her. "Very well, if you shan't reveal your name, tell me a secret no one else knows instead."

Rowan shifted against him, her fingers twisting in his chest hair. After a long silence, she replied, "I bought a spell today even though I distrust magic."

Hawke stiffened and narrowed his eyes. No wonder he'd felt such instant attraction. He should have realized magic was responsible. "A seduction spell, I suppose."

"No!" Rowan jerked back to caress his face. "I'd never purchase a love or seduction spell, Hawke. Merely a small spell for courage."

He relaxed at her earnest expression. She couldn't be deceiving him. He kissed her palm then tugged her back into his arms. "So what is the price for courage?"

Rowan shrugged as she nestled against him again. "A purse of marks plus whatever the magic demands."

Unable to resist, Hawke wrapped her vibrant hair around his fingers. It smoldered like flame trapped in wood. Gorgeous. "The magic demands? Sounds ominous."

"Not particularly; the witch said magic needs something from the buyer to work." Rowan chuckled and kissed his chest. "Perhaps it simply made me reckless enough to seduce a stranger."

His pulse leaping, he grinned and ran a finger up her spine. Thank the Goddess for her spell then. "I should buy a spell for courage too."

"Absolutely not." Rowan prodded his ribs. "If you possessed more courage, you'd challenge half the gentlemen at court to duels. And if you became more reckless with your lovers, you'd acquire a venereal disease within a fortnight."

Hawke tensed at her barb. Did she really think that? He relaxed. No, she must be teasing—she'd come home with him and given him her virginity, after all. To repay her teasing, he tickled a leaf on her waist. "How harsh you are of mortals, even for a magical tree spirit."

Rowan squirmed from his hand. "Enough nonsense. Now that I told you a secret, you tell me one."

He stilled, his breath catching. Rowan already seemed to

know him, so what could he tell her? He shrugged. "My mother means to see me settled this season."

Snorting, Rowan prodded his ribs again. "That's no surprise, considering the duchess. Tell me a real secret."

Hawke winced but sighed. She was right; Mother's meddling was no surprise. And his upcoming venture with Buford lacked significance. So he must reveal his rakish reputation was a facade. But would she still want him then? "I've suffered from increasing boredom over the past two years."

Rowan shoved out of his arms to gape at him. "What? You have not."

A flush burned his neck as he shrugged. "I have, but I've never admitted it to anyone, even my best friend. Wren would just scold me for wasting time at court events."

Rowan frowned, her hazel eyes dark. "But you're forever busy with various lovers and court events."

Hawke grimaced. "Busy doesn't mean interested." Tonight was the first time he'd felt interested in years. All because he'd met her.

Rowan pursed her lips. "True, but if court events bore you, why do you bother attending?"

He sighed, hollowness echoing inside his chest. "At first, I believed attending more court events and seducing more lovers would cure my boredom, but they exacerbated it."

Rowan blinked then tilted her head. "So why continue attending?"

Hawke caressed the leaves adorning her breast to distract himself. His body tightened. Goddess, she was bewitching. "To maintain appearances. I couldn't allow Mother to note my boredom—her meddling would become unbearable. Besides, I've little else to do."

Rowan scowled and thrust his wrist from her breast. "Then find something! Learn a challenging piece on your violin. Or discover a new hobby. Or try helping others. The orphanage—" Her mouth snapped shut.

Was she about to reveal a clue to her identity? His senses sharpening, he craned forward. "The orphanage?"

Rowan's gaze skittered away as she flushed a deep scarlet and began sliding from his embrace. "Never mind."

Hawke encircled her waist to halt her retreat. He must reveal another secret to distract her from her slip. "Only because you're so bewitching. Did you know you're the first woman I've brought home since last season?"

Rowan stilled. "But I thought you were maintaining appearances?"

He coughed with a shrug. "By attending court events. Lovers were too tiresome." Until he'd met her. He arched a teasing brow. "Are you certain that spell of yours wasn't a seduction spell?"

Rowan wrinkled her nose at him. "I already told you it wasn't."

She was adorable. Heat flooding him, Hawke glided a hand up her back. "Perhaps the witch who created your spell misled you. Where did you purchase it?"

Rowan's jaw tightened. "A witch shop."

He sighed. Her tone was the same as when she'd refused to reveal her true name. She'd flee if he didn't cease probing. So he tickled her ribs to distract her.

Rowan giggled and swatted his hand. "Stop that!"

Laughter bubbling inside him, Hawke waggled his brows yet ceased tickling her. "But your giggles are sweeter than a siren's song." And with the right song, sirens could bewitch any creature able to hear them.

Rowan snorted. "I'm a dryad, not a siren."

His heart surged as he squeezed her waist. She was certainly as shy as a dryad, who remained hidden unless their forest was threatened. "Perhaps you're both." He certainly couldn't resist her.

"Flatterer." Rowan cocked her head. "Are you certain it's been nearly a year since you seduced anyone? You don't appear lacking practice."

Did that mean she couldn't resist him either? Hawke flashed a crooked grin and winked. "You inspire me."

Rowan's changeable eyes softened to a tender green. "You inspire me too." She leaned forward and brushed a kiss against his lips. As he pulled her closer and deepened their kiss, she purred and fisted her hands in his hair.

He wrenched his head back when his body became painfully hard. Despite his hunger, they couldn't make love again tonight. She'd been a virgin until an hour ago. "Rowan, we must stop."

Rowan licked her swollen lips. "Why?"

Burning to kiss her again, Hawke stilled. "Because..." He coughed. Must he truly explain? "You might be sore from before."

A coy smile lit Rowan's face. "I feel fine. Better than fine. Glorious."

He shuddered as his body hardened further. How could he resist? He rolled Rowan beneath him and braced himself above her. He scrutinized her for weariness or regret, but only passion shone in her face. So he kissed her again.

Rowan threw her arms about his neck and pulled his weight fully atop her. She parted her lips to kiss him deeper.

Hawke rumbled as their mouths fused. Rowan's hunger mirrored his, and unlike with previous lovers, one night, or even one month, would never be enough. He'd ask to court her after they made love again. Mother might see him settled, after all.

CHAPTER 9

*W*ren awoke when the pale light of dawn filtered through Hawke's window. Though her head throbbed with fatigue, she must leave before Hawke woke or one of his servants found her in his bed. Being discovered would ruin her plan to preserve their friendship. So she sighed and eased from his embrace.

She glanced down at Hawke with a soft smile, her fingers aching to caress his unshaven cheek. She'd always treasure last night—he'd been all she'd expected and more. Seductive and rakish, yet oddly tender. What had been her favorite part of their enchanted night? Making love, cuddling, or exchanging secrets?

Her breath quickening, she licked her lips as she stared at Hawke. Making love had been thrilling and passionate. If only they could do it again. Yet although making love had been glorious, the cuddling and exchanging secrets afterward had warmed her heart even more. She'd never expected such intimacy. Too bad she'd received it as a lady who didn't exist rather than herself.

Wren shook herself from her reverie, her stomach tightening. She must cease ogling Hawke. He could wake at any moment, and their enchanted night was over. In the bright light of day, he probably wouldn't find her near as alluring.

She sighed and padded across the room and slipped on her crumpled undergarments and ballgown without tying the back laces. Once she scooped her mask and cloak into her arms, she glanced over her shoulder at Hawke.

Goddess, if only she could stay forever. But he didn't love her, so he'd not want that. Her heart squeezed. Unable to resist, she glided back to the bed and brushed a kiss on his forehead. Still bending over him, she whispered, "I love you, Hawke."

Despite her confession, Hawke didn't stir, and his breathing remained even.

A lump clogged her throat. Straightening, she shook her head at her foolish yearning. Even if Hawke had been awake, her confession wouldn't have touched him. Rowan was merely a mysterious lady he'd met last night. One he'd forget as soon as she left. And she must do so at once.

Wren set her jaw as she tossed her cloak about her shoulders, donned her mask, and pulled up her hood to hide her vibrant hair. She darted downstairs then unlocked the front door and slipped into the quiet morning. Her pulse thundering, she skulked down the alley that cut across several streets to her parents' townhouse. Yet the dawn air was still, and she encountered no one on the short walk.

Breathless and lightheaded, she circled around to the front door, even though the alley ran behind the townhouse. At this hour, the kitchen servants would be busy in the back. Her hands trembled when she unlocked the door, but the entrance hall was as empty as the street. She slipped inside then darted upstairs to her chambers.

She began to relax until she glanced about the room. Abby was sleeping in a chair beside the fireplace. When the maid woke, she'd doubtless scold Wren for staying out so late. Wren muffled a sigh then crept across the floor to begin eradicating all traces of Rowan. She built up the fire, attempting to be as quiet as possible.

However, Abby jerked awake just as the fire began to blaze. "Miss Wren?"

Wren stiffened but kept her back to her maid as she fed her mask to the flames. Of course, Abby would wake now. Wren rubbed her brow. Goddess, she was too exhausted for the impending interrogation. "Morning, Abby. I told you not to wait up."

Abby bustled over to her. "I was worried when you didn't return. Plus, I knew you'd need help removing your ballgown."

Wren gripped her cloak closed and fought not to blush. She would have, except Hawke had removed it last night. And Abby would see her unlaced ballgown if she shed her cloak. She swallowed then rose and shooed the maid toward the door. "I can manage."

Abby's eyes narrowed as she looked her up and down. "Where've you been all night?"

Wren forced herself to shrug. "Attending the king's summer masquerade." Then seducing Hawke. Tingling warmth swept over her. Goddess, making love to him had been glorious. Well worth Abby's scold.

Abby humphed and crossed her arms over her chest.

Before the maid could scold further, Wren managed a faint smile. "And I'm exhausted beyond reason. I simply want a bath and bed. I'll ring when I want breakfast." Hopefully, 'twould prompt Abby to leave.

Abby pursed her lips as she eyed Wren for a long moment. Then she snorted and uncrossed her arms. "The bath'll be cold. I prepared it not long after midnight." She whirled and strode from the room.

Finally alone and safe in her chambers, Wren plopped on the edge of her bed, her muscles as limp as the wet pulp-clay the orphans used to construct their theater sets. She sagged with a shuddering sigh. She'd continue eradicating Rowan once her trembling eased.

After several deep breaths, she slid her hand into her cloak pocket. She couldn't burn the enchanted bird along with her dryad costume. So she must hide the clue to their enchanted night some place Hawke would never discover it.

Yet her fingers found nothing. "Dear Goddess!"

The muffled thud when she'd donned her cloak in Hawke's chambers echoed in her ears. Oh, Goddess. She must have lost the enchanted bird then. She shivered and closed her eyes. What if Hawke found it and decided to burn the odd carving he discovered? 'Twould end the glamour spell, and he'd realize she'd seduced him as Rowan.

She rubbed her aching chest. No matter how glorious, their enchanted night wasn't worth destroying their lifelong friendship. She lifted her chin. But surely Hawke wouldn't bother to burn the enchanted bird, no matter its eerie appearance. And as long as he didn't burn it, everything would be fine.

But she'd better finish eradicating Rowan before she fell asleep or Abby returned. So despite the fatigue dragging her limbs, Wren pulled herself upright and removed her cloak. She sliced it into long strips and tossed the strips into the fire one by one. Then she tugged off her ballgown and destroyed it as she had her cloak.

While the remnants of her costume burned, she removed her emerald earrings. After last night she'd no need for a contraceptive charm since she'd never make love again. Her throat cramped while she tucked her earrings into the jewel box on her dressing table. Then she shed her undergarments and slid into her icy bath with a squeak.

Her teeth chattered as she scrubbed her skin raw to remove the leaf designs. Shivering, she staggered from the bath then dried herself and donned her nightgown. She rubbed her chilled skin as she glanced about her chambers. All traces of Rowan had been eradicated, except for the enchanted bird she'd left at Hawke's. Only Wren remained.

Hollowness filling her chest, she stumbled across the room. Her aching body trembled as she crawled into bed and pulled the covers over her whirling head. She'd actually done it. She'd seized her one chance to express her love then vanished. She now had one night of memories to cherish when he wed another. His ravenous kisses and their bodies joining echoed through her. And what memories they were.

She sighed. She'd never experience passion like that again. And her love must remain buried in her heart to avoid destroying their friendship. She'd miss the freedom she'd enjoyed as Rowan. But that was all over, and her relationship with Hawke would return to normal. And having his friendship was better than having nothing.

Tears pricking her eyes, Wren succumbed to slumber, and dreams of their passionate night consumed her. If only she'd more than dreams left.

CHAPTER 10

*H*awke awoke bursting with energy for the first time in months. All because of the delectable Rowan. His eyes still closed, he smiled and reached for her. He'd wake her with a kiss then ask if he could court her as he'd intended last night. Yet nothing but cool sheets met his touch.

His eyes sprang open, and he bolted upright. He glanced about for Rowan, but his chambers were empty. She'd vanished like a venus who seduced men in their sleep. Yet he'd not dreamt his enchanted night with Rowan. She was real, and he must find her.

He leapt from bed, landing on an unexpected lump. He grunted and bent to gather the offending object. 'Twas a small, wooden bird that gleamed like pearl, obviously magical in nature. Rowan's spell for courage, no doubt. Had she meant to leave it when she fled? Regardless, the enchanted bird was a clue, one of the few he possessed, to her identity.

Hawke clenched the little bird in his fist. "I *will* learn your true name, Rowan."

Why had she fled? Last night had been extraordinary, and he'd felt closer to Rowan than anyone, except perhaps Wren before their Longnight kiss. He rubbed his head as searing pain pierced his skull. "The second headache in a day. I hope I'm not developing chronic ones like Mother."

Despite his aching head, Hawke inspected the enchanted bird for an emblem but found none. He'd have to take it to witch shops to find its creator. He grimaced and set the bird on his bedside table.

He yanked on a dressing gown then hurried to his desk to write a list of clues about Rowan. As his list grew, so did his headache, and by the time he'd described her appearance, pain almost blinded him. He staggered across his chambers to ring for his valet. He rasped when John arrived, "A tonic for my head, and not one for alcohol."

John darted from the room and returned a few moments later with a steaming tonic.

Hawke gulped the tonic then sighed as it loosened the headache's grip. "Thank you, John."

Still unable to bear reading, he glanced at the list on his desk. He'd show it to Wren so she could help him discover Rowan's true identity. No doubt Wren would say 'twas time he was serious about a lady. He chuckled. Hopefully, he could withstand her smug comments. He dressed, snatched the list and enchanted bird, then left to visit Wren.

Hawke strode to the Keyes's townhouse, the warm morning air clearing the remnants of his headache. He grinned while he rapped on the front door. With Wren's help, he'd soon find Rowan. He brushed past the Keyes's butler, who was the younger brother of his parents' butler. "Morning, Perkins. Where's Wren?"

"I haven't seen her this morning, my lord. If you'll wait here, I'll have someone find her." Perkins Two whisked away.

After a few moments, Wren's maid bustled downstairs. "I'm afraid Miss Wren is indisposed, my lord."

"Really?" Hawke frowned. Oh yes, she'd planned to finish her orphanage play. He smiled and shook his head. "She must have stayed up all night writing again." When Abby jerked a nod, he chuckled. "Very well, I'll see her tomorrow then."

He bounded down the front steps. He'd visit his parents instead. He must ensure Mother's meddling didn't wreck his courtship of Rowan. His stomach growled. Plus, he could get some breakfast.

Hawke hurried to his parents' townhouse two doors down then rapped on their door. When it glided open, he nodded at his parents' longtime butler. "Morning, Perkins. I trust everyone is still eating breakfast."

"Yes, Lord Beza." Perkins One ushered him inside.

Hawke winced but didn't chasten the butler for using his proper name. The old stick never listened anyway. He breezed into the breakfast room to join everyone, but his parents were alone at the table. Mel's absence wasn't surprising, but where were Aragon and Selena? Was she too nauseous to eat again?

Hawke nodded at Father and kissed Mother's cheek. Then he heaped his plate with food and sat between them. "Is Selena well?"

Mother grimaced. "As well as any pregnant lady in the morning, so she and Aragon prefer to eat breakfast in their chambers." She paused then beamed at him, her expression suspiciously impish. "I'm pleased you joined us this morning. I've just had the most marvelous idea for my fete and can't wait to tell you."

His stomach tightened, but he made himself swallow a forkful of eggs. What was Mother plotting now? To announce his betrothal at the fete as well? He frowned. She'd better not. He wanted to court Rowan, not marry whomever Mother decided would suit. "What idea?"

Mother's eyes gleamed. "Wren must write one of her plays for the fete."

Hawke gaped at her. Wren would *loathe* that. He must dissuade Mother. "Wren shan't agree to writing a play for court."

Father chuckled as he finished his toast. "I'm certain your mother can convince her."

Hawke scowled. No doubt, but she shouldn't. How could he dissuade Mother? "A sirenic play would be more impressive than one of Wren's." Sirens performed spectacular plays full of aerial duels, intricate arias, and torrid affairs, so court adored them.

Mother blinked with a faint frown. "Nonsense. Diana says Wren's plays are delightful."

True, but Wren would loathe the attention court would show her afterward. He must quash Mother's plan. Hawke set his jaw and leaned forward. "But, Mother..."

Mother raised her palm. "Enough. Wren's play shall be perfect."

Hawke sighed and pushed away his half-eaten plate. Considering her resolute tone, further attempts to dissuade Mother would be futile. She was determined for Wren to write that play. He must warn Wren when he next saw her.

Mother added, "Now tell us about the masquerade."

His shoulders tensing, Hawke forced a shrug. "The masquerade was well enough, I suppose."

Mother frowned. "You sound as if you didn't enjoy it."

Hawke shrugged again. Not until he met Rowan, but he'd not mention her. Mother would definitely meddle in his courtship then. "Merely bored. I might stop attending court events for a bit." That should explain his time spent hunting and courting Rowan.

Mother and Father exchanged a glance, but Mother only replied, "As long as you still attend family events, like Kit's water party tonight."

Hawke almost winced. Although he'd planned to avoid that party even before Rowan, now he'd better attend to appease Mother. Except then he must deal with Kit's flirting. He straightened. But Rowan might be there. Only near recluses like Wren wouldn't attend the fashionable countess's party.

· · ·

So AFTER DINNER, Hawke rode to the royal bay just north of Ormas. Although usually tranquil and empty, tonight it teemed with barges bearing paper lanterns that shifted from white through every color of the rainbow before fading to white to start again.

Her smoky eyes gleaming, Kit pursed a coy smile when he reached her in the queue to board the first barge.

He said to forestall her flirting, "Lovely water party. Those witchlights must have cost a fortune." Any shop Kit patronized would be fashionable—he could start his hunt for Rowan's witch there. Energy darting through him, he managed a bland smile. "Where did you purchase them?"

"A darling shop called Charms and Nonsense on Morning Street." As the queue behind him surged, Kit fluttered her lashes and leaned toward him. "We must talk once all my guests arrive. I barely saw you at the masquerade."

Hawke grunted. He mustn't allow her to find him later. He escaped Kit and boarded the first barge. Once he accepted a glass of strawberry wine, he strolled along the edge of the barges and hunted for a familiar lady with auburn hair. He sighed after his fourth circuit. Rowan mustn't be here. So he wandered over to his eldest brother and sister-in-law.

Hawke clapped Aragon's shoulder and smiled at Selena. "I'm surprised to see you here, considering your delicate condition."

Selena grimaced, her freckled face wan. "If this wasn't Kit's party, and your parents hadn't a prior engagement, we wouldn't be. But we shan't stay long."

Poor Selena must still be suffering nausea. Hawke winced then flashed a crooked grin at Aragon. "I should tell Devon of your shockingly disloyal decision to attend the Countess of Blaine's water party rather than his summer masquerade."

Aragon returned his brother's grin. "Too late. I told him after the council meeting this morning. Devon said he wished he could have also skipped the masquerade until he met his mermaid."

Mermaid, what mermaid? However, Hawke merely replied, "A pardon straight from the king. Another plan to discredit you foiled."

Aragon arched a brow. "Another plan? What was your first? Pursuing fast widows?" He gave Hawke a pitying glance. "You shan't manage that much longer. Mother has *plans* for you this season."

Plans he'd not succumb to, especially now that he'd met Rowan. Hawke shrugged and snagged a krab turnover from a passing servant. "Wren had heard as much."

Aragon shuddered. "I recall those trying days before I met Selena. Mother was relentless."

Selena chuckled and kissed Aragon's jaw. "I'm glad I've been of some use to you, particularly after all the hassle I caused when we met." An enormous yawn split her face. "I believe we must depart; otherwise, you may be forced to carry me home."

Aragon grinned at his wife. "Well, 'twould demonstrate my prowess to court."

Selena scowled. "Home. Now."

"Yes, my love." Aragon tossed his brother a departing wave.

His ribs squeezing, Hawke watched his brother solicitously escort Selena from the barge. If only Rowan was here. Then he could begin courting her and see if their attraction burgeoned into love like Aragon and Selena shared.

He sighed then sauntered along the edge of the barges to study the guests once more. Rowan still wasn't among them, so he slipped away before Kit could corner him for the talk she'd threatened. He'd visit Wren tomorrow and get her advice about Rowan before starting his hunt in earnest.

CHAPTER 11

When she finally drifted awake, Wren blinked and rubbed her hollow stomach. How long had she been asleep? An entire day, considering her ravenous appetite and the early morning sun. Yet exhaustion still hung over her like a shroud—making love was more rigorous than she'd imagined. But she couldn't sleep forever, so she pushed aside her covers.

Abby burst from the chair by the fireplace, her cry piercing Wren's aching skull, "Thank the Goddess! I was so worried. First, you stayed out until dawn. Then you slept *all* day. You didn't even rise for Lord Beza."

Wren winced. Because she'd been too weary to rise when he'd visited. Even more than she was now. "I'm fine, Abby. I simply danced too much at the masquerade. You know I'm not accustomed to such affairs." Especially when such affairs included making love—twice.

Abby frowned. "But..."

Wren raised a weary hand as her stomach growled. She couldn't handle Abby's scolding right now. "Enough. Go fetch some breakfast. I'm famished."

Abby muttered but bustled from the room.

Wren sighed then dragged herself out of bed. Perhaps food would revive her. She was braiding her hair when Abby returned with a covered tray.

Abby set the tray on the table by the fireplace with a rattle. "Breakfast."

"Thank you, Abby." As Wren devoured her breakfast, her energy trickled back, but languor still filled her bones. If only she could return to bed.

She tensed when Abby asked, "What happened to your costume? I wanted to clean it yesterday but couldn't find it."

A chill skittered across Wren's skin as she shrugged and gulped the last of her shokolat. She adored the hot beverage made from melted dark shokolat, cream, eggs, honey, and cinnaspice. She licked the sweet beverage from her lips. "I burned it."

Abby gaped at her. "Why? You looked lovely in it."

"Never mind my costume." Wren's heart fluttered. "Did Hawke mention why he called yesterday?" Had it been about the enchanted bird or Rowan?

"No." Abby laid a periwinkle dress on the bed. "Though he appeared perturbed you were still abed, as we all were."

Wren scowled at Abby as the maid helped her dress. "I *told* you I'm fine." She wasn't a child to be coddled.

Abby snorted but said nothing further.

Ignoring her maid, Wren glided downstairs to find her parents. She must check they didn't realize she'd seduced Hawke. Mother was reading in the conservatory, so Wren kissed her papery cheek and sat in the chair beside her. "Morning, Mother. Where's Father?"

"Morning, Wren." Mother set aside her book. "The daft man is hawking with the Duke of Childes. When shall he learn that such strenuous pastimes only aggravate his aching bones?"

Warmth imbued Wren at her mother's usual quip over Father's boundless energy. She grinned and replied as she always did, "Probably after we bury him, and not until then."

Mother chuckled, but her eyes sobered as she peered at Wren over her reading spectacles. "Are you well? Your father and I were concerned yesterday."

Wren avoided her mother's probing gaze, her chest tightening. "I'm fine, Mother. I stayed up until dawn working on my play for the orphanage the night before, so I was exhausted."

Mother shook her head with a sigh. "I know how you get in the throes of writing. I do wish you'd take more care."

"I'll do better in the future." After all, she'd never have another night with Hawke. A lump rose in Wren's throat. She stood then kissed her mother's cheek again. "Since I missed Hawke's call yesterday, I'm off to visit him."

Mother nodded and reopened her book. "Have fun."

As Wren strolled to Hawke's townhouse, her heart began pounding. Why had he called right after the masquerade? Surely he couldn't have realized she was Rowan. She swallowed. Not unless he'd burned the enchanted bird.

Unusually winded by her gentle stroll, she paused before his front steps. Goddess, please let him not have burned the enchanted bird. He'd never forgive her deceitful seduction. She gulped a bracing breath then climbed the steps and rapped on his front door.

The door jerked open, and Hawke grinned at her. "Wren, finally!"

As he grabbed her raised wrist and yanked her inside, Wren locked her knees to slow their flight with little success. "Hawke, *what* are you doing? Where's Hobb?"

Hawke shrugged then impelled her into his study and onto the sofa. "Selecting wine for dinner or some such like a good butler should."

Wren's heart galloped as she wrenched her wrist free. Why was Hawke dragging her? "Why are you answering your own door?"

Hawke blinked. "I wasn't. I was on my way to visit you."

Her stomach lurched. Because he'd burned the enchanted bird and realized she was Rowan? "Oh?"

Hawke leaned toward her with a feverish glint in his pale-blue eyes. "Something wondrous happened at the king's summer masquerade, and I need your advice."

Her throat constricting, Wren rasped, "The king's summer masquerade?" Oh, Goddess.

"Yes." Hawke grasped her limp hands and flashed an impish grin. "I met the most delectable lady. A dryad called Rowan."

Heat swept through her at his touch. Why was he holding her hands? Her heart skipped, and she swallowed. "Rowan?"

"Yes." Hawke shrugged. "Although Rowan isn't her true name, which is why I need your advice."

"My advice?" Wren leaned away from Hawke, chill sweat trickling down her back. Was he teasing her? Had he burned the enchanted bird or not?

Hawke nodded. "To help find her."

"Find her?" Wren's breath froze in her chest. Hawke wanted to find Rowan? Why? He'd never pursued past lovers before. He wasn't supposed to do that.

"Yes." Hawke frowned as he squeezed her icy hands. "Wren, why are you repeating everything I say? Is something wrong?"

She managed a tremulous smile. "No, I'm simply surprised you want to find her." At least he didn't appear to realize she'd been Rowan. Perhaps he hadn't found the enchanted bird yet, and she could sneak upstairs to retrieve it.

"How could I not?" Hawke's voice deepened, "'Twas an enchanted night."

Tingling flooded Wren as memories of passionate kisses and entwined bodies echoed through her. It *had* been an enchanted night, and not because of her glamour spell. She forced herself to drawl, "So they all are."

Hawke tsked. "So cynical for one so young." He squeezed her hands again. "'Twas different with Rowan."

Different? Their night shouldn't have been different for

Hawke. Her fingers aching to caress him, she made herself tug on her hands instead. "Very well, but I don't perceive how I can help find your mystery lady."

Hawke released her hands at last to pat his coat pocket. "I've gathered clues to Rowan's identity, and since you're a lady, I thought you'd possess insight that would help."

Wren choked back a cackle. Considering she'd been Rowan, she possessed marvelous insight. Not that she could admit that —'twould destroy their friendship. She swallowed. "What clues do you have?"

With a flourish, Hawke withdrew her small bird carving and a folded piece of paper from his pocket. "The first is this bird. I believe 'tis a spell for courage."

Her ribs tightened. He'd found the enchanted bird, after all. She shied away as he attempted to hand her the pearly carving. She'd not touch it again. "How do you know 'tis not a dastardly seduction spell?"

Hawke withdrew the enchanted bird. "Because she swore she only bought a courage spell."

Wren almost snorted. Such faith in a mysterious lady he'd known for one night. "But how shall an enchanted bird help you find this Rowan?"

Hawke pocketed the bird with a grin. "Simple. I'll learn her true name from the witch who created the spell. There can't be that many fashionable witch shops in Ormas."

She began to relax. Being in a poor neighborhood near the docks, Rhiannon's Veils wasn't fashionable. So her secret might be safe if he hunted elsewhere. "How do you know she bought it at a fashionable shop?"

Hawke handed her the folded paper. "That brings me to my list."

Wren swallowed and unfolded the list then read aloud Hawke's bold scrawl, "Clues to Rowan's Identity. One: Enchanted bird for courage. Two: Genteel breeding." She peered at him. "How did you infer that?"

Hawke chuckled. "'Twas obvious. Her mannerisms and opinions indicated a lady reared by a superior governess. And such a lady would never purchase a spell from a less than fashionable shop. She wouldn't even know where to find one."

She hid a wry smile. Not unless she'd friends in less than fashionable places, like an orphanage. She nodded then returned to the list, "Three: A virgin." A blush scorching her cheeks, she muttered, "How did you recognize that?"

Hawke eyed her askance. "Has your mother never explained?"

Wren blushed harder and shook her head. She'd never asked, so Mother didn't realize her interest, and Mother had never explained since she wasn't betrothed.

Hawke ran a hand through his hair. "A man can feel when he breaches a woman's maidenhead, which only happens her first time."

"I see..." Her eyes widened. So *that* was why the first time had stung at first. Eager to cease discussing that, she read, "Four: Orphanage?"

Hawke relaxed. "Yes, Rowan mentioned an orphanage. But she halted before she revealed more."

Her stomach quivering, Wren almost winced. Well, at least he hadn't noticed her slip about seeing his chambers before. To distract him from the orphanage, she returned to the list again, "Five: Recognized Lantos."

Hawke flashed a crooked smile. "Who, as you know, is a vastly unappreciated bard. We only discovered her because your lute tutor adored music from the previous century."

She did wince at that. She'd forgotten Lantos's obscurity when he'd hummed the other night. She rushed to the final item, "Six: Smoldering auburn hair like flame trapped in wood, changeable hazel eyes like a forest canopy, and a dainty figure like a true dryad."

While she bent her head to disguise her blush at his poetic

description, a matching blush tinted Hawke's cheeks. He said, "I suppose that's a bit much, but Rowan is beautiful."

Wren wrinkled her nose. Yet it had taken a glamour spell for Hawke to see that. She gazed blindly at his list. How could she dissuade him from hunting for Rowan? He must forget about her so their friendship could return to normal. But why was he driven to find her? Because her mystery roused his curiosity? Despite all her careful planning, she'd not anticipated that. She licked her lips. "This is all you know about the mysterious Rowan?"

Hawke nodded and leaned forward with an eager grin. "Yes, what do you think?"

She set her jaw and thrust the list toward him. "That she's too perfect to be real, and you'd be wise to leave your enchanted night as a pleasant memory rather than pursuing a will-o'-the-wisp." Because like the magical ghost lights who misled travelers, Rowan was nothing more than a mirage that led nowhere.

Hawke scowled and pocketed his list. "So you refuse to help me?"

"In perpetrating this folly, yes." Wren rose, gritting a serene smile. He mustn't see her perturbation or he'd wonder at it. And then he might decide to burn the enchanted bird. "I must go. I told Mother I'd join her for luncheon."

Hawke grunted but saw her to the door. "I'll see you later then."

She flicked a wave and fled. Before she saw him again, she must decide how to handle his unexpected hunt for Rowan. 'Twas painful to keep deceiving her best friend.

CHAPTER 12

After Wren left, Hawke began pacing about his study with his hands clenched behind his back. Why had she refused to help him? She should have been excited for him.

He frowned. 'Twas almost as if Wren was jealous of his interest in Rowan. But that made no sense—she regarded him as a friend, not a lover. He shuddered. Their Longnight kiss had proved that. If she regarded him as more, she wouldn't have scolded like a banshee portending a family death.

Shoving that aside, Hawke perched on the edge of his desk and withdrew his list of clues. He must find Rowan, despite what Wren thought. His delectable lady was no will-o'-the-wisp, and she fit better than any other lover. He'd find her, no matter how arduous the hunt.

He scrutinized his list. He'd focus on the most concrete clue, the enchanted bird, but he'd also pursue the orphanage. The remaining clues wouldn't help him find Rowan, but they'd help identify her. His temple aching, he rang the bellpull. When Hobb arrived moments later, Hawke said, "I want a list of Ormas's witch shops patronized by court as well as a list of Ormas's orphanages."

Once the butler left, Hawke tapped his folded list against his chin. Hobb would have nothing until tomorrow at least. In the meantime, he'd visit that witch shop Kit had mentioned at her water party. Perhaps he wouldn't even need Hobb's lists.

So after luncheon, he rode to Morning Street to find Charms and Nonsense. He chuckled at the witch shop's painted sign. Clustered above the ornate shop name were three baskets, one of writhing aether, another of glittering jewelry, and a third of bubbling vials. How whimsical.

Hawke ducked inside then halted at the throng. The rest of court must have decided to visit the fashionable countess's favorite witch shop too. Most of the patrons crammed inside the shop were ladies, but Rowan wasn't among them.

A pang darting through him, he edged along the wall and squeezed into a gap beside the counter to wait for a clerk to become available. He rummaged through the basket of charms nearest him, labeled Perfume Amulets.

As he selected a gray amulet, a young female clerk whisked over. "Bergamot, a nice choice for such a handsome lord."

"Is that what it is?" Hawke dropped the amulet as if scorched. "Truthfully, I'm not interested in perfumed amulets."

"No?" The girl giggled and waved toward the next basket, labeled Perfect Cosmetics. "'Tis clear you need no appearance charm." She whirled around to grab a glittery ring from a basket behind her. "Perhaps you'd like a gift for your sweetheart?" She twisted the ring, and a misty face appeared above it. "Our witches can spell this to show whatever you wish."

He flung up a hand. He must stop the clerk before she described every other unwanted charm in the shop. "I merely want to ask about a spell I found."

The girl stilled and arched her brows. "Oh?"

Good, she quieted enough to listen. Hawke withdrew the enchanted bird from his pocket and set it on the counter. "A lady I met at the king's summer masquerade left this behind, and I want to return it, but I never learned her name. Did she purchase it here?"

The clerk hissed and prodded the pearly carving. "Absolutely not. At Charms and Nonsense, we specialize in magical trinkets with minimal magical cost." Prodding the enchanted bird again, she shuddered. "And this bird is no trinket. 'Tis powerful magic and doubtless extracting a high magical cost from your lady friend."

He blinked with a frown. Powerful magic? "But she said 'twas only a spell for courage."

The girl slowly shook her head. "If so, 'tis a *very* unusual one."

Hawke swallowed. Yet Rowan couldn't have lied to him—she'd been so earnest. "And you're certain she couldn't have purchased it here?"

The clerk eyed Rowan's spell and nodded. "Definitely."

His chest sinking, he tapped the enchanted bird. "Can you think of another witch shop where she might have purchased it?"

The girl shrugged. "Almost any witch shops in Ormas. Most don't share our philosophy of only selling low impact spells."

He tensed and eyed the clerk. She must know more. He flashed a cajoling smile. "Surely you could guess where she might have bought it."

The girl grimaced then replied, "Toil and Trouble at the corner of Broad Street and Amaryllis Road."

Hawke echoed her grimace. Toil and Trouble? How sullen. But perhaps he'd have better success there if they sold more powerful spells than Charms and Nonsense. He pocketed the enchanted bird. "Thank you, miss. You've been most helpful."

"Are you certain you don't want anything?" The clerk flourished the glittery ring. "You could give a picture ring to your mysterious lady when you return her spell."

He almost chuckled as he flicked the girl a silver coin. She certainly was determined to sell him one of her charms. "Not today, but perhaps when I find her."

Adroitly catching the coin, the clerk bobbed a small bow. "Well, ask for Anya when you return. I'll give you the best bargain."

Hawke nodded at her then thrust through the crowded witch shop and equally crowded street to return home. He'd visit Toil and Trouble tomorrow as soon as the shops opened to avoid the throng.

So STRAIGHT AFTER breakfast the following morning, Hawke rode to the corner of Broad Street and Amaryllis Road. His neck prickled as he eyed Toil and Trouble's black door. It definitely suited the shop's sullen name. He strode inside then grimaced at the silence, shadows, and stale air. Black witches would adore this gloomy shop.

A thready voice drifted across the room, "Greetings, my lord. How may I be of service?"

Hawke peered through the gloom. At the back of the shop, a cadaverous man was hunched over a massive tome. Although his long beard was white, his dark robe made him disappear into the shadows. Hawke swallowed then approached the witch and withdrew the enchanted bird. "I'd like to learn about this."

The witch rose and stretched forth his gnarled hands, a fervid gleam lighting his eyes.

His stomach tightening, Hawke dropped the enchanted bird into the ancient witch's eager grasp. After the witch had caressed it for several moments without a word, Hawke said, "I believe 'tis a courage spell."

The witch chuckled. "Is that what she told you?"

Hawke frowned at the witch's sardonic drawl. "Yes." And 'twas the truth.

"Doubtful." The ancient witch petted the enchanted bird. "Unless the courage was for you."

"Of course not." Rowan had scoffed at that idea. Still frowning, Hawke eyed the witch. "Why would you think that?"

The witch shrugged and shot him a glance. "Because you're a focus of the spell."

A chill skittered across Hawke's skin. Why was Rowan's spell focused on him? She'd sworn she hadn't purchased a love or seduction spell. He swallowed. "Can you tell the purpose of the spell?"

"No." The witch scowled. "There's a strong warding on the spell preventing anyone from deciphering it."

Hawke relaxed. The witch's words were just supposition then. He leaned forward. "How can you tell I'm a focus of the spell?"

The ancient witch stroked his tangled beard. "Because I can sense it working on you."

Hawke's stomach lurched. He clenched his hands behind his back. "The spell is still active?"

"Yes." The witch shook his head. "The lady who commissioned this spell certainly believes in being thorough. I wonder if she realizes the magical cost for that."

Hawke tensed as another chill engulfed him. Goddess, what had Rowan done? "Are you certain you can't determine the purpose of the spell?"

"Yes, and all the witches in Ormas will tell you the same, except for the spell's creator." The ancient witch shook his head again. "The spell is ingenious and powerful—I've never seen its like. It can only be the work of a Rhiannon descendant."

Hawke nodded. Because descendants of the early witches bloodbound to the founder of human magic were more powerful than their fellow witches. "I assume by your tone you aren't one."

"If only that were true." The witch caressed the enchanted bird still cradled in his hand. "Just imagine all the spells I could cast, like this lovely little bird here."

Hawke suppressed a shudder at the witch's lust. "How can I find a Rhiannon descendant?"

The ancient witch grunted. "As to that, I don't know. True Rhiannon descendants are shy about announcing their power."

Hawke almost snorted. So that people like this witch wouldn't exploit them. He drummed his fingers against the counter. "Do you know any that might be a Rhiannon descendant?"

The witch shrugged. "No."

Hawke's jaw tightened, but he drawled, "So I must visit every witch shop in Ormas and ask if they created the enchanted bird?"

The ancient witch shrugged again. "I can't see what else you could do."

"Very well, thank you for your time." Hawke wrested the enchanted bird from the witch's grasp and dropped a silver coin onto his empty palm.

He strode outside into the golden sunshine and rode home. Although he'd learned about the spell's creator at the gloomy witch shop, he'd learned nothing about Rowan. If only Wren had accompanied him. Surely she'd have gleaned more from the ancient witch.

He grimaced as he climbed the steps to his townhouse. Except once Wren saw Toil and Trouble, she'd have refused to enter the witch shop. She'd avoided magic since the incident with the charmed pen, and the shop's sullen name and door would have only heightened her distrust.

After pouring a snifter of spiritwine from the gamesroom bar, Hawke tramped to his study. He missed Wren, and not just because she could aid his hunt. He sighed. Why had she been upset about Rowan? She'd never cared about his past lovers. And her unexpected disapproval had confounded him, so he'd forgotten to warn her about Mother's fete plans. His throat tightened. Now Mother might ambush Wren with her ridiculous plan.

He drained his spiritwine then set aside his snifter. He'd warn Wren when he next saw her, but for now, he must focus on finding Rowan. Unfortunately, Hobb hadn't brought those lists he'd requested yet, so all he had was the list of clues he'd written. He withdrew it from his pocket and studied it again but saw nothing new. When his head began pounding, he closed his eyes and rubbed his temple. His hunt for Rowan was going to be painful.

CHAPTER 13

The afternoon after her dispute with Hawke, Wren burst into the matron's study at the orphanage. Talking with Kiera would surely help her not fret about his unexpected hunt. Plus, last night she'd finally finished the orphanage play. "Afternoon."

"Wren!" Kiera raised her head with a smile that became a frown as she eyed Wren. "Is everything all right? You appear exhausted."

Wren grimaced and sat in the chair before Kiera's desk. Was it so obvious? "I was up past midnight finishing the play." And her sensual dreams of Hawke hadn't made for restful sleep.

Kiera's eyes narrowed.

Before her friend could speak, Wren tossed the finished play on the desk.

Kiera arched a brow but flicked through the play. "*Kat's Tail.* Intriguing. The children shall love it, as always. But you shouldn't have missed sleep to finish it."

Wren blushed and gazed at her hands. "I had to. The ending was giving me some trouble." Mostly because she'd not worked on it since learning of Hawke's imminent betrothal.

Pursing her lips, Kiera eyed her friend. However, she only

asked, "So has Abby forgiven you for not wearing that masquerade costume?"

Yes, because she'd worn it to seduce Hawke. Tingling warmth flooded Wren as making love with him echoed through her. She forced herself back to Abby, who still hadn't forgiven her for destroying the costume after wearing it. She shrugged. "As much as she ever does."

Kiera chuckled. "Next year you should wear the costume and pretend to attend to stop her fussing. Use tales from Hawke to convince her. What did he say about this year's masquerade?"

Wren shifted in her chair, her hands fisting in her lap. That he'd met a delectable lady, but one who didn't exist. "Not much."

Kiera's brows flew upward. "Really? But he usually shares everything with you."

Wren leapt to her feet. Visiting Kiera hadn't distracted her from Hawke at all, and her perceptive friend saw too much. She must leave before Kiera realized she'd seduced Hawke. "I must go. I'll return next week for play rehearsals."

Before Kiera could reply, Wren darted back to her carriage. Then to distract herself, she spent the rest of the afternoon rereading her favorite book, the volume of Lantos verse Hawke had secretly given her the natalday Kit had given her the charmed pen.

At dinner, Mother mentioned Hawke's mother wanted Wren to join her for a private luncheon the following day. Wren's skin prickled, but she nodded without protest. She couldn't refuse a summons from the duchess, no matter how suspicious.

If only she could visit Hawke to learn if he knew the reason for his mother's invitation. She suppressed a wince. Except he'd probably want to discuss Rowan again. Surely if she waited another day or two, he'd have forgotten his vanished lover, and everything would be normal again.

· · ·

So when Wren entered his parents' family dining room the following day, she still had no inkling why the duchess had invited her. Hopefully, it didn't involve the king's summer masquerade or Hawke's imminent betrothal.

The duchess kissed Wren's cheek then gestured toward the tea table. As always, the duchess's blonde perfection made Wren itch to smooth her dress. Yet despite their disparate appearances, the duchess beamed at her as they sat. "How are you, Wren?"

Wren swallowed at the duchess's dulcet expression. That expression usually meant Hawke's mother was matchmaking. "I'm well, thank you."

After the servants brought the first course, the duchess chuckled and leaned toward Wren. "I expect Hawke told you our happy news."

Wren's stomach quivered, but she swallowed the formerly succulent fish clogging her mouth. The duchess would only consider one thing happy news, and Hawke had been too distracted by Rowan to mention something as insignificant as his betrothal. "No, I'm afraid not."

"How odd." The duchess hummed for a long moment. "Well, Selena is with child."

Her stomach relaxing, Wren finished her fish. Selena's pregnancy must explain the duchess's invitation and dulcet expression. "That is happy news. Congratulations."

"I'm exceedingly eager to hold my first grandchild in my arms." The duchess grinned as the second course was served. When they were alone again, she drawled, "Since you've volunteered at Waterstreet Orphanage for eleven years, you must adore children too."

Wren choked on her wine and eyed Hawke's mother over her glass. Why was the duchess quizzing her about children? "Yes."

The duchess nodded as she began cutting her beefsteak. "You should marry then. 'Tis not as if you dislike men. Why, you and Hawke have been inseparable since you were born."

Wren shifted in her chair and almost blushed. And they'd

been even more inseparable four nights ago. "Yes, but we're just friends."

The duchess's pale-blue eyes gleamed, exactly like Hawke's at his most impish. "Friends often make the best husbands. The duke and I were friends before we married."

"But husbands must also be lovers, and I don't think of Hawke like that." Heat scorched Wren's cheeks as them making love echoed through her again. She bent her head to hide her blush and finished her beefsteak.

The duchess arched a brow as trifle was served, but once the servants left, she only said, "I invited you to luncheon today to ask a favor."

A frisson flashed across Wren's skin. Please don't be about Rowan or Hawke's betrothed. "What would you like?"

The duchess beamed while she poured them cups of kahve. "One of your delightful plays for my fete celebrating my first grandchild."

Wren forced herself to breathe. She couldn't write a play for court. "One of my plays wouldn't be grand enough. Perhaps a sirenic play instead?" With flying battles, exquisite duets, and passionate romances, sirenic plays were always stunning.

The duchess pursed her lips. "Hawke suggested the same."

Pain slashed through Wren's chest. Hawke knew about this and hadn't told her? Had his infatuation with Rowan completely consumed him?

The duchess nodded. "But one of your plays shall be perfect."

Wren eyed Hawke's mother. From her resolute smile, doubtless she'd persist until Wren relented. Her stomach heavy, Wren sighed. "Very well."

Not bothering with her trifle or kahve, Wren fled before the duchess could ask any more favors. The next one *would* be about Rowan or Hawke's betrothed.

Focused on escape, she almost crashed into the lady ascending the front steps. "I'm *so* sorry." She glanced up and stiffened. "Good afternoon, Kit. What are you doing here?"

A smirk curved Kit's lips. "I'm here to leave an invitation to my card party. You?"

Wren forced a serene smile. "The duchess invited me for luncheon."

"Really?" Kit leaned forward. "Did she discuss Hawke's betrothal?"

Wren's pulse stuttered. "No, the fete she is planning." She'd not mention the fete play—Kit would only needle her about it.

Kit arched a brow. "Odd. The duchess should have since you're *such* a close family friend."

Wren maintained her smile, but her tone sharpened, "Well, she didn't."

"Did she mention the gossip from the king's summer masquerade?" When Wren shook her head, Kit purred a chuckle. "Mysterious ladies monopolized both of court's most coveted unwed gentlemen. King Devon met a mermaid and danced with her rest of the night. And Hawke whisked away a dryad as soon as she arrived, then neither were seen at the masquerade again."

"So?" Wren almost winced. Of course court had noticed Hawke's disappearance. At least no one had recognized her. Kit would have gloated if they had.

Kit's eyes glinted. "Doesn't Hawke's peculiar behavior concern you?"

Wren shrugged. "His behavior at the masquerade doesn't sound peculiar. Hawke often disappears with lovers." Although until Rowan, he'd never pursued one after their affair ended.

Kit moued and tilted her head, her sable hair gleaming in the summer sun. "I'd have thought those lovers would vex you, considering how *close* you are to Hawke."

Wren flashed a glittering smile. They did, but she'd never admit that to anyone, especially Kit. "Why would they? Those lovers mean nothing to Hawke, while I've been his best friend for ages."

Wren nodded at Kit then swept down the front steps. Hopefully, Kit believed her lie.

. . .

AFTER AN AFTERNOON SPENT READING to distract herself about Hawke and avoid the fete play, Wren dressed for dinner and strolled to the family dining room. Her parents beamed when she joined them.

As they began their whitekrab soup, Mother asked Wren, "How was your luncheon with Caro?"

Wren wrinkled her nose. "'Twas very—interesting. The duchess asked me to write a play for her fete to celebrate her first grandchild." Finishing her soup, she eyed Mother. "I suspect you'd something to do with that."

Mother beamed while Father served them roast chicken. "I mentioned your plays when Caro said she was hunting for entertainment. They're always so diverting. 'Tis a shame you've only written them for the orphanage."

Wren swallowed as she pushed her chicken around her plate. "Writing diverting plays for an orphanage is entirely different than writing them for court."

Father's eyes gleamed with laughter. "I'm certain you'll think of something clever, my dear. After all, you are my daughter."

Wren smiled and relaxed. Like always, Father's loving teasing heartened her—although she'd still rather not write the fete play. "Thank you, Father."

As her parents began discussing King Devon and his mysterious mermaid over the next course, Wren toyed with her spiced apples. At least they weren't discussing Hawke and his mysterious dryad.

She stiffened when Mother said, "Do you think the mermaid used a glamour spell to capture the king's attention?"

Father snorted. "Doubtful. The magical cost to subvert the protection charm King Sarastor gave him would probably kill her."

A chill skittering across her skin, Wren swallowed. "What?"

Father's expression was solemn for once. "Strong spells can

have grave magical costs. And a spell to overcome a protection charm created by the royal witch would need to be strong indeed."

As strong as her glamour spell from the veiled witch? Wren forced herself to sip her wine. "What sort of costs?"

Mother shook her head. "With strong spells, no one can say until afterward."

Wren almost shivered. Oh, Goddess. "Then why did you risk the spell to conceive me? Surely that was a strong spell."

Father exchanged a glance with Mother then threaded his fingers through hers. "We'd been married twenty years, and we'd never conceived, so we knew a strong spell was our only chance for a child."

Mother gave Wren a tender smile. "We would have gladly paid any cost for you."

Wren's ribs constricted. Any cost? That sounded ominous. What would she pay for her night with Hawke? "What cost did you pay?"

Mother touched her throat. "I loved to sing and had a beautiful voice, but after the spell, only air emerges when I sing."

Wren flinched. That must be why Mother had chanted rather than sang lullabies. She turned to Father. "And you?"

He shrugged. "My aching bones."

Wren closed her eyes. Those aching bones crippled an active gentleman like Father. "So for a child to love, magic took something else you loved."

Mother's mellifluous voice was warm, "Yes, but your father and I have never once regretted it."

Wren opened her eyes. And she must do the same. If only she could determine what her cost was.

Without waiting for dessert, Wren returned to her chambers to work on the fete play, but inspiration remained absent. Her ideas might amuse children from a poor orphanage, but they were too simple to satisfy court. She grimaced and threw down her pen. Normally, she'd discuss ideas with Hawke or Kiera. But

Kiera had no experience with court, and she was avoiding Hawke.

She sighed. They'd only been apart two days, but she missed him. And since Hawke hadn't stopped by, he must still be obsessed with his hunt. Could she risk seeing him while he was hunting Rowan? Perhaps if she pretended to aid him instead of ignoring him. Then she could encourage him to forget Rowan and deflect his hunt, so their friendship would return to normal. Until he married someone else.

Wren glanced at the fete play's blank page. She could offer her help in exchange for his help with the play. Hawke would never suspect her of obstructing his hunt. A strangled cry bursting from her lips, she flung herself into bed. She'd never practiced such tricks until the masquerade. Why had she allowed Kit's needling to tempt her into seducing Hawke?

CHAPTER 14

*H*aving endured various court events to find Rowan since his visit to Toil and Trouble two mornings ago, Hawke struggled from his tangled sheets much later than usual due to explicit dreams about her. He glared at his empty bed and rubbed his still throbbing head. How could a bed that had been the perfect size have become so massive after she'd spent one night in it? He sighed as he rang for his valet.

Once Hawke had shaved and dressed, John asked, "Shall I have Cook prepare breakfast?"

Hawke's stomach lurched. His head pounded too much to eat. "No, just have kahve sent to the study."

He scooped up the enchanted bird from his bedside table then strolled downstairs. Setting the wooden carving beside his list of clues, he sprawled into the chair behind his desk and rubbed his temple until Hobb arrived.

The butler set a tray of kahve and breakfast rolls on the desk then offered Hawke some papers. "The lists you requested, my lord."

Hawke snatched the lists. At last! Now he could cease attending court events to find Rowan. Without Wren or his family insulating him from husband-hunting ladies, court events were painful to attend. Plus, they'd been pointless since he couldn't ask about Rowan without rumors starting, and she'd not appeared at any of the events. She must be almost as reclusive as Wren. His temples tightening, he waved the butler from the study. "Thank you, Hobb. I've difficult business and don't wish to be disturbed."

As Hobb left, Hawke began studying the list of fashionable witch shops, but the butler's scrawl made his throbbing head clench. He shuddered and set aside the lists. Perhaps a steaming cup of kahve would ease his headache and allow him to read. He poured himself some kahve, ignoring the breakfast rolls. He shut his eyes and cleared his mind as he sipped the dark, bitter brew. When he'd finished, the pounding in his head had muted, and he could think again. So he must resume his hunt for Rowan.

He poured himself more kahve then eyed the butler's lists again. Visiting each witch shop alphabetically would take too long, so he must devise a strategy, but what? None of the shops seemed obvious choices. And how could he possibly use the list of orphanages? He'd no inkling how Rowan was involved with the one she'd mentioned.

Rubbing his temple, he sighed and sipped his kahve. He needed Wren's help to analyze his lists. But she'd disapproved of his hunt, so how could he convince her to help him? Perhaps if he explained how special that night with Rowan had been and begged for her help. Wren was too tenderhearted to resist a plea from her best friend. Even if she thought his desire foolish.

Hawke glanced at the clock on the mantel. 'Twas almost noon, so he'd visit Wren after luncheon. But first he should select the first witch shop to visit. He scanned the list of witch shops again. Where would a lady purchase a spell for courage? Mirage or Esrever? Or perhaps Bewitching Raiments?

A spritely knock on his study door startled him. His head pounding anew, he didn't look up from his list. He must pick a witch shop. "I told you I didn't wish to be disturbed, Hobb."

"'Tisn't Hobb," a familiar alto replied.

"Wren!" Warmth radiating through him, Hawke dropped the list of witch shops and leapt to his feet. "I was just about to call on you."

"Then I saved you a trip." Wren slipped into the study and lifted the basket hooked on her elbow. "I brought nutbread."

His stomach rumbled despite his aching head. He couldn't refuse his favorite treat. He strode across the room and liberated the basket. "You know me so well."

A wry smile curved Wren's lips. "I should. We've known each other all our lives."

"So we have." Tingling swept across his skin as he set the basket on his desk beside the enchanted bird. "I'll ring for fresh kahve."

Wren shook her head before he reached the bellpull. "Don't bother. I requested some from Hobb when I arrived."

The butler entered the study as if her words had summoned him and replaced the old kahve tray.

Hawke couldn't resist grinning at Hobb. "How did Wren wheedle herself into my study? I told you I didn't wish to be disturbed."

As Hobb stiffened, Wren tsked. "Cease teasing your butler, Hawke. Such orders have never applied to me, as you well know."

Yes, but Hobb was amusing to tease. Hawke chuckled and waved the butler from the study. As Hobb left, he dragged a chair for Wren to the side of his desk. "I suppose that's true."

Wren's smile was wooden as she sat and poured them kahve. "Although doubtless that's about to change. Your wife shan't wish another lady to run tame in her household."

He blinked as he plucked several slices of nutbread from her basket. Was that why Wren had refused to help him? Yet her concern was unfounded. Surely Rowan would understand he and Wren were simply friends. "I shan't marry a lady who doesn't allow us to remain best friends."

Wren snorted and slanted him a flat glance while she stirred several spoons of sugar into her kahve.

His jaw stiff, Hawke devoured his first slice of nutbread. "Besides, I never said I wanted to marry Rowan." Although their night had been extraordinary, he didn't know her well enough for that—yet.

Wren's lips tightened as she buttered a slice of nutbread. "Then why are you so keen to find her? You want another night or two before you tire of her? Or perhaps you can't bear for a lover to tire of *you* first?"

Fire flashed through him, and he crammed another slice of nutbread into his mouth. Then he swallowed and said, "That's not it at all. I want to find Rowan so I can court her and see if our attraction burgeons into love. I'll only marry when I love a lady who loves me in return."

Wren bent her head and set down her nutbread. "And you think Rowan might be that lady? Why her and not another of your many lovers?"

His heart surged as memories of their hungry kisses and tender rapport darted through him. "Because she differed from any lady I've ever met."

Wren crumbled her uneaten slice of nutbread. "Differed how?"

Tingling warmth filled Hawke. "Rowan fit better than any other lover ever has."

Wren lifted her chin, a blush staining her cheeks. "I suppose by that you mean the coupling was good."

A slice of nutbread halfway to his mouth, he stared at Wren. She never spoke so crudely. Why now? "It was, the best in fact, but that's not why I want to court Rowan."

Wren arched a brow and gestured for him to continue with her cup of kahve.

How could he convince her? Hawke set down his nutbread. "'Twas more than mere coupling, Wren. I've been with enough lovers to recognize that. I felt as if I'd known Rowan forever and could be my true self with her."

Wren's cup clinked as she set it beside the basket of nutbread. "More than you are with me?" Hurt echoed in her soft words.

His heart squeezed. He grasped her hands, a zing darting from his fingers to his chest. "No, but we're not attracted to each other."

Her face scarlet, Wren yanked her hands free. "How are you certain your sense of intimacy wasn't an illusion? Your mysterious dryad vanished after a night."

Hawke's head throbbed. Why was he so certain? Rowan's face flashed through his mind. Because of the tenderness in her hazel eyes. He met Wren's gaze, his headache sharpening. "Believe me, it was real."

Wren huffed a sigh. "Very well, but why did Rowan vanish without a word? She must be unable to pursue a relationship. Perhaps she's ill or dying."

He snorted. Wren's concern was conjuring wild suppositions. "Rowan acted too lively to be dying."

Wren wrinkled her nose. "Then she must be ineligible for another reason. Perhaps she's married and sought a dalliance. Masquerades are ideal for that."

Hawke chuckled. Which was why Wren despised them. "True, but Rowan couldn't be married—her husband would rise from his deathbed to consummate their marriage, and she'd been a virgin."

A blush darkened Wren's cheeks. "Well, perhaps she's betrothed and seduced another gentleman to escape it."

He stilled. Had Rowan become his lover to escape an unwanted betrothal? Surely not. She'd appeared focused on him. Although she had refused to dance with him in the ballroom. He shook his head to dispel his doubts. "Rowan would never act so dishonorably."

Wren grimaced and raised her eyes skyward. "Well, she must have had *some* reason to vanish."

His stomach tightened, and he scowled at her. "Why are you determined to see the worst in Rowan?"

Wren started as if shocked by an energy spell. "I'm not. I merely find her vanishing suspicious." She touched his hand. "I worry about you, Hawke."

Hawke relaxed as his heart softened at her tender concern. He flashed a crooked grin and squeezed her hand. "You worry about everyone."

Wren glared as she snatched back her hand. "I do not."

He shook his head at her. She'd not dedicate herself to the orphanage if she didn't. "You do."

Wren pursed her lips. "I'm attempting to offer to help find your Rowan, but you're making it difficult to do so."

"Are you?" Hawke arched a brow. "It seemed to me you were attempting to disparage her." Which was unusual for his tender-hearted friend.

"I was being realistic," Wren gritted. She thrust out her hand. "Just give me that list you showed me the other day."

He brightened and handed her that list as well as the ones for the witch shops and orphanages. Thank the Goddess she was helping him at last.

Wren perusing the lists with a frown. "Do you recall anything else?"

Hawke strained to recall further details about Rowan. Pain pierced his skull. He rubbed his brow as his head began throbbing in time with his heart. "Cursed headache."

Wren stiffened and glanced up at him. "What?"

Still rubbing his head, he grimaced. "Ever since the masquerade, my head has ached throughout the day, particularly when I try to recall Rowan."

Wren caressed his temple, her hazel eyes darkening. "I'm sorry."

Hawke blinked. Why did Wren almost appear guilty about his headache? He shrugged. "Why? 'Tisn't your fault."

CHAPTER 15

*W*ren suppressed a wince as she touched Hawke's temple. Except if he suffered headaches when thinking of Rowan, then doubtless they were her fault. She glared at the enchanted bird sitting on his desk. The glamour spell must be causing his headaches to prevent him from recognizing her as Rowan.

She gulped and dropped her hand. Her parents had both sacrificed something they loved for the spell to conceive her. What if Hawke's headaches were more than obfuscation, and her cost for their enchanted night was his life? Goddess, 'twould be so much worse than when her pet faebird had died when she was seven.

Both she and her faebird had contracted wraith flu that winter. And although wraith flu drained people to pale shades of themselves, it rarely killed them—unlike more fragile creatures like the tiny, jewel-like songbirds beloved for their bewitching songs. Yet at least when her pet faebird died, she'd had Hawke to comfort her. He'd asked to create their friendship stone the morning she'd emerged after her illness. The heart-shaped stone he'd chosen had made her realize she loved him, and she'd assumed he loved her back until he kissed Kit first. Then she'd known he saw her as nothing more than a friend.

His brow furrowed, Hawke leaned toward her. "Are you well? Your skin is the color of whey."

Dragging her mind back to the present, Wren dredged up a smile. "Of course. I simply realized how difficult our hunt for Rowan shall be. We know so little. What have you done the past few days?"

Hawke relaxed into his chair. "I visited two witch shops about the enchanted bird. I started with the one Kit recommended—"

Her chest squeezed as if seized by a massive kraken's many tentacles. She clenched Hawke's lists in her hands. "You told *Kit* about Rowan?" Oh, Goddess.

"Of course not. I noticed she'd some ingenious witchlights at her water party, so I asked her where she purchased them." Hawke shuddered. "I'm not in the habit of sharing confessions with Kit. Especially with her on the prowl for a new husband."

Wren sighed and smoothed out the lists. "I see."

Hawke flashed a crooked grin. "Besides, you're the only one who knows about Rowan, and that's how I intend to keep it until I find her. Can you imagine Mother's *help* if she knew?"

Wren winced. If the duchess learned about Rowan, she'd soon realize Wren was Rowan. The enchanted bird would prevent the duchess from revealing that to Hawke, but it wouldn't prevent her from pestering Wren. "Then I'll not mention Rowan to anyone."

"Good." Hawke smiled and nodded. "As I was saying, I visited Kit's witch shop, but the clerk only directed me to another shop. And the clerk there told me a Rhiannon descendant must have created the enchanted bird. But he didn't know any."

Wren stared at him. The veiled witch was a Rhiannon descendant? Well, that explained her shop's name and her reputation for being able to magic anything. She arched her brows. "Did they offer how to determine if a witch is a Rhiannon descendant?"

Hawke grimaced as he ran a hand through his inky-brown hair. "No."

She leaned forward with a tight smile. She must pretend to further his hunt. And pursuing his list of witch shops should be safe since it didn't include Rhiannon's Veils. "So we've no way to filter your list of witch shops?"

"No." Hawke sighed and turned to his other list. "What about my list of orphanages?"

"I don't know." Wren eyed that list, which *did* include Waterstreet Orphanage. So she needed a plausible reason to avoid pursuing it. "We don't know how Rowan is connected to an orphanage. She only mentioned one mid scold."

She froze, her mouth drying. Hawke hadn't told her why Rowan had mentioned the orphanage. Damn her loose tongue. Had he noticed?

Yet Hawke merely nodded. "True, but she did mention one, so she must be connected to an orphanage somehow."

Wren relaxed. Hawke hadn't noticed her slip, but he was still determined to pursue the orphanages. She needed a better excuse. How about not having a sketch of Rowan? Even if he'd attempted to sketch her, no one would recognize her from it—he excelled at the violin, not sketching. "Do you possess a sketch of Rowan?"

"No." Hawke pursed a wry smile. "Not that I could provide one. As you well know, my sketches would make a chimera laugh." And the three-headed hybrid of a lion, goat, and snake wasn't known for its sense of humor, but its destructive rage. Which seeing one of his sketches might inspire.

She pursed her lips to disguise her grin. "Then I doubt the orphanages would be much help. We've nothing to show them, and your description, while poetic, is too vague."

Hawke's jaw tightened. "Auburn hair, hazel eyes, and dainty figure seem specific enough to me."

And perfectly described her. Her heart quivered, but Wren slanted him a flat glance. "Except those traits mean different things to different people. Auburn ranges from near red to brown, hazel from brown to blue, and dainty from diminutive to frail." Thank the Goddess for that. Although if he provided his description with her beside him, anyone would realize she'd been Rowan.

"I suppose." Hawke scowled. "So we're stuck with the witch shops then."

"Yes." She sighed then tapped the lists against her knee. Now that she'd misdirected his hunt, she must delay it as well. "Could I borrow these lists for a day or so? I'd like to rank the witch shops, so we know which to visit first."

Hawke beamed at her. "Would you?"

"Of course." His grateful expression curdled her stomach. Deceiving Hawke like this was wicked, especially considering how she loved him. Yet what else could she do? If he realized she'd disguised herself with a glamour spell to seduce him, 'twould destroy their friendship.

Wren crushed his lists in her lap. Even though their enchanted night had been the best of her life, she never should have purchased that wretched spell. But no sense crying for spilt unicorn water. Relaxing her hands, she shoved Hawke's lists into her reticule. She *must* shift their conversation from Rowan before she crumbled with guilt. "I finished my play for the orphanage the other day."

"The one about the clever cat and her bumbling master?" When she nodded, Hawke asked, "Would there be a part for a violinist?"

She blinked. Hawke was offering to be in an orphanage play? He'd not taken part in one since she'd begged for his help two summers ago. He was always too busy with court events and his many lovers. And although she'd been his first lover in nearly a year, he still attended countless court events. "What about the social season?"

Hawke flicked his fingers. "I've decided to cease attending court events that bore me, which are most of them. I can't understand why I ever started attending so many."

Wren almost winced. She did. She'd never forget their wretched first season. That spring and summer, she'd cried whenever he'd attended a court event rather than joining her at the orphanage. "As I recall, the duchess nagged until you did so." Fortunately, Mother hadn't done that to Wren.

"Right." Hawke grinned at her. "If I only attend interesting court events, I'll have plenty of time, so I thought I could help at the orphanage again."

Her heart lightened. Like he had before their come out. "The orphans shall definitely appreciate that. In fact, some," like the scampish Bedsford twins, "shall adore you at once."

Hawke winked. "I look forward to meeting them."

Wren giggled. And inspiring them to new mischief. "No doubt. Well, I can add you to the play. Rehearsals start in a few days."

Hawke inclined his head. "Just let me know when."

She grinned in response then deflated. But could she manage the orphanage rehearsals while writing the duchess's onerous play? She sighed. "'Twas fortunate I'd finished the orphanage play. Your mother asked me to write one for her fete celebrating Aragon and Selena's baby."

Hawke winced. "I meant to warn you but forgot because of our disagreement the other day. I'm sorry, Wren."

Warmth welled in her chest. Perhaps his infatuation with Rowan hadn't consumed him, after all. She'd just fled before he could warn her. "'Tis fine."

"No, 'tis not." Hawke glanced at her. "I'm surprised Mother convinced you. I thought you'd refuse."

Wren grimaced. If only she could have. "I tried, but I could tell she wouldn't relent until I agreed."

Hawke echoed her grimace. "I recall thinking the same when

I started attending those boring court events." He arched a brow. "Would you like help writing the fete play?"

She beamed at Hawke. She'd been about to ask him exactly that. "Yes, please."

After a brief knock, Hobb entered the study with the post. The butler handed it to Hawke then departed.

Riffling through the stack, Hawke paused at a vellum letter. "The Westons are having a musical evening a week and a half from now. Shall we attend?"

Wren shrugged. The Westons' musical evenings were more bearable than most court events, and as a musician, Hawke adored attending, so she often joined him. She didn't love music like he did, but she enjoyed it well enough, and the Westons were always amiable. "If you like."

Hawke snapped his fingers. "Which reminds me, a selection of Lantos's songs are being performed tomorrow at The Nightingale. I meant to invite you several days ago but kept forgetting. A theme for me lately."

She straightened. Lantos music actually sounded tempting. But only if they could listen to it without constant interruptions. "Shall the duchess be attending?"

"Avoiding my mother, perchance?" When she wrinkled her nose at him, Hawke chuckled. "Perhaps because unlike most of court, you attend concerts to hear the music rather than be seen?"

They both did. Wren repeated his phrase from earlier, "You know me so well."

Hawke nudged her skirt with his boot. "Fortunately for you, she and Father are attending the Campbells' ball."

She nodded. "Oh yes, my parents are too." She'd forgotten that since she rarely attended balls. "I'll look forward to attending the concert." She glanced at the clock on the mantel. "I should go—Mother is expecting me for luncheon."

Hawke dropped the enchanted bird in his pocket then threaded his arm through hers.

Heat flashed through Wren, like it had when he'd taken her hands and denied their attraction. As he escorted her out, she buried her reaction to his touch. Although their one night had whetted her desire for him, she must learn to ignore it. Their enchanted night was over.

Hawke squeezed her elbow before releasing her at the front door. "I'll fetch you tomorrow at half past seven."

She nodded then waved and descended his front steps. Hopefully, by then she'd have contrived another excuse to delay Hawke's hunt as well as learned to ignore her desire.

CHAPTER 16

Straight after dinner the following evening, Hawke bounded up Wren's front stairs to fetch her for the Lantos concert. But he was early, so Perkins Two showed him to the morning room. As he sprawled into a damask chair, energy jittered across his skin. Had Wren ranked the witch shops yet? Perhaps he'd ask her before the concert.

Yet when Wren joined him, his breath stilled, and his question vanished. She looked lovely in her deep green evening gown with an emerald firegem flickering at the hollow of her throat.

Wren glided across the morning room. "I swear, you arrive early so I feel guilty for keeping you waiting."

Hawke rose. Who did Wren remind him of in that gown? Agony stabbed his head, and he rubbed his temple. Foolishness, she doubtless reminded him of herself. "I simply didn't wish to be late."

Wren pursed her lips. "You were in such a rush to arrive, your cravat is crooked."

While she tweaked his cravat, he studied her auburn hair, whose subdued knot couldn't disguise its fiery gleam or delicate violet scent. For some reason, his heart fluttered.

"There," Wren murmured as she finished, her hands stilling to rest on his shoulders.

His pulse surged. Why? He gulped a steadying breath then tapped her firegem. "Considering your opinion on magic, I'm surprised you're wearing a firegem."

Wren jerked away as if burned. "Although hardened dragon flame, firegems only contain residual magic, and everyone knows they're harmless. Besides, as a family heirloom from Lantos's era, I thought it appropriate tonight."

Hawke escorted her to his carriage then settled in the backward seat across from her. "It certainly lights up the carriage." Although the dragon flame trapped inside the emerald firegem made Wren's face an inscrutable mask. As inscrutable as Rowan's in the moonlight behind her leaf mask. Pain pierced his head again, and his breath caught in his throat.

Wren fingered her flickering firegem as the carriage started forward. "Perhaps I shouldn't wear it to the concert because it shall attract too much attention."

Forcing himself to breathe until his head eased, he leaned back and crossed his ankles. "I could draw the curtains to the box if it bothers you."

Wren winced and shook her head. "Absolutely not. Salacious gossip would start within minutes."

And court adored nothing more than salacious gossip, even if 'twas impossible, like an affair between him and Wren. Weight compressed his chest. "I suppose it would."

Wren crossed her arms. "So the box curtains shall remain open, no matter the attention my firegem necklace garners."

Hawke shrugged. "As you wish. I'm not the one who despises attention." Hopefully, the necklace wouldn't attract any, for her sake.

Wren scowled and kicked his ankle. "No, you seek it instead to conceal your true emotions, even from yourself."

His stomach hardened. What did she mean by that? He eyed

her as he straightened from his sprawl. "My, someone is in a scathing mood."

Wren grimaced and shook her head. "Sorry. I spent most of the day attempting to rank your list of witch shops without success, which soured my mood."

Hawke sighed. Wren had found the list impossible too? Before he could ask her about that, the carriage halted, so he extended his hand and said, "Well, Lantos's music shall cheer you."

"No doubt." Wren curled her fingers about his.

His hand tingling, he took her arm. He shoved that odd reaction aside and escorted her into The Nightingale's teeming lobby. They paused to greet a few acquaintances, but soon he led her upstairs to his family's box. "No one is joining us, so now that we've survived the social gauntlet downstairs, we should be left alone to enjoy the music."

Wren smoothed her skirt then primly folded her hands in her lap. "Good."

Hawke chuckled and sat beside her, resisting the urge to thread his fingers through hers. Why did he want that? His head throbbed again. And why did his head keep plaguing him? If it didn't ease, it might spoil the concert.

The house lights dimmed, so he and Wren turned their attention to the stage. The haunting yet beautiful strains of Lantos's music floating to their box, his headache faded by the second song, and they remained rapt throughout the entire first half.

During intermission, Hawke turned to Wren, who was propped against the box's parapet with her chin resting in her palm. And her soft smile shone even in her firegem's unsteady light. Adorable. "Did the music sweeten your sour mood?"

Wren blinked and straightened then chuckled. "I suppose it did. I'd forgotten that until you mentioned it."

Unable to resist, he tweaked the hair that had escaped her subdued knot during the performance. "I apologize for mentioning it then."

Wren swatted at his errant hand. "Stop that. Go fetch us some sparkling wine."

Warmth welling in his chest, Hawke rose and swept a playfully servile bow. He loved when she feigned hauteur. His tenderhearted friend could never quite manage it. "Yes, mistress."

He strode from the box and battled through the crowd to purchase refreshments. The second half was just starting when he returned and handed Wren her flute of sparkling wine then settled beside her again.

Midway through the first song, a sultry drawl interrupted, "I hope I'm not intruding, but the boxes of all my other friends were full."

He and Wren exchanged a resigned glance. Kit was almost as irritating as Mother during performances. Setting his sparkling wine on the parapet, he hid his grimace as he turned to face Kit. "Of course you aren't intruding."

Wren set her flute beside his with a saccharine smile. "How did you find us?"

Her crimson ballgown gleaming, Kit swished across the box and sat too close to him. "Your parents mentioned at the Campbells' ball that you were attending. And since the ball was dull, I decided to join you."

Hawke almost shuddered. Because she was pursuing him. He slid toward Wren until he pressed against her. "How nice."

Wren hissed in an undertone, "What *are* you doing?"

His body tingling, he matched her tone, "Trying to escape Kit. Would you care to switch seats?"

While Wren slanted Kit a narrow glance, Kit returned it with a coy smile and said, "What are you two whispering about?"

Wren sighed but rose. "We were arranging to exchange seats, so I've a better view of the stage."

Hawke leapt to his feet and abandoned his seat for Wren's. Thank the Goddess she was too tenderhearted to refuse him.

Yet he winced when Kit drawled, "Such chaotic conduct.

How fortunate I arrived to act as chaperone. 'Tisn't proper for you two to be alone."

Her lips compressing to nothing, Wren remained silent, but fire flashed through him. He gritted, "Nonsense, I'm not about to ravish Wren in a crowded music house."

Kit's gaze flicked over Wren. "No, I suppose not."

His jaw clenched. How dare Kit disparage Wren so? Despite her sultry beauty, she was nothing compared to Wren. He covered Wren's hand with his. "You may be my cousin's widow, but you're our age and in no way an appropriate chaperone."

Kit fluttered her lashes at him and said in an entirely different tone than before, "No, I suppose not."

Hawke recoiled, prickles skittering across his skin. Couldn't Kit see he was uninterested?

Fingering the firegem at her throat, Wren turned her gaze from the stage to Kit. "If you can't remain silent, you should leave. I can't hear the music over your chatter."

Kit smirked at Wren. "This isn't your box, so you've no say in the matter."

A flush burned his neck at Kit's hauteur. Unlike Wren, she always managed it perfectly, especially when needling Wren. He squeezed Wren's hand to hearten her. "Perhaps not, but 'tis my family's, and I agree with her."

"Very well." Kit turned toward the stage with a huff.

Though the box was silent except for Lantos's intricate music, tension hung in the air like before a thunderstorm, so Hawke tugged Wren to her feet when the current song ended. "I feel another headache descending. We should leave."

Wren whirled toward him, her eyes wide. "What?" When he winked at her with the side away from Kit, she relaxed. "Of course."

Kit began following them, but he waved her back to her seat. "Don't allow our departure to spoil your enjoyment of the concert." Except she'd not come to enjoy the concert. He shuddered and whisked Wren from the box then through the lobby as if chased by a hungry hellhound. He flung her inside his carriage then leapt in behind her.

As he pounded on the roof to spur the carriage forward, Wren collapsed on her seat and giggled. "You're horrid, Lord Beza."

Not grimacing at his given name for once, Hawke relaxed with a grin. Thankfully, Wren had already recovered from Kit's insults. He chuckled as he dropped into the seat across from her. "I know, but she deserved it. Imagine her agreeing I wouldn't ravish you in such an insulting tone."

Wren's giggles silenced. "You said as much the other day."

His throat thickened. He grasped her shoulders and pulled her toward him. He frowned and peered into her eyes. Had he wounded her? "If I did, I didn't mean it *that* way. I merely meant we're close as siblings."

Her face cast in shadow by her emerald firegem's flickering flame, Wren slid his hands from her shoulders. "I know."

A pang darted through Hawke. He sighed as he settled back in his seat. Why did comparing Wren to a sibling feel mendacious? They'd been best friends forever, and there was no attraction between them. If there was, their Longnight kiss would have gone differently all those years ago. His emotions must be tangled because he'd found the perfect lady and lost her. Goddess, he must find Rowan before he destroyed his friendship with Wren.

He forced a crooked grin. "Since 'tis still early, shall we review the witch shops? Perhaps together we can rank them."

CHAPTER 17

$\mathcal{W}$ren suppressed a wince. Of course Hawke wanted to discuss his hunt for Rowan. As she'd mentioned earlier, she'd attempted to rank the witch shops today between attempts to start the fete play—although not the way he assumed. She'd attempted to rank them by risk of discovery, but she'd visited none of them, so 'twas proving difficult. How could she delay for a few more days? "Not tonight, please. Lantos's music sweetened my mood, and I don't wish to sour it again by ranking witch shops, especially after dealing with Kit."

Hawke drooped and ran a hand through his hair. "Very well, but we must start visiting witch shops soon, else I'll never find Rowan."

She almost winced again. He'd never find Rowan regardless because she didn't exist. "I know. Just give me a few days to ponder the list. I'm sure I'll have a strategy by then." She'd have to—she couldn't delay Hawke's hunt forever without him becoming suspicious.

Hawke beamed at her as he helped her alight from the carriage. "You're the best, Wren."

Her throat cramping, Wren swallowed. She wasn't. She was deceiving him. If only he'd forget about Rowan and their enchanted night. Surely his infatuation wouldn't last much longer. Waving good night, she fled upstairs to her chambers and went straight to bed.

When Abby brought a breakfast tray at the usual time the following morning, Wren only roused enough to recognize the maid before succumbing to slumber again. Some time later, her maid's shaking roused her from a dream where Hawke had drawn the box's curtains and ravished her. More, she wanted more. She whimpered and buried her face in her pillows. "What?"

"'Tis almost midday, miss." Abby shook her again.

Already? Wren rubbed the grit from her eyes and swung her legs over the side of the bed. She rarely slept so late. Why had she required so much sleep recently? She sighed. Her tangled relationship with Hawke must be fatiguing her. "I suppose I should rise then."

Wren glanced at the breakfast tray, but her stomach spasmed at the shokolat pot. Although she normally adored the rich beverage, her stomach was too asleep to bear it today. "Abby, please bring me some tea instead of the shokolat."

Abby narrowed her eyes but collected the shokolat pot without a word. Then she returned several moments later with a steaming pot of tea.

Wren relaxed when the tea's refreshing scent soothed her stomach. She set aside the pastry she'd begun nibbling to pour herself tea. "Where are my parents today?"

Abby held up two dresses for Wren's approval. "Sir Alaric went riding several hours ago, but Lady Keyes is in the conservatory."

Unsurprising. Wren nodded then gestured toward the plainer dress, disregarding Abby's heavy sigh. She finished her pastry and tea then dressed and strolled down to the conservatory. She kissed Mother's papery cheek and sat beside her. "Morning, Mother."

Mother set aside her book and removed her spectacles with a

smile. "Morning, Wren—although 'tis perilously close to afternoon."

"I know." A blush heating her neck, Wren grimaced. Of course Mother had noticed her late appearance. Not that she could explain without revealing her sensual dreams about Hawke. She asked to distract Mother, "How did the Campbells' ball go last night? I was already asleep when you returned home."

Mother narrowed her eyes, but she replied, "'Twas a crush, like the Campbells' parties always are, but Caro and I found time for a comfortable talk."

Wren's skin prickled. Considering the duchess's proclivity for matchmaking, their comfortable talk wasn't comforting at all. "Did you discuss anything interesting?" Like Hawke's imminent betrothal?

Mother shrugged. "This and that. We decided the families should dine together tonight." She slanted Wren a stern glance. "You're expected to attend, so be ready to leave at half-past five."

Wren relaxed and nodded. At least their talk had produced nothing more alarming than a family dinner with the Hawkes. It could have been much worse. "Very well."

An amused glint flickered through Mother's eyes. "We also decided to go shopping next week for ballgowns to wear at Caro's fete. And you must join us."

Wren sighed. Although not news about Hawke's betrothal, dress shopping with Mother and the duchess was almost as unpalatable. She'd be draped and pinned and fussed over for most of a day. Atrocious. Yet like always, she'd the perfect excuse to avoid that. "Unfortunately, rehearsals for the orphanage play start in a few days, so I shan't have time."

Mother shook her head. "You must make time. You can't wear an old ballgown to the duchess's fete."

Wren wetted her lips. Mother sounded adamant—like Hawke's mother when determined. Clearly Mother wouldn't permit her usual refusal. Why was this fete so special? Perhaps because court would be watching her thanks to the fete play the duchess had coerced her into writing. She almost shuddered but said, "Yes, Mother."

Before Mother could reply, Wren managed a smile and rose. "Speaking on the fete, I must work on its play. No ballgown, no matter how lovely, shall atone for botching that."

Then she drifted back upstairs to her chambers. Although she'd told Mother she'd be writing the fete play, she couldn't bear thinking about it again. Without Hawke's input, she'd just spend another afternoon coming up with ideas then discarding them for being too simple.

Wren plopped in her desk chair. She could visit Hawke, but he'd want to discuss Rowan again, and she needed a respite from that. She eyed the list of witch shops on her desk. She could rank those, but that wouldn't be a respite. No, she'd read instead. A good book could absorb her like nothing else, so 'twas the perfect respite.

Since yesterday she'd finished rereading the book of Lantos verse from Hawke, she grasped one of her favorite novels instead. She lost herself in the passionate tale of the crippled soldier who won the heart of a fae princess. If only she could do the same with Hawke.

AFTER DRESSING FOR DINNER, Wren sauntered down to the empty entrance hall, arriving at half-past five. She couldn't resist grinning when her parents, arm in arm, joined her several minutes later. "I thought we were leaving at promptly half-past."

Father tweaked her nose as they passed. "Saucy miss. I can't *imagine* who taught you that. Must have been your mother."

Mother lightly slapped his arm. "Wren's impudence is entirely your doing, you rogue."

Warmth filling her chest, Wren giggled at their banter as they descended the front steps. "You're equally to blame, Mother. You chose to marry him, after all."

Father winked at Wren. "Best decision she ever made too."

Mother tsked as they reached Hawke's parents' townhouse.

While her parents were greeting the duke and duchess, Wren turned to Aragon's wife. "Evening, Selena. How are you?" Wonderful, no doubt. She'd been fortunate enough to marry the gentleman she loved, who adored her in return.

Her freckled face radiant, Selena dimpled. "Fairly well. I tire easily, so I've started napping in the afternoons, but other than that, I feel wonderful. And since I tried nibbling on dry toast and crackers throughout the day as my healer suggested, I no longer suffer nausea."

Wren blinked at Selena's candor. Although twenty-three, she'd never heard such things since she wasn't betrothed or married. Pregnancy sounded demanding, not that she'd ever experience it herself. She inclined her head. "I'm pleased you aren't suffering unduly."

Selena cast Aragon, who was laughing with Hawke and Mel across the room, an adoring glance. "Any suffering I endure is worth bearing Aragon's child."

Wren's ribs squeezed as if crushed by a sea serpent. She'd never know the joy of bearing Hawke's child. Instead, she'd watch him have children with another. She forced a bland smile. "I imagine so." To distract herself from her hopeless yearning, she said, "I suppose you've heard the duchess asked me to write a play for the fete in honor of your baby. Do you have any requests?"

Selena blinked then grinned at Wren. "No, but I'm certain whatever you write shall be perfect. Hawke is forever saying how clever your plays are."

Wren grimaced with a shudder. "I almost wish he and my parents hadn't been so complimentary. Perhaps then the duchess wouldn't have fancied my play worthy of her fete. I feel unequal to the task." She sighed. "Since you've no requests, do you know what the duchess wants?"

"No, but we can ask her." Selena waved over her mother-in-law, who excused herself from Wren's parents to join the two younger ladies. "Wren wants to know the details for the fete play."

The duchess's patrician brows flew upward. "I'd intended to leave all that to you, Wren. You're the writer, after all."

A chill sweeping over her, Wren swallowed. "Do you have a particular troupe of players you want me to hire?"

"Players?" The duchess frowned and tilted her head. "Nothing so plebeian. I'd thought family members could perform it."

Wren eyed Hawke's mother askance. Family members? Had they agreed to that? "Whom did you intend to cast?"

The duchess shrugged. "Hawke and Mel shall perform, of course. You could perform the female roles."

Wren's heart pounded in her ears. "Me?! You want *me* to act in the fete play?" Dear Goddess, 'twas so much worse than the upcoming dress shopping.

"I can't imagine anyone more perfect." The duchess flashed Wren a candescent smile and took Selena's arm. "Come, Selena, Lady Keyes wants to speak with you."

As the duchess and Selena swept away, Wren stared after them, bile burning her throat. She couldn't act in front of all of court—having others perform her play would be bad enough. Ceasing to breathe, she swayed as black spots danced before her eyes. She simply couldn't do it.

CHAPTER 18

$\mathcal{L}$aughing at an exchange between Aragon and Mel, Hawke glanced across the room at Wren, who was ashen as she stared after Mother and Selena. What had happened? Wren was eyeing them like scythe-bearing thanatoses who'd come to collect her soul. His laughter extinguished, he strode across the room and grasped her elbow. "Wren, what's wrong?"

Wren clutched his shoulder. "Hawke, please tell me you didn't know."

His throat tightened as she blinked up at him. Goddess, she appeared about to faint. Wren never fainted, not even when they'd gotten lost at the docks or faced an angry troll. He swallowed and led her to the nearest sofa. "Know what?"

Her face white against her auburn hair, Wren collapsed on the plush seat. "That your mother expects me to act in the fete play."

"What!" Hawke dropped beside her, slashing Mother a hard look. How could his normally perceptive mother propose such a ridiculous scheme? "Of course not. I'll speak with her about it."

Wren sighed. "I'd prefer if you didn't. The duchess said she only wanted family members to act, and she mentioned me specifically."

He grasped her icy hands. "No doubt she intends to match you with one of my cousins." Damn Mother and her incessant matchmaking. Wren was too shy to be forced to perform before court. Being coerced into writing the play was bad enough.

"No doubt," Wren echoed in a dull voice. But then she inhaled and straightened. "Although I could do that just as well while directing the play like at the orphanage."

Hawke relaxed. Good, she seemed to be recovering her composure. He smiled and squeezed Wren's hands. "I suppose you could."

"Then that's what I'll do." Wren nodded then beamed at him. "Thank you, Hawke."

He flashed a crooked grin. "Why? You solved your conundrum yourself." He released her hands to tap her nose. That should banish any lingering fright.

While Wren wrinkled her nose at him, Mother called over, "Hawke, cease fondling Wren and escort her to dinner."

Wren's cheeks darkened, but Hawke glowered at Mother. He wouldn't have been fondling Wren if not for Mother's thoughtless demand. But he replied, "Yes, Mother."

He turned back to Wren and raised his eyes skyward until her blush faded. Warmth filling his chest, he tugged her to her feet, and they followed the others to the dining room and sat between Father and Mel.

From the head of the table, Father craned around Hawke to address Wren. "Are you certain you want to sit between these reprobate offspring of mine?"

Wren chortled while she arranged her napkin on her lap. "I should be fine—provided they swear not to throw boiled vegetables over my head."

Mel's eyes gleamed as he tugged his robes. "Priests would never be so uncouth as to throw food at dinner."

Not now perhaps, but he had ten years ago. Hawke smirked and ladled fish soup into Wren's bowl then served himself. "And I can swear to not throw boiled vegetables, although I make no promises about fried ones."

Wren sipped her soup and grinned at Father. "I may not want to sit between your reprobate offspring after all, your grace."

Father returned her grin as he buttered a roll. "I'm afraid you must persevere since you already started eating."

Wren pouted with a sigh. "I suppose I'll grow accustomed."

Hawke chuckled along with Father and Mel. Wren's exaggerated resignation was amusing, especially considering she saw worse behavior at the orphanage.

When they quieted, Father arched a brow. "How goes the play Caro inveigled you into writing for her fete?"

Hawke grimaced. Of course Father had to remind Wren about the fete play. Hopefully, being reminded wouldn't make her worry again about Mother expecting her to act.

Wren's playful pout drained from her face, but she didn't turn ashen like earlier. Good. Instead, she sighed and shook her head. "Well enough, although your wife volunteered Hawke and Mel to perform in it."

Mel choked on his soup, yet Hawke merely sighed. Of course they were some of the family members Mother wanted in the fete play. But unlike Wren, they could handle performing before court. They were Mother's sons, after all.

Mel wiped his mouth with his napkin. "Mother volunteered us to act? How delightful."

Hawke snorted. "You know Mother."

Father chuckled and flashed a crooked grin. "Yes, Caro is never shy about managing the affairs of others. If you boys are opposed to acting in the play, I'll speak with her."

Hawke and Mel exchanged a glance over Wren's head. If Father did, Mother would harp on it for ages. And performing the fete play would only be one night. So Hawke shrugged again. "No, we'll perform. Although being asked rather than volunteered would have been nice."

Setting down her spoon, Wren scowled at Hawke. "Your mother means well."

Hawke shrugged. Perhaps, but that didn't make her meddling any less vexing. He nudged Wren while serving her roast chicken and tubers. "You didn't think so when she volunteered *you* to act."

Wren shuddered then sniffed and cut her chicken. "That was entirely different."

Father inclined his head, murmuring, "Of course it was." When Hawke snorted, Father pointed his fork at Hawke. "You've a great deal to learn about the gentler sex. Never disagree with them, especially when they're at their most illogical."

Wren stilled, her eyes narrowing. "I can hear you, your grace."

Father's expression was seraphic. "Can you? How marvelous."

When Wren turned from Father and queried Mel about his work at the temple, Hawke coughed to disguise his laugh. "I believe you riled her." So deftly too.

Father winked at Hawke and poured himself another glass of wine. "I heard a rumor about you the other day."

The back of his neck prickling, Hawke arched his brows then served himself more chicken. Doubtless 'twas about Rowan. Why couldn't he have found her before any rumors reached his parents? Mother was too eager to see him settled and would interfere if she knew he was hunting a lady. "Oh?"

Father eyed Hawke over his wine glass. "That you disappeared with some lady at the king's summer masquerade."

Hawke shrugged. He'd not explain Rowan to Father—Mother would learn of it before the evening ended. "I can't imagine why 'twould cause gossip." Perhaps because Rowan was too delectable to forget.

Father cocked a brow while the servants brought the next

course. "Apparently, you whisked her away from the masquerade as soon as she arrived. You didn't even dance with her. Everyone assumes 'twas a planned assignation."

Hawke almost winced. Not planned, but definitely an assignation. Yet he must convince Father that Rowan was meaningless until he'd found and courted her. He snorted then served Wren and himself creamy salmon and broccoli. "A planned assignation? 'Twas a mere flirtation, and I never bothered to learn the lady's name."

Father grunted, his eyes narrow. "You missed the king's summer masquerade for a mere flirtation?"

Hawke forced another shrug. He'd miss any court event for an enchanted night with Rowan. "The masquerade was dreadfully dull. Besides, if it had been planned, I'd have told Wren beforehand. Wouldn't I, Wren?"

Drawn from her conversation with Mel, Wren blinked at him. "Would you what?"

Hawke gritted a nonchalant smile. "Have told you about a planned assignation." She'd catch his silent plea. She always understood him, even when no one else did.

Wren squeezed his hand beneath the table with a wry grin. "He always has before. Sometimes his ribald tales cause my maiden's ears to burn." She paused. "Is this regarding the rumor about Hawke and the dryad? Kit mentioned it the other day."

Hawke's breath froze as Father nodded. Why was she mentioning Rowan after she'd promised not to? He eyed Wren. 'Twasn't like her to betray his trust. What was she about?

Wren giggled and squeezed his hand again as the servants brought dessert. "As usual, court misunderstood matters. That dryad was shameless—she pursued Hawke then abandoned him for a bandit."

Hawke relaxed and served Wren a generous slice of shokolat torte, her favorite. Her fabrication made Rowan sound like another flirtation, so Mother wouldn't bother to interfere. And that was worth his pride. He feigned a chagrined wince when Father and Mel stared at him then guffawed.

"As I said, you've a great deal to learn about the gentler sex." Still chuckling, Father sipped his wine. "You're fortunate I heard the rumor before your mother."

Hawke shuddered and set down his fork. True, Mother would have continued interrogating him until she unearthed Rowan's name. "If you feel any fondness for me, you'll explain the truth when she does hear."

Mel snickered. "Although that may not save you from Mother."

Hawke shrugged. "I don't expect it shall, but it may delay her." Hopefully, long enough he could find Rowan and court her without Mother's meddling.

Wren finished her shokolat torte and rose. "Be nice, Hawke." She slanted him a chiding glance before following the other ladies from the dining room.

As Father, Sir Alaric, and his brothers discussed the king's upcoming talks with the nightmara herds, Hawke fingered the enchanted bird in his pocket and allowed the conversation to flow past him. Concealing Rowan from his family was tiresome. And with rumors about him and Rowan circulating through court, his time to find her before someone else did was dwindling. He and Wren must discuss ranking those witch shops.

So when they joined the ladies in the drawing room, he strode straight to Wren and drew her upright. "You look exhausted. I'll escort you home."

Wren blinked as he took her arm. "I'm a bit tired, but I look exhausted?"

Hawke winced. 'Twas insensitive to denigrate her appearance, but they must talk without others overhearing. So he remained silent until they were alone outside. "You look fine. I just wanted privacy to discuss meeting tomorrow about the witch shops."

Wren paled and licked her lips. "We must meet about the fete play as well." She flashed a bright smile. "Stop by late morning. I'll have the witch shops ranked by then."

He stared after Wren as she trudged up her front steps. She must be fretting about the fete play again. Mother never should have asked her, but Wren wouldn't renege now that she'd agreed. Somehow, he must get her through it. He'd start by finding out tomorrow what help she needed with the fete play.

CHAPTER 19

*H*aving overslept again, Wren had just finished a late breakfast when Abby announced Hawke was waiting downstairs. Wren winced. She'd meant to finish ranking the witch shops this morning, but she'd slept too late. Yet she couldn't delay again—he'd begin to suspect her offer to help.

She sighed and trudged over to her desk. Studying Hawke's list of witch shops and jotting notes, she approved the first dress Abby offered without looking. Once dressed, she scooped up Hawke's other lists and her notes for the fete play then headed downstairs.

Sprawled on a chair in the morning room, Hawke blinked when she joined him, and his brows flew upward. Then he coughed a laugh. "*What* are you wearing?"

"Huh?" Wren glanced down, gawking at the frilly peach dress she'd refused to wear for the past year. She grimaced and smoothed her skirt in a futile attempt to disguise its embellishments. "Mother bought it last year. She said I would look adorable in it."

Hawke snickered. "I suppose, but having known you forever, I can tell it doesn't suit you at all. You look like a massapan doll from a lady cake."

She scowled and kicked his outstretched ankle. Made of almond paste, massapan dolls were oversweet and ornate, especially on the elaborate layer cake favored by court during Lantos's era. She couldn't stand eating them, never mind being compared to one. "Oh, hush." When he snickered harder, she shook his lists at him. "If you don't, I shan't help you find your Rowan."

Hawke ceased laughing, although his pale-blue eyes still glimmered with suspicious brightness. "I shan't tease you about your frilly dress again."

"Good." Her chest tightening, Wren gestured for him to follow her. She'd best offer her advice about the witch shops. If only her frilly dress could distract him forever. But he was too determined to find Rowan for that. "Come on then. I'm not about to discuss your secret lover in the morning room where callers could interrupt us. Abby said Mother is visiting your mother, so the conservatory should be empty."

Hawke stood with a crooked grin. "Except for the plants and birds."

His teasing loosened the knot in her chest. Surely she could pretend to help while hiding that she'd been Rowan. She tsked as they strolled to the back of the townhouse. "Must you be so literal?"

Hawke quirked a brow. "No."

Wren almost smiled. Definitely teasing. She must reciprocate. She slapped his shoulder with the lists, but he merely guffawed, so she slapped him with the papers again.

Hawke twisted the lists from her grasp and wagged them in front of her. "Massapan dolls shouldn't be so fractious."

"Hawke!" She glared at him, her hands fisted on her hips. He'd promised not to tease her about her dress. Perhaps she could use that as an excuse to delay again. He'd not suspect her of obstructing his hunt then. "Since you keep teasing about my dress, you must no longer want my assistance with Rowan."

"I do. Your frilly dress is just too droll to resist teasing you about." His grin infectious, Hawke dropped onto a stone bench beside a fragrant lymon tree. "Goddess, I've not laughed so hard in weeks. Thank your mother for me."

Her heart swelled, and her lips began curving in a smile. Before he could see it, she whirled and examined the glossy lymons. They were yellow with a green tint, so they'd be ripe soon. "I'll do no such thing. Now, give me back the lists." She sat beside him on the bench and held out her hand.

Hawke returned the lists with a chuckle.

Wren began perusing her notes about the witch shops until Hawke grasped her chin and turned her face to his. Tingling warmth suffusing her skin, she ceased breathing and eyed his lips. If she were still Rowan, she'd only need to lean forward and raise her chin to kiss him.

Hawke's lips stopped moving.

Her skin chilled. What had he just said? She'd not heard a word since he touched her. She swallowed. "What did you say?"

A frown furrowing his brow, Hawke leaned closer. "Are you well, Wren?"

Now all she'd needed to do was raise her chin. To prevent herself from kissing him, Wren wrenched her chin from his fingers. "Of course. I was pondering the witch shops. So what did you say?"

Hawke scrutinized her for a moment then sighed. "I said, before we rank the witch shops, why didn't you tell me about the rumors you heard from Kit about Rowan?"

Her stomach fluttered. He'd grasped her chin to ask about some rumors? He never touched her so casually. She forced herself to shrug. "Because Kit often tells me rumors about your lovers, so one about Rowan wasn't surprising."

Hawke grimaced. "I wasn't aware anyone noticed me and Rowan."

Wren shook her head at him. "You're handsome, wealthy, and the son of a duke. Of course, someone noticed. Although the rumors don't mention Rowan's identity." Thank the Goddess.

Hawke drummed his fingers against his knee. "With all the rumors, I'm afraid someone shall discover her first and use our night against her."

She suppressed a snort. His hunt was using their night against her, and he'd no idea. But at least the enchanted bird prevented him from finding her. "Your Rowan shall remain unscathed until we find her."

Hawke sighed. "Hopefully so. But to find her, we must start visiting witch shops. Have you ranked them yet?"

Wren swallowed and licked her lips. "Yes. We'll start with the witch shops in the fashionable district." She pointed to three shops on the list, all of which specialized in magic completely different from the veiled witch's. So her identity probably wouldn't be revealed at them. "These are near the most fashionable dress shops in town. We can visit them tomorrow midmorning."

Barely glancing at the list, Hawke cocked his head. "The shops might be crowded then. Perhaps we should go earlier."

She shifted in her seat. Except she couldn't manage earlier. Sensual dreams of Hawke disrupted her sleep too much since the masquerade. "The shops near Broad Street are always crowded, no matter the time. And I might be up late working on the fete play."

Hawke nodded. "Very well. I'll fetch you midmorning then." He arched a brow. "What help do you need with the fete play?" His tone turned wry, "Besides acting in it, of course."

Wren winced. Poor Hawke, to be forced to perform before court when she'd managed to evade it by directing instead. "I'm sorry for that."

Hawke snorted. "Why? 'Tisn't as if you control Mother. Not even Father can do that. So what do you need?"

She heaved a sigh. An idea that was intricate enough to satisfy court without confusing them. She grimaced. "An idea would be nice. I can't fathom the right one."

An impish grin flickered across Hawke's face. "How about how Aragon and Selena met?"

Wren gaped at him. In a brothel? To escape a black witch? The duchess's fete would be the scandal of the season if she wrote a play about that. She scowled. "I think not. Your mother would be furious."

Hawke snickered. "Yes, but she'd never ask you to write another play for court."

She prodded his arm. True, but court would scrutinize her for ages if she wrote such a scandalous play. Her stomach lurched. So hideous. "I need a real idea."

Hawke shrugged and rubbed his chin. "How about a tale promoting the benefits of children?"

Wren nibbled her lip. 'Twould serve if the tale were intricate enough. "Perhaps..."

Hawke grinned. "Add magical creatures and spells, and the court shall adore it." He waggled his brows. "Maybe you could include an enchanted bird."

She shuddered. She'd not hint at the glamour spell or their enchanted night before court. Someone might realize she'd been Rowan. She tilted her head. But what other strong spells did she know about? She drew a quick breath. Her parents' conception spell.

The tale for the fete play began to emerge. Her fingers itching for a pen, Wren muttered, "After years of hoping, a king and queen are blessed with a daughter through the aid of a kind elf, and the princess grows up to be wise and beautiful and kind, so much so that a demon lusts after her and seizes her kingdom, but she rescues everyone using her wits and a magic heirloom, and the demon is cursed..."

Hawke chuckled, halting her tide of words. "I'd definitely want to watch that play, if I wasn't acting in it. May I be the demon?" He flashed a crooked grin. "Please?"

She giggled behind her hand as he widened his eyes like a brownie begging for milk after completing his household chores.

She couldn't resist such a plea. "Very well, but then I'll have Mel play the elf, so your mother isn't insulted. How many of your cousins shall act in the play?"

After a pause, Hawke began with his maternal cousins, "Elise would be glad to play the princess. Edouard shall act if she does." He continued to his Hawke cousins, "Dane, Xavier, and Pippa would probably act as well. Since Mother foisted this play upon you, I'll write and ask them to participate."

"Thank you, Hawke." Her heart lightening, Wren nodded and began inventing parts for his cousins. Edouard and Pippa could be the king and queen. Dane and Xavier...

Hawke rose with a low chuckle. "Since I no longer have your attention, I'll take my leave. See you tomorrow."

She murmured a vague farewell as he left the conservatory. Dane could play a soldier, and Xavier a courtier. With all her players decided, she darted upstairs. She must write her ideas before she forgot them.

CHAPTER 20

Hawke grinned as he strode from Wren's conservatory. Now that she'd gotten started, she'd be lost in the fete play for the rest of the day. 'Twas good they'd already discussed the witch shops.

He sighed. If only they could start visiting those shops today. He must find Rowan soon. But Wren needed to write the fete play, so he'd have to wait. He wasn't visiting fashionable shops in the middle of the day without her. Unless she accompanied him, husband-hunting ladies would mob him.

To distract himself from his delayed hunt, Hawke retreated to his music room after luncheon and spent the afternoon lost in soaring sonatas, rollicking fiddle tunes, and intricate Lantos melodies. Like Wren and writing, playing the violin could absorb him for hours. He only left the music room when Hobb told him dinner was ready.

He grinned at the first course. Fish pie! Aragon would be jealous; he adored the hearty dish, especially from The Gold Griffin. And Cook's fish pie was almost as good as the one served there. Maybe she'd pilfered the recipe.

Hawke chuckled as he devoured his fish pie. He and Mel

should take Aragon out for that private celebration he'd proposed earlier. Aragon would love visiting The Gold Griffin again—if they could pry him away from his pregnant wife. And tonight would be perfect since they'd no family events for once.

So after dinner, he headed to the Great Temple on Our Lady's Way. His chest lightened as he strode through the balmy evening. A night with his brothers would be another excellent distraction. He couldn't dwell on his delayed hunt while drinking and jesting with Aragon and Mel.

When Hawke rapped on the discreet wooden door of the priests' quarters, the view panel slid open, and a suspicious eye peered through the slim opening. "Yes?"

To placate the priest, Hawke flashed a crooked grin and said, "Hawke to see his brother, Priest Melchior Hawke."

The eye narrowed before withdrawing. "Wait here." The panel slammed closed.

Hawke chuckled. My, that priest was surly. 'Twas like he'd desecrated the Goddess's altar by requesting to see his brother.

The wooden door creaked open after a few moments, and Mel stepped outside. "Hawke? The porter had to fetch me from Vespers."

Hawke cocked his head. The evening service featuring lengthy prayers thanking the Goddess began at sundown, and that wasn't for another half hour. "Should Vespers have started yet?"

Mel snorted with a wry smile. "Normally not, but tonight's priest moved it an hour early, so he could talk longer."

Hawke almost shuddered. Such a drawn-out service sounded painful. He could never manage it. Unlike Mel, who would endure anything for his calling to serve the Goddess. "I hope he doesn't lead services often."

Mel shrugged but chuckled. "Often enough. Although garrulous, he's related to the high priest." He arched his brows. "But why are you here? Clearly not to attend Vespers. Did something happen between you and Wren that you must discuss?"

Hawke frowned at Mel. What could possibly happen between him and Wren? His temples tightened. They were just friends. "Of course not. No, I'm here to fetch you to take Aragon out to celebrate his first child."

Mel smiled and shook his head. "You simply want an excuse to drink too much, seduce barmaids, and gamble away your fortune."

Hawke suppressed a grimace. Not since his first season, and definitely not since he'd met Rowan. But he couldn't admit that to his brothers. If they learned about Rowan, they'd mention it to Father. Then Mother would know and meddle. So to maintain his rakish facade, Hawke widened his eyes with a feigned gasp. "How did you know?"

Mel snickered, his wicked grin unbefitting a priest. "We grew up together, remember?"

Hawke nodded as they began toward their parents' townhouse. Which meant he must take care to conceal his disinterest in flirtation. Like Mother, Mel was too perceptive. To distract him, Hawke quizzed Mel about his work. They discussed that until they reached their parents' townhouse where Hawke knocked and asked after Aragon.

Perkins One inclined his head. "Both Lord and Lady Treyvan are in the drawing room, Lord Beza."

His jaw twitching at his given name, Hawke strode to the drawing room with Mel close behind him. But only his sister-in-law was there. He grinned at her. "Evening, Selena. Where's Aragon?"

Selena glanced up from her sketch journal to beam at them. "He's fetching me a snack from the kitchen. Why?"

Mel sat on the sofa across from her. "We've come to take him out to celebrate your pregnancy as Hawke mentioned last week."

Hawke chuckled and stole the chair beside Selena. Aragon's no doubt. Stealing it was the perfect way to tease him without a word. "I thought we'd take him to The Gold Griffin."

A dimple quivered in Selena's cheek. "Just swear to not let

him become too drunk. Both of us needn't suffer nausea tomorrow morning."

Aragon burst into the drawing room with a plate of sweet biscuits. "I thought you stopped suffering nausea once you began eating dry toast and crackers in the morning."

Selena raised her gaze to the ceiling. "I did, dear coddler. I was jesting with your brothers."

"Oh?" Aragon slapped away Hawke's hand when he attempted to filch a sweet biscuit. "Those are Selena's."

Laughter bubbling in his chest, Hawke smirked at his eldest brother. He was so amusing to tease, even more than Hobb. And teasing involving Selena always succeeded. "She can eat some of her crackers instead."

While Aragon growled at Hawke, Mel snorted a laugh. "Stop it, Aragon. Can't you see Hawke is tormenting you?" When Aragon subsided with a grumble, Mel continued, "We've come to take you out to celebrate your upcoming fatherhood."

Aragon frowned as he perched on the arm of his wife's chair. "I don't know if I should leave Selena alone."

Selena coughed on a sweet biscuit. "Please do. Your hovering is beginning to vex me. I'm pregnant, a condition women have survived since time began, not ill. I'll be fine spending a quiet night at home."

Aragon eyed Selena for a moment then sighed. "Very well." He turned to Hawke and Mel. "Where are we going?"

Hawke leaned forward with a crooked grin. "The Gold Griffin." That should end Aragon's reluctance, no matter how protective he was of his pregnant wife.

Aragon brightened. "I've not been there in ages." He kissed Selena's cheek. "Don't wait up for me, my love."

"I shan't," Selena murmured as the three brothers departed.

Taking the least ostentatious carriage, Hawke and his brothers arrived at the rowdy tavern near the docks within half an hour.

While Hawke instructed the driver to return for them at midnight, Aragon grinned at the peeling sign of a gold griffin swinging above the tavern's door. "'Tis good to be here again."

Hawke grinned at the gold griffin as well. Land creatures weren't often emblems for taverns near the docks. But griffins were renowned for taking lifelong mates and inspiring truth, so the gold griffin alluded to the tavern's special gold ale that glowed when the drinker remained truthful. And that special ale was doubtless why his brother loved this tavern. He shoved Aragon toward the door. "We aren't there yet."

As they strode into the teeming tavern, the cacophony was near deafening, but across the room a deep voice boomed, "Lord Treyvan! It's been an age." A huge man with a bristling beard and a tattered apron barreled over to them.

Aragon smiled and shrugged. "Alas, Micah, married life has kept me too busy to frequent my former haunts."

His ribs squeezing, Hawke forced a snicker. "Hence why I'm glad I haven't got a wife." Although he'd not mind one if he loved her like Aragon loved Selena.

Mel clapped Aragon's shoulder. "But we wrested Aragon from his wife tonight to celebrate."

When Micah arched his brows, Aragon beamed and puffed his chest. "I'm about to become a father."

"Congratulations!" The huge tavern keeper led them to a small table along the back wall. "The first round is on me." He waggled his finger. "But all the ones after that you must pay for."

"Of course," Aragon said as he sat with Hawke and Mel flanking him.

Micah barreled away, and a plump barmaid returned within moments with three glowing tankards of gold ale.

Aragon sipped his gold ale and glanced about the tavern. "Not much has changed here, except," he gestured with his tankard, "that fiddler over there is new."

Hawke studied the gypsy playing a haunting fiddle tune. The

woman's red kerchief, brightly patterned skirt, and dangling belt of coins further heightened the music's exotic air. His pulse quickened at her skill. "She's good." When his gold ale dimmed, he chuckled. "Very well, she's exceptional. I'd forgotten how the ale detects even understatements."

Aragon toasted his brother. "That's why The Gold Griffin is my favorite place to play cards. The games are always honest."

Mel snickered. "Although I imagine the glowing ale makes wooing the barmaids more difficult."

Aragon took a deep draft. "Except only Hawke bothers with that."

Not hardly. Hawke gulped down his gold ale so it couldn't betray him. "As you say."

Suddenly the teeming tavern hushed. The three brothers glanced toward the door to see why. A woman concealed by black veils was slipping through the crowd to reach the bar. An air of mystery swirled about her like magical smoke about a djinn.

His skin prickling, Hawke leaned toward Aragon and whispered, "Who's that?"

Aragon toyed with his half-empty tankard. "The owner of the witch shop around the corner. She provides the magical ingredient that makes the gold ale glow."

A jolt surging through him, Hawke fingered the enchanted bird in his pocket. Rowan couldn't have purchased it from a shop near the docks, but perhaps the veiled witch could see more than the other witches had.

The veiled witch's gaze met his, and a shudder raced up his spine. 'Twas as if she could sense he'd a spell in his pocket.

"I shall return," he muttered to his brothers then strode across the tavern. However, before he could reach the veiled witch, she disappeared into the back room. He sighed and returned to his brothers.

Both Aragon and Mel eyed him with arched brows. When he

sat, Mel slanted him a narrow glance and murmured, "What was *that* about?"

Hawke shrugged. Nothing he could explain until he'd found Rowan. To distract them from his odd behavior, he asked, "So Aragon, how do you *really* feel about becoming a father?"

CHAPTER 21

*W*hen Abby brought a breakfast tray at the usual time, Wren forced herself to rise. She'd retired early after writing half the fete play yesterday, but her body ached for more sleep. Would those sensual dreams of Hawke *ever* let her rest? She stumbled to her washstand and doused her face in cold water then sat down to breakfast.

She selected a flaky pastry and eyed the shokolat pot. Although she'd abstained from her favorite breakfast drink for the past several days, she'd try some this morning. Her stomach quivered at her first sip but settled by her second. Her aversion must have been a temporary aberration.

While she ate, Wren watched Abby. She'd not wear another frilly dress like yesterday's peach one. Not after making sure to ruin that eyesore by spilling ink in her lap while working on the fete play. But when the maid laid a teal silk dress on the bed, Wren shook her head even though 'twas free of embellishments. "I want the olive wool today."

Abby scowled at her. "But miss, this dress emphasizes your coloring."

Wren shrugged. "So it does, but I want something more sober.

Fetch the olive wool." She mustn't attract more attention than necessary at the witch shops today. If the witches examined her too closely, they might notice her connection to the enchanted bird.

Abby grumbled but brought the olive wool and helped her dress.

Once the maid left with the breakfast tray, Wren began working on the fete play again. The princess had just found the magical heirloom but hadn't decided how to use it. Perhaps to curse the demon to spend eternity granting the wishes of others? Her pen flew across the page. She continued writing until Abby told her Hawke was downstairs.

Her heart lurching, she swallowed and set down her pen. Time to visit the witch shops. Wonderful. Too bad she couldn't delay more—forever perhaps. But then he'd suspect her offer to help. She sighed and slid his lists into her reticule then trudged downstairs.

Hawke's eyes gleamed when she met him in the entrance hall. "Ready?"

Wren wrinkled her nose. As much as she'd ever be. "Of course."

Hawke chuckled as he took her arm. "Not anticipating this, are you?"

Tingling flashed through her at his touch, but she grimaced and shook her head. Definitely not. If only he'd stop his futile hunt for Rowan.

Hawke chuckled again while escorting her into his carriage. "Where are we visiting again?"

She gulped a breath then folded her hands in her lap. "The Arte of Spells and Magic of the Sea on Broad Street, then Panacea Potions around the corner on Silk Road." Goddess, let the witches at those fashionable shops not see she'd purchased the enchanted bird. None of them specialized in glamour spells, so hopefully, she'd be safe.

Hawke relaxed back into his seat. "Good. I told my driver to drop us at Broad Street and return for us in three hours." The carriage soon slowed, and he helped her alight.

Wren glanced around Broad Street to find the first witch shop. The fashionable street was already swarming at this relatively early hour. Lovely. She grimaced as she pointed across the street. "The Arte of Spells is over there. Beside Celeste's." Where Mother and the duchess would be dragging her in a few days.

His gaze following her finger, Hawke nodded and escorted her through the traffic.

She eyed The Arte of Spells as they approached. 'Twas much more impressive than Rhiannon's Veils. A magical mosaic bearing the shop's name hung above the elegant door. Powerful witches must work here. She almost shuddered. Would they realize she'd been Rowan even though they sold magical art rather than glamour spells?

Yet when Hawke escorted her inside the witch shop, no stifling sense of magic imbrued the air like it had at Rhiannon's Veils. She blew a silent sigh. Her identity wouldn't be revealed here.

Giddiness bubbling in her chest, Wren glanced about the magical art gallery. Moving paintings hung in splendor on the walls, dancing statues twirled about the room, and elegant music wafted through the air without musicians. Although infused with magic, everything was exquisite. No wonder Selena, a lady passionate about art, adored this witch shop.

A clerk in a sleek black gown glided over to them. "What type of magical art are you seeking today?"

Hawke scanned the room. "Where's that music coming from?"

Wren smiled. Of course, the music would intrigue Hawke. She glanced at her nickname flitting through a dappled forest. She preferred the paintings herself. Not that she'd ever purchase magical art.

The clerk gestured toward a row of tiny wooden chests along the opposite wall. "That's one of our music boxes. They're enchanted to play any piece of music. You simply tell it what you want to hear."

Hawke arched a brow. "Interesting."

Meaning he hated them. Wren almost laughed at his bland tone. When the clerk drew her breath to speak, Wren nudged him. If the clerk began pitching the unwanted music boxes, they might never escape.

Hawke withdrew the enchanted bird from his pocket. "Did any of your witches enchant this?"

The clerk sniffed. "How common. No, none of our witches enchanted *that*. We specialize in magical art, not trinkets."

Wren bit the inside of her cheek to contain a snort. The enchanted bird was no trinket. If the clerk couldn't see that, she was much less powerful than her shop's facade indicated.

Hawke pocketed the pearly bird with a tight smile. "Thank you for your time."

As he steered Wren toward the door, the clerk rushed after them. Although she couldn't see the enchanted bird's power, she could at least see she'd lost a sale. "Don't you want to examine the music boxes or the statues or the paintings?"

Wren smiled at the clerk over her shoulder. Thank the Goddess for the clerk's blindness to powerful magic. 'Twas even better than she'd hoped when selecting this witch shop. "Perhaps another time."

Hawke muttered once they were on the street outside, "How dare that clerk sneer at Rowan's bird?" He shuddered. "Especially when they sell those soulless music boxes."

Wren swallowed a giggle. Only a musician would be so horrified by an inconsequential music box. She patted his arm. "Perhaps we'll fare better at Magic of the Sea." Hopefully not. She pointed down the street. "Which, I believe, is that way."

Hawke grunted, and they strolled the several blocks to the next witch shop.

As they approached Magic of the Sea, her heart quickened. The sea was powerful, so witches tied to it had extra power and saw more. But the glamour spell didn't involve sea magic. Would her secret be revealed here?

Wren tensed at the iridescent mermaid above the door. The mermaid's gaze seemed alive and knowing. However, when they entered the witch shop, she relaxed. Like at The Arte of Spells, the air here lacked the stifling sense of magic. Plus, the shop was filled with glowing seashells, miniature ships, and other nautical artifacts. Nothing from a forest in sight.

As they headed toward the counter along the back wall, she whispered to Hawke, "I doubt they sold an enchanted songbird here. 'Twould have to be a seagull or an albatross or maybe even a duck."

Hawke's lips twisted in a wry smile, but he pulled the carving from his pocket to show the clerk behind the counter. "Did you sell this enchanted bird?"

The weatherbeaten clerk, who seemed as if he'd be more at ease on a ship than in an Ormas witch shop, snorted as he eyed the gleaming carving in Hawke's palm. "Not hardly. We don't sell land-beasties here."

Hawke sighed and pocketed the enchanted bird again.

Wren couldn't resist a giggle once they left Magic of the Sea. "I told you."

Hawke glowered at her. "Gloating is unattractive."

"And so I'll remind you the next time you start." She pointed left down the crossing street with an airy smile. "I believe Panacea Potions is that way." Considering how little they'd learned at the other witch shops, this last one would pose no danger. The glamour spell was much more than a mere potion.

Hawke grumbled as they turned down Silk Road, which was only slightly less crowded than Broad Street, but she had to stifle her grin. Soon they'd finish visiting witch shops for today without him learning anything about the enchanted bird. Her strategy so far was a success.

A few steps later, they reached Panacea Potions. Unlike the other witch shops, this shop had no fancy sign above its red door. Wren's neck prickled. Panacea Potions looked like Rhiannon's Veils, except a bit larger and not so shabby. Perhaps Hawke might learn something here after all. Oh, Goddess.

However, when they entered, the stifling sense of magic was again missing. Her tension eased, and she glanced around the witch shop. 'Twas cluttered with potions, dried herbs, and preserved animals. Nothing like the veiled witch's nearly empty shop.

Wren pursed her lips as they weaved through the clutter to the back of the shop. The sense of magic at Rhiannon's Veils must be because the veiled witch was a Rhiannon descendant. So she'd be safe at witch shops lacking that. Ordinary witches shouldn't be able to unravel a powerful glamour spell created by a Rhiannon descendant.

When they reached the counter, Hawke held out the enchanted bird to the plump old woman. "Did you create this?"

The witch plucked the spectacles from her disheveled, white hair and perched them on her nose to examine the carving. "Oh dear, oh dear. This little birdie is much beyond my skills."

Wren almost smiled. As she'd suspected. But she must make sure. She leaned forward. "Another witch said a Rhiannon descendant created it for a friend of ours."

The plump witch tilted her head. "Most likely, most likely. I wonder where your friend purchased it. Last I heard, no Rhiannon descendants lived in Ormas."

CHAPTER 22

His stomach tensing at the old witch's words, Hawke exchanged a frown with Wren. Rowan must have purchased the enchanted bird in Ormas—her accent had been that of court, which was held in Ormas throughout spring and summer. "Could our friend have purchased it from an itinerant witch?"

The witch rubbed her plump chin. "Possibly, possibly. But if your friend was highborn like you, I don't know where she'd find one."

He sighed. So where could Rowan have purchased her spell? He grimaced as pain seized his head. "Must we find the Rhiannon descendant that created the spell to unravel it?"

The old witch fluttered her hands. "Maybe, maybe. Although I could..." She puttered behind the counter, pulling various potions and powders from the shelves. Humming, she mixed her ingredients in a pewter bowl.

Hawke glanced at Wren, who was ashen while she watched the witch work. Goddess, she appeared as unwell as when Mother had proposed she act in the fete play. If she wasn't dedi-cated to helping him, she'd flee the witch shop at once. To reassure her, he took her hand and pulled her close. "I know you abhor magic, but nothing dreadful shall happen."

A tremulous smile quivered on Wren's lips. "Of course."

Hawke eyed Wren. How else could he reassure her? He squeezed her hand then turned his gaze to the old witch. Hopefully, 'twould be enough to bolster Wren while the witch performed her magic.

Her white hair wild, the plump witch stirred the last ingredient into her bowl. She snatched the enchanted bird and poured her brown sludge on the carving. A blinding flash, thunderous boom, and smoke reeking of charred feathers erupted from Rowan's spell.

His head throbbed as he and Wren recoiled and choked on the smoke.

The witch muttered, "Oh dear, oh dear, oh dear. This spell is tricky, tricky. Doesn't like anyone examining it. And it seems to be—" she paused to frown at them then shook her head. "No, no, that can't be right. It couldn't be pulling power that way."

While Wren paled further, Hawke leaned forward, his pulse surging. "What do you mean?" Would he finally learn *something* concrete about the enchanted bird?

The old witch began clearing her counter. "'Tis nothing, young man. Couldn't possibly be true. If it was, the creator would be more than a Rhiannon descendant; she'd be a goddess."

Although Wren gasped, he grimaced. Gods rarely visited Damensea in corporeal form since the Age of Gods. If the witch believed *that* likely, she couldn't help them. He slipped the enchanted bird back into his pocket and pressed a gold coin in her hand. "Here, for your trouble."

The old witch beamed at him. "Thank you, thank you, young man."

Hawke ushered Wren, who was whiter than a banshee before a family death, from the shop. His chest tightened. She looked even worse than earlier. Was she actually going to faint this time? Scrutinizing her, he waited until they were outside before asking, "Are you well?"

Her eyes dark, Wren clenched his arm. "I'm not sure we should pursue your mysterious Rowan further. I don't want to be tangled in the affairs of the gods."

To reassure her, he chuckled while they threaded through the traffic back to his carriage. "Don't take the old witch's words seriously. She seemed batty, and 'twas clear she doesn't possess enough power to read the spell." Unfortunately.

Wren slanted him a sidelong glance. "Do you think so?" When he nodded, she relaxed. "Very well, I suppose I was too nervous about being near so much magic to notice that."

A sultry voice behind them purred, "Hawke, were you visiting Panacea Potions? Why the sudden fascination with witch shops? And however did you convince Wren to accompany you? I thought she'd shunned magic since the charmed pen incident."

Hawke almost groaned as he and Wren turned to face Kit. They kept encountering Kit lately. Was she desperate enough for a husband she'd begun following him? He inhaled to respond but paused when Wren took his hand.

Wren flashed a glittering smile. "Hawke is purchasing a faegift for me, and he wanted me to choose it."

He blinked but managed to nod. A faegift? Gentlemen only gave magical gifts to family, wives, or ladies they were courting. But he and Wren had been best friends forever, so him purchasing a faegift for her shouldn't raise any brows.

Kit narrowed her eyes. "Is he really?"

Hawke threaded his fingers through Wren's, and tingling ran up his arm. Just like at the Lantos concert. Goddess, he really must find Rowan before he destroyed his friendship with Wren. He forced a crooked grin. "Wren deserves one."

Kit quirked a brow. "What selfless thing has she done now?"

Warmth surged in his chest. Managed his hunt for Rowan, even though she thought it foolish and hated witch shops. He squeezed her hand. "She's been the best friend a gentleman could have."

Wren tugged her hand free, a blush staining her cheeks.

"How sweet." Kit fluttered her lashes at him. "If you treat a *friend* so generously, I can scarce imagine how you'd treat a wife."

Hawke stiffened. Kit would never learn that firsthand, despite her obvious pursuit. How could he get her to stop pursuing him?

Wren grasped his arm. "We must be off. We've more witch shops to visit."

He relaxed when Wren tugged him toward his carriage and Kit remained behind. They'd escaped.

Once they were out of earshot, Wren murmured, "Sorry about the faegift excuse. A faegift was the first reason I could think of to visit a witch shop."

Hawke shook his head. "'Twas a good one." He grinned at her. "And you do deserve a faegift for helping me hunt Rowan."

Her gaze darting away, Wren took his hand to climb inside the carriage. "Nonsense."

He eyed Wren as he settled across from her. Could she endure visiting more witch shops today? They'd such wretched success so far, but that might change if they visited more. And he must find Rowan soon.

He'd opened his mouth to ask when Wren closed her eyes and leaned her head against the carriage seat with a sigh.

Hawke shut his mouth. No, Wren was too weary to visit more witch shops. And although he must find Rowan, he'd not torment Wren to do so. He waited until the carriage halted before her townhouse to ask, "What witch shops shall we try tomorrow?"

Wren sighed as he helped her alight. "There are more witch shops near Broad Street. We'll try those."

"Very well." He escorted her inside then returned home. To distract himself from Rowan and his inability to find her, he spent the evening playing his violin. Since the rehearsals for the orphanage play should start soon, he focused on the rollicking fiddle tunes he'd need for the play.

THE NEXT MORNING, Hawke had just finished breakfast and was about to fetch Wren when Hobb handed him her note.

Hawke—

I heard from Kiera that the orphanage rehearsals shall start tomorrow, so I've too much to accomplish to hunt for Rowan today. My apologies. Below I've enclosed a list of the moods for the different scenes in the play for you to select songs. I'll be leaving for the orphanage directly after luncheon tomorrow. See you then.

W

Scanning her list, he chuckled. As he'd expected, mostly rollicking fiddle tunes. He set aside her list. Too bad Wren couldn't help him today. But he didn't know which witch shops to visit next, so he must wait until Wren was free. Hopefully, the delay wouldn't prevent him from finding Rowan before someone else did.

He sighed. He must think about something other than Rowan and his frustrating hunt. Since he'd spent last night playing his violin, he strolled to the gamesroom to play some elementball.

Just after his second game, Hobb brought a package from Buford.

Wincing, Hawke accepted the package then strode to his study. He'd forgotten about the arachne's magical fabric since Rowan had vanished, so he'd not promoted it at court, even when he'd attended events to find her. Damnation. He must start attending again to promote the fabric, or no one would purchase it when it arrived.

He plopped in his chair behind his desk. Yet attending court events would be difficult since he'd his hunt for Rowan and he'd committed to the orphanage play. Plus, to avoid husband-hunting ladies, he should only attend family events or ones meant for gentlemen. But perhaps he could start rumors about the magical fabric at several select events before Mother's fete then reveal the fabric there. The fete was right before the shipment would arrive too.

Opening the package, Hawke eyed the clear fabric. He'd meant to give the sample bolt to Mother, yet perhaps he should give it to Wren instead. After all, she *did* deserve a faegift. And Wren wearing an extravagant ballgown would be more dramatic than Mother wearing one. If Mother praised Wren's ballgown, all of court would need one too.

He nodded. He'd give the arachne's magical fabric to Wren tomorrow after they visited the orphanage. His heart quickened. She'd look lovely in an extravagant ballgown, even more than she had at the Lantos concert.

Who knows? Perhaps 'twould even inspire some gentleman into making her an offer. His stomach tightened. Although no gentleman was worthy of his best friend. Yet if Wren loved the gentleman, he'd accept the match, like she had with Rowan.

So after luncheon the following day, Hawke gathered his violin and sample bolt then took his carriage to Wren's townhouse. She was still eating, so he joined her in the family dining room. He paused in the door with a frown. She was pale, and her movements listless. She must have stayed up late writing the fete play. Surely that's all it was. He shook his head then strolled to the chair beside her.

CHAPTER 23

Her limbs heavy after another restless night, Wren was laying her napkin in her lap when Hawke sauntered into the family dining room. He sprawled into the chair beside her and filched a slice of cheese from her plate. "Afternoon, Wren."

She glared at him and pulled her plate beyond his reach. Must he steal her luncheon? He was as bad as when they were children. She could never control his food thievery then either. "Afternoon, Hawke. Don't your servants feed you?"

Hawke shrugged with a crooked grin. "Yes, but I can always eat more." He beamed when a servant arrived bearing a second plate.

As he devoured the cold meat and cheese with crusty rolls, Wren shook her head and toyed with her full plate. How could he possibly eat so fast? "You're *such* a glutton." Yet she loved him anyway.

Hawke swallowed and winked at her. "Guilty."

Her heart fluttered. He flirted with Selena and other ladies with winks. So why was he winking at her? He saw her as nothing more than a friend.

Hawke waved his roll at her plate. "You'd better start your luncheon unless you want us to be late."

Wren stiffened and pressed her lips together. She stuffed some meat and cheese in a roll then bolted it and quaffed her tea. Not as fast as Hawke, but fast enough. "I'm done."

Hawke eyed her half-finished plate. "Is that all you plan to eat?"

She jutted her chin as she rose. Just because he was a glutton didn't mean she must be. "Yes. Are you ready to go now? Or did you want to eat my plate too?"

His brows arched, Hawke rose as well. "My, my. Someone is cross today. Did a nightmara plague your sleep?"

Wren rubbed her forehead. A horse-like magical creature, night-mara could control dreams and even inspire nightmares, although they rarely did so in Calatini since the Nightmara-Calatini Treaty which the king and the nightmara queen-heir were renewing next week. But her enchanted night with Hawke, not a nightmara, had inspired the sensual dreams that had plagued her sleep.

She sighed. And her restless sleep had drained her and dead-ened her appetite. Hopefully, she'd enough energy to handle the orphans. "I simply stayed up too late preparing the details for today."

Hawke's eyes narrowed as he took her elbow. "I know you love helping others, but you must consider yourself first occa-sionally."

And she had at the summer masquerade. Tingling flooded her as echoes of his kisses brushed her skin. Shoving that aside, she arched a brow when they left the family dining room. "I'll remember that the next time you want help with your hunt for Rowan."

Hawke slanted her a flat glance while handing her into his carriage. "Don't turn this into a quip. I'm serious, Wren."

Her jaw tightened. Must he be so overbearing? He'd not scold her for considering others first if he knew she'd seduced him with a glamour spell. But he must *never* realize that, so she asked instead, "Have you selected songs for the play?"

As his carriage started forward, Hawke frowned, but he sighed after a moment. "Yes, I selected them last night. Fiddle tunes mostly."

Wren relaxed against the carriage seat. He'd accepted her obvious evasion. She beamed at him. "The orphans shall like that."

"No doubt." Hawke chuckled. "But their musical palates have yet to taste Lantos."

"Perhaps you could introduce them." She giggled then hummed a lilting waltz, one of her favorites. "That one might work well during the ball scene."

Hawke eyed her askance, rubbing his temple. "Do you know, that was the song I sang with Rowan."

Heat scorched her cheeks. Goddess, it was. She'd forgotten that. Fortunately, the carriage halted before they could discuss the waltz further. Giddiness sweeping through her, she leapt for the door. "We're here!"

Still managing to exit first, Hawke helped her descend then released her and turned to scrutinize Waterstreet Orphanage. "It looks much the same."

Wren cocked her head. Of course it did. The orphanage hadn't enough money to improve. "Did you expect it to change?" When Peter opened the door with a grin, she said, "Afternoon, Peter. How are things?"

Peter chuckled as he shut the door behind them. "Well enough, except the Bedsford twins locked themselves in the attic yesterday and threw turnip greens at passersby on the street. Kiera was right mad."

She choked back a laugh. She could see John and Jacob hurling greens while ignoring Kiera's scold.

Hawke's brows rose. "Turnip greens? Twins I can relate to."

Peter grinned at him. "No doubt, Mr. Hawke—or should I call you Lord Beza; it's been so long."

Hawke raised his violin case at Peter. "If you do, I'll brain you with my violin."

Wren raised her eyes skyward. Why did gentlemen enjoy threatening violence on one another? Although she'd known Hawke forever, sometimes she still didn't understand him.

Peter chortled. "I think me hard head would break your wee fiddle."

Hawke sighed. "So it would. I suppose I'll have to settle for punching you instead." He exchanged a grin with Peter.

Men. She tsked but simply asked, "Is Kiera in her study?" When Peter nodded, she grabbed Hawke's arm. "Come on then, enough dawdling." They must start rehearsals before her energy waned.

Saluting her, Hawke followed her down the hall. "Yes, play mistress!"

Wren almost giggled at his teasing as she knocked on the door of the matron's study then entered. "We're here, Kiera."

"We?" Kiera glanced up from the papers on her desk. "Oh, I see! Hawke, it's been too long." She bustled around her desk to embrace him.

Once Kiera released him, Hawke pursed a wry smile. "So it has, but I'm glad to be back."

Kiera rubbed her hands together. "Since you're here, you can supervise the set designers, so I only need to supervise the costume makers."

Wren's heart swelled. 'Twas just like before their first season. She grinned. "What children want to participate this time?"

Kiera rifled through the papers on her desk. "I've lists here." After handing Wren the play and a list of players, she jotted some notes on another list then handed it to Hawke. "I've written a list of children who'd prefer to be musicians below the list of set designers."

Wren scanned her list. She'd a few more players than usual. She'd need to split a few of the parts to make sure everyone received lines. Warmth filled her chest. The orphans must have truly loved *Kat's Tail.*

Hawke coughed a laugh. "I see a John and Jacob Bedsford on my list of set designers. Are those the turnip green throwers Peter mentioned?"

Although Kiera grumbled, Wren giggled. The twins would adore a dashing gentleman like Hawke. He'd no doubt inspire their next escapade. "Yes, you'll *like* them."

Hawke flashed a crooked grin. "I imagine so."

Kiera's curls bobbed as she shook her head. "Why am I suddenly afraid of what might happen?" When Hawke shrugged, she chuckled. "Try not to rile them too much. You don't have to settle them afterward."

Wren grinned when Hawke assumed an innocent expression and replied, "Of course." His promise might be impossible to keep.

Kiera narrowed her eyes at him then collected the pattern book Wren had donated last year from her desk. However, she only asked, "Shall we meet for tea in my study after rehearsals?"

While Hawke beamed, Wren inclined her head. If she managed to last the three hours, she'd definitely need refreshments. The orphanage plays were strenuous, but the orphans' joy made them worthwhile.

Kiera rose and gestured for Hawke to proceed her. "Hawke, I'll take you to the set designers."

As Kiera led Hawke in the opposite direction, Wren drifted to the library where her players waited. She sighed. The orphanage's library was barely a library—it only had one case of books, and most she'd donated over the years. The orphans deserved more, but the orphanage never received enough to build a decent library in addition to feeding and clothing the sixty-odd orphans.

But at least they had her plays. If only she could do more, but her parents had refused to allow her to donate her dowry to the orphanage. They insisted she'd need it one day, but she never would since Hawke wasn't interested in her. No, he was only interested in a will-o'-the-wisp that didn't exist.

Forcing her mind back to the play, she entered the library and grinned at her players. "Afternoon! Are you ready to act?"

The orphans mobbed her like a flock of ravenous sprites about a ripe raspberry bush. "Miss Wren!"

Warmth swamped Wren as she dispensed hugs to the children enveloping her. Hopefully, she could keep up with them this afternoon. She beamed at everyone. "Who wants to explain how we decide parts to those who've not been players before?"

Janelle bounced up and down. "First, we tell you what part we want. I want Kat!"

Wren hid a smile. With her verve, Janelle would make a perfect Kat, but the others must have a chance. "Anyone else who wants to play Kat, go stand by Janelle. Everyone else stand by me. What's next?"

From beside Wren, Sarya raised her hand then replied, "Everyone reads a few lines from the part they want. Once everyone reads for a part, Miss Wren selects the player."

Wren grinned at Sarya until the girl smiled back. The solemn girl needed to laugh more. "That's right. But don't fret, everyone who wants a part shall have one. If your first part goes to another, you can read for the next part you like. Any questions?"

All the orphans shook their heads.

Wren sat at the table by the bookcase and opened her copy of the orphanage play. "Then everyone open the play you copied last week to page six. We'll start with Kat's lines at the top. Janelle, why don't you go first?"

CHAPTER 24

Monitoring John and Jacob Bedsford, who'd slung wet pulp-clay at each other within moments of Kiera introducing them, Hawke turned to his budding musicians. "So you four want to perform the music for the play?"

The two older boys bobbed nods, and the older girl inclined her head, while her much younger sister bounced and shouted, "Yes!"

Hawke grinned. Adorable. How he'd missed the orphans—he never should have stopped visiting. He leaned toward his musicians. "Smart decision. Music makes the play because without it, the audience doesn't know what emotion to feel, no matter how clever the words." He winked. "But don't tell Miss Wren I said that."

The older children giggled, but the little girl blinked at him.

To avoid provoking the orphans' grief-filled memories, Hawke kept his tone light, "Are any of you familiar with a specific instrument?"

The boys glumly shook their heads, while the older girl shrugged and murmured, "Not really."

The little girl wiggled in place and beamed up at Hawke. "I sing!"

The dark-haired boy snorted. "That's not an instrument." He yelped when the older girl kicked his shin.

Hawke hid a smile. He'd not scold such a fierce protector. Instead, he ginned at the little girl. "Then you'll be our singer, Miss—?" Kiera's list of musicians had only listed not described them.

"Amaranth." The little girl danced to her sister and tugged her toward him. "And this is my sister Cassandra."

After giving Cassandra a half bow, Hawke began turning to the boys, but furtive movements from the Bedsford twins caught his gaze. He'd handle the twins later. He smiled at the boys before him. "And you are?"

The dark-haired boy announced, "Will," and the sandy-haired boy chimed in, "Jace."

Hawke nodded at the boys then eyed the four children. He hadn't instruments to give them today. "Go help the others build the sets. We'll start the music tomorrow."

While the others dashed across the dining hall to where the others were molding pulp-clay into trees for a magical forest, Amaranth hugged his knees before darting after her sister.

Now that the musicians were settled, he'd better handle the twins. Hawke strode across the dining hall to halt behind Jacob. "I doubt Mistress Kiera would be pleased if pulp-clay wandered away from the stage decorations."

Jacob sighed and extracted wads of pulp-clay from inside his sleeves.

When his twin made no move to do the same, Hawke arched a brow despite the laughter bubbling in his chest. "You too, John."

As John grumbled but obeyed, Hawke coughed to disguise his laugh. No wonder Wren had said he'd like them. He'd have done the same as a child.

The children continued molding pulp-clay until Kiera appeared in the doorway and announced, "Time for tea."

With cheerful shouts, the set designers thundered across the room to the trestle tables like a herd of starving centaurs.

Warmth welled in his chest at their rowdy glee. He took Kiera's arm while the rest of the orphans bounded into the dining hall. "For us too, I hope."

Kiera patted his hand as they started for her study. "As I promised."

Hawke flashed a crooked grin. "Good, I'm famished after watching those scamps." He sobered and eyed her. "How have things been here since I last visited?"

Kiera shrugged. "Much the same. Children who grow up or run away are replaced by children abandoned on our doorstep or whose parents have died. And there are so many more we can't help." She sighed. "Sometimes I feel as if we're using our hands to scoop out bilge water from a ship with a cracked hull in the middle of the ocean."

His brows flew upward. She'd become a pessimist in the past two years. What had happened?

Kiera glanced up at him and grimaced. "But perhaps I've lived at the orphanage too long. Yet I know that without Wren, our ship would have sunk years ago."

Hawke almost winced. He should have helped too, rather than attending tiresome court events. His jaw firmed. He would henceforth.

When he said nothing, Kiera smiled at him. "How have things been with you, Hawke? Did you attend the king's summer masquerade two weeks ago?"

His heart stilled as they entered the matron's study where Wren was already pouring tea. Why would Kiera ask him about the masquerade? Had Wren mentioned Rowan? No, she'd promised not to mention Rowan to anyone, and that included her best female friend. "Briefly."

Kiera sat behind her desk and accepted a teacup from Wren. "Only briefly? I thought masquerades lasted for hours."

Hawke forced himself to devour a sweet biscuit. Although

Kiera was a close friend, his enchanted night with Rowan was too private to share with her. So he must feign nonchalance. "They do, but 'twas dull, so I left early." With Rowan.

Her skin wan, Wren sipped her tea and crumbled the sweet biscuits on her plate. "Hawke has decided to cease attending court events that bore him."

Kiera arched her brows over her teacup. "Really? Why?"

He shrugged. "I wanted a change, I suppose." And he'd found one when he met Rowan. If only he could find her again.

Kiera's gaze dropped to her tea. "I understand that." After a pause, she asked them how the first rehearsal went.

While they talked with Kiera, Hawke eyed Wren, who appeared even more exhausted than before. And she'd eaten none of her sweet biscuits. Wren needed a decent meal and some sleep to recover from her late nights writing the fete play. When their conversation paused, he stood and offered his hand to Wren. "We should be off."

Wren drained her tea before taking his hand.

His hand tingled as he pulled her upright. He suppressed his reaction to her touch. They were just friends, and he'd cease reacting to Wren once he found Rowan. He began escorting Wren out until Kiera pulled him into another embrace.

Kiera whispered in his ear, "Try to find out what ails Wren."

Hawke met her eyes and nodded. So Kiera had noted Wren's exhaustion as well. Damn that fete play. He drew a deep breath. To help her recover, he'd make sure Wren ate a decent meal then retired as soon as she got home. So when they left the orphanage, he handed Wren into his carriage and muttered to his driver, "Head straight home, James."

He frowned as he settled across from Wren. She was curled against the side of the carriage with her eyes closed. Dark smudges underscored her eyes, and for the first time since she'd contracted wraith flu at seven, her dainty figure appeared fragile, as if a strong wind would shatter her. His throat tightened.

Goddess, what if 'twas more than late nights and something serious was wrong?

When the carriage halted before his townhouse, Hawke collected his violin and sample bolt then helped Wren alight. He'd give her the faegift inside.

Wren's brow furrowed as she smoothed her hair. "Why are we at your townhouse?"

He threaded his arm through hers with a crooked grin. He must mask his concern, or she might balk. She disliked being coddled, even when she desperately needed it. "I thought we could have dinner together."

Wren heaved a sigh when he escorted her up his front steps. "To discuss Rowan, I suppose."

Hawke grimaced. If only. But Wren hadn't the energy to discuss witch shops tonight. Not when they distressed her so. "No, another matter entirely." When Hobb opened the door, he told the butler, "Tell Cook to hurry dinner along, please."

Wren shook her head as they started down the hall. "Cook needn't bother on my account. I'm not particularly hungry."

At her disregard for her own health, he couldn't help glaring at her as he steered her to the sofa in the study. Obviously, she needed to hear the truth. "Yes, she does. You must eat a decent meal. You ate nothing at tea, and you barely ate luncheon." She'd not be so exhausted if she ate properly.

Wren returned his glare as he set down his violin and dropped beside her. "I ate plenty, perhaps not enough to fill the abyss called your stomach, but plenty for a *normal* person."

Hawke grasped her chin and leaned forward until their lips almost touched. His heart stuttered for some reason. "Cease fighting. You'll eat a decent meal if I have to chew your food and spit it into your mouth like a mama roc." The gargantuan bird was notoriously fierce about feeding and protecting its nestlings.

Her hazel eyes darkening, Wren blinked before jerking back. "Fine, you bully."

Why was his pulse uneven? Shoving that aside, he thrust the

sample bolt at Wren. "I wanted to discuss this. 'Tis Buford's latest find."

Wren blinked when she unwrapped the package. "Clear fabric?" She threaded her fingers into the fabric and wiggled them at him. "How, er, brash."

What would Wren look like in a transparent gown? His breath quickening, Hawke swallowed. "Only until someone bonds with it using a drop of blood. Then it becomes whatever color they imagine. And the color can be reset with another drop of blood. 'Tis woven by the arachne on Mist Isle. Magical, but harmless residual magic like firegems."

Wren's eyes widened. "Court shall adore it. What are you calling it?" When he shrugged, she caressed the fabric. "It feels silky—call it arachne silk."

He beamed at her. She'd devised the perfect name. Calling it arachne silk would make it even more irresistible to court. His clever friend always knew the right words to use. That's why she was such a gifted writer.

Wren attempted to return the sample bolt.

Hawke chuckled. He'd not explained. Idiot. "No, 'tis yours. A faegift. For helping me find Rowan."

Wren paled and thrust the sample bolt at him again. "Oh no, 'tis too extravagant for me."

"You deserve it." When she shoved anew, he captured her hands. Tingling warmth flooded him. Not again. Disregarding that, he leaned toward her. "You do. Use it for a ballgown for Mother's fete." He flashed a wheedling grin. "The shipment is due shortly after the fete, and your ballgown shall sell the entire lot."

Wren pursed her lips. "Very well. But I'm surrendering under duress."

His retort was halted when Hobb announced dinner. "Shall we?" At Wren's nod, Hawke drew her to her feet by her still captured hands then led her to dinner. He must ensure she ate a decent meal then retired for the evening.

CHAPTER 25

As Wren walked into the fete, the duchess thrust papers into her hands. "Here. I've rewritten your *simple* play. You're playing Rowan. Hawke can play himself."

Her chest freezing, Wren attempted to retreat, but the duchess shoved her into the middle of the crowded ballroom. Although Hawke effortlessly read his lines, she stumbled over hers, and the swarm of faces stared at her like derisive fae at a barbarian who'd stumbled into their queen's court.

Then Hawke kissed her and recoiled with a grimace, while the faces smirked and jeered. Unable to breathe, she wrenched free from his arms then bolted across the ballroom, but the doorway remained as distant as the north star...

Wren started awake. She shuddered then sighed. "Thank the Goddess 'twas only a dream." But after such a dream, she'd not return to sleep even though she ached for more—another four hours at least.

So she thrust aside her tangled blankets and stumbled across her chambers to pull back the drapes. The faintest hints of dawn lightened the horizon. Disgusting. She should still be asleep. Although she'd retired when she got home like Hawke had ordered last night, dawn was no time to be awake, unless you were an actual bird, not just called one.

Wren sighed again and rubbed her face, her stomach queasy from lack of restful sleep. 'Twas too early to ring for Abby, so she selected a gray dress she could lace herself. Once dressed, she returned to the window and watched the dawn since she couldn't focus enough to even read.

When the sun finally cleared the horizon, she rang for Abby and said, "Have Cook prepare my breakfast with my parents. But no shokolat, please, just tea." Since she'd risen so early, she could join her parents for once.

After Abby bustled out, Wren tread downstairs to the family dining room. Her parents returned her tepid greeting with such exuberance that she almost winced as she took her seat between them.

While Mother poured Wren a cup of tea, Father waggled his brows at their daughter and said, "It's been a while since you've joined us for breakfast."

Wren wrinkled her nose at him, adding a spoon of sugar to her tea. "That's because you two are unseemly early risers, even with your social engagements often running past midnight." How could they manage on so little sleep?

Mother smiled at Wren over her half-eaten toast. "Neither of us has ever needed much sleep, and as we age, we need even less."

Wren shook her head. She needed a full eight hours of restful sleep to function. Although she'd not gotten that since her night with Hawke due to her recurring sensual dreams. To obscure her flushed cheeks, she ate a forkful of eggs, but her stomach quivered. She frowned and set down her fork. Apparently, she'd be consuming only tea and toast this morning. Stupid dreams.

Mother's voice pulled Wren from her thoughts, "We're visiting Celeste's tomorrow, so today we must shop for the perfect fabric for your ballgown."

Wren suppressed a smile as she spread apple preserves on

toast. At least she could avoid today's shopping. "Hawke gave me some fabric yesterday for the fete. Besides, I have plans."

Father's eyes gleamed. "Hawke did, eh?"

Wren sighed. "'Tis nothing like *that*, Father." She studied her slathered toast then ate a bite. Her stomach remained steady. Good. She began devouring her toast. "Hawke has a new find he wants displayed before court, so he convinced me to wear it at his mother's fete."

Mother tilted her head. "That's too costly a gift for a gentleman to give an unconnected lady."

Wren shrugged. "We're not unconnected. We've been best friends forever." Her chest tightened—and Hawke had been determined she accept the arachne silk for her mendacious help with Rowan. Goddess, she was a terrible friend.

Mother tsked. "Very well, do as you like. I suspect you simply want to avoid a day of shopping. Just make sure you're free tomorrow."

Wren grimaced into the dregs of her tea. If Mother only knew she and Hawke would be a few streets away visiting Nature's Gifts. She'd almost prefer Celeste's over the witch shop. "Of course, although I can't stay too late because I've rehearsals at the orphanage in the afternoon." Thankfully.

Mother pursed her lips, but Father chuckled and said, "Do the poor orphans know you're using them as an excuse to curtail dress shopping?"

Wren shrugged again. "They're not an excuse—exactly." She shifted her eggs until it appeared she'd eaten more than a bite. Then she rose and smiled at her parents. "I'll see you tonight. I must work on the fete play until Hawke arrives to take me to the orphanage."

She returned to her chambers and worked on the fete play until Abby told her Hawke had arrived. Wren set down her pen with a sigh. Now she must endure another of those blasted witch shops. She swallowed to soothe her aching throat.

When she met him in the entrance hall, Hawke scrutinized her for a moment. Doubtless he was checking if she'd retired early like he'd ordered.

She stiffened. He'd no cause to study her so. She'd listened to him and retired early last night, but lack of restful sleep and her dawn awakening had undermined that.

Hawke waved toward the front door. "Shall we go?" Then once they'd settled in his carriage, he glowered and drawled, "So how late did you stay up writing?"

Wren glared back. She wasn't a child to be chided. "I retired as soon as I got home, as *ordered*."

Hawke eyed her up and down. "It doesn't appear so."

She almost snorted. That was entirely his fault. She'd get some rest if he ceased invading her dreams. She gritted a saccharine smile. "Do you wish for my aid finding Rowan?" When he nodded, she dropped her smile. "Then cease coddling me."

Hawke reached across the carriage to grasp her hands. "I don't mean to, but you look wretched."

At the concern darkening his eyes, she softened and squeezed his hands. "I swear to get more sleep tonight." If the dreams would let her.

"Good." Hawke absently caressed her palms with his thumbs. Why was he touching her again?

Tingling warmth flooded Wren. She ached to seize a kiss. 'Twas getting harder to resist her whetted desire. How could she survive it for the rest of her life?

The carriage halted, and Hawke grinned at her. "We're here." He pulled her from the carriage by her captured hands.

She almost winced at the green and brown sign swinging before Nature's Gifts. Her skin prickled. A dryad? Dear Goddess.

Hawke followed her gaze and chuckled. "A dryad on the sign seems promising, doesn't it?"

Hopefully not. Wren tensed as he escorted her inside. However, like the other witch shops she'd visited with Hawke, Nature's Gifts was missing the stifling sense of magic. She relaxed and glanced about at the shop's bounteous plants and natural treasures.

"Look!" Hawke nodded at the far wall. "Wood carvings. Rowan must have purchased the enchanted bird here."

Giddiness swept through her. No, she hadn't. She gestured toward the motherly woman behind the counter by the carvings. "Go speak with the clerk then."

Wren trailing behind, Hawke strode across the shop and extracted the enchanted bird from his pocket. "Morning, did you make this spell?"

The genial beam fled the clerk's face. "By the bounty of the Goddess, no." She shuddered. "Whatever that spell's about, it's definitely against nature."

Wren's heart stuttered. Against nature? 'Twas a mere glamour spell. A strong one, but still.

Hawke deflated and pocketed the enchanted bird. "Do you know a way we could locate the witch who created it?"

"No, I'm sorry." Relaxing with the spell out of sight, the motherly woman glanced between Hawke and Wren. "But I could provide you and your wife a similar carving with a fertility spell."

A weight compressed Wren's chest. Wife? If only. "We're not married, or even betrothed." Although if loved her as she loved him, they would be.

The clerk blinked, cocking her head. "Really?"

"Yes." Hawke coughed and flicked the clerk a coin. "Thanks for your time." He grabbed Wren's elbow and dragged her from the witch shop. Once the carriage started for the orphanage, he snorted. "That clerk was clearly mad. Imagine us married."

Wren glanced down at her hands. She had, many times. But 'twas an impossible fantasy. She blinked back the tears burning her eyes. If he talked to her about Rowan or marriage, she might begin sobbing. Her lack of restful sleep was making her weak and peevish as a fae changeling after years of living among humans without magic. Damned dreams.

To avoid questions about the next witch shop they should visit to find Rowan, she curled against the side of the carriage and feigned sleep. She could sense Hawke's gaze boring into her during the ride, but she forced herself to stay still. Would he say something?

Yet when the carriage halted, Hawke remained silent, only retrieving two pairs of drum sticks and a bulky case from beneath his seat.

Wren stretched and smoothed her hair. Her feigned sleep wouldn't be convincing otherwise. "What's in the case?"

Hawke flashed a crooked grin while helping her alight. "Water glasses. I thought they'd be ideal for Cassandra to play while her younger sister sang."

She blinked. Amaranth sang? The little girl hadn't mentioned that before, but it made sense considering her celestial voice. "During the ball scene, I suppose."

Hawke nodded as they entered the orphanage. He slanted her a final narrow glance then strode to the dining hall.

Wren turned toward the library. Just before entering, she inhaled to settle her perturbed emotions. She must focus on the orphans. She swept into the library and beamed at her players. "Shall we start at the top, everyone?"

CHAPTER 26

*S*ince he'd ordered Wren, again, to rest when he took her home after the orphanage rehearsal, Hawke headed to a horse auction the following morning rather than dragging her to another witch shop before her dress fitting. She'd better take this respite to recoup sleep rather than working on the dratted fete play.

He usually only attended horse auctions when he wanted a new horse, but he must start rumors about the arachne silk. Mother's fete was just two and a half weeks away, and the horse auction would be his first time promoting it. And he needn't worry about ladies pursuing him since they rarely attended horse auctions. Gentlemen wouldn't be his principal buyers, but some would want the magical fabric, either for themselves or their ladies.

Because the summer morning was balmy and not humid for once, he strolled to Bowers Street rather than taking a carriage. If he wanted a ride back, he'd obtain one from a friend at the auction. He entered Aherne's and wandered the stables, glancing at the horses being groomed for auction, but none interested him.

On to promoting the arachne silk. Hawke inhaled then

drifted to the auction block and corral. He joined several older gentlemen who'd served on the council with Father, and now Aragon, for years. As advisors to the king who also headed government ministries, councilors were among the most influential members of court, so their interest would bolster the arachne silk's success. "Good morning, my lords. See any horses you fancy?"

Lord Nolan, a bluff baron known for his prime racing stock, chortled. "A few, but don't expect me to inform you which ones." He winked at Hawke. "Can't have a young rakehell stealing my fillies."

Hawke almost snorted. As if he'd want to steal any the baron had chosen. But he mustn't reveal his distaste—he'd the arachne silk to promote. He flashed an innocent smile. "I'd never do such a thing."

The portly Count of Osteen snickered. "That's not what I heard, although as I recall, 'twasn't with horses."

Hawke stiffened but clung to his smile. Would the myth about how he'd acquired his first mistress ever cease amusing court? A drunken rival for the lady had fabricated most of it. But he'd never convince these gentlemen of that, so he forced a shrug. "I steal nothing that doesn't wish to be stolen, my lords."

The gentlemen guffawed, and the nearest, the lanky Lord Dabar, slapped him on the back. Hawke's jaw twitched. They resembled imps cackling over an ingenious prank.

When the gentlemen quieted at last, Hawke leaned forward and lowered his voice, "Although don't spend all your funds today. My shipping partner and I made the most extraordinary find, which Miss Keyes shall wear at Mother's fete. Your ladies shall demand one as soon as they see it."

Having a wife, four daughters, and a mistress, Lord Osteen crossed his arms over his chest. "And what is this extraordinary find?"

He almost had them. Hawke wagged his finger at the older gentlemen. "A secret until you see it adorning Miss Keyes." He arched a brow. "I can take your orders now and reserve them from our first shipment to ensure your ladies get one."

Lord Nolan laughed as the auctions began. "Without seeing it? I think not. Although I'll look for Miss Keyes at the duchess's fete."

Hawke smiled but shrugged. "Hopefully, others feel the same. I'd hate if Father's friends missed the most modish find of the season." That should be enough to make the arachne silk irresistible.

Hawke nodded at the older gentlemen and sauntered away to join a cluster of young gentlemen fresh to Ormas. They weren't as influential as councilors, but they loved to gossip, especially about the latest novelty. He tantalized them with hints about the arachne silk then continued to the next group and did the same. He circulated the auction area twice before stopping. No one had offered to purchase the arachne silk unseen, but rumors would proliferate after today.

Although his work was done, he couldn't leave yet. 'Twould appear suspicious. So he leaned against a pillar and watched the auctions until a surge in the crowd thrust another gentleman into him. His eyes slitting, he tensed. "Winston."

Herrick Winston, a despicable fortune hunter despite being a future baron, glared back as he straightened and smoothed his coat. "Lord Beza." His expression turned lecherous. "How's that delectable *friend* of yours been? Such a feisty filly."

Hawke's fingers twitched as fire flashed through him. At Mother's ball celebrating Aragon and Selena's marriage last year, Winston had followed Wren onto a secluded balcony and attempted to kiss her. When Hawke had joined them, he'd pitched the cad over the balcony. Unfortunately, they'd been on the first story, so the fall hadn't done permanent damage.

Goddess, if only he could punch Winston, but 'twould engender gossip. Hawke relaxed his fists but gritted a sharp grin. "If you ever speak of Miss Keyes in that tone again, I'll thrash you until even your eyes bleed. And if you touch her, I'll kill you." Gladly.

Winston stiffened. "You can't speak to me that way, you lout."

Hawke smirked at him. "I just did." And he'd do more to protect Wren.

Winston raised his chin. "I'll be a baron one day."

Hawke snorted. A destitute one with no influence. And a title wouldn't save him from a thrashing. "True, but no matter your rank, you'll still be the slime between a troll's toes."

Winston sputtered and turned purple before storming away.

A familiar voice rumbled behind Hawke, "Well said. Although I wish I'd been the one to say it. I caught him pestering your cousin Pippa the other day. Damned fortune hunter."

Hawke's tension vanished as he grinned at his maternal cousin. "Morning, Edouard. I didn't see you here."

Edouard, the Count of Blaine, chuckled and shook his head. "No, because you were too busy *hawking* your latest find. Something Wren shall wear at the duchess's fete. How did you get her to agree to that?"

Hawke shrugged. "I begged." But perhaps he shouldn't have. Wearing the arachne silk would magnify the attention she'd receive after the fete play. His chest tightened. Yet she deserved a faegift for helping with Rowan. Shoving that aside, he arched a brow at Edouard. "Found any horses you like?"

Edouard thrust his hands in his pockets and leaned on the pillar beside Hawke. "Not yet. Although I don't mind—I'm here to escape my dear stepmother's company."

Hawke coughed to disguise his laugh at Edouard's sardonic drawl. The same age as Hawke and Kit, Edouard had never liked her—he'd considered her brazen and grasping even before she'd persuaded his father into marrying her. And having her as his stepmother for the past six years had only hardened his dislike. Hawke tsked. "And what has Kit done to vex you today?"

Edouard groaned. "Asked for more money. Again. I swear, she must eat gold for breakfast."

Hawke shook his head. She would if 'twas the fashion. "It requires a fortune to remain as fashionable as Kit."

"I know." Edouard shuddered. "At least now I control the coffers. Father never denied her whims."

Hawke almost winced. Kit had effortlessly manipulated Edouard's father, both before and after marriage. To distract his cousin from the past, he asked, "Did you receive my note about Mother's fete?"

Edouard slanted him a wry glance. "The one where you requested I perform in some play? Yes." He grimaced. "How could I decline? You insinuated the duchess would be displeased if I did. I was still attempting to pen a suitably elegant reply."

Hawke smirked at his cousin. No doubt he'd hoped if he'd ignored the note, the play wouldn't occur, or at least wouldn't involve him. To no avail. "I'll inform Wren all her players are confirmed then. You were the only one who dared ignore my threat of Mother."

Edouard arched his brows. "Who else besides me and Elise have you blackmailed into performing?"

Hawke chuckled. Of course Edouard knew about Elise's note. Although they'd lived apart since her marriage, the twins still saw each other every day and never kept secrets. Hawke grinned at Edouard. "My cousins Dane, Xavier, and Pippa. Mother conscripted me and Mel."

The cherry bay being brought out drew his eye, and he pushed away from the pillar. He'd missed her during his scan of the stables. "Do you see that mare? Her coat is the exact shade of Wren's hair. Perhaps I should buy the mare for her."

Edouard snorted as he followed Hawke to the front. "You should give it to her on the day of your wedding."

Raising his hand to bid on the mare, Hawke frowned at his cousin. Wren would never marry him, so why would Edouard say that? "What?"

Edouard snorted again. "Why don't you just marry Wren? You two are practically married. You're either together or thinking about each other."

Hawke placed another bid, his chest compressing. "Wren and I are just friends." And if he married anyone, 'twould be Rowan. After he'd courted her, and their attraction burgeoned into love. As the auctioneer proclaimed him the winner, he muttered, "Would I have pursued all those lovers if Wren was more?"

Edouard's eyes narrowed. "I suppose not. You must forgive me." His tone turned scathing, "Your unwed status is all Kit natters about to Elise. And Kit happened to be home when Elise visited this morning."

Hawke winced as they returned to the pillar. Of course Kit was obsessed with his unwed status. She was pursuing him. He shuddered. To distract his cousin from that, he asked, "How is your sister?"

Edouard shrugged and quirked a smile. "Well. Still blissful with Farson. Although she wishes she was expecting like Selena."

Hawke nodded while turning his gaze back to the auction. Elise had married a year before Selena, so her longing wasn't surprising. "I'm sure she and Farson will be similarly blessed soon." And probably bear twins like her and Edouard.

As the horse auction continued, Hawke eyed the clock on the front wall. Wren's dress fitting should be soon. His pulse stirred. He'd remain with Edouard until almost luncheon then ride over to Celeste's to give Wren the cherry bay and check Mother wasn't fatiguing her.

CHAPTER 27

*W*ren awoke late morning when Abby burst in with a laden breakfast tray. As the maid bustled toward the bed, Wren stretched like a sunbathing tygris in the sweltering grasslands far south of Calatini. Her nightmare yesterday morning and rising at dawn had exhausted her enough that she'd enjoyed her first dreamless sleep since the masquerade. If she managed another unbroken night, she'd feel herself again and not a sickly fae changeling.

Abby scowled as she plunked the tray on the small table beside the bed. "Cook noticed you didn't eat yesterday, so I promised to make sure you did today. You know sent-back food wounds her."

Wren gulped at the heaped plate. How could she manage to eat all that? But considering Abby's expression, the maid would stand over her until she did. So Wren choked down the eggs, bacon, and toast, but she drank water rather than the shokolat. Her stomach overfull when she finished, she dropped her fork. "There. Not a morsel left. Satisfied?"

Abby snorted and nodded. "I suppose. Don't you want the shokolat?"

Wren shuddered, her stomach roiling. If she drank the rich

drink, she'd expel that enormous breakfast she'd just choked down. "Absolutely not."

Once Abby helped her dress, Wren said, "I've become weary of eggs and shokolat. Tomorrow I want porridge and tea." The blander foods should rest better in her now delicate stomach. The Rowan imbroglio must be giving her an ulcer.

Her lips pressed flat, Abby collected the breakfast tray before nodding and bustling from the room.

Wren gathered the sample bolt of arachne silk then joined Mother and the duchess in the morning room. "Morning."

Mother studied her. "Barely. I was about to send someone to drag you from bed." Her eyes narrowed. "You wouldn't be attempting to avoid your dress appointment, would you?"

Wren smiled despite her queasy stomach. "Of course not." Although she would have if that could have succeeded.

Mother and the duchess exchanged a glance before the duchess rose, saying, "Shall we go? One dares not arrive late for a fitting at Celeste's."

Once her carriage started down the street, the duchess eyed Wren. "Diana and I were discussing Kit's card party tomorrow night, and she mentioned your family hadn't received their invitation yet."

Wren laced her fingers over her bloated stomach. Knowing Kit, they'd not been invited—she was pursuing Hawke and wanted no other competition, no matter how slight. Wren's heart squeezed. At least without an invitation, she'd not have to attend the wretched card party. She despised cards, and watching Kit flirt with Hawke would be tortuous.

Mother beamed at Wren. "So Caro offered to bring you as her guest. Your father and I shall stay home since we dislike card parties anyway."

Wren almost grimaced. If only she could stay home too. A sour taste flooded her mouth. Goddess, why must the duchess meddle? Provoked by Wren's unexpected appearance, Kit would be sure to exacerbate her flirting with Hawke to needle Wren. "'Twouldn't be right attending without an invitation."

The duchess waved a hand as the carriage halted. "Nonsense. The party is for family. You belong there."

Wren sighed but followed Mother and the duchess into Celeste's. The duchess was too determined. So Wren couldn't escape the wretched card party. Just like she'd not escaped today's dress fitting or writing the fete play. But perhaps she could delay the dress fitting awhile. She skirted the edge of the anteroom. "You two should take the first appointments."

Mother shook her head and pulled Wren into the center of the room. "The appointment is yours alone. Our dress fittings were the other day. We're simply here to ensure you don't bolt."

How well Mother knew her. Wren sighed again as Celeste and two assistants entered the anteroom. At least she'd eaten enough at breakfast to withstand a lengthy dress fitting.

The duchess's eyes shimmered with laughter. "Now, let's see that fabric Diana said my son gave you."

When Wren unwrapped the transparent arachne silk, Celeste and her assistants twittered, and Mother groaned, but the duchess only arched her brows. "Although I understand why my son would want to see you naked, I can't approve of his desire to do so in public."

Wren blushed. Except he only wanted that when he'd not recognized her. "Once I bond with the arachne silk, it becomes any color I wish." She'd waited to do so since gossiping dressmakers would increase the demand for Hawke's fabric.

She pricked her finger with a pin, allowed a drop of blood to soak into the arachne silk, and concentrated on her favorite color. Starting where the blood fell, a dark green flooded the clear fabric until only a peculiar luster indicated its magical nature. Impressive.

Mother fingered the arachne silk but shook her head. "You should have desired something more exotic than a plain green."

Wren shrugged. "I'll wait until the dress is sewn to add embellishments." She glanced at Celeste, whose dreamy eyes were riveted on the fabric, and gestured toward a fitting room. "Shall we?"

"Of course, miss." Celeste snapped her fingers at her assistants. When Mother and the duchess moved to follow, the dressmaker imperiously pointed at the sofa in the anteroom. "You two know only the recipient in the fitting room."

Wren suppressed a laugh as she stepped on the stool and handed Celeste the arachne silk. No wonder the duchess loved this dressmaker; she'd found a likeminded soul. Once the assistants drew the curtain closed and began measuring, she smiled at Celeste. "I surrender to your superior taste. I only request no frills."

The dressmaker glanced up from her scrutiny of the arachne silk. "Certainly, those wouldn't suit you at all. Now strip."

Wren pursed her lips as she removed her dress. "My mother seems to think so." Hence the peach dress Hawke had snickered over.

Celeste cocked her head while she began pinning the arachne silk into place. "She still sees you as a little girl, but you're a woman."

Tingling swept over Wren. An experienced one, thanks to her glamour spell. Her enchanted night with Hawke echoing through her, she remained silent until the dressmaker pinned her neckline perilously low. "What are you *doing*?"

"Showing you're a woman." When Wren sputtered, Celeste fixed her with a gimlet glare. "You promised to yield to my superior taste, Miss Keyes. Now let me work."

Wren met the Celeste's gaze and nodded. The dressmaker was the best in Ormas, so if anyone could accentuate her ordinary beauty, 'twould be Celeste. Perhaps with the dressmaker's aid, she might even eclipse herself as Rowan.

Wren swallowed as weight tightened her chest. Hawke wouldn't kiss her again, but perhaps desire might flicker in his eyes when he first saw her. So she held still as Celeste muttered to herself, pinned, cut, and commanded her assistants. During the lengthy dress fitting, Wren's overfull nausea faded to comfortable fullness.

Celeste straightened at last. "There. All finished."

Wren turned to glance at herself in the mirror, and her lips parted. Dear Goddess, she couldn't be the vision reflected there. Although her coloring and green arachne silk fit a dryad, the perfectly cut ballgown transformed her into a wingless siren—both ethereal and entrancing. Her blood bubbling in her veins, she breathed, "Celeste, you're a true artist."

The dressmaker shooed out her assistants and flashed a grin. "I know. I'll fetch Lady Keyes now."

Still gazing at herself in the mirror, Wren nodded. She definitely eclipsed Rowan. She grinned and whirled around when the curtain rustled. "What do you think, M—"

Instead of Mother, Hawke stood in the doorway, his pale-blue eyes dark and intent. He'd not stared at her so since she'd been Rowan.

Her pulse surged, and she stopped breathing. His reaction was more than she'd just wished for. Would he kiss her after all? Fire throbbed beneath her skin, and she swayed toward him.

Hawke blinked then shook his head. When his gaze returned to her, his eyes were no longer hungry.

Numbness swamping her, Wren gasped and stumbled from the stool. "Hawke, what are you doing here?" And what had just happened?

Hawke coughed while running a hand through his inky-brown hair. "Mother told me to escort you to the anteroom for them to inspect."

She shuddered. Then they'd notice her disappointed desire. She crossed her arms across her chest, careful to not disrupt the pins. "And ruin this masterpiece? Absolutely not."

Hawke inclined his head. "I'll inform them of your refusal."

Wren gazed after him as he bolted from the fitting room. Had he been about to kiss her? Impossible. Not when she was herself.

Celeste and her assistants bustled through the curtain. As they began the painstaking process of extracting Wren from the unfinished ballgown, Celeste smiled at her. "Your young gentleman is fierce on your behalf, miss."

Wren's heart stuttered. Hawke wasn't hers. She'd merely had him for one night. And he'd soon belong to another. She heaved a sigh as her gaze fell. Scraps of arachne silk were strewn across the floor. She frowned. Since the fabric was bonded to her by blood, they might provide a magical link to her. "I'll require all the scraps of arachne silk back."

"Of course." Celeste snapped her fingers, and one of her assistants swept them into a small bag.

Accepting the bag, Wren checked for stray scraps then nodded at the dressmaker and returned to the anteroom.

Hawke grasped her arm. "I'll escort Wren back. If we don't leave now, we'll be late for the orphanage."

Tingling warmth suffused Wren at his touch. As he swept her outside, she scrutinized his face, but his expression was blank. His earlier reaction must have been an aberration. Her tingling faded. "Why are we hurrying? We're not expected at the orphanage for several hours."

CHAPTER 28

His pulse still erratic after his bizarre reaction to Wren in her unfinished ballgown, Hawke forced a smile. "I've a surprise for you." He gestured toward the cherry bay tied to a nearby post.

Wren glided to the mare with a soft smile. She chuckled when the mare nickered and butted her outstretched hands. "She's beautiful. Sweet too."

As Wren petted the mare, his heart squeezed. He'd been right. The mare's coat matched Wren's auburn hair. Lovely. As lovely as Rowan at the masquerade. Pain gripped his temples, but he nodded. "She's yours."

Wren jerked around to gape at him. "You can't buy me a *horse*. Our parents could barely accept the arachne silk. And what if court finds out?"

Hawke stiffened as weight compressed his chest. If anyone found out, they'd assume he and Wren were more than friends. He managed a crooked grin. "How you got her must remain secret then." Only Edouard would know, and he'd not mention it to anyone.

Wren shook her head and turned to pet the mare again. She

sighed when the mare leaned into her caress. "I shouldn't accept, but she's too sweet to refuse."

He untied the mare and swung into the saddle. "Come, we'd best leave before our mothers see us with your new mare." He offered her his hand, and his breath quickened for some reason. "We must ride double. I left my carriage at home."

Her gaze skittering away, Wren gave the mare a final pat then accepted his hand and settled behind him.

Hawke swallowed. They'd not been so close in years. His body tightened as her delicate violet scent weaved around him. What was the matter with him? They were just friends. Pain bolted through his head again. He urged the mare to a canter. This uncomfortable ride must end soon, but a gallop would attract too much attention.

At his townhouse, he relaxed once he helped Wren alight. Thank the Goddess. After instructing a groom to deliver the mare to Wren's, he said, "We should eat luncheon before we head to the orphanage."

Wren wrinkled her nose. "Very well, but I shan't eat much. Abby forced me to eat an enormous breakfast."

Hawke almost snorted. No doubt because she'd been too tired to eat much the night before. Yet she'd glare if he said that, so he winked instead. "I'll eat your portion then."

A blush shading her cheeks, Wren tsked when they entered the family dining room. "You always do. You're worse than a starved manticore."

Hawke chuckled as servants brought two full plates. When he and his brothers were boys, Father had often called them manticores. Rare yet invincible magical creatures, manticores were renowned for eating half their weight every day. Not that Hawke and his brothers had eaten quite that much, and none of them ate near as much now. Yet he winked at Wren again and replied, "I know."

While Wren nibbled on a roll, he devoured his luncheon and

the rest of hers. Then they took his carriage to the orphanage. As Wren stared out the window, tingling suffused him again, so he remained silent the entire ride. Yet the rowdy rehearsal at the orphanage settled him.

But the rehearsal drained Wren. Hawke eyed her as she dozed on the carriage ride home. She'd not eaten much at tea, and she was wan again. She must need more sleep. Tomorrow he'd wait as long as possible to fetch her. He helped her alight, saying, "I'll collect you midmorning tomorrow. We can visit a witch shop then have luncheon and head to the orphanage."

Wren nodded and drifted inside.

He stared after her, his chest tight. Surely she'd be better tomorrow. He returned home and played his violin to distract himself from Wren's exhaustion and his curtailed hunt for Rowan. He played until his fingers were stiff and his bow arm burned then bolted dinner and retired for the evening.

ALTHOUGH HAWKE FELL ASLEEP QUICKLY, Rowan plagued his dreams yet again, so his sleep was restless. Most of the dreams featured him making love to her again, until the last one.

Her auburn hair blazing against the dark green arachne silk, Rowan turned with a saucy grin when he joined her in Celeste's fitting room.

His body throbbed as he pulled her into his arms, pinned her against the mirror, and captured her mouth in a fierce kiss.

She shoved him to the floor. "*Never* do that again!"

As he gaped up at Wren, the dream dissolved around him. Pain crushing his head, he stumbled from bed to ring for a tonic. Goddess, what a mad dream. Somehow Rowan had merged with Wren at Celeste's then scolded him like she had after their Longnight kiss.

Once he drank his tonic, Hawke lay with a cold cloth over his eyes until his headache eased. Then he quaffed another tonic with his light breakfast before collecting Wren. As he escorted her to his carriage, he managed a smile. "Where are we headed today?"

Her brow furrowed, Wren eyed him for a moment then replied, "Charmed Blessings."

His brows rose. The sacred witch shop? A lady who seduced a stranger outside of matrimony wouldn't have purchased a spell there. However, he instructed his driver to head to the Great Temple.

Wren pursed her lips as the carriage began forward. "Are you well? You don't seem your ebullient self."

Hawke grimaced, her scornful decree from his dream echoing in his ears. "A nightmara curdled my sleep. And I awoke with an excruciating headache."

"Oh dear." Wren paled with a tremulous smile. "We're quite the pair. Both of us have forgotten how to sleep in the past few weeks."

He grunted. "Yes, but I know why my sleep is disturbed—Rowan. Why is yours?" Surely it couldn't only be late nights spent writing.

Wren shifted her gaze out the window. "The fete play, I suppose. Look, we're here!" Her enthusiasm at a witch shop must be fake. What was she hiding?

Hawke scrutinized his best friend as he helped her alight. Had she found someone but was waiting until he found Rowan to tell him? His headache pierced his temple again. The tonic from before must be waning. He'd drink another at luncheon. Please let the visit to Charmed Blessings be brief.

Unlike the other witch shops they'd visited, the clerks at Charmed Blessings were all priests, and relics for the Goddess predominated the displays. As soon as they entered, he extracted the enchanted bird and waved over the nearest priest. "Morning, holy sir. Did a witch from your shop enchant this carving?"

The ascetic priest shuddered. "Absolutely not. That nasty

spell does *not* bear the blessing of the Goddess. Doubtless 'twas crafted by a black witch."

Wren turned ashen. "What?"

The priest inclined a solemn nod. "You'd be wise to destroy that cursed thing straightaway."

As the priest scuttled away, Hawke's head throbbed. What exactly was Rowan's spell? Yet he couldn't destroy his only link to her. He sighed and pocketed the enchanted bird. Then he took Wren's trembling hand and pulled her from the sacred witch shop. At least the visit had been brief.

He and Wren were both pale and silent during luncheon, but their rehearsal at the orphanage cheered them, even though they had to skip tea with Kiera. Somehow Mother had convinced Wren to attend Kit's card party. Since Wren despised cards, he'd attend to support her even though Kit was sure to pursue him.

When Hawke arrived at Blaine House that evening, Kit immediately grasped his arm with a coy smile, just as he'd expected. "I'm so glad you could come, my dear Hawke. Now I've a worthy partner."

He wrenched his arm free and glanced about the room to find an excuse to escape. His parents and Wren hadn't arrived yet—doubtless Mother was planning her usual stately entrance. So he must rely on one of his cousins, and Elise was the closest. "I'm already spoken for, Kit. Excuse me, your stepdaughter must speak with me."

Kit's glare burning his back, Hawke strode over to Elise. "Pretend you need me. *Please.*"

Edouard's twin chuckled and tilted her head. "Stepmother is hunting you, hmm? Perhaps you should have Wren solve that."

He frowned at his cousin. How could Wren end Kit's pursuit? "What?"

Elise chuckled again then said, "Never mind. Tell me about Wren's play."

His chest lightening, Hawke leaned forward. "It'll be delightful, naturally. I play the demon that lusts after the nubile princess." He waggled his brows. "Which is you, dear cousin."

Elise laid a playful hand over her heart. "Whatever shall I do?"

He flashed a crooked grin. "You curse me with some heirloom, so everyone else can live happily ever after." Wren's plays always ended happily for everyone but the villain.

Elise arched her brows. "Poor demon. Whoever shall love you?" She pointed toward the door. "Wren has arrived with your family. Now that she's here, I must go find my husband."

As she left to find Farson, Hawke glanced across the room. His parents, Wren, and Mel were greeting Kit. His brows flew upward. Mother had convinced Mel to attend too? Mel rarely attended Kit's events—he said they were too frivolous.

When Mel and Kit began bickering like usual, his parents and Wren glided over to Hawke.

After nodding at Father, Hawke grinned at Mother and Wren, his chest warming. "Evening. How lovely my two favorite ladies look."

A blush pinked Wren's cheeks, but Mother arched a brow. "Do you think so? I thought Wren should change into a fancier gown."

Why? Hawke eyed Wren's amethyst gown. Its elegant simplicity suited her. Although she looked better in green. His head cramped. "Wren looks fetching."

Wren glared and pursed her lips. "Must you two discuss me as if I weren't here?"

Ignoring her, Mother beamed at Hawke. "I do believe you're right." She gave Father a smug glance then patted Wren's hand. "We must greet Edouard."

Hawke stiffened as his parents bustled across the room. He frowned at Wren. "What was that about?"

Wren grimaced. "Considering 'twas the duchess, some matchmaking scheme."

He almost snorted. No doubt. But matchmaking whom? Could Mother intend to match Wren with Edouard? His stomach hardened. 'Twould be a suitable match, not that Wren had shown interest in his cousin before. Shoving that from his mind, he grinned at her. "Would you be my partner?"

Wren gazed up at him, her hazel eyes shimmering. "No..."

CHAPTER 29

$\mathcal{W}$ren whirled away from Hawke and blinked back foolish tears. Why had his simple request made her maudlin? 'Twas as if, since that night as Rowan, she could no longer control her emotions. Perhaps *that* was the cost for the glamour spell. If so, how long could she hide her love from Hawke? Although not as dire as him realizing she'd seduced him, she'd still lose their friendship if he realized she loved him.

Hawke touched her shoulder. "Wren, what's wrong? I swear I'll fix whatever's troubling you."

She shrugged off his hand then faced him. If he knew he was the trouble, he'd not promise that. "Nothing is troubling me. 'Twas dust, nothing more."

Hawke's eyes narrowed. "Then why won't you be my card partner?"

Wren almost grimaced. She'd not been thinking about cards. She waved a hand. "Because I'm wretched at cards; you know that."

Hawke leaned toward her until their faces were a handbreadth apart.

Warmth flooded her at his intense gaze. Although she managed not to sway forward and kiss him, she couldn't step away. She was entranced like a sailor by a siren's song. And she was about to wreck her ship against the rocky coast simply to keep hearing that bewitching song.

"How cozy," Kit drawled from beside them.

As she and Hawke sprang apart, Wren battled a blush. When had Kit joined them? Had anyone else noticed them staring at each other?

Kit's eyes glinted. "Why are you here, Wren? I meant to ask earlier, but Mel distracted me." Kit arched a brow. "This is a family event, so I didn't send you an invitation."

The duchess glided forward with a lofty smile. "Well, you should have done. But no matter, I corrected your error by bringing Wren myself. And I convinced Mel to come to keep the numbers even."

Kit paled and lifted her chin. "Thank you, your grace." Once the duchess sailed away, Kit glowered at Wren. "I suppose you can stay to ensure everyone has a card partner." She tossed her head. "Now excuse me, I must announce tonight's entertainment."

Wren and Hawke exchanged a glance as Kit swished across the room. Only Kit would dare needle Wren after the duchess's censure.

Kit tapped a flute of sparkling wine, and everyone quieted and turned toward her. She smiled then said, "Before we begin playing cards, I'm pleased to announce I hired a gypsy witch to read our fortunes. She awaits in the adjoining room. But for now, everyone please take your seats."

As everyone drifted to the card tables, Hawke escorted Wren to the nearest one, and she was just about to sit when Kit stole the chair Hawke was pulling out. Wren sighed. How like Kit.

Hawke glared at Kit. "That was for Wren."

A smirk curving her lips, Kit began shuffling the cards. "But I love this chair. And Wren doesn't mind, does she?"

Wren forced a serene smile as she sat in the opposite seat. She refused to reveal how Kit's needling annoyed her. "One chair is much like another." She patted the chair beside her. "Although I can't say the same for partners."

Hawke settled beside Wren. "Yes, where's your partner, Kit?"

"Here." Mel strolled over and sat beside Kit. "Kit scuttled across the room so fast I couldn't keep up with her." He tsked and straightened his priest robes. "Not the best way to start a partnership."

Kit stiffened, her hands pausing mid-shuffle. She glared at Mel. "We don't have a partnership. You're merely my partner for the evening."

Mel plucked the cards from her still hands and finished shuffling them. "As you say." He smiled at Wren and Hawke. "Shall we start?"

Wren almost beamed. Thank the Goddess Mel was partnering Kit. He was the sole person who could distract Kit from needling her. Even as children, Mel could handle Kit, either by deflecting or confronting her. And he always saw the truth and knew exactly what to say. Doubtless 'twas why he was such an excellent priest. She inclined her head. "Of course."

His fingers swift, Mel dealt the cards, and the game began.

Wren's muscles tightened. She'd not lose to Kit tonight. She paid attention to the game for once, so she and Hawke didn't fare as badly as usual. Yet her eyes widened when they drew the five strongest cards of the white arcana during their fourth hand. A good fortune? She'd never such luck at cards.

With Hawke smirking beside her, Wren fanned the cards on the table and said, "A good fortune, I believe."

While Kit sputtered, Mel laughed. "Unbelievable. We should trade partners."

Hawke threw an arm around Wren's shoulders. "Oh no, Wren is mine, and I intend to keep her."

Tingling then fire flashed through her. She was his, not that he noticed. But he'd *never* seek to keep her. "I think not. Release me."

Hawke jerked back and held up his palms. "I was jesting, Wren."

Which was the problem. Her heart throbbed as she glowered at him. If only he truly wanted to keep her. Then she wouldn't have needed to seduce him as Rowan.

Kit purred a laugh. "Dear Hawke, haven't you learned in your twenty-three years that ladies don't appreciate jests about keeping them, especially those in—"

"I'd like my fortune read." Wren leapt to her feet, her pulse skittering. She must prevent Kit from revealing she loved Hawke. She managed a smile. "In the adjoining room, you said?"

Although Kit appeared smug and Mel amused, Hawke gaped up at Wren then said, "But you hate fortune readings."

Wren clung to her smile. "Not tonight. If you'll excuse me."

She scurried away, almost tripping on her skirt in her haste, but halted before the door to the adjoining room. As Hawke had said, she hated fortune readings. Yet she'd claimed to want one to silence Kit. 'Twould appear odd if she returned without entering. She swallowed then made herself to open the door.

Sitting behind a table in a dark corner, the gypsy witch was dressed in sober colors that blended into the shadows. Only the coins dangling in her hair and about her waist drew the eye. She beckoned Wren forward. "Come, my child."

Wren swallowed again, but she glided inside and shut the door. "I'm not your child."

The witch deftly shuffled the deck on the table. "Perhaps not, my child would never be so rude. Sit."

Wren perched on the chair before the table, the gypsy's magic tingling her skin. She'd not sensed magic like that since the veiled witch. She gulped a breath. Goddess, would the gypsy see she'd been Rowan? At least Hawke wasn't here.

The witch arched her brows. "I presume you want a quick reading." When Wren nodded, the gypsy fanned the cards across the table facedown. "Think of yesterday and point to the first card you notice."

The sense of magic now stinging her skin, Wren concentrated then selected a card. She shivered. Why had she allowed Kit's needling to provoke her into getting her fortune read?

The witch slid the card toward Wren. "Now think of today and point." Wren pointed again, and the gypsy slid that card beside the first. "Think of tomorrow." Once Wren selected a third card, the witch slid it to the others then swept the rest of the deck into a pile and set it aside.

The gypsy touched the first card. "This is your past." She flipped the card, revealing a young man cavorting by a cliff. "The Fool."

Wren choked a laugh. "I've certainly been that." Only a fool would have disguised herself with a glamour spell to seduce her best friend.

The witch frowned. "No, the Fool doesn't mean you were stupid. It represents potential and innocence."

Wren pursed her lips. She'd been an innocent until their enchanted night. "I suppose that applies as well. Please proceed."

"Your present." The gypsy flipped the second card, revealing a moon beaming down on a howling wolf and dog. "The Moon, confusion and secrets. Not necessarily bad, but you should listen to your instincts."

Wren sighed. Confusion and secrets defined her tangled relationship with Hawke since the masquerade, although her instincts were as confused as the rest of her. If only he'd stop hunting Rowan. Then their lives would return to normal.

"And finally, your future." The witch flipped the third card, revealing a skeleton bearing a scythe.

The gypsy needn't explain *that* one. Wren froze and whispered, "Death." This morning the priest had called her enchantment a curse, and now the witch was hinting 'twould kill her.

The gypsy shook her head, jingling the coins in her hair. "Not always physical death, as you clearly imagine. It represents dramatic change."

Wren clenched her hands in her lap. Like losing your best

friend since childhood. Whether to his wife or due to her deceitful seduction. Oh, Goddess. What had she done by invoking that glamour spell? "I see."

The witch swept the three cards back into the rest of the deck and shuffled. "A good fortune, I'd say. You're transforming from a child to a lady, but like the caterpillar, you'll be grateful to be a butterfly once the pain has passed."

Wren licked her lips. Another good fortune? Somehow it didn't feel like one. "That's the second time this evening. How remarkable." She inclined her head then rose. "Thank you for the reading."

She fled the room as swiftly as her shaky knees allowed. She must leave. The duchess wouldn't take her home so early, but Hawke would. She darted over to him, even though he was talking with his cousin Xavier.

Hawke halted mid-sentence to smile down at her. "How was it?"

Wren swallowed then shrugged to feign nonchalance. "The same mystical trumpery." Only true.

Hawke rubbed his chin. "I wonder if I went, I could get insight on some matters."

Her stomach roiled. Goddess, he wanted to ask about Rowan. The gypsy's magic would unravel her deception if she read them both. The enchanted bird should prevent her from telling Hawke —unless she managed to break the veiled witch's spell. And she might, considering how strong her magic had been. So Hawke speaking with the gypsy witch was much too risky. She grasped his arm. "I'm rather fatigued. Could you escort me home?"

Hawke nodded, his brow furrowed as he eyed her. He whisked her from Blaine House into his carriage.

Tears pricked her eyes again. If the gypsy's fortune was right, Hawke's tender care would end soon, so she must treasure it while it lasted.

CHAPTER 30

*S*hortly after breakfast the following morning, Hawke had just finished his business correspondence when Hobb arrived bearing a letter with the royal seal. He grinned as he opened the seal and read his cousin's note.

Hawke—

Certainly you may ride in the royal forest. Has a certain dryad inspired your recent desire? If so, your mother shall harp on it until you wed the lady. Try not to poach too many of my rabbits.

Devon

He chuckled and pocketed the letter. He requested his iron-gray gelding from Hobb before bounding upstairs to change. Now that he'd royal permission, he must pry Wren away from her writing for a good ride. Although 'twould probably be more arduous than obtaining permission from Devon.

When he arrived at Wren's townhouse, she'd yet to emerge from her room. As her maid returned upstairs to inform Wren of his visit, he called, "Make sure she dresses for riding."

After what seemed an age, Wren descended scowling but

attired in a brown riding habit that heightened her pallor. "Why are you here at such an unseemly hour? I'd barely begun breakfast when you arrived."

Hawke eyed Wren. Why did she look tired again? On the carriage ride home last night, she'd said she was retiring for the evening as soon as she returned. When would she recover from late nights writing the fete play? He forced himself to smile at her. "Devon gave me permission to ride in the royal forest. I thought we could test your new mare's paces." Plus, a ride might assuage the oddly mercurial behavior she'd shown at Kit's card party.

Wren sighed. "I suspected as much, so I sent someone to the mews to saddle her."

They strolled outside to their waiting horses, but Wren staggered as she attempted to place her boot in the stirrup. He stiffened. Although not horse mad, she'd never had trouble mounting a horse before. He stepped forward. "Allow me."

Hawke's breath quickened as he grasped her about the waist and began hoisting her atop the cherry bay mare.

Wren slapped his chest. "What are you doing?"

He jerked and lost his grip, and she tumbled into him and slid to her feet. They stilled with their bodies pressed together. As they stared into each other's eyes, her violet scent filled his lungs.

Hunger roared through Hawke. He'd not held Wren like this since their Longnight kiss eight years ago. Yet she felt familiar in his arms. Why? Agony pierced his head, and he released her and stepped back.

Wren glared up at him, a blush darkening her cheeks. "I can mount a horse myself." She jammed her boot in the stirrup and swung into the saddle.

His body tight, he rubbed his temple. Dear Goddess, what had just happened? He mounted as well. "I can see that now, but you were struggling earlier."

Wren urged her mare forward with a snort.

His body settled as he joined her. He eyed her while they rode through Ormas. Her temper was as mercurial as last night. He should wait until they were out of the city to talk. Then if she became irate, no one would observe her shouting, and she wouldn't trample any bystanders.

They rode out the eastern gate, but Hawke studied Wren and remained mute. A frown still pinched her face. Roasted by the late summer sun, they rode in silence past several farmsteads amid the ripening fields.

He relaxed when they reached the meandering path beneath the thick boughs of the royal forest. Relief at last. He glanced at Wren, whose frown had smoothed into a faint smile, so he asked, "How's the mare?"

Her auburn hair muted by the dappled shade, Wren rubbed the mare's neck. "Quite fine. She's the best mount I've ever owned."

Hawke chuckled. He'd known the cherry bay mare would be perfect for her. "That's because you're too engrossed in your writing to attend to mundane matters like purchasing a horse."

Wren wrinkled her nose but chuckled as well. "True."

He flashed a crooked grin as he steered his gelding around a fallen log on the path. "'Tis fortunate you have me to attend to such matters."

Wren's eyes flickered, then she snapped the twig brushing her shoulder and threw it at him. "Very fortunate."

Warmth surging in his chest, Hawke caught the twig and wagged it at her. "Didn't anyone ever tell you not to throw things, young lady? You could have cost me an eye."

Wren giggled. "Not likely. You possess the reflexes of a tygris. Speaking of felines..."

As she began chattering about the orphanage play, he almost smiled. She seemed her usual self again—the forest ride and his teasing had worked. So he'd not mention visiting witch shops until after the orphanage play. Visiting them always soured her mood. Plus, she could use the rest, and the orphanage play was only three days away.

Laughing at Wren's description of the girl playing the cat, Hawke hid a frown. Hopefully, his hunt for Rowan wouldn't suffer from another delay. 'Twasn't her spell that was cursed as the priest had claimed. His hunt was. Yet he must find Rowan again, so he'd not quit.

Wren eyed him. "Hawke, have you heard anything I said?"

He tensed, scouring his mind for her last words. After a moment, he relaxed and replied, "You were describing Janelle washing her face with her hand."

Wren hummed and pursed her lips. "So I was."

If he didn't cease musing over Rowan, he'd curdle the cheerful mood he'd created. His gaze drifted to the cherry bay mare. "I suppose I *was* distracted. I was attempting to find a place for us to race."

Wren cocked her head. "Race?"

Hawke arched a brow. "Yes, how else were we to test your mare's paces?" Plus, Wren had always loved a good race.

"In that case..." Wheeling around, Wren prodded her mare into a gallop.

He barked a laugh and pivoted his gelding to follow. By the time he had, Wren and her nimble mare had already disappeared down the meandering path. He urged his gelding to a gallop, ignoring the branches slapping him. But due to his greater weight and larger horse, he didn't catch up with Wren until he burst from the trees. "Truce, unicorn spawn! I forfeit."

Wren giggled as she slowed to a walk. "As you should." She patted her mare's neck again. "Yes, definitely the best mount I've ever owned."

Hawke couldn't help but grin at her disheveled hair and bright face. His heart quickened. Adorable. They must race more often.

He halted his gelding at a quaint tavern near the eastern gate. "Shall we eat here then ride straight to the orphanage?"

"If you like." Wren slid from the saddle and allowed him to escort her inside.

Hawke devoured a hearty meal of ham stew with dark bread. He smiled when Wren ate three-quarters of hers before giving him the rest. She'd spent more time toying with her food than eating it in recent days.

He and Wren headed to the orphanage after luncheon. During another rowdy rehearsal, an inspired idea struck him. He should invite his cousins to the orphanage play so they'd see what they must do for the fete play. He'd invite his parents and brothers too, even though they'd seen Wren's plays before. He'd mention inviting everyone to Wren at tea.

However, Wren's eyes kept drifting shut when she joined Hawke and Kiera for tea. He and Kiera exchanged frowns and silently agreed he should escort Wren straight home.

Since Wren couldn't manage to ride alone, Hawke tied her mare to his gelding then placed Wren behind him.

Without a word of complaint, Wren sighed and wrapped her arms about his waist. She was soon limp against him. Asleep, no doubt.

Heat flooded him at her innocent snuggling. Goddess, why did he keep reacting to Wren like this? His head began to pound. He urged his gelding as fast as he could without her falling. This tortuous ride must end as soon as possible.

At her townhouse, Hawke carried the still sleeping Wren upstairs to her bed. He penned her a brief note about inviting his family to the orphanage play then abandoned her to the care of her hovering maid. He massaged his aching head as he rode home.

As he'd written Wren, the following morning he ate breakfast with his parents and invited them to the orphanage play. Before he left, he stopped by Aragon and Selena's room to invite them as well, but Aragon was meeting the nightmara delegation with Devon during the orphanage play. Then he headed to the Great

Temple and invited Mel, who promised to clear his duties to attend so he could support Wren.

Afterward, Hawke spent the rest of the morning visiting his cousins to invite them to the orphanage play. Everyone accepted except Elise's husband Farson—as the councilor for the Golddell duchy containing the Nightmara Plains, he was meeting the nightmara delegation with Devon and Aragon.

While visiting his cousins, Hawke also mentioned the arachne silk. Them knowing about it should further the rumors he'd started at Aherne's. But he was careful not to reveal exactly what his latest find was, only that Wren would wear it at the fete. The continued mystery should keep the rumors circulating through court.

After his final visit, Hawke returned home to bolt luncheon. Then he fetched Wren for the orphanage. As his carriage pulled up, she darted outside. She was still pale, but the shadows beneath her eyes had almost faded. Good.

As Wren climbed into his carriage and sat across from him, she glanced at him and blushed. "I'm sorry for falling asleep on you yesterday."

He shrugged to mask his concern. "I should have recalled how much energy the orphans require and not taken you on such a lengthy ride beforehand."

Wren stared at her hands as she laced her fingers together. "I enjoyed our ride."

Hawke smiled at her. "So did I." 'Twas the most in tune they'd been since he told her about Rowan.

Wren studied him through her lashes then returned his smile. "Did you invite your family to the orphanage play? I invited my parents after I read your note."

A zing darting through his chest at her smile, he nodded. "Yes, and everyone was eager to accept."

Wren licked her lips. "Was Kit around when you spoke to Edouard?"

Hawke eyed her mouth as his pulse stirred. He couldn't stop

staring for some reason. "No, fortunately she was out. So she doesn't know about the orphanage play, and I avoided her irksome flirting."

Wren relaxed and beamed at him.

He swallowed then made himself describe this morning's visits in detail until the carriage halted. He inhaled and offered her his hand. "Shall we?"

Wren nodded and took his hand, and they entered the orphanage together.

CHAPTER 31

*A*fter another successful rehearsal, Wren grinned at Kiera and Hawke over her teacup. "I think we're ready for tomorrow's dress rehearsal. I only hope *something* goes awry then, else it shall during the performance." Like the time Roger had tripped and knocked over all of the stage decorations three years ago. The poor boy hadn't performed in a play since.

Kiera's curls bobbed when she chuckled. "I doubt that. As usual, you've matters well in hand."

"I certainly hope so." Wren gave Hawke a wry smile, her stomach fluttering. "Considering all the nobles Hawke invited." Hopefully, they'd enjoy her little play.

Hawke sipped his tea. "They're just family."

"Yes, but your family includes the king." Wren's chest seized. "He's not attending, is he?" Hawke hadn't mentioned him during the carriage ride, but she had to ask. King Devon might enjoy her play, but if he attended, others from court might too, and they probably wouldn't. No doubt they'd sneer at her simple play and the orphan's rough performance.

Hawke chuckled. "No, Devon, Aragon, and Farson have a meeting with the nightmara delegation that afternoon, remember?"

Wren relaxed and sipped her tea. That's right, Hawke had mentioned that.

Kiera's teacup clattered on her desk. She blanched. "You were planning on inviting the king *here*?"

"Why not? He'd enjoy it." Hawke waggled his brows at Kiera. "Just imagine the donations you'd receive if he did."

When Kiera glanced at her, Wren nodded. King Devon and their families would doubtless donate to the orphanage, and the rest of court would rush to mimic them. 'Twas what always happened when Selena and her friends arranged an art sale for charity. Once the king bought a piece, the rest sold within an hour. Unfortunately, the orphanage hadn't benefited from such a sale yet—last year they'd supported the Great Temple's Center for Healing and this year the Ormas Veteran's Society.

Kiera blinked at Wren's nod, and her expression turned dreamy. "We could afford new clothes for the children, hire better tutors, and send the older ones to trade school." Her gaze refocused on Hawke. "Invite the king next time."

Wren muffled a smile. For her orphans, Kiera was as fierce as a mama roc defending her house-sized nest. Too bad she'd no family of her own to love and nurture. A pang darted through Wren, but she only said, "Plus, having Hawke's family attend shall be good practice for the fete play."

Kiera's brow furrowed. "What's this? Are you writing another play for us so soon?"

Hawke choked on a sweet biscuit. "No, for my mother."

Wren shuddered. "Yes, the duchess coerced me to write a play for the fete celebrating her first grandchild. I hope court enjoys it." She sighed and set down her teacup. "Speaking of which, we should leave so I can work on it."

As Wren and Hawke rose, Kiera shook her head. "No wonder you've been distracted."

Wren almost winced. No, she'd been distracted by her seduction of Hawke and his unforeseen hunt for Rowan. Shoving that aside, she beamed at Kiera. "See you tomorrow."

Hawke escorted her home, and as they climbed her front steps, he slanted her a gimlet stare. "Remember to retire early tonight. We can't have you falling asleep tomorrow like you did yesterday."

She grimaced. True, but must he chide her about it? She could manage her own affairs. However, she simply nodded and went inside. Since her parents were out, she ate dinner in her room then retired early.

When Wren rose midmorning the next day, she winced at her aching lower back and breasts. No doubt she'd hurt herself acting out sensual dreams of Hawke. She sighed and downed her bland breakfast of porridge and tea despite her uneasy stomach.

After breakfast, she finished the fete play. She gave the completed play to Abby to send to a scribe to make copies. Unlike the orphans, Hawke's cousins couldn't be expected to make their own as part of their lessons.

Once Abby returned, Wren had her maid fetch a sturdy, beige dress. Who knew what today's dress rehearsal might require? Unfortunately, tomorrow she must wear a stylish dress because of Hawke's family.

She descended to the family dining room and grimaced at the substantial luncheon awaiting her. Everyone except her stomach had decided she must eat more. She selected a slice of cold meat and bread. She was nibbling on her food when Hawke burst into the room.

Hawke eyed her food as he sat beside her. "Barely eating again? You're starting to appear gaunt."

Wren shrugged. Stress had made her stomach sensitive, which deadened her appetite. Yet if she mentioned that, Hawke would insist she visit her healer over nothing. "Cease nagging. I'm fine."

Hawke wrapped bread about a chunk of meat and cheese

then took a hearty bite. "You should be eating like this." Devouring the rest, he shook his head. "Sometimes I think you need a keeper."

A keeper? She bristled as she tore her food into pieces. "If I need a keeper, you need one more, Lord Rakehell." She wasn't the one hunting a lady who didn't exist.

Hawke glared at her. "You know that isn't true since I met Rowan."

Wren swallowed and dropped her food onto her plate. According to his confession during their enchanted night, it hadn't been true for the past year. Somehow her mysterious air as Rowan and determination to seduce him had convinced him to bring her home. Too bad she couldn't convince him to forget Rowan as easily.

Hawke's pale-blue eyes darkened. "By the Goddess, if you don't eat your luncheon, I'll tie you down until you do."

She stiffened then wrinkled her nose at him. "If you tie me down, I'll have no hands to eat with." At his wordless growl, she forced herself to eat. He was right; she'd not been eating enough lately. That and her sensual dreams of Hawke were doubtless why she was tired all the time.

His gaze stern as a gargoyle protecting his castle, Hawke watched as she ate and handed her more when she finished. When she grimaced but ate her second portion, he nodded and drawled, "Have you ever thought that Rowan is my keeper?"

Wren choked on her tea, scalding her mouth. "No. You don't even know her true name." And she didn't exist.

Hawke's jaw hardened. "But I shall."

A shiver skittering across her skin, she swallowed. Why hadn't his desire to find Rowan waned yet? "I'm surprised at your persistence. Your other lovers rarely lasted longer than a night."

Hawke glanced away. "I might be able to love Rowan one day."

Her heart spasmed. Except he wouldn't. If he could, she

wouldn't have needed the glamour spell to seduce him. "But you only knew her for one night before she vanished as if she'd never been."

Hawke ran a hand through his hair. "I know, but she felt as if she belonged in my arms. And such visceral attraction could burgeon into love given time."

If only that were true. Wren forced herself to breathe through her tight chest. "I suppose I'll understand your persistence once I meet her."

His gaze returning to her, Hawke squeezed her hand. "Thanks, Wren. We should leave for the orphanage. Take the rest of your food with you."

She sighed as he released her hand and rose. Why couldn't he have forgotten that amid his confession about Rowan? Grimacing, she wrapped her food in a napkin and followed him. She nibbled on her food during the silent ride to the orphanage, which took twice as long as it should due to an upset produce cart blocking the road.

Peter grinned at them as they entered the orphanage. "'Bout time you two got here. Your urchins is makin' a ruckus, Master Hawke, although your players are readin' their lines, as pretty as you please, Miss Wren."

Laughter lightening her chest, Wren smirked at Hawke. The din spilling from the dining hall was already noticeable. "My children are better behaved than yours."

Hawke flashed a crooked grin as they strode down the hall. "But I have the Bedsford twins."

She giggled and followed Hawke rather than heading to the library. What could his children be doing to cause such racket? When she and Hawke entered the dining hall, children were frolicking about and whooping, and the Bedsford twins were teasing Amaranth. The little girl was giggling at their antics until they pulled snakes from their pockets. As Amaranth shrieked, a stifling sense of magic swept across the room.

Hawke sprinted toward the commotion. "John, Jacob, stop tormenting Amaranth!"

The twins stumbled backward, and their snakes flew from their hands. One of the orphans must be using magic—likely Cassandra.

Wren scrutinized the dining hall for the older girl. She'd not felt such powerful magic since the veiled witch. Not even with the gypsy witch the other day. She stiffened when she finally located Cassandra in the far corner.

Her skin ashen, Cassandra was panting while glaring at the twins. She clenched her hands, and the sense of magic thickened —she wasn't finished yet.

The hair on the back of her neck rising, Wren strode across the dining hall and stepped between Cassandra and her targets. "Stop it *now*, before you injure someone."

Cassandra's mulberry eyes flew to meet Wren's. After a moment, she inhaled then relaxed her fists.

Wren sighed as the sense of magic dissipated. Thank the Goddess. Who knew what Cassandra's uncontrolled magic might have unleashed? "Go rescue Hawke from your sister. We'll discuss this later."

Cassandra winced but nodded then scurried over to Amaranth.

Wren watched Cassandra pry a teary Amaranth from Hawke's shirt. Cassandra and Amaranth must be Rhiannon descendants like the veiled witch. She needed to take Cassandra to the veiled witch for training. Perhaps the week after the orphanage play. Hopefully, 'twould be soon enough.

She sighed then hurried to fetch her players from the library. Once they'd donned their costumes, they thundered back to the dining hall, and the dress rehearsal began.

CHAPTER 32

*L*ater that evening, Hawke bounded up the steps of Wren's townhouse and rapped on the door. When it glided open, he strode inside then joined Wren in the morning room. His pulse quickened as he scrutinized her. Her silver-blue gown made her hair smolder like flame trapped in wood. And although slightly pale, her expression was alert. Better than he'd expected after today's grueling rehearsal. Perhaps she'd recovered from her late nights writing the fete play. "You look well."

"I took a nap before dinner." Wren's eyes narrowed. "I don't require your superfluous advice or a keeper to tend myself."

He hid a smile and offered his arm. Yet his advice had probably made her realize she must actually do so. Therefore, he'd keep offering it, even though it annoyed her. "Are your parents joining us?"

Wren threaded her arm through his. "You know they dislike musical evenings. Father hates remaining still that long, and I think they remind Mother of what she lost. No, the Campbells invited our parents to the kelpie races." Since kelpies raced both on land and under water, kelpie races were exciting and unpredictable, and the sports-mad at court adored them.

His arm tingling at her touch, Hawke swallowed as he escorted Wren outside. He must stop reacting to her and remember their friendship. He set his jaw then handed her into his carriage and leapt after her. "What did your mother lose?"

"You recall my parents resorted to a spell to conceive me, yes?" When he nodded, Wren continued, "Well, that spell cost them both something they loved. In Mother's case, her beautiful singing voice."

He swallowed and frowned out the window. If magic had taken that much from Wren's mother, what had it demanded from Rowan? So far the visits to the witch shops had hinted 'twould be substantial. He shoved that aside when his carriage halted before the Westons' front steps. "We're here."

Hawke grinned while he whisked Wren inside. He'd been attending the Westons' musical evenings for five years—they were court events he actually enjoyed. Their musical taste was always superb, and they never permitted talking during the performances, unlike some hosts.

Lord Weston, an older gentleman with pensive lines etched into his face, wrung Hawke's hand. "Evening, Hawke. I think you'll enjoy tonight's performance. We've a delightful quartet who perform historic pieces, including those by Lantos."

Hawke's pulse quickened. His and Wren's favorite. Rowan's too, but he'd not see her here. He knew everyone who attended the Westons' musical evenings. "Sounds magical." He arched a brow. "Speaking of magical, have you heard about my latest find?"

Lady Weston, whose graying brown hair and dark eyes now reminded Hawke of someone, smiled. "Yes, all of court is gossiping that Miss Keyes shall wear it at your mother's fete." She turned to Wren. "How nice to see you, Miss Keyes. How's your charity work? At an orphanage, I believe your mother said."

Wren beamed. "Yes, on Waterstreet."

Hawke chuckled and recaptured Wren's arm then jested, "She's dragooned me into volunteering too."

Her brows arched, Lady Weston glanced between them. "Doing what?"

Hawke flashed a crooked grin. She must be imagining something scampish. How true, yet not in the way she imagined. "Helping the orphans to perform one of Wren's plays. If you're free tomorrow, you should attend. We'll be marvelous."

Wren sighed but smiled at the Westons. "Yes, our families are attending, so you'll be in good company."

Lord Weston and his wife exchanged a heavy glance, then he said, "We'll be glad to come."

A shadow flitted through Lady Weston's eyes. "Our daughter loved to put on amateur theatricals as a child. She was always a joy to watch, and no doubt your orphans shall be too."

Hawke tensed then swallowed. How could he respond? The Westons rarely mentioned Anne, who'd run off when he and Wren were five. Yet their grief over their lost daughter pervaded their lives.

A gentle smile illuminating her face, Wren grasped Lady Weston's hands. "They are. That's why I spend so much of my time at the orphanage."

"You're a sweet child." Lady Weston extracted her hands and shooed them away. "Now go procure refreshments before the music starts."

He was handing Wren a flute of sparkling wine when Kit sashayed into the room. Goddess, why? Mother, despite her meddling, would be preferable. He groaned and pulled Wren beside a potted tree to hide. "Kit's here. No doubt to pursue me." The Westons' musical evenings weren't modish enough for Kit to bother attending before.

Her lips sardonic, Wren eyed him. "Have you considered informing her you're not interested?"

Hawke shuddered and quaffed his sparkling wine. "That's never worked. Not now nor when we were seventeen." Kit had only stopped then because she'd captured his cousins' father instead.

Wren tsked then sipped her drink. She grimaced. "This sparkling wine tastes vile."

He blinked. What? The Westons' refreshments were never vile. He stole her flute and took a sip. "It tastes fine to me."

Wren grimaced again. "Then you drink it. I'll fetch some tea."

Hawke eyed the room from beside the tree while Wren visited the refreshments table. He stiffened at the new guest greeting the Westons. What was *Winston* doing here? He was even less likely than Kit to attend the Westons' musical evenings. Too cultured.

Once Wren returned with her steaming tea, he jerked his chin toward the door. "That cad Winston just arrived." He'd better not pester Wren.

Winston met his gaze from across the room then turned away without acknowledging him.

Wren gasped. "How rude. He can't still be mad that you threw him into your parents' ornamental lake last year."

Hawke shrugged. At least Winston hadn't leered at Wren. His threat the other day had worked. Good. "Well, there's that, but we also exchanged words at Aherne's recently." He slanted Wren a stern look. "And some of those words concerned you, so take care around him."

Wren grimaced with a shudder. "Definitely. I never want to fend off his kisses again. They're doubtless viler than that sparkling wine."

He relaxed, chuckling. "No doubt, considering 'tisn't vile at all. You simply possess staid taste." When she kicked his ankle, he grinned and waved toward the chairs. "Shall we secure seats before Kit or Winston approach?"

Wren nodded, and they emerged from beside the tree, but Kit intercepted them just before the chairs. Hawke stiffened again. Damnation.

Kit fluttered her lashes and purred, "How delightful to see you, Hawke." Her eyes narrowing, she nodded at Wren. "Wren."

He scowled. Goddess, why couldn't Kit stop pursuing him? And must she be so rude to Wren? To block Kit, he drew Wren against him. His skin tingled as her dainty body nestled against him and her violet scent filled his lungs.

A blush darkening her cheeks, Wren squeezed his hand. "Likewise, Kit."

Kit's eyes glinted. "You've certainly monopolized Hawke in recent days. At the Lantos concert, at my card party, and now here. Perhaps you should allow another lady a turn."

Winston sidled over to them, leering at Wren. "I'd be glad to assist with that."

His pulse surged as fire roared through him. How *dare* Winston approach Wren? He forced a smile. "I was wondering when you'd slither out from under your rock, Winston."

Kit smirked and grasped Hawke's free arm. "How belligerent. Hawke, we should allow Wren and Mr. Winston to converse privately."

Glaring at Kit and Winston, Hawke bit back a growl and wrenched his arm free. He'd *never* allow Winston alone with Wren. The cad would attempt to kiss her again.

Wren tilted her head. "No, thank you, I've nothing to say to him." While Winston sputtered and turned purple, she flashed a saccharine smile. "But perhaps you might, Kit. You're both hunting for spouses, unlike me and Hawke. We'll leave you two to converse privately instead."

Hawke's pulse slowed at Wren's deft dismissal. He almost laughed as she tugged him to two empty seats at the end of a row with no free seats nearby. "Well played."

Wren shrugged while settling on the inside chair. "They're fortunate I didn't toss my tea at them. Although I would have if it had been necessary to escape."

Warmth filling his chest, he squeezed her hand. Wren was wonderful. "And I'd toss my sparkling wine after to demonstrate my support." Though the Westons would probably never invite him to another musical evening.

Before Wren could reply, four musicians glided into the room. The string quartet bowed while the chattering audience fell silent. Then they began a thorny Lantos sonata, followed by equally complex pieces. Exquisite.

Yet during the middle of the concert, Wren's head drifted into his shoulder. Hawke tensed, his delight in the music vanishing. Why was she sleeping again? She'd taken a nap this afternoon. She mustn't have recovered from her late nights, after all.

He sighed then tucked a strand of hair behind her ear, his heart fluttering. He roused Wren enough to escort her outside without attracting undue notice but scooped her into his arms once they left the Westons' townhouse.

When Hawke attempted to deposit her on his carriage seat, Wren moaned and tightened her arms about his neck. Heat suffusing him, he swallowed and settled in his carriage with her in his lap. Hopefully, this ride would be brief.

Wren continued cuddling against him until his body burned. *Why* was he reacting to her like this? They were friends, nothing more. He winced as pain seized his head. And what about Rowan? His chest tightened, but his body still burned as the carriage rumbled toward Wren's townhouse.

CHAPTER 33

ren started awake when Abby slammed a breakfast tray on the tea table. Her body sluggish, she rubbed sleep from her eyes. What had happened last night? The last she recalled was struggling to remain awake as the quartet's music soothed her like a lullaby. "How did I get in bed last night?"

Abby scowled at her. "Master Hawke carried you up. *Again.*"

Wren winced. Oh dear, Hawke would chide her again. She sighed and slid from bed but stilled when she eyed the heaped breakfast tray. "Why are meat and cheese on my breakfast tray?"

Abby's scowl darkened. "Because 'tis almost luncheon."

Wren wrinkled her nose. If she didn't choke down some meat and cheese, Abby would nag her about not eating enough. And she didn't need that in addition to Hawke's chiding.

Wren sighed. She'd better get started. Hawke would be here soon. She ate her porridge and a slice of meat and cheese, all her stomach could stand. Sipping her tea to calm her roiling stomach, she requested a stylish day dress for the orphanage play.

Once Abby helped her don the amber silk, Wren strolled downstairs and intercepted Hawke in the entrance hall. She tensed as she waited for him to mention falling asleep last night or her modish dress.

Yet Hawke only eyed her and said, "I hope you don't mind sharing the carriage with some rather large hampers."

Hampers? She climbed inside the carriage then gaped at the two covered hampers on the backward seat and the third occupying over half of her seat. Rather large, indeed. "What are those?"

Hawke wedged himself on the seat between her and the door, draping an arm behind her. "I had Cook..."

Wren's pulse surged. Goddess, he was practically holding her again, which he'd done often in recent days. Why? Before the masquerade, they'd both avoided touching each other except when necessary. 'Twas as if the glamour spell misled his mind, but his body knew the truth. She swallowed and forced herself back to Hawke's words.

"...their refreshments. Kiera nearly cried with relief when I told her."

The large hampers must contain refreshments for their families. She licked her lips. "I hope the children preparing refreshments aren't upset."

Hawke shrugged and flicked his fingers. "Kiera assured me she'd explain it to them so they wouldn't be."

Tingling warmth swept through Wren at his movement. She could kiss him if she turned her head. She gulped a breath. "I hope you didn't expect me to carry a hamper. They appear to weigh as much as I do."

"I'd planned to ask Peter, but if you'd like to attempt one, I'd love to see it." Hawke paused, his eyes narrowing. "Are you well?"

She would be if his body wasn't tempting her beyond reason. She managed a grin. "Of course, 'tis simply hot being crammed together like this." And how she burned. But she must learn indifference—their enchanted night had been over for more than two weeks.

Hawke studied her then nodded. "Fortunately, we've arrived." He extracted his arm from about her and sprang from the carriage. If only she could be as nonchalant.

Wren buried her desire as he helped her alight. She must focus on the orphans. So without another word, she bustled to the dining hall, which had been converted to a theater. The stage had been erected at one end, the trestle tables were removed, and chairs for their guests lined the back wall.

Children in various stages of dress swarmed her as soon as she arrived. She knelt to straighten and lace their costumes while they chattered at her.

Janelle, adorable in her tabby costume and askew ears, bounced before her. "Miss Wren, we heard some of Master Hawke's family is comin'—and Cassandra said his mama is a *duchess*."

Smiling at Janelle's reverent tone, as if a duchess was a goddess, Wren adjusted the girl's headpiece. "She is, but don't fret, she'll love you."

Sarya frowned while Wren helped her don her royal robes. "Is she why you wore a honey princess dress?"

Yes, she'd worn a fashionable dress because of the duchess and Hawke's cousins, but revealing that would increase the children's nerves. So Wren chuckled and tweaked Sarya's nose. "No, I wanted to match your splendor, your majesty. Besides, see how well it twirls."

The girls and little boys giggled as Wren pirouetted, although the older boys snorted.

Once Wren stilled, Amaranth hugged Wren's legs. "You look beautiful, Miss Wren."

Wren smoothed the girl's loose curls, warmth filling her chest. "So do you. Like a little siren." She straightened and clapped her hands. "Places, everyone! Our audience shall arrive shortly."

As the orphans scurried to their opening positions, Hawke

strolled into the room with his violin beneath his arm. "My parents' carriage just arrived."

Wren's mouth dried. Already? "For once the duchess is early."

Hawke flashed a crooked grin. "That's because she feels no need to make a stately entrance here. Shall we?" He waved his bow toward the stage.

She nodded despite her skittering pulse, and they strode behind the curtains before the stage. Please let their noble audience enjoy her little play. The orphans would be devastated if they didn't, and she'd have no players for the fete play. Shoving aside her nerves, she calmed the children on the right wing of the stage, while Hawke calmed those on the left.

Once the orphans not performing burst into the dining hall and sat on the floor, Wren's parents, Hawke's family, and the Westons strolled to their chairs in the back. Children serving refreshments darted forward and offered the sparkling wine and victuals Hawke had brought. Unlike the children, the adults were permitted refreshments during the performance.

Then Kiera came onstage and spoke a brief introduction. After she'd left, Wren drew a bracing breath and shooed David, the narrator, onstage. Her muscles tensed as the boy lifted his chin and began belting his lines. She mouthed along in case he forgot them.

At her cue, Janelle bounded onstage with Wren also mouthing her words. Her chest lightened when the audience cooed at Janelle then chuckled as she tumbled into the Pool of Tongues and wandered the Enchanted Forest. Everyone was enjoying her little play so far.

When Arliss, the cat's master, bumbled onstage from the other curtain, the audience laughed again. Excellent. Wren grinned, still mouthing lines, as Janelle and Arliss romped about the stage. Then Sarya, the evil queen, appeared with a fearsome clatter from Hawke's percussionists, and the audience hushed. They were engrossed.

Energy darted through Wren as the play continued without

issues. The audience sighed when Arliss fell in love with Emma, the queen's abused handmaiden, and they gasped when Janelle and Arliss barely escaped the kingdom. They clapped when Arliss convinced Janelle to return, and they cheered when the duo tricked the evil queen into eating her own poisoned candies. They oohed when Emma admitted she was the kingdom's true princess forced to serve the evil queen. And they aahed when Arliss begged Emma to marry him.

Then Amaranth glided onstage to sing for Arliss and Emma's marriage ball, and a strangled gasp drifted from the audience. Wren frowned and peered past the stage. Who had gasped? And why? Before she found them, Amaranth lifted her head and began to sing. The little girl's celestial voice soared with the glasses played by Cassandra backstage. As the sisters performed, the audience was silent and still.

The curtain slid closed when their song ended, but the audience remained silent. Her heart swelling, Wren inhaled with a grin. Everyone had definitely enjoyed her little play. When the silence continued, she gestured for the curtain to rise and the performers to take their bows. Both Janelle and Amaranth received thundering applause. Whose was louder?

Hawke came around behind the sets and dragged her onstage despite her garbled protests. A blush burned her skin when the audience cheered during their bows.

She glanced out past the orphans to smile at her beaming parents. Yet her smile stiffened as her gaze drifted past them. Sitting in the row behind her parents, Kit was clapping halfheartedly, unlike the rest of the audience. Wren's chest tightened. What was Kit doing here? Hawke had said she'd been out when he told Edouard.

She relaxed when the curtain closed again. She shooed the performers to join the other orphans. Kiera had begun passing out refreshments, and they couldn't miss those.

"Marvelous, just as I said." Hawke winked as he handed her a glass of water. Where had he found that?

She nodded and guzzled the water. She was parched after mouthing all the lines. Her stomach fluttered as she tidied her hair and smoothed her dress, but she inhaled and accepted Hawke's arm. Time to face everyone and hear their true thoughts about her play.

The Westons accosted them as soon as they stepped out from behind the curtain. Her eyes wild, Lady Weston quavered, "That little girl who sang. You must introduce us. *Please*."

Why was Lady Weston so desperate? Wren glanced at Hawke, who shrugged. She opened her mouth to ask the older lady.

But a stifling sense of magic swept through the room. "What do you want with my sister?"

CHAPTER 34

*H*awke and the others turned to face Cassandra. The girl was glaring at the Westons with her hands clenched beside her. He winced. She resembled a chimera about to erupt. And when that monstrous magical creature erupted, it always left behind a trail of disaster—'twas how the Goddess's Great Temple in Oress had been razed during the Stone Wars.

Wren darted over to Cassandra then leaned and murmured in the girl's ear.

Cassandra blinked, relaxing her fists. She shot the Westons a parting glower then scurried away.

Hawke gaped at Wren as she turned to face the Westons. Goddess, how had she mollified the angry girl?

Frowning, Wren sighed. "Cassandra has gone to fetch Amaranth. But be gentle with them; they lost their parents not long ago, and Cassandra is protective of Amaranth."

Lady Weston gasped and clutched her husband's hand, while Lord Weston paled and drew his wife close.

Staring at the older lady, Hawke stiffened. Cassandra and Amaranth would look just like her in fifty years—*that's* who Lady Weston had reminded him of yesterday. He eyed the sisters as they approached. Definitely the same features and hair, and Amaranth had the same eyes.

Wren knelt before Cassandra and Amaranth with a soft smile. "These friends of Master Hawke wish to speak with you." She returned to Hawke and waved toward the Westons.

Lady Weston opened her mouth but only a croak emerged, so Lord Weston said, "Miss Keyes mentioned you lost your mother recently."

Hawke exchanged a glance with Wren. Lord Weston's tack would perturb the sisters.

As expected, Amaranth's chin wobbled, and Cassandra glared at Lord Weston then replied, "*And* our father. To a runaway carriage owned by some *noble*."

Lord Weston nodded, the lines on his face deepening. "Did she tell you her name? Or about her parents?"

Wren reached for Hawke's hand as Cassandra embraced Amaranth. No doubt to keep herself from interfering.

Once her sister's watery expression cleared, Cassandra shrugged. "No, she only said her parents were small-minded fools. But Papa called her Annie."

As in Anne Weston? Hawke squeezed Wren's hand while Lady Weston whimpered. How extraordinary the Westons found their missing daughter's children in a poor orphanage near the docks.

Lord Weston swallowed. "And your father, was he a gypsy fiddler? Shandor, perhaps?"

Cassandra's lips flattened as she jerked a nod.

Wren winced, clenching Hawke's hand. He eyed her. Why was she so alarmed? Cassandra had merely nodded. Angrily, but 'twas to be expected.

The Westons clung to each other for a moment before Lord Weston coughed and said, "Our daughter Anne ran off after we refused to allow her to wed Shandor, her fiddle tutor. She was right—we were small-minded fools. We lost our only child due to our haughtiness."

A twinge darted through Hawke's chest. And they'd regretted it ever since.

Cassandra narrowed her eyes. "Are you saying you're our grandparents?"

Amaranth bounced. "Grandparents?"

Hawke and Wren exchanged another glance. The little girl was adorable.

Lady Weston spoke at last, "You must be. You two look just like our Anne as a child, especially Amaranth."

Amaranth mobbed her newfound grandparents, but Cassandra crossed her arms with a glare.

Wren strode over to Cassandra and murmured something, then Cassandra grimaced and murmured back.

Hawke's stomach fluttered as he watched them. Wren would somehow mollify the girl again. She'd be a perfect mother one day.

Meanwhile, Amaranth was chattering at the Westons, "...your house like? Will we get to live there?"

Her eyes sparkling for once, Lady Weston grinned at her young granddaughter. "We'd like that above all things."

Amaranth vibrated like a sprite trapped in a jar. "When?"

Hawke suppressed a chuckle. Amaranth looked even more excited than when she'd admitted she sang. Quite a feat.

Lord Weston ruffled the little girl's loose curls. "Today, if possible."

Amaranth bounced to her sister, who was still conversing with Wren. "Cassie, Cassie!" She yanked her sister's skirt. "They want us to come live with them. Today!"

As Wren murmured something else, Cassandra stared at her sister then sighed. She nodded with a tight smile. "How nice." With Wren's hand on her back, Cassandra glided over to the Westons. "Amaranth and I would be glad to come live with you, Lord and Lady Weston."

Amaranth frowned at her sister. "Grandpa and Grandma!"

Hawke winced. Cassandra couldn't call the Westons that yet. She could barely smile at them.

Wren shooed the girls across the dining hall. "Amaranth, go have some more refreshments. The starpeaches are almost gone, and I know you adore them. Cassandra, fetch Mistress Kiera and introduce her to the Westons."

After the girls left, Hawke clapped Lord Weston's back. He and his wife deserved some happiness after years of regret. "Congratulations."

Lord Weston beamed in return, looking ten years younger than he had last night. "And 'tis thanks to you we've a family again."

Lady Weston threw her arms around Wren. "And Miss Keyes, of course."

Wren patted the older lady's back. "I'm glad you've found each other." She glanced across the room. "And here's Kiera now. We'll leave you to discuss matters."

Once Wren freed herself, Hawke escorted Wren over to their parents. She must hear everyone praise the orphanage play. 'Twould bolster her enough to endure the fete play.

Lady Keyes embraced Wren with a proud smile. "Lovely, as always, my dear."

Sir Alaric's hazel eyes gleamed, exactly like Wren's when teasing Hawke, as he nodded toward the Westons. "And the after play was a superb touch."

Wren smiled and shook her head. "I'd nothing to do with that. Hawke invited them."

Father grinned at Hawke as he squeezed Mother's arm. "Our son must have foresight. It runs in your family."

Hawke snorted. Foresight, him? He'd not have such difficulty finding Rowan if he did. "I'd no idea the Westons would discover their granddaughters here. I just thought they'd be generous patrons for the orphanage."

Mother arched a brow. "They certainly shall be after today."

She turned to Wren. "If your play for my fete is half as delightful as this one, I'll count myself pleased."

While Wren blushed, Hawke winked at Mother. "It'll be twice as delightful because *I'll* be the villain." And he could be much more wicked than little Sarya.

As their parents chuckled then sauntered away, warmth filled his chest. They'd praised Wren as expected, but she should hear more. So he led her to his Hawke cousins—the bubbly Pippa would surely rave. "How did you enjoy the play?"

Pippa beamed and stepped away from her older brothers to grasp Wren's hands. "'Twas marvelous. I can't believe you penned it. I'm so excited to be performing one at the duchess's fete."

Wren blushed but smiled. "Be warned though, I'm a strict taskmaster during rehearsals."

His heart lightening, Hawke chuckled. Wren almost appeared cheerful about the fete play. "Yes, she actually expects her players to practice."

Xavier sighed and smoothed his mustache. "The first rehearsal is the day after tomorrow?"

When Hawke and Wren nodded, Dane's brawny shoulders stiffened, and he rumbled, "Could we know our parts?"

Dane and Xavier's reluctance would spoil the cheer Pippa had created, so Hawke slapped Dane's shoulder before Wren could reply. "Not until the first rehearsal." He winked at Pippa, who giggled. "Savor the possibilities."

As Dane and Xavier groaned, Hawke whisked Wren over to Edouard, Elise, and Selena. Elise would ensure her twin didn't say anything negative. "Well?"

Selena dimpled and embraced Wren. "'Twas fantastic. I'm eager to see what you pen for the fete."

While Wren stepped back with a shrug, Elise winked and leaned toward her. "No wonder Hawke rhapsodizes about your plays."

Edouard chuckled. "We should have attended one sooner."

He flashed a wry smile. "Seeing this *almost* makes me dread performing less."

Hawke glowered at Edouard. That wouldn't encourage Wren.

As Selena tsked, Elise punched her twin's arm and said, "Edouard, don't be churlish." She turned to Wren. "Sorry for his dreadful behavior."

Wren wrinkled her nose. "I felt much the same when the duchess asked me to perform, but I could direct the play instead."

When Edouard rubbed his chin, Hawke snorted. "Not an option." Wren had already written a part for him, and she'd not have time to rewrite the fete play.

Edouard sighed. "I suppose not."

As the twins joined Pippa and her brothers, Selena embraced Wren again then said, "Truly wonderful, Wren. Aragon will be jealous to have missed your play to meet the nightmara delegation."

When Selena followed the twins across the dining hall, Kit abandoned her quarrel with Mel to swish over to Hawke and Wren.

Hawke stiffened. Doubtless Kit had only attended to pursue him. And how had she found out about the orphanage play? She'd been out when he'd invited Edouard, and Edouard had said he'd not mention it to her.

Kit gave him a coy smile then turned to Wren, her smile sharpening. "Fascinating play. Do you imagine yourself the clever cat or the bumbling master?"

He almost growled. Goddess, why must Kit needle Wren?

Wren lifted her chin. "Neither, but I know who I imagine as the evil queen."

Kit purred a laugh as Mel joined them. "Your imagination has always been nonsensical. Lonely trolls, wounded kelpies, talking cats..."

Wren paled, while fire flashed through Hawke. How dare Kit mock Wren about her clever plays? The harpy.

Mel frowned at Kit. "Stop needling Wren, Kit. You're simply envious of her talent." When Kit glared in response, he added, "Don't deny it. You probably wish Mother had asked *you* to write the play for her fete."

Hawke almost groaned. Why had Mel mentioned the fete play? Now Kit would needle Wren about it or attempt to inveigle her way into performing.

Kit whirled to face Wren. "You're writing a play for the duchess?" At Wren's weak nod, Kit pursed her lips.

Hawke tightened his grip on Wren's arm. They must escape before Kit unleashed whatever she was plotting. He made their excuses then swept Wren from the dining hall. Hopefully, Kit hadn't made Wren dread the fete play again.

CHAPTER 35

*H*er stomach roiling after her light luncheon, Wren was sipping her third cup of mentha tea when Hawke burst into the library. She tensed. No doubt he wanted to resume his hunt for Rowan.

Hawke sprawled beside her on the sofa. "So yesterday went well."

She blinked as she marked the page she'd been rereading for the past half hour. Why hadn't he mentioned Rowan? "Yes, the orphans were marvelous, and the Westons finding their granddaughters was a happy twist not even I could pen."

"Plus, our families praised your delightful play afterward." An impish glint flickered in Hawke's pale-blue eyes. "Although no one complemented my superb fiddling." He sighed. "Such is the curse of musicians."

Laughter bubbling in her throat, Wren hid her smile behind her teacup. His banter soothed her stomach better than thirty cups of mentha tea. "You were magnificent—the best fiddler to ever grace Waterstreet Orphanage."

Hawke drooped, his lips twitching. "Why am I always condemned to such faint praise? I should run off and join a gypsy fiddling troupe to prove my skill."

Weight compressed her chest at him joining a traveling fiddling troupe. She'd never see him. 'Twould be worse than him wed to another lady. She clung to her smile. "The duchess would love that."

Hawke waggled his brows. "She would if I told her I was eloping."

Wren tsked and set aside her teacup. Not hardly. "If you eloped, she couldn't plan your wedding." Which the duchess would hate.

Hawke shuddered. "Mother is *never* planning my wedding. I remember the spectacle she made of Aragon's."

She echoed his shudder. Such a wedding would be hideous. The duchess couldn't resist arranging grandiose affairs, like a fete for her first grandchild where her family was forced to perform a play. But to distinguish herself from Rowan, she asked, "What if Rowan wants her to?"

Hawke flashed a crooked grin. "Impossible. She was so shy she refused to dance with me in the ballroom."

Wren pursed her lips and almost snorted. Only so no one would recognize her. "Not *that* shy. She danced pressed against you in the gardens, after all." Her breath froze. He'd never mentioned that. How could she have slipped again?

Hawke winced and rubbed his temple. "What did you say? A sudden headache distracted me."

Her throat cramped. Every time she slipped, the glamour spell hurt Hawke. She must get him to forget Rowan, so they could cease discussing the masquerade. "I said most ladies would want the duchess's help, if only to prove she accepted them."

Hawke shook his head. "Not Rowan. But speaking of Rowan, what witch shop shall we visit this afternoon?"

Wren stiffened. She'd known he would ask. But she must persuade him to stop visiting those witch shops. Each one risked exposing her. She forced a wheedling smile. "We've visited at least half of the witch shops on your list in the past two weeks, and we're still no closer to finding your mysterious dryad."

Hawke jutted his chin. "We still have the other half left."

Perhaps he'd listen if she begged. She widened her eyes like her pet faebird had whenever she'd brought faeberries. That had always inspired her to feed the faebird too many. Hopefully, 'twould work on Hawke too. She leaned toward him. "Please, Hawke. I hate those shops. I don't want to visit any more." And not just because she might be exposed, but because so much magic unnerved her.

Hawke ran a hand through his inky-brown hair. "We have to. 'Tis the best way to find Rowan. You said so when you agreed to help."

Wren touched his arm. "But at every shop, the witches have called that enchanted bird dangerous, and the priest called it a *curse*." Perhaps that would convince him. Please, Goddess.

Hawke scowled and crossed his arms. "The enchanted bird isn't a curse or dangerous. 'Tis a spell for courage—Rowan said so."

Her stomach hardened. How could he possess such unwavering faith in a lover he'd only known one night? Granted, that lover was actually her, but he didn't realize that. She snorted and poked his chest. "You're certain of that, after *everything* those witches have said. Perhaps 'twould be best to not rouse sleeping dragons."

Hawke leapt to his feet. "Rowan wasn't lying, and I refuse to forget her."

Wren lifted her chin to meet his gaze. How could she convince him? She must end his futile hunt before he realized the truth or she shattered with stress and guilt. She pursed her lips. "Hawke, your obsession with a lover you knew one night isn't healthy."

Hawke glared and clenched his hands. "I'm not obsessed!"

Fire flashing through her, she leapt to her feet as well. "You are! Because that cursed bird won't let you forget." Surely 'twas the only reason he was still hunting her. She thrust out her hand. "Give it to me so you stop obsessing over it." Then she could hide it like she'd meant to that night, and their relationship would return to normal.

Hawke snorted an almost laugh. "You'd burn it to ensure I forgot, wouldn't you?"

A chill suffused her skin. Except burning the enchanted bird would allow him to remember everything, including that she was Rowan. She suppressed a shiver. "Trust me, I'd never burn it."

Hawke sighed and relaxed. "I trust you." He grasped her hands and pulled her down to the sofa beside him.

Wren swallowed as tingling warmth darted up her arms to her chest. Goddess, she could lean forward and kiss him. If she did, would he return her kiss? Her breath quickened.

Hawke squeezed her hands. "That's why I need your help to find Rowan. Please, Wren. I must find her. *Please.* She may be my only chance at love."

Her chest froze, and tears welled in her eyes. She wasn't, but if only she was. Then she never would have needed to disguise herself as Rowan. She jerked her hands free and whirled away. She mustn't let him see her tears. How could she possibly explain them?

Hawke cleared his throat. "Are you crying?"

Tears spilled down Wren's cheeks. "No."

Hawke turned her to face him. "You are. Why?" When she shook her head, he pulled her into his arms. "Please don't cry."

Inhaling his scent, she snuggled into his chest and sobbed as he rubbed her back. If he knew the truth, he'd not hold her so. "I can't help it. I've not slept properly in weeks." Thanks to sensual dreams of Hawke. "Everything has been so stressful." Mostly because of his hunt for Rowan. "Your mother coerced me into writing a play for court. Then you asked your family to attend the orphanage play." Which they'd enjoyed, but still. "And now the first rehearsal for the fete play is tomorrow, and I've so much to prepare. I had a scribe copy the play, but what about sets and costumes? Your family won't do those—I'll be fortunate if they memorize their lines."

Hawke continued rubbing her back. "Everything shall be fine."

Wren sobbed harder. No, it wouldn't. She'd ruined everything by seducing him. Why had she been so foolhardy?

Hawke hugged her. "Do we even need sets for your fete play? How about colored curtains that suggest rather than depict the scene? We could hide behind them when not onstage, and we could have servants draw them."

She sniffed as her tears ebbed, but she didn't pull away. She needed his embrace too much. "That might work."

Hawke squeezed her. "As for costumes, we couldn't wear anything elaborate over our ball clothes. How about one accessory per character, like a hat or mask or some such? And make everyone find their own accessories and bring them to the dress rehearsal for you to check." He raised her chin and wiped her damp cheeks. "Does that help?"

Wren managed a tremulous smile. "Yes, but why couldn't I think of those? Your solutions were so simple." Her mind must have dissolved since seducing him. Damn fatigue. And stress.

Hawke released her chin. "Perhaps due to that lack of sleep you mentioned." His expression darkened. "I blame Mother for this. She shouldn't have coerced you into writing a play for court."

She wrinkled her nose. True, but without the fete play, she'd have nothing to blame her fatigue and stress on, so perhaps she should be grateful to the duchess.

Hawke sighed. "Although I don't wish to, we must postpone our visits to witch shops until after the fete. You can't handle them with the fete play looming over you."

Wren gaped at him. What? He was abandoning his hunt? "But you just said you must find Rowan."

Hawke grimaced. "I must, but my hunt can wait a couple weeks. No matter how long it takes, Rowan shall wait for me. I know it."

Fresh tears pricked her eyes. She'd wait for him forever, not that he'd want her if he knew she was Rowan. She forced a smile. "Thank you, Hawke."

Hawke winked at her as he rose. "Just be ready for more witch shops after the fete. I can't go without you, you know. I'd get mobbed by hordes of husband-hunting ladies."

Wren arched a brow, her chest lightening at his teasing. "One or two ladies aren't hordes."

"Well, they certainly feel like it." Hawke tossed a wave. "I'll see you tomorrow at my parents' for the fete play rehearsal. Get some sleep tonight."

As he strode from the library, she picked up her book. She'd try, but sensual dreams of him would probably foil her attempt. She sighed and opened to the chapter she'd marked. At least he'd agreed to stop taking her to witch shops until after the fete. His aversion to husband-hunting ladies should prevent him from continuing his hunt without her.

Unless he decided to try another approach. Like the orphanages. Her skin prickling, she swallowed and forced herself back to her book. Surely he'd not pursue those when she'd advised against them.

CHAPTER 36

When Hawke entered his parents' ballroom the following afternoon, Wren was bustling amid the circle of chairs arranged in the center. Tingling flooded his chest. She resembled a fae queen dancing amid a fae ring on Summerday. And the shadows beneath her eyes were faint, so she must be recovering. At last.

"Do you require any assistance?" His baritone reverberated through the ballroom.

Wren gasped and whirled around, a tendril of auburn hair falling across her cheek. "Hawke, you startled me!" She relaxed and set a script on the last chair. "No, we just need to wait until your cousins and Mel arrive." She sank into the chair farthest from the door.

His fingers itching to tuck her stray hair behind her ear, Hawke sprawled in the chair beside her. "Do you mind if I read before the others arrive?" He grinned as he waved his copy of the script.

A blush darkened Wren's cheeks. "Please proceed."

He lost himself in her play by the third line. As always, her words were enthralling. And the demon's part would be perfect for evil cackles and mad grins. Marvelous.

The princess had just found the magical heirloom when Pippa swirled into the room flanked by Dane and Xavier. With a sigh, Hawke closed his script. If only he could keep reading.

Pippa's brown eyes glowed. "Afternoon! I can't wait to start. My very first acting performance."

As she bounced toward the chair beside him, he hid a grin. His younger cousin was as enthused as before. That should encourage Wren.

Wren coughed before Pippa sat beside him. "Could you sit on my other side but leave an empty chair? I'd like the players arranged by part. Reading through the play shall be easier."

As Pippa whirled to her designated chair, Dane gestured to himself and Xavier then rumbled, "Where should we sit?"

Hawke eyed Dane and Xavier. Unlike after the orphanage play, they were relaxed and smiling. Pippa's influence, no doubt.

Wren pursed her lips. "Xavier next to Hawke, and you next to Xavier."

While the brothers sat, Edouard and Elise strolled into the ballroom. Edouard smirked at his twin and said, "I told you we weren't late."

Elise narrowed her eyes. "We would have been if you'd delayed any longer. Afternoon, everyone."

Hawke shook his head as everyone greeted the twins. Edouard was still as reluctant as before. Hopefully, 'twouldn't dishearten Wren.

Yet Wren merely smiled at Elise and Edouard then pointed at the chair on the other side of Pippa. "Edouard, sit next to Pippa there. Elise, you sit between him and Dane."

Pippa beamed at Edouard as he sat beside her, and he grinned back.

Hawke muffled a laugh. Pippa would sweeten Edouard's reluctance. Edouard had shown a marked preference for Pippa since her come out this spring, and she'd returned his interest. Doubtless Wren had paired them because of that. Was she taking matchmaking lessons from Mother?

Wren eyed the door. "Once Mel arrives, we can begin the rehearsal. Everyone can read the play until then."

Hawke grinned and flipped back to where he'd stopped. The demon was reeling from the princess's curse when Mel strode into the room. He sighed and closed his script again. Why couldn't Mel have been later? He'd only a few pages left.

"Sorry I'm late, everyone." Mel slid into his chair by Wren. "Sext went overlong—the priest giving the sermon rambled."

Wren straightened, folding her hands in her lap. "Now that everyone's here, let me explain how we'll proceed. This play is simpler than the orphanage play, so meeting every day for an hour or two after luncheon should be sufficient."

Hawke chuckled when the other players sighed as one. Apparently, no one had been anticipating performing a complicated play before court in just ten days.

Wren's hazel eyes gleamed with laughter. "Instead of sets, we'll have colored curtains. We can have servants draw them, or perhaps players with smaller parts."

Xavier smoothed his mustache. "I'd wondered how we'd build such complicated sets without the horde of energetic children."

Hawke flashed a crooked grin. "We could manage it if we locked you in the ballroom and Wren gave me a whip." 'Twould be excellent practice for playing the demon.

Wren tsked. "The duchess would never allow such a vulgar act to occur in her ballroom." Once everyone chuckled, she resumed her explanation, "Besides no sets, your costumes shall be an accessory you can wear over your ball clothes."

Elise tilted her head. "I'd imagined frantic attempts to change without my maid, but this should work better."

Wren nodded. "You'll each select your accessory based on your part and bring them to the dress rehearsal."

Pippa bounced, her brown hair almost tumbling from her chignon. "Speaking of parts, which do we have?"

Laughter lightened Hawke's chest. His bubbly cousin would absolutely sweeten Edouard's reluctance.

Wren gestured to each player in turn. "Hawke is the demon. Mel the elf. Edouard and Pippa are the king and queen, and Elise their daughter. Dane and Xavier are suitors of the princess; Dane a soldier and Xavier a courtier."

Edouard arched a brow. "Of course, Hawke receives the best part."

Hawke shrugged with a wry chuckle. Privilege of being the writer's best friend. "I put forth a persuasive argument that Wren couldn't refuse, but I doubt you want my part—it has more lines."

When Edouard shuddered, Pippa laid a hand on his arm. "Since we've paired parts, we could practice together if you're concerned about memorizing your lines."

Edouard placed his hand over hers. "That would be nice."

Hawke almost laughed when Wren hid her smile behind her script. Definitely matchmaking.

Once her smile faded, Wren lowered her script. "Now that everyone knows their parts, we'll read through the script aloud." She opened her script, and everyone rushed to follow her. "Mel, please start."

Mel introduced the play as a tale from his past, with everyone joining when their parts appeared.

Unlike the others, Hawke read his lines with evil cackles and mad grins. As diverting as he'd imagined. And this time, he finally reached the end.

When Mel concluded the play after the princess's wedding, Wren beamed at everyone. "Splendid reading." She rose and rang the bellpull. "I believe that's enough for today. How about some tea?"

Once servants had served tea and left, Elise asked, "Have you heard the most recent news about the nightmara treaty?"

Along with the others, Hawke shook his head. He'd not spoken with Aragon, Devon, or Farson since before their meeting with the nightmara delegation during the orphanage play. But doubtless Farson had discussed everything with his wife, so Elise knew the latest gossip.

Elise leaned forward. "Apparently, the talks have foundered. Before the treaties have been between Calatini's queen and the nightmara queen or queen-heir."

Wren nodded as she sipped her tea. "Not surprising. Dominant mares lead nightmara herds, with the strongest being their queen. Nightmara don't respect kings as leaders and won't negotiate with them."

Hawke frowned. "But Devon has no queen to negotiate. Are the nightmara declaring he must wed before they'll sign a treaty?" Dear Goddess, wedding someone for political reasons would be dreadful. Another reason not to be king.

Elise nibbled her sweet biscuit. "No, but they're hinting that. Some articles swiftly agreed upon in the past have been stalled or outright denied. If King Devon continues to negotiate without a betrothed, Calatini might fare terribly in the renewed treaty."

Pippa blinked. "But I thought he and Lady Snow, er, Lady Annalise, were practically betrothed."

Elise shook her head. "Not since he abandoned her at the masquerade."

Edouard's eyes narrowed. "I suppose King Devon is still mad for that mermaid he met."

Mel set down his tea with a sigh. "Aragon said he is but has made no progress in unearthing her. Almost as if she never existed."

Hawke stiffened. Just like Rowan. Could they be connected somehow? Perhaps he and Devon should compare their progress. They might discover new clues about their mysterious ladies. As soon as returned home, he'd send a note inviting Devon for a ride.

His pulse surging, Hawke smiled behind his teacup. He could hunt for Rowan without forcing Wren to visit more witch shops. With the fete play looming, she truly needed the respite.

When he glanced up, Wren was eyeing him rather than discussing the nightmara delegation like the others. She must sense his plans. Yet he couldn't share them. She might insist on joining his ride with Devon, and the last time she'd ridden, she'd fallen asleep in his arms. She appeared better today, but he'd not risk her recovery.

So he flashed an innocent smile then rose. "Sorry to interrupt, but I must be off. Urgent matters regarding my latest find."

Edouard chortled. "As your closest relations, aren't you going to tell us what your mysterious find is yet? Everyone at court keeps expecting us to know."

Hawke arched a brow. With the fete closer, court learning exactly what his latest find was should fan the rumors until then. "Arachne silk, a magical fabric that transforms to whatever color you imagine." To distract Wren from his plans, he added, "But Wren can tell you more about that—I gave her the sample bolt the other week."

As Elise and Pippa began interrogating Wren about the arachne silk, he slipped from the ballroom. He must escape before Wren finished answering them and could ask about his plans.

CHAPTER 37

*A*fter a small luncheon the following day, Wren breezed into Hawke's parents' townhouse. With his hunt for Rowan postponed until after the fete, she'd not visited, or prevented him from visiting, a witch shop in days. And Hawke hadn't mentioned trying another approach.

She hugged her script to her chest. Plus, they'd not discussed Rowan or the masquerades, so their relationship felt almost normal again. Except for the sensual dreams still plaguing her. But since she'd no morning commitments, staying abed until just before luncheon had compensated for her restless sleep.

Wren whisked to the ballroom where the chairs were already arranged in a circle. She sat in the same one as before, smiling as she waited for everyone. They'd make decent players, considering their splendid first rehearsal.

His script tucked beneath his arm, Hawke soon strode through the door. He sprawled into the chair beside her. "What are the plans for today?"

Her heart swelled. Yes, normal again. If only she could get him to forget Rowan for good. She tilted her head. "You'll read from your seats again today, but instead of going straight through, I'll interject suggestions."

Hawke smiled at her. "I think we did well yesterday—especially me."

Wren chuckled. "Yes, everyone did well, but you must watch your embellishments." Although his evil cackles and mad grins were hilarious.

Hawke flashed a crooked grin. "But they're so much fun."

She tsked even though her mouth twitched. "The play isn't a farce." The duchess wouldn't approve of that.

Before Wren could say more, Pippa bounded into the ballroom. "Afternoon! Same seats as yesterday?" Pippa sank into her seat at Wren's nod. "Dane and Xavier should be along shortly. They began arguing over which Hawke ancestor had a pet wyvern."

Wren arched a brow. "Why are they arguing over *that*?" Owning a wyvern hadn't been fashionable at court since Lantos's era, although wilder gentleman still watched wyvern fights held in rougher areas.

Pippa shrugged as she opened her script. "Because Xavier wagered that Dane didn't know." She beamed at Wren. "But why bother with my daft brothers? This play is marvelous, just like the one at the orphanage."

A blush burned Wren's cheeks. The fete play was decent, not marvelous.

Pippa turned to Hawke, waving her script. "You agree, don't you?"

Hawke nodded and winked at Wren. "As always."

Wren blushed harder. "I'm pleased you enjoy it." Hopefully, court would too.

Pippa leaned forward with a bubbly grin. "Why have you only written plays for the orphanage? Once court sees your talent, everyone shall request your plays for their parties. Or perhaps King Devon shall sponsor a play at the royal playhouse."

Wren shuddered. Goddess, how horrifying. She'd become a

recluse first. "I write my plays for my own amusement. I couldn't bear the scrutiny that a professional playwright receives."

Hawke winked at her. "You'd be fine."

A chill skittered up Wren's spine. No, she wouldn't. If court scrutinized her, someone might realize she'd been Rowan. And even if the glamour spell prevented them from telling Hawke, rumors about the straightlaced Miss Keyes's scandalous behavior would doubtless titillate court.

Pippa's brothers burst into the ballroom before Wren could reply. Dane was smirking at Xavier, who was scowling back. Dane must have been right about the wyvern owner. Without prompting, they slid into their chairs beside Hawke.

Everyone had just exchanged greetings when Edouard stormed into the ballroom. Pippa beamed at him, but he barely smiled back.

Wren frowned. Edouard always had a smile for Pippa. What had upset him? Something to do with his missing twin? "Where's Elise?"

Edouard grunted and gestured toward the door as he plopped into his seat beside Pippa. "Out there, attempting to handle Stepmother."

Wren tensed, her stomach roiling. Kit must have followed Edouard and Elise to inveigle a part in the fete play. No doubt she'd planned to do so the moment Mel had mentioned it. Then she could flirt with Hawke every day until the fete, and she could outshine everyone during the play before court, especially Wren.

Trailed by a glowering Elise, Kit swished into the ballroom and said, "Afternoon. I'm here to take part in Wren's little play."

As Kit stole the chair beside her, Wren forced a polite smile. "Unfortunately, all the parts are assigned." Thank the Goddess.

Elise snorted. "I attempted to explain that, but Stepmother insisted upon joining us. I'm sorry, Wren."

Kit fluttered her lashes at Hawke. "I'm sure 'twould be simple for Wren to add a part for me."

Simple? Simple?! Wren gurgled. Was Kit truly so senseless? Adding another part meant rewriting the entire play, and the fete was only nine days away.

Hawke glared at Kit. "Rewriting an entire play isn't simple."

Kit tossed her head, her cinnaspice perfume swamping Wren. "Nonsense."

Almost sneezing at Kit's overpowering scent, Wren managed to say, "No, he's correct. And there's not enough time to rewrite the entire play."

Kit's eyes glinted as she turned to Wren. "You could add a part for me if you wanted."

Wren lifted her chin and met Kit's gaze. "Not in time for the fete." But even if there had been, she'd not rewrite the play for Kit.

The ballroom remained silent as Wren and Kit stared at each other.

But their deadlock was broken when Mel strode into the ballroom. His brows arched, he halted before the circle of chairs. "I see my seat has been usurped. I didn't think I was *that* late."

Kit's gaze slid from Wren to Mel, and a feline smile curved her lips. "Intriguing idea. As a priest, Mel has many responsibilities and can't give the play his full attention. I could take his part. I'm sure he wouldn't mind not having to act."

Wren stiffened. True, the duchess had coerced Mel into acting. But if Kit replaced him, she'd have to bear Kit flirting with Hawke and smirking over the fete play. For the next nine days. Excruciating.

Mel strode around the circle to grasp Kit's elbow and haul her upright. "I might not, but Mother would. With Hawke playing the demon, if I don't play the kindly elf, it appears like Wren disapproves of our family."

Hawke shrugged. "When in truth, I had to beg Wren for the part."

Wren winced when Kit purred a laugh then said, "Oh, I *doubt* you had to beg her very hard."

Although Hawke frowned, everyone else exchanged knowing looks.

Wren flushed. Goddess, did everyone but Hawke realize she loved him? She set her jaw then glanced at Mel, who still grasped Kit's elbow. "Please escort Kit out."

"Gladly." Mel smiled and propelled Kit toward the door.

"How dare you—" Kit sputtered. When Mel muttered something in her ear, Kit recoiled and jerked her elbow free. She swirled to face Wren with a smirk. "Best of luck with your little play."

Everyone sighed when Kit swirled back around and swept from the ballroom.

Wren relaxed, almost chuckling. So she wasn't the only one to not welcome Kit. Surely unusual for the fashionable countess. But Hawke and his relatives were from influential families, so they'd the freedom to not like the leaders of fashion.

Wren glanced about her circle of players and drawled, "Now that that's settled..." Once everyone laughed, she continued, "Let's return to the *penned* drama." She turned to Mel, who'd recaptured his stolen seat. "Mel, start from the beginning."

As everyone read their parts, Wren paused them to offer ideas on how to display their characters' emotions, or in Hawke's case, how to not overplay them. Directing Hawke's family differed from directing the children at the orphanage. Although none of Hawke's family had performed before and required guidance there, they didn't require help pronouncing words or understanding the emotions in a scene. And they were more focused than the orphans.

After they'd read through the entire play, she had them return to a few crucial scenes and reread those before ending the rehearsal. "Excellent rehearsal. We deserve tea."

Once everyone had tea and sweet biscuits, Pippa bounced in

her seat. "This play is the most diverting activity I've done in ages."

Edouard sighed into his teacup. "I still would rather not have to perform."

Wren crumbled a sweet biscuit. And she'd rather not have written a play for court, but the duchess had insisted. She managed a grin despite her quivering stomach. "Well, I suppose I could give your part to your stepmother—since she's so eager for one."

Edouard shuddered. "No, no, don't do that. She'd not make a good king."

Hawke chortled and waggled his brows. "True, but imagine her donning a fake beard as her accessory. The more garish, the better."

Hawke and his family glanced at one another and burst into laughter, but Wren only grimaced. Kit would never stand for such treatment. If she joined them, Kit would usurp Elise's part as the princess, and likely assume credit for the entire fete play.

Wren nibbled her lip. Hopefully, today's confrontation had convinced Kit not to return. Yet Kit loved needling Wren and was pursuing Hawke, so she'd probably return tomorrow to steal a part.

When Kit did, how could she eject her? She must devise a way. Kit would distract everyone, and they must focus on practicing the fete play. Otherwise, they'd never be ready to perform before court in just nine days. Wren swallowed.

Then Pippa asked what accessory she should find, and somehow Wren managed a coherent reply. She rejoined the conversation with Hawke and his family. She'd decide how to handle Kit later.

CHAPTER 38

$\mathcal{A}$s Mel and his cousins filed from the ballroom, Hawke eyed Wren. She was smoothing her hair with a frown between her brows. Fretting over Kit, no doubt.

He tensed when Wren drifted after his cousins. She shouldn't have to fret over that harpy. He must handle Kit for her. But how? He winced. Mother, of course. She could persuade Kit to quit pestering them. Besides, Mother owed Wren after coercing her into writing the fete play.

Hawke frowned. But if he involved Mother, she'd attempt to meddle. Especially if she truly wanted Kit as his bride like Wren had warned. He sighed. He'd just have to remain wary and not mention Rowan. Surely he could manage that.

So he left a note with Perkins One requesting a private luncheon with Mother tomorrow. He grimaced when he received her assent a few hours later. Mother's probing was apparent in her penned lines. He rarely met with her in private, but his request couldn't become fodder for family gossip. Wren would despise that.

The following morning, Hawke forced a crooked grin as he strode into the family dining room. "Morning, Mother. Shall anyone else be joining us?"

Mother arched a brow and rang the bellpull. "No, you requested a private luncheon."

Swallowing at her smile, he nodded as servants burst into the room and arranged the first course on the dining table before setting the second course and dessert on adjoining tables.

Mother shooed them toward the door once they finished. Good, not even the servants would overhear his request. She said, "That will be all. I'll ring when we're finished." After he served the first course, she narrowed her eyes. "So why did you send me that *peculiar* note?"

Hawke shrugged and swirled his wine. "I've a favor to ask concerning the fete play, and I wanted to do so privately."

Mother pursed her lips while buttering a roll. "Don't bother to ask to be excused from the fete play. If my own sons don't perform, your cousins shan't either. And a play requires players."

During her scold, he inhaled half of his savory lamb stew. 'Twas one of his favorites. Mother must have requested it for him. Sometimes her loving regard was wonderful—just not when it involved meddling in his life. When she finished, he lowered his spoon and shook his head. "Acting in Wren's play is fine. 'Tis about Kit. She interrupted yesterday's rehearsal, demanding a part, but Wren hadn't written one for her."

Mother hummed and sipped her wine. "Why did Wren exclude Kit? She's family, after all."

Only by marriage. His stomach tightening, Hawke shuddered but finished his stew. And now she was pursuing him. "Wren asked me for a list of players, and I didn't include Kit. She's hunting a husband, and I'm not interested, but she never notices my hints."

Mother's mouth twitched as he served the second course. "I see."

Hopefully so. He quaffed his wine. Then she'd not attempt to match him with Kit. Too bad he couldn't get Mother to abandon her matchmaking altogether. He shrugged. "Besides, Wren and Kit don't get along."

Mother paused with her knife midway through a chicken medallion. She narrowed her eyes at him. "And why is that?"

Hawke swallowed a bite of the succulent chicken and mushrooms. Another of his favorites. He sighed. "Because Kit has always been jealous of Wren. Her parents adore her, and she possesses a comfortable fortune." Kit's situation had been the opposite growing up.

Mother nodded then began eating again. "And is Wren jealous back? Kit is gorgeous. Her beauty was enough to beguile my cousin into marrying her."

He shook his head, his heart softening. Wren was too sweet for that. "No. Wren always felt for Kit, despite Kit's constant needling. Which brings me back to my favor."

Mother nodded again and laid her utensils on her empty plate. "Please proceed."

Hawke flashed a beseeching smile as he served the decadent shokolat sweetice, his favorite dessert. "Kit appeared determined to secure a part yesterday. If she manages to insert herself into the fete play, she'll make Wren miserable. Wren doesn't deserve that, especially since she only wrote the blasted play because you *coerced* her."

Mother stilled with a spoonful of sweetice before her mouth. She arched her brows. "What exactly do you wish me to do?"

He leaned toward her. "Use your influence to keep Kit away from the fete play."

Mother shook her head and lowered her laden spoon. "If Kit is as determined as you say, how shall I accomplish that?"

Hawke chuckled and devoured his sweetice. Mother could accomplish anything she put her hand to. Except marry him off unless he loved the lady. He grinned at Mother. "You'll find a way. Say whatever you deem necessary, short of my hand in marriage or my firstborn child."

A smile hovering about her mouth, Mother scrutinized him. "Wren's serenity means that much to you, does it?"

He blinked. "Naturally, Wren is my dearest friend." He'd do anything for her, other than quit hunting Rowan.

Mother's eyes gleamed. "Very well, I'll handle Kit."

Hawke smiled at her. Excellent. Now Wren could relax—as much as she could with the fete play looming over her. "Thanks, Mother." He rose and kissed her cheek. "I must be off. Rehearsal has no doubt begun."

As he started to leave, Mother called, "Before you go..." When he turned with arched brows, she continued, "Your father and I expect you to dine with us tomorrow night."

He nodded, even though his neck prickled. What was Mother plotting now? He winced. Was she finally going to subject him to marriage candidates like she had Aragon? Shoving that aside, he strode to the ballroom, but he was the last to arrive.

Wren brightened when he sprawled into the chair beside her. "Hawke, finally! I thought you'd forgotten."

Hawke flashed a crooked grin to reassure her. "No, merely late."

As Mel's eyes narrowed, Wren gestured toward the curtain at the back of the ballroom beneath the musicians' balcony. "I was telling the others we would try acting on stage with our scripts today." She began explaining the stage movements.

While everyone followed her toward the curtain, Mel grasped Hawke's elbow and muttered in his ear, "Perkins said you arrived over an hour ago. Where have you been?"

His shoulders tensing, Hawke muttered back, "Meeting with Mother."

Mel arched his brows. "About Kit, I assume."

Hawke nodded. "Yes, now shhh." Wren would notice their muttering soon and scold them.

Finishing her explanation, Wren smiled at Mel. "Start from the introduction."

Hawke and his cousins scurried behind the curtain. They performed the play on stage for the first time, halting for instructions from Wren, missed entrances, or bungled lines. However, they eventually managed to complete the final scene.

After that, Wren had them redo a few scenes before ending the rehearsal by ringing for tea. When it arrived, the players fell upon the tea and sweet biscuits like ravenous hellhounds after a lengthy hunt. Then everyone took their seats in the circle.

As he devoured a sweet biscuit, Edouard grinned at Wren. "When Pippa said you claimed to be a strict taskmaster, I couldn't believe it. But now I do."

Hawke waggled his brows over his teacup. "And her sweetly reasonable manner when she corrects you for the hundredth time somehow makes it worse."

A blush staining her cheeks, Wren shifted in her seat. "I don't mean to make this difficult for anyone."

Elise pursed a wry smile, smoothing blonde hair behind her ear. "But you do hold us to a certain standard."

Wren winced and whirled her free hand. "When I pen the words, I possess a clear vision of how they should be played, you see."

Pippa winked at Wren. "I daresay that's what shall make our performance shine—just like for the orphanage play."

Wren inclined her head at Pippa as she drained her tea. "I certainly hope so. I know our performance shall engender talk, but I'd rather it be praise than snickers."

Hawke's pulse surged. He'd ensure it was. Wren despised public scrutiny of any kind, and snickers would wound her, so they must perform well. Her play would shine if they did. He set aside his empty dishes then narrowly eyed Mel and his cousins. "We all want that."

His fellow players nodded in response then rose and made their goodbyes.

As Wren moved to follow, Hawke grasped her hand to tell her about Kit. Tingling skittered up his arm. Not again. When she turned toward him with an arched brow, he dropped her hand, but he still tingled. "Please stay."

"Very well." Wren crossed her arms before her chest. "Why were you late today?" She swallowed. "Rowan?"

If only. Weight compressed his chest. His hunt was stalled until Devon wrote him back. Not that he could mention that to Wren. He still couldn't invite her to join their ride and risk her recovery. He shook his head. "No, I was convincing Mother to handle Kit for us."

Wren's face brightened, and her arms fell to her sides. "Truly?"

Warmth suffused Hawke at her palpable relief. Definitely worth risking Mother's meddling. He winked at her. "Yes."

Wren flushed, her gaze darting toward the door. "Thank the Goddess. What does she plan to do?"

He blinked at Wren. Why had she looked away? Ignoring her odd reaction, he shrugged and replied, "No inkling. Although she informed me I was joining her and Father for dinner tomorrow."

Wren paled and nibbled her lip, her gaze still avoiding his. "I wonder why."

Hawke grimaced as he took her arm to escort her from the ballroom. "Again, no inkling. Yet knowing Mother, it involves matchmaking or a lecture or both." But he'd discover for certain tomorrow.

CHAPTER 39

$\mathcal{W}$hile sipping her tea after rehearsal the following day, Wren eyed her players. The past four rehearsals had gone fantastic, even though she was always drained afterward. Her players were sure to give an excellent performance next week. If they weren't performing before court, the fete play would no longer worry her.

Hawke turned to Wren as everyone finished their tea. "I just learned I've an appointment during tomorrow's rehearsal. May I miss it? I swear this shall be the only one."

Wren tilted her head. "But we can only rehearse a few scenes without you." She glanced at the others, who'd all leaned forward. Clearly they'd be grateful for a respite. "However, we've worked hard these last few days, so we're far beyond where I'd expected. We can afford to miss tomorrow's rehearsal."

Drooping since the last scene, Elise brightened. She'd the meatiest part of the princess, so she must be especially eager for a respite. "Truly?"

Wren ached to droop like Elise, but as play mistress, she must conceal that to hearten her players. "Yes." She shook her head with a playful scowl. "But don't use my leniency as an excuse to shirk. I expect everyone back the day after tomorrow, working hard again."

Edouard saluted her, an impish gleam in his pale-blue eyes. "Yes, strict play mistress."

Wren almost smiled. Edouard and Hawke were definitely cousins. Wearing that expression, Edouard appeared remarkably like Hawke despite his blond hair. She pointed at the door. "Out. Enjoy your day of respite."

"We will." Edouard took Pippa's arm and whisked her from the ballroom.

Hawke chuckled as the others vanished. "I didn't mean to cancel tomorrow's rehearsal."

Wren shrugged then allowed her shoulders to sag since they were alone. She needn't feign cheer for him about the fete play. He knew how she truly felt—about the play anyway. "No matter. They deserve it." Besides, an afternoon free would allow her to rest.

Hawke flashed a crooked grin. "*They* do? And I don't?"

Her lips twitched, but she arched a brow to tease him. "No, you requested one, you shirker." Plus, his mother was to blame for the fete play.

Hawke snickered. "I love your wit, Wren."

Wren's heart clenched. Yet he didn't love her. She forced a blithe smile. "I know." She'd begin sobbing if they continued discussing love, so she asked, "What appointment do you have tomorrow?"

Hawke shrugged and glanced away. "Meeting with Buford about the arachne silk."

She tensed. Again? And why was he avoiding her gaze? What was he hiding? "Couldn't you schedule your meeting for the morning instead?"

Hawke shrugged again. "The afternoon was the only time he could meet."

A chill skittered across her skin. He wasn't meeting with Buford, and his appointment must concern Rowan. But why was he being secretive? Had her outburst the other day inspired him to exclude her from his hunt? If so, how could she obstruct it?

Wren swallowed then made herself rise and almost staggered. Goddess, she was exhausted. Stupid fete play. "I must be off. After yesterday's rehearsal, Mother informed me we're also dining as a family tonight, and I've something to attend to before then." A nap, or she'd never last through dinner.

Hawke grimaced and rose as well. "Our mothers must be colluding again."

As they strolled down the hall, she wrinkled her nose. "That's what I thought when she told me. I hope it shan't be as painful as last time." Or about Rowan. Or Hawke's betrothal.

Hawke coughed a laugh. "You mean when Mother invited me to luncheon to lecture me about dowdy attire while your mother did the same to you two doors down? As I recall, our mothers even used the same phrasing for most of it."

Wren poked his arm while Perkins One opened the front door. "That lecture inspired Mother to purchase that dress you said made me a massapan doll." Thank the Goddess she'd ruined the frilly eyesore.

Hawke guffawed as they strode down the front steps. "Surely this lecture shan't inspire anything as bad as *that*."

Hopefully not. She shuddered, waving when she reached her front steps. "I'll see you the day after tomorrow." Please let him discover nothing at his secret appointment. Shoving that aside, she slipped inside then headed straight to her chambers and sank into slumber.

WREN JOLTED awake after a nightmare where Hawke had burned the enchanted bird. He'd been furious and had glared at her with heavy disgust as he'd vowed never to speak to her again. She shivered while she rubbed sleep from her eyes. Somehow she must convince Hawke to forget Rowan and return the enchanted bird to ensure that nightmare never happened. But how? Everything thus far had failed.

She glanced at the clock on the mantel and sighed. She'd slept for several hours, so despite her nightmare, she was probably refreshed enough to withstand her parents' lecture, no matter the subject.

She rang for Abby and selected a simple violet-blue gown, ignoring the maid's habitual grumbles over her plain taste. Even if she was dining out, which she wasn't, this gown would be entirely appropriate.

Yet when Wren strolled downstairs, her parents were in the entrance hall rather than the family dining room. She stilled, blinking at them. Were they dining out, after all? If so, why hadn't Mother mentioned that before?

Mother beamed at her. "At last, my dear. Are you ready to go?"

Wren stiffened. Oh, Goddess. Mother's beam resembled the duchess's when asking Wren to write the fete play. But Mother rarely meddled like her best friend, so what was she about? Wren swallowed. "Where are we going?"

Father arched his brows as he took Mother's arm. "To Childes House, of course."

Wren gulped a deep breath. Hawke was wrong; this lecture promised to be much worse than the last. She shivered. Had their parents discovered she'd been Rowan? If they had, the enchanted bird should prevent them from revealing that to Hawke. Right?

Her skin prickled as she followed her parents to the Hawkes' townhouse. When they entered the drawing room, only Hawke and his parents awaited them.

The duke and duchess rose. The duchess slipped her arm through her husband's and gestured toward the door. "Shall we proceed to dinner?"

Hawke frowned from his chair across the room. "Aren't we waiting for Aragon, Selena, or Mel?"

The duchess widened her eyes with a bright smile. What exactly was she plotting? "Oh no, they're dining with Kit. I couldn't deny her request after I spoke to her about the fete play."

Her stomach roiling, Wren glanced at Hawke, who grimaced back before rising and offering her his arm. Unaffected by his touch for once, she hissed as they followed their parents down the hall, "Have you any inkling what this is about?"

Hawke ran his free hand through his hair. "No. Although their alliance and lack of witnesses can't bode well."

Wren shuddered. Precisely. Plus, their parents rarely lectured them together. They must find some way to avoid it. She clutched Hawke's arm when they entered the family dining room. "So how can we escape?"

"I doubt we can now," Hawke murmured in her ear as he pushed in her chair. Then he slid into the only empty seat, beside her.

Although Wren tensed for the forthcoming lecture, conversation remained innocuous during dinner. Yet she could hardly eat, and when Hawke served her eel stew, normally a favorite, she gagged and pushed her reeking bowl away. Anxiety, no doubt. She grabbed a roll to quell her stomach then waved over a servant.

Their parents continued their conversation, but Hawke slanted her a narrow glance. "Is everything all right?"

Wren nodded and nibbled on her roll as a servant whisked away her bowl. She'd consume plain fare tonight. Hopefully, their parents wouldn't notice. Goddess, would this interminable meal ever end?

His lips tight, Hawke offered her another roll, and dinner resumed its smooth course.

After dinner, everyone adjourned to the drawing room with Wren and Hawke taking the sofa at the far end. Perhaps if they remained unobtrusive, their parents would forgo the lecture.

Her heart froze when their fathers each lined up two chairs

before the sofa. The dreaded lecture was about to begin. She swallowed and burrowed her hand beneath her skirt to not grasp Hawke's hand. Dear Goddess, this couldn't be good. *Please let it not involve Rowan.*

Their parents sank into their chairs, with hers on the right before her and Hawke's on the left before him.

The duchess arched a brow. "How long have the two of you known each other?"

Hawke narrowly eyed her. "All our lives, as you know."

Mother smiled at Wren. "And how long have you been best friends?"

Wren shifted in her seat. Why were they asking about that? "Not too long after our births."

The duke nodded. "And have either of you done anything important without the other?"

Her chest tightening, Wren glanced at Hawke, who frowned back. As one, they drawled, "No..."

Father's eyes were unusually solemn. "And who do you first turn to when in need?"

"Hawke," Wren replied as Hawke said, "Wren." Her stomach cramped. Although since the masquerade, 'twasn't quite true. She'd spent the past several weeks deceiving him.

Their parents nodded and exchanged a glance, then the duchess said, "Which is why we've decided you must marry." When Wren and Hawke gaped at her, she added, "*Each other.*"

Wren's vision darkened as rushing filled her ears. Out of all the ladies at court, their parents had chosen *her* as Hawke's betrothed? They'd never pushed her at Hawke before. Why now when 'twas too late?

How could she possibly explain her missing virginity? Hawke would never believe he'd taken it but didn't recall due to a glamour spell. Not unless he burned the enchanted bird. But he'd never forgive her, much less marry her, if he realized her deceitful seduction.

Plus, Hawke was obsessed with finding Rowan. No doubt he

believed himself halfway in love with his mysterious dryad. But he'd never find her unless he burned the enchanted bird, and he'd no longer want her once he did.

Unshed tears burned her eyes. But even without the Rowan situation, she'd never accept an offer inspired by family pressure. She'd only marry Hawke if he loved her like she loved him. Which he didn't. She swallowed, not glancing at Hawke. His scorn would shatter her.

CHAPTER 40

*H*awke gaped at Mother after her pronouncement. Marriage to Wren? He glanced at Wren, who was also gaping at their parents. Weight compressed his chest. Marriage between them would never work.

Wren had spurned his kiss eight years ago, so she'd never wed him. She regarded him as a friend, and if he undid even one lace on her gown, she'd slap him so hard his ears would ring for days. Tingling flashed through him. Although seeing her naked might be worth getting slapped.

He winced as agony seized his head. What was the matter with him? True, Wren was as attractive as Rowan, but he and Wren could be nothing more than friends. Imagining her naked would destroy their friendship. If he had Rowan, such thoughts wouldn't trouble him.

His muscles tensed. He must find Rowan. Then he'd court her, and if their attraction burgeoned into love, he'd marry her. He'd not settle for marrying his best friend because their parents decided they should. 'Twouldn't be fair to him or Wren.

When he and Wren remained mute, their parents began spouting arguments without waiting for them to reply.

Mother arched a brow. "We expected you to tend to the matter ages ago."

Lady Keyes added, "However, you've made no move to do so, and you passed the age of majority three years ago."

Father nodded. "We decided we must nudge you past whatever has delayed you."

Sir Alaric's eyes gleamed. "Especially since we want grandchildren before *you* become old and gray."

Mother tsked, shaking her head. "In truth, 'twould be impossible to find others to marry you."

Lady Keyes pursed her lips. "You're always together and tell each other everything."

Father snorted. "If I was married to Wren, I'd *never* allow you so close to my wife."

Sir Alaric grinned and drawled, "And if I was Hawke, I'd be plotting how to kill her husband."

When their rapid arguments paused, Hawke eyed them. Why had their parents assumed they'd marry? And since when was *ordering* marriage a nudge?

Hawke glanced at Wren, whose hazel eyes were glazed. She couldn't possibly respond, so he inhaled then replied, "Not being in love with each other delayed us. Wren and I refuse to settle for less."

Wren paled and jerked a nod, but their parents burst into laughter. When they quieted, Mother asked, "Aren't you?"

Hawke stiffened and glared at her. "Certainly not. If we were, we'd have married ages ago." At eighteen in a romantic ceremony on Longnight. But Wren had shoved him away after a simple kiss, so *that* had never happened.

A smile trembling on her lips, Wren lifted her chin. "Hawke's right. We're merely friends."

Father arched a brow and glanced between Hawke and Wren. "Caro and I were friends before we married."

Taking his hand, Mother chuckled. "We were furious when our parents arranged our marriage, but within a month we were madly in love, and within a year, we couldn't imagine not being married."

Father kissed her hand. "And we weren't near as close as you and Wren."

Hawke's jaw tightened. "Yes, but 'tis because we're so close that we know we don't suit." And he'd met Rowan, who did suit.

Wren swallowed and turned to her parents. "Your marriage wasn't arranged, was it?"

Lady Keyes inclined her head. "No, it wasn't."

Wren spread her hands with a tight smile. "All Hawke and I want is that—the chance to choose our own spouses rather than settling for friendship."

Hawke nodded. Exactly. He'd only marry for love. And Wren had always felt the same.

Sir Alaric arched a brow at Wren. "If that's true, why do you rarely attend court events?"

Hawke suppressed a snort. Didn't the baronet know his daughter?

Wren wrinkled her nose and shuddered. "You know I despise those."

Lady Keyes sighed. "But, my dear, how do you expect to meet someone if you don't?"

When Wren crossed her arms and looked away, Mother interjected, "And you're no better, Hawke. Always consorting with inappropriate women, not counting Wren."

His neck and ears hot, Hawke shifted but shrugged. "I've plenty of time to find a suitable wife." Which he might have with Rowan. He simply must find her again.

Father narrowed his eyes. "How about we consider you and Wren betrothed, and if neither of you find other spouses in the next year, you'll marry each other?"

Wren winced and turned ashen, but Hawke nodded. He'd find Rowan before then. "Very well, but the betrothal mustn't be announced," he slanted Mother a hard glance, "to *anyone*."

Sir Alaric chortled. "That *would* make it awkward to hunt for another wife."

Her hands clenching, Wren cackled. "I can imagine one who'd not mind in the least."

Hawke shuddered. Except he'd *never* marry Kit. "Well, I can't." When Wren said nothing further, he eyed her. She was still ashen as a banshee. His throat tightening, he rose. "Wren and I should go, as you can imagine, we've matters to discuss."

Mother nodded then stood, pulling Wren upright to embrace her. "I look forward to gaining another daughter soon, especially one so dear to us."

Somehow, Wren paled further. "Thank you, your grace."

When Wren swayed, Hawke grasped her arm. Goddess, let her make it to his carriage. He nodded at their parents. "We'll see you later." Then he hustled her outside.

As he ordered his driver to tour Ormas, Wren collapsed in the corner of the forward seat with her eyes squeezed shut.

He frowned and settled beside her rather than taking his normal seat. She needed his help recovering. Damn their parents' mad proposal. He lit the inside lanterns and drew the drapes so no one else could see her distress then took her hand. "Everything shall be fine, Wren. I'll find Rowan and wed her, and you'll be free to wed a gentleman you love." Although no one was worthy of her.

Wren flung herself forward and buried her face into his chest then burst into tears.

As Wren pressed against him, her violet scent surrounded him, and his body hardened. Not again. Why did he keep reacting to her? Pain bolted through his head, but he crooned nonsense and smoothed her hair. She'd not been this upset since her faebird had died after she and her beloved pet had contracted wraith flu. But asking to create a friendship stone wouldn't cheer her this time.

Perhaps teasing would work. Hawke tickled her neck. "I

know you aren't in love with me, but I'm no troll. I'll become insulted if you continue to sob like that."

Wren sat upright and slapped his chest. "Do hush. My tears weren't at marrying you, but at an arranged marriage."

A pang darted through him. At an arranged marriage to *him*. He gritted a crooked grin and extracted his pocketcloth from beside the enchanted bird then handed it to her. "You simply must redouble your assistance in my hunt for Rowan."

Wren glared at him over the pocketcloth as she dried her face. "And even if I redouble my assistance, what do we do if we never find her?"

Hawke set his jaw. There was no chance of that. He'd not quit until he found Rowan. "We only must refuse to marry. We're of age, so they can't force us."

Wren hurled his balled pocketcloth into his lap. "That works for *you*. You possess your own fortune and a townhouse. I possess neither and only receive my inheritance when I marry or my parents die."

He shrugged. "If your parents disinherit you for refusing to marry, I'll buy you a townhouse." Not that they ever would.

Wren snorted and raised her eyes skyward. "Rowan would *love* you supporting another lady. I'd chase my husband around the house with a knife for such an offense."

Hawke shifted. She would too. "I suppose 'tis good we aren't marrying then. Besides, Rowan shall understand our friendship."

"Shall she?" Wren shook her head and muttered, "I somehow fail to."

He tensed, his head pounding anew. "What?"

Wren shoved his shoulder. "Never mind. Go sit in your seat."

Hawke's throat constricted, but he nodded and flung himself onto the backward seat. He'd only been attempting to help.

Wren sighed as she rubbed her forehead. "I'm sorry to be short, but I'm too exhausted to handle this ridiculous situation. I must focus on the fete play."

He grimaced. And he must focus on finding Rowan. 'Twas

the only way to end their ridiculous situation. "I'll take you home." He rapped on the roof of his carriage to signal his driver.

"Thank you, Hawke." Wren creaked a laugh. "It *is* ridiculous, you know. We can't marry when you're hunting another lady."

Hawke eyed her haggard face, his stomach hardening. Wren was right; she couldn't handle an unwanted betrothal in addition to the fete play. He'd ensure everything went as it should. "I know."

When the carriage halted before Wren's townhouse, he squeezed her hand as he helped her alight. "I'll see you the day after tomorrow. Now get some rest." Otherwise, she'd never recover.

Wren nodded then trudged up her front steps.

As Hawke climbed back into his carriage, he rubbed his still aching head. He must find Rowan to end their parents' meddling. Fortunately, his ride with Devon was tomorrow, and that should provide new clues.

CHAPTER 41

*A*fter reading the same Lantos poem for the fourth time, Wren snapped her book shut then leapt to begin pacing about the conservatory. What was Hawke doing right now? Was he investigating witch shops or orphanages on his own? Or had he somehow found the veiled witch? Surely professional ethics, along with the glamour spell, would mute her tongue.

Wren swallowed when nausea surged again. If only she knew what Hawke's secret appointment was. Then she could have enjoyed her free afternoon. As it was, she couldn't even read, and her stomach was threatening to expel the two rolls she'd choked down at luncheon.

She rubbed her queasy stomach. She needed a distraction from Hawke's secret appointment before she made herself ill. She should visit Kiera—she'd not seen her friend since the orphanage play because of the fete play rehearsals.

Engrossed in her thoughts, Wren bumped into a low branch of a lymon tree. She eyed its bright yellow fruit. They were fully ripe now, and the tart lymons would be a perfect treat for the orphans. So she gathered all the ripe lymons then requested a carriage to the orphanage.

On the ride across Ormas, she closed her eyes and inhaled

the lymon's citrusy scent to quell her stomach. Thankfully, her nausea faded by the time she reached the orphanage. She climbed from the carriage then smiled at Peter. "Where's Kiera?"

"In her study, Miss Wren." Peter chuckled with a grin. "Disciplin' those Bedsford twins again."

Wren tsked. Again? The twins were always in trouble nowadays. More than even Hawke used to be. "What did those scamps do now?"

Peter shrugged. "Went fishin' then mounted their catch above the door to the dinin' hall. When everyone ate luncheon, the twins made the fish dance and sing with fishin' twine. Scared the little ones somethin' awful, though the older children laughed."

She almost giggled. An escapade worthy of a childhood Hawke. "Kiera might be a while." She lifted the canvas sack with the ripe lymons. "Before I visit her, I'll take these lymons to Mary."

Wren gave Mary the lymons then accepted the laden tea tray in return. She headed upstairs, but unable to knock without spilling the tea tray, she tapped on Kiera's closed door with her foot.

The Bedsford twins burst from Kiera's study but halted before Wren, chorusing, "Afternoon, Miss Wren!"

She pursed her lips to curb a smile. She mustn't encourage them. "John, Jacob, I hear you made a fish dance."

John chortled. "And sing!"

Jacob flashed a grin. "'Twas great!"

Then the twins barreled down the hall without waiting for her to reply.

Wren tsked as she entered the study. "Those two scamps need a constructive outlet for their exuberance." Although amusing, their escapades would soon become impossible to handle.

Kiera grimaced while Wren set the tea tray on her desk. "Maybe so, but at twelve, the basic schooling we provide bores them, yet they're too young for employment." She sighed and poured herself some tea. "Although they've been worse since

Cassandra and Amaranth left. They adored Amaranth, so they miss her something fierce."

Wren chuckled as she accepted a steaming teacup from Kiera. That explained the snakes last week.

Kiera arched her brows. "What?"

Wren grinned. "I was recalling the twins teasing Amaranth. I should have realized they liked her, but I was distracted by Cassandra's fury." And her powerful magic.

Kiera shook her head over her teacup. "Cassandra is fierce when defending Amaranth." She paused then added, "Have you visited them at their grandparents' yet?"

Wren toyed with the sweet biscuit on her plate. "I've been too busy with the fete play to visit the Westons." But she must take Cassandra to the veiled witch before the girl injured someone. She'd write to the Westons as soon as she returned home.

Kiera lowered her teacup and leaned forward. "How's that going?"

Wren shrugged. "The rehearsals are going well." Especially now that the duchess had handled Kit. "'Tis different from directing orphans. But the rehearsals aren't the issue—the performance is." She sighed at that upcoming ordeal.

Kiera's eyes narrowed as she sipped her tea. "I suppose fretting over the fete play has disturbed your sleep in recent days. You appear exhausted."

Wren nearly winced. No, sensual dreams of Hawke and fretting over his hunt for Rowan were responsible for that. Although last night their parents' mad plan had helped. Because of everything, she'd barely slept.

When Wren said nothing, Kiera's frown burgeoned.

Avoiding her friend's gaze, Wren sipped her tea. She'd better explain her exhaustion, or Kiera would probe until she confessed about Rowan. "I didn't sleep much last night, but not because of the fete play. Do you remember I mentioned the duchess was plotting Hawke's betrothal?"

Kiera nodded and set down her teacup.

Wren made herself shrug. "Well, our parents informed us last night that *I* was his chosen bride." So impossible.

Kiera chuckled, her frown vanishing. "I told you the duchess would pick you."

So she had. Wren scowled at Kiera. "I'm not about to allow our parents to force us into an arranged marriage. Particularly since 'tis too late."

Kiera's brow furrowed. "Why too late?"

Wren tensed. Damn her loose tongue. How could she explain without revealing she'd seduced Hawke as Rowan? "Hawke is obsessed with finding some dryad he met at the king's summer masquerade. Even though she vanished like a will-o'-the-wisp, he's convinced himself he's halfway in love with her."

Kiera gaped at her. "He what?"

Wren forced a blithe smile as she set down her teacup. "'Tis true. I've been helping him hunt for her without alerting his parents."

Kiera reached across her desk to grasp Wren's hands. "No wonder you appear dreadful. Helping the gentleman you love find another."

Wren lifted her chin. "I told you before I feel nothing for Hawke but friendship." What a lie. "'Tis the places we've gone to hunt his vanished dryad—witch shops. She left behind a spell, you see."

Kiera released Wren's hands to cross her arms. "A love spell, I suppose."

Wren shrugged. No, a glamour spell to prevent Hawke from recognizing her. But if she'd not been Rowan, she'd share Kiera's cynicism, so she drawled, "Hawke said she *claimed* 'twas for courage."

Kiera snorted. "And you believe that?"

Wren wrinkled her nose. "What matters is Hawke believes that. So we've been visiting fashionable witch shops across Ormas since the masquerade, but I despise them. They're eerie, and none can decipher the spell." But one might some day.

Kiera uncrossed her arms and leaned toward Wren. "Have you thought of visiting the witch shop beside the Bedsfords' old miscellany shop?"

Wren stilled. "No, because Hawke is convinced his dryad is too genteel to visit a shop like that." Thank the Goddess.

Kiera nodded. "Probably, but the veiled witch might offer insight into the spell."

Wren glanced down at her plate, a blush warming her cheeks. Yes, the veiled witch would since she'd created it. "I'll have to suggest her to Hawke. Enough about witch shops."

Kiera tsked and arched her brows. "The king's summer masquerade was almost a month ago. Why didn't you mention Hawke's dryad when I first asked about the masquerade?"

Wren fingered a sweet biscuit. "Hawke wanted no one to know." And she couldn't risk revealing she'd been Rowan. Kiera saw too much.

Kiera tsked again and picked up her teacup. "I can't help but wonder what else you failed to mention about the king's summer masquerade."

That she'd been Hawke's mysterious dryad. Wren gulped a breath. She must distract Kiera before her friend realized that. So she shrugged and said, "The only other masquerade gossip I know involves the king, but I didn't hear about it until recently."

Kiera's brows rose as she began sipping her tea. "Oh?"

Wren nodded, her tension easing. Kiera had bit on her distraction. "Like Hawke, King Devon was enthralled by a mysterious lady who vanished, although in his case, 'twas a mermaid."

Kiera choked mid-swallow. "Really?"

Wren blinked. What made Kiera choke? "Are you well?"

Kiera inclined her head with a faint smile. "'Tis nothing. Swallowed wrong."

Unpleasant. Wren winced but returned to distracting Kiera, "According to Hawke's family, the king's obsession with his mermaid is damaging the talks with the nightmara herds."

Kiera's mouth fell open. "Why?"

Wren shrugged. "Nightmara are matriarchal, and he needs a wife, or at least a betrothed, to negotiate with them. Until the masquerade, everyone assumed he'd offer for Lady Annalise Greysnowe, but now he only wants his mermaid." Her stomach tightened. Just like Hawke only wanted Rowan.

Kiera's teacup clattered onto the desk. "Oh dear."

Wren eyed her friend, who was as pale as a wailing banshee before a family death. "Are you *certain* you're well?"

Kiera rubbed her forehead. "No, I'm afraid this tea made me ill for some reason."

Wren rose. Kiera needed time to recover, and she must escape while Kiera had forgotten about Rowan. "Do you need me to fetch someone?" When Kiera shook her head, Wren continued, "Then I'll see you later."

Wren returned home then wrote the Westons and asked if she could take Cassandra out one morning later this week. She left why vague since the Westons might object to their granddaughter learning magic. She'd devise an excuse before their outing.

After writing the Westons, she attempted to read, but her mind kept drifting to Hawke's secret appointment. What if it inspired him to burn the enchanted bird? Oh, Goddess. She must ask him about his secret appointment after tomorrow's fete play rehearsal. Hopefully, she could manage her nerves until then.

CHAPTER 42

*B*ursting with energy, Hawke galloped to the palace stables to meet Devon straight after a hearty luncheon. Surely their ride would provide new clues to find Rowan. But when he arrived, his cousin wasn't in the stable yard —doubtless he'd gotten absorbed in state affairs and forgotten their ride.

After ordering grooms to prepare mounts for Devon and his guards, Hawke strode into the palace and up to the royal wing. He nodded at the two royal guards flanking the king's study before entering without a knock.

His crownless brow furrowed and lines bracketing his mouth, Devon sat hunched behind a desk strewn with papers. He was so focused on his reading he didn't stir at Hawke's arrival.

Hawke suppressed a chuckle as he leaned against the door frame. "Still hard at work, I see."

Devon glanced up at him with a smile. "As I should be. 'Tisn't yet luncheon." When Hawke smirked at the tray of food beside the desk, Devon eyed the clock on the mantel and winced. "But I see that it is. How did it get so late?" He ran a hand through his hair and rose. "I'll go change and then we can be off."

Hawke tsked. "Planning on skipping a meal? I've time if you want to eat first." Devon was bound to sicken if he kept skipping meals to work. Besides, he'd be sharper after eating, so comparing their hunts would go better.

Devon grimaced. "No, I'll grab something to eat in the saddle from my luncheon tray. Unfortunately, *I* shan't have the time."

Hawke shook his head as Devon bolted from the study. Being a good king was a heavy burden, especially alone. Hopefully, exchanging information today would help Devon find his mermaid and Hawke find Rowan. They both needed their mysterious ladies.

Devon soon returned in riding clothes, stuffed some rolls with meat and cheese then waved Hawke forward. They strode down to the stable yard with the two guards from the door following them.

Once everyone vaulted into their saddles, Hawke grinned at Devon. "Where do you want to ride?"

Devon shrugged and devoured one of his stuffed rolls. "Doesn't matter as long as it hasn't crowds or nightmara."

Hawke nodded. He'd want to avoid the nightmara too in Devon's situation. "How about the royal forest?" Devon always enjoyed riding there, and 'twould be private enough to discuss their mysterious ladies since riding there required royal permission.

"Sounds good." Devon urged his black gelding forward, eating another stuffed roll.

One of the royal guards spurred his horse until he rode before the king, while the other waved for Hawke to proceed him.

Hawke joined Devon, and they rode through Ormas with stern royal guards at their front and rear. Much more tense than his ride with Wren last week. He grimaced. How did Devon stand it?

Hawke relaxed when they rode through the eastern gate and sped to a trot. Now that they were alone, the royal guards should unbend. Plus, slightly cooler than last week, the summer afternoon was perfect for a brisk ride through the ripening fields.

Devon halted when they entered the royal forest. "Smith, join Johnson behind us. And keep out of earshot." When his guards began to protest, the king straightened and jerked his chin. "Hawke is no danger to me, and we're alone, except for the odd poacher."

The royal guards exchanged a resigned glance then withdrew.

Devon urged his gelding forward again. "So, Hawke, what favor did you want to ask me? Something about your latest find, perhaps? Arachne silk, was it?"

Hawke flashed a crooked grin. "No, that's handled. All of court shall purchase the arachne silk once they see Wren wearing it at Mother's fete." He widened his eyes to feign innocence. "And why would you assume I want a favor?"

Devon arched a brow. "Because you've never requested a private ride before, not even when we were children."

Hawke chuckled. True. He'd just joined Aragon and Devon without asking, usually with Wren along. "Your wits are as sharp as ever."

Devon's eyes flickered. "I'm pleased you think so. No one else seems to right now."

Hawke almost winced. The council must be after Devon to abandon his mermaid and marry another, so they'd a queen to renegotiate the Nightmara-Calatini Treaty. But if Devon wanted his mermaid like Hawke wanted Rowan, 'twould be impossible. He studied Devon. "Because of the mermaid you met at your masquerade three weeks ago?"

Devon stiffened. From his demeanor, he was expecting censure. "Yes..."

Hawke leaned toward his cousin with a grin. He was about to provide the opposite. "Remember those rumors about me and a dryad at the masquerade? Well, I've been attempting to find her. I thought we could compare our hunts and perhaps learn something new since we've not made progress alone."

Devon relaxed and eyed him. "Do you know, you're the first to offer to further my hunt for my mermaid."

Hawke grimaced. That's because no one else understood their hunger to find their vanished ladies. "I can imagine. I almost couldn't convince Wren to help me."

Devon guffawed. "You asked *Miss Keyes* to help you?"

Hawke blinked at him. "Of course. Why wouldn't I?" She was his best friend.

Devon snorted as he steered his gelding around a fallen tree. "Hawke, you're shrewd with investments, but sometimes you're the stupidest man in Calatini."

Hawke frowned. What did Devon mean by that? But he only replied, "In any case, Wren and I haven't had luck finding my dryad. All she left behind was a spell. We've been visiting witch shops to learn more, but all the witches have been able to decipher is that a Rhiannon descendant created it. What have you tried?"

Devon rubbed his forehead. "With the nightmara negotiations and pacifying the council and the Greysnowes, I've not possessed the time to do much."

Hawke sighed. Poor Devon. Ruling was a terrible onus. Thank the Goddess he was related to Devon's mother and not in line for the throne. He cocked a brow. "I suppose Lady Annalise is vexed she'll no longer be queen."

Devon shook his head. "The lady herself is indifferent, but her parents are decidedly not."

Hawke blinked. If Lady Annalise wasn't interested in being queen, why had she allowed Devon to escort her to court events for over three years? He shrugged. But who cared about that? He and Devon must find their mysterious ladies. "Even with your limited time, you must have learned something."

Devon halted and glanced back at his guards before

extracting a pocketcloth from his riding coat. Unfolding the white linen, he murmured, "This is my only clue."

Hawke studied the ragged scrap of fabric nestled in the pocketcloth. As a clue, 'twas even less than he had. "What is it?"

Devon refolded his pocketcloth and slipped it back inside his coat. "A piece of my mermaid's ballgown snagged in her haste to flee before the unveiling at midnight."

Hawke frowned at his cousin. "But the fabric doesn't appear rich enough to dazzle all of court."

Devon shrugged. "Her ballgown was enchanted—she admitted as much before she fled. I showed it to the royal witch, but Lady Juliet refused to analyze it. She said stronger magic would erase the wisps of magic remaining in the fabric."

Hawke snorted and shook his head. Interesting their ladies left behind contrary clues. He extracted the enchanted bird from his pocket. "This is the spell my dryad left behind. Unlike your clue, 'tis too strong to analyze."

Devon prodded the pearly carving. "Even *I* can sense the magic burning inside, and I've barely a drop of witch's blood. Put it away." Once Hawke had pocketed the enchanted bird, Devon asked, "Would you like an appointment with the royal witch to analyze your clue?"

Hawke grinned. The royal witch was powerful, so she'd decipher *something* about the enchanted bird and Rowan. "I'd appreciate an appointment with Lady Juliet."

Devon grimaced. "I only hope you possess better fortune than I did."

He would. His pulse surging, Hawke leaned toward his cousin. "When I find the Rhiannon descendant who created my dryad's spell, she can examine your scrap of fabric. Doubtless she'll unearth more for you."

Devon inclined his head. "Thank you, Hawke." He sighed. "I suppose we should return. I've reports to attend."

As they turned their geldings, Hawke leaned toward Devon. "Could we keep our discussion today private? I don't want even

Aragon to know—Mother would find out somehow." And then she'd meddle.

Devon chuckled and nodded. "Of course."

Relaxing, Hawke winked at Devon. "Shall we race back to Ormas?"

A smile curved the corners of Devon's mouth. "My guards would panic."

Hawke snickered. 'Twould do them good. "An excellent reason to race back. Unless you fear losing."

Devon arched his brows. "I never lose."

Hawke smirked back to tease his cousin. "Only because you're the king."

"Oh really?" Devon crouched in his saddle then prodded his gelding forward.

Hawke chuckled and dashed after Devon. Unlike with Wren, he and Devon weighed about the same and rode similar-sized horses, so they were soon even. However, just outside of Ormas, Hawke's gelding stumbled over rough ground, allowing Devon to reach the gate first.

As his scowling guards joined them, Devon patted his sweating gelding and grinned at Hawke. "Told you I'd win."

Hawke chuckled. He must stop proposing races from the royal forest. He was doomed to lose. Although losing was a small price for the appointment with Lady Juliet. "Don't worry, I'll win next time."

CHAPTER 43

Sipping her tea after the next fete play rehearsal, Wren sighed as everyone discussed court gossip. Would Hawke's family ever leave? She must ask him about his secret appointment yesterday. Not knowing itched like pruries burrowing beneath her skin, although fortunately without leaving behind glowing faemarks revealing her worry.

She glanced at Hawke over her teacup, her stomach quivering. Whatever his appointment had been, at least it hadn't inspired him to burn the enchanted bird. He'd not be so mellow if he had. She suppressed a shiver and forced herself back to the ongoing conversation.

Elise raised her pale-blue eyes skyward. "And now the Greysnowes are accusing the Ravenstones of concocting the mermaid to divert the king from Lady Annalise."

Edouard snorted while he drained his tea. "Considering their feud, I'm not surprised."

Mel sighed as he brushed crumbs from his priest robes. "I never understood why Devon escorted Lady Annalise. Any problems would inflame the Greysnowe-Ravenstone feud."

Pippa giggled into her teacup. "Lady Annalise *is* the most beautiful lady in Calatini."

Wren almost smiled. A fact which doubtless vexed Kit. Yet the icy Lady Annalise never acknowledged Kit's needling. Wren sighed. If only she could be as stoic.

Hawke shuddered while he devoured his last sweet biscuit. "Even so, escorting someone dubbed Lady Snow doesn't seem pleasant to me."

Elise shrugged and rose. "Her dispassion no doubt made it easier for the king to abandon her whenever affairs of state intruded."

With that, Elise made her excuses and left. Fortunately, her departure inspired the others to leave as well. At last.

Once only she and Hawke remained, Wren pounced like a ravenous manticore on a pegasus, intent on devouring his secret to the bones. She must learn everything so she could continue delaying his hunt. "Where were you yesterday in truth?"

Hawke chuckled and arched a brow. "I suppose there's no harm in telling you now. I'd a ride with Devon."

She blinked. His secret appointment hadn't concerned Rowan? "Why bother to prevaricate about a ride with the king?"

Hawke tensed, slanting her a sidelong glance. "Because I thought a ride would be too taxing for you."

Wren wrinkled her nose. True, she had fallen asleep in his arms after the last one. Damn her sensual dreams of Hawke. If she could get decent sleep, she'd not be so exhausted. "Why did King Devon request a private ride?"

Hawke relaxed with a sigh. "He didn't; I did. Since we're both hunting mysterious ladies, I thought we could learn something if we compared our hunts."

Her heart pounded in her throat. She'd *known* his secret appointment had concerned Rowan. She buried her hands in her skirt to hide their trembling. "And what did you learn?"

Hawke shrugged but flashed a crooked grin. "Not much, but Devon arranged an appointment with Lady Juliet about the enchanted bird."

Oh, Goddess. Wren swallowed to soothe her roiling stomach.

The royal witch was powerful—would she decipher the veiled witch's spell? The veiled witch was a Rhiannon descendant, but Lady Juliet might be too. She managed a smile. "When's your appointment?"

Hawke grinned. "The day after tomorrow before rehearsal. You should come."

Damnation! She nibbled her lip. Last night, the Westons had written back she could take Cassandra out that morning. "I can't. I'm visiting Cassandra then." And she couldn't delay introducing Cassandra to the veiled witch again.

Hawke sighed, running a hand through his hair. "Too bad. Your insight would be beneficial at my appointment."

Wren winced. "Lady Juliet shan't require my insight about a glam—" Coughing wracked her entire body until tears trickled down her cheeks.

His eyes darkening, Hawke leaned toward her. "Are you well?"

She nodded and rose, wiping away her tears. The glamour spell must have caused her coughing fit to prevent her from slipping again. Fortunate. "But I should return home. I'll see you tomorrow at rehearsal."

Hawke frowned as he took her arm. "I'll escort you."

Wren sighed. She'd prefer time alone to consider his appointment with the royal witch, but her heaving coughs had drained her, so his arm would be welcome. Yet she remained silent during the short walk home.

At the base of her steps, Hawke halted and frowned down at her. "Are you *certain* you're well? You're white as a banshee."

She forced a shrug. "I'm just tired after the fete play rehearsal. I'll be recovered by tomorrow." If she got decent sleep.

His gaze probing, Hawke released her arm. "Until tomorrow then."

Wren nodded then trudged inside and up to her chambers. If only King Devon hadn't arranged for that appointment. Then she'd be safe until after the fete. At least without her there, Lady

Juliet wouldn't see the spell impacting her as well as Hawke like the disheveled witch had.

To cease brooding over Hawke's appointment, she curled on her bed to read Lantos, although she slipped into a doze by the third poem.

A FROWNING Abby woke Wren some time later and helped her dress for dinner. She rubbed her face to revive herself and drifted down to the family dining room. She really must get some decent sleep tonight. To mask her fatigue, she grinned as she greeted her parents and took her seat. Then she asked, "So where are you off to tonight?"

"Lady Staghorn's ball." Mother cocked a brow. "You should join us."

Wren shuddered, her mushroom soup curdling in her mouth. "Even if I enjoyed such events, I'd never attend one thrown by Mr. Winston's great-aunt. She always invites her poor relations, so 'twould be impossible to avoid Mr. Winston."

Father's eyes gleamed with laughter. "For shame, Wren, you're speaking about a future baron."

Wren snorted. "Who's still a cad, not to mention a fortune hunter." And as her parents' only child and heir, she was his preferred type of prey.

Mother studied Wren over her wine glass. "You could avoid his odious attentions by announcing your betrothal to Hawke."

Wren's stomach clenched. Except she and Hawke weren't betrothed. She glared at Mother. "I shall not. And you agreed not to do so either."

Mother pursed her lips. "Very well. Although I can't understand all the fuss. From the day you two met as babes, 'twas apparent you'd wed some day."

Perhaps to their parents, but not to Hawke, so nothing would come of it, no matter how much she loved him. Wren tightened her jaw and pretended to eat more soup.

When Mother opened her mouth to continue, Father touched her hand and shook his head, so she halted mid-breath. Silence reigned over the table while the servants brought a course of roasted pheasant and scalloped tubers.

As Wren cut her food into tiny pieces rather than eating it, Mother said, "Celeste sent a note today informing me your ballgown is ready."

Wren set down her knife to sip her wine. "I'll stop by tomorrow morning to fetch it." She might as well, since she'd no plans except for the fete play rehearsal.

Mother arched her brows. "Do you want me to accompany you?"

Wren shook her head. "I'll be fine alone." Her stomach lurched as she swallowed a bite of scalloped tubers. Attempting to eat would be futile, so she rose. "I'll see you both later. Enjoy the ball."

Mother and Father exchanged a glance but bid Wren good night.

The following morning, Wren overslept after another restless night, so she hadn't time to visit Celeste's before rehearsal. She took a carriage to Broad Street afterward. Hopefully, the fashionable dress shop wouldn't be too crowded in the afternoon.

It wasn't, but Kit was lingering in the anteroom. Wren tensed. How could she avoid Kit?

Before Wren could slip out, Kit swirled to face her with a feline smile. "So you've visited Celeste's at last. What convinced you?"

Wren shrugged. "Mother and the duchess insisted I have a new ballgown for the duchess's fete." No doubt because they meant to push her at Hawke.

Kit's eyes glinted. "Ah yes, court rumors claim 'tis made from Hawke's latest find. Arachne silk or some such?" When Wren nodded, Kit purred a chuckle. "You must wear your new ballgown for me. I'm sure you look well... for you."

Wren managed a serene smile. Why must Kit always needle

her? "I can't. You know how Celeste feels about multiple ladies in a fitting room. You must wait to see it with everyone else at the fete."

Kit moued, but her protests were halted by Celeste's arrival. The dressmaker imperiously beckoned Wren. "Right this way, Miss Keyes."

Her chest easing, Wren hurried to follow the dressmaker into a fitting room. She allowed the assistants to replace her dress with the ballgown then climbed on the stool.

Muttering to herself, Celeste made a few slight alterations before stepping back with a smug grin. "All finished. I believe 'tis one of my best creations, although the extraordinary fabric helps."

Wren turned toward the mirror, her breath catching in her throat. Dear Goddess. Somehow the ballgown looked even better than before. "Definitely a masterpiece. Thank you, Celeste."

As the assistants wrapped her ballgown, she sighed and licked her lips. Hawke had almost kissed her when he'd seen the unfinished ballgown. How would he react to it now? Would he pull her into an alcove and kiss her like he had Rowan? Tingling heat suffused her. But after a moment, she shook her head. No matter how much she wished it, he'd never kiss her like that again.

CHAPTER 44

*T*aking a deep breath, Hawke knocked on the door to the royal witch's wing in the palace for his late morning appointment. Lady Juliet was the most illustrious witch in Calatini—perhaps he'd receive answers about the enchanted bird at last. He swallowed to wet his dry throat.

A little maid in starched livery ushered him inside. "Right this way, Lord Beza."

He winced at his given name but followed her into the immaculate and stylish chambers. His brows rose. Where were the enchanted artworks, dusty tomes, and magical accoutrements?

The maid led him to an airy workroom, which *was* filled with magical accoutrements, but they were meticulously arranged on shelves. Not like any witch's workroom he'd ever visited. "Lord Beza, Lady Juliet."

A canvas apron protecting her modish gown, the royal witch finished stirring the brew in her cauldron then rapped the spoon against the rim and set it on the table. After thanking the maid, she removed her apron and gestured for him to sit on the sofa near the door. Once he sat, she perched beside him. "King Devon said you'd a spell for me to examine?"

His pulse surged as he extracted the enchanted bird from his pocket and held it out for Lady Juliet. "Yes, here it is."

The royal witch started, her eyes narrowing. "Wherever did you find a spell like *that*?"

Hawke tensed. What did her barbed drawl mean? To mask his tension, he flashed a crooked grin. "My companion at the king's summer masquerade abandoned it. She said 'twas a spell for courage."

As she accepted the pearly carving from him, Lady Juliet cocked her head. "Did she really?"

Again with that drawl. The back of his neck prickled, but he maintained his grin. "Yes, although one witch I visited told me I was a focus of the spell."

Her brow furrowed, the royal witch eyed Rowan's spell and turned it over and over in her hands for several moments. Then she rose, muttering to herself, and drifted over to a worktable along the wall.

Hawke leapt from the sofa and followed her. The enchanted bird mustn't leave his sight. 'Twas his only concrete clue to Rowan's identity. He'd never find her without it.

Lady Juliet set down the enchanted bird and turned toward the orderly shelves behind her worktable. She gathered a glass bowl, several herbs, a vial of amber liquid, and a powder that glittered like stardust. She began chanting in some melodic tongue, placed Rowan's spell in the glass bowl, and sprinkled it with the glittering powder.

As the wooden carving began glowing like a tiny star, the weight of the royal witch's magic compressed his head. He winced at the sudden pain. He'd never witnessed such powerful magic.

Lady Juliet waved her hands over the bowl three times. Then she dropped the herbs into the glass bowl and drizzled the amber liquid on top. The enchanted bird flared as bright as the sun, and his headache grew until he could barely see.

When her chant rose to a shriek, Rowan's spell exploded with a thunderous boom and smoke reeking of charred feathers.

Agony piercing his skull, Hawke staggered into the worktable. Dear Goddess. He gripped the edge to remain upright, squeezing his eyes shut and gulping air. When his head merely ached again, he squinted about the workroom.

Her brows arched to her fashionable coiffure, the royal witch was gaping at the enchanted bird, which no longer glowed but shimmered as it had before.

His stomach clenched. From Lady Juliet's expression, she'd deciphered little more than the other witches. Damnation. He coughed to draw her attention. "What did you discover, my lady?"

The royal witch tore her gaze from Rowan's spell. "Absolutely nothing. The warding on your spell was too strong. That's never happened to me before, so whoever created your spell must be *incredibly* powerful. A Rhiannon descendant like no other." She scowled.

Hawke grimaced and pocketed the enchanted bird. Of course, Rowan's witch was impossible for even the royal witch to trace. "Can you tell me anything at all?"

Lady Juliet frowned as she tapped her finger against her lip. "Only that I know I've seen this witch's work before. Now, if only I could recall where... I feel as if I should know, but I don't. I'm sorry, Lord Beza."

He drooped, his chest burning. Yet again, his hopes had been dashed like flotsam against the rocks during a tempest. Would he ever find Rowan? Maybe she really was the will-o'-the-wisp Wren had called her.

The royal witch escorted him from her workroom. "But if I realize anything about the spell, I'll write, my lord. And if you discover the identity of the witch, please let me know."

Hawke almost snorted. Not likely. An incredibly powerful Rhiannon descendant wasn't a witch to cross and wouldn't appreciate being exposed to a rival. However, he only inclined his head and said, "Thank you for looking into my spell for me."

He hurried from the palace and into his carriage. Since his appointment with Lady Juliet had run long, he instructed his driver to head straight to his parents' townhouse. He'd eat luncheon there before heading to the fete play rehearsal.

Yet when Hawke strode into the family dining room, he tensed and almost groaned. Why was Kit dining with Mother? He should have gone home for luncheon and been late. Now he must endure Kit's pursuit again. He sighed and settled in the chair farthest from Kit then heaped a plate with fish pie, roasted tubers, and stuffed peppers.

Mother's eyes gleamed over her wine glass. "Shall you have time to eat all that? You've rehearsal for the fete play soon."

He shrugged as he began devouring his fish pie. He'd be fine if he bolted his food. And he'd better—Wren hated when anyone was late for rehearsal.

Kit purred a chuckle. "Such a hearty appetite."

Hawke shrugged again and finished his fish pie. Responding to Kit would only encourage her.

A smile curving her lips, Mother said, "I invited Kit to luncheon today to help with certain elements of my fete. Her opinions have been most valuable."

He almost chuckled as he sipped his wine. So *that* was how Mother had handled Kit. Mother had been planning elaborate court events well before he or Kit had been born, so her request for help must be a ruse.

Kit fluttered her lashes at him. "I've been considering those elements, your grace, and I think I'll require Hawke's assistance."

Hawke stiffened. Absolutely not. Even if Kit wasn't pursuing him, he'd not help plan one of Mother's events. 'Twould be like herding pixies—exasperating, exhausting, and ultimately futile. "I'm much too busy with the fete play."

As he began inhaling his roasted tubers, Mother tilted her head. "Yes, you should ask Mel instead."

Kit's eyes narrowed. "Mel has a part in the play too."

Mother arched a brow. "True, but Hawke's part is larger, and he must support Wren."

Exactly. He jerked a nod as he finished his tubers. And stay far, far away from Kit. If they spent time together, she might eventually manage to entrap him into marriage.

Kit dabbed her mouth with her napkin. "Of course he does. Poor Wren can't survive without him."

Fire flashed through Hawke, and he quit eating, leaving his stuffed peppers untouched. He glared at Kit. "What do you mean by that?"

Kit smirked and leaned toward him. "Only that you're always forced to escort Wren to court events since she's too shy to attend alone."

His blood still burning, he gritted a smile. "No one forces me to escort Wren. I escort her because I prefer her company. Unlike *some*, she doesn't pursue uninterested gentlemen because she desires their fortune."

Kit's smirk vanished. "Yes, but Wren shall possess her own when her parents die."

Hawke snorted. "Even if she wouldn't, she's too sweet and honorable to marry for anything other than love." So their parents' mad proposal would never succeed. His chest squeezing, he sighed.

Kit tossed her head. "Such a paragon. How can the rest of us compete?" She leapt to her feet and swirled to Mother. "I'll speak to Mel about the fete before I leave."

Once Kit swished from the family dining room, he turned to Mother. "Why did you steer Kit to Mel? As a priest, he has more important duties than handling Kit." Surely Mother wasn't plotting a match between Mel and Kit. Not even Mother would dare influence the will of the Goddess.

Mother finished her wine with a faint smile. "Because you wanted to escape Kit, and Mel always could distract her." She arched her brows. "But why are you asking about that? Don't you have rehearsal?"

Hawke glanced at the clock across the family dining room and winced. So he did, and now he was late. Damn Kit for distracting him. Wren would be vexed, and she didn't need missing players with the fete play looming over her.

He strode to the ballroom, but when he arrived, everyone was assembled except Wren. All his cousins were in their seats, while Kit was storming away from Mel in the corner. His throat tightened. Where was Wren? She was never late. Was she unwell again?

CHAPTER 45

*W*ren woke when the late morning sun reflected off her mirror. Goddess, she was late for her visit with Cassandra. She leapt from bed. As her stomach roiled and vision blackened, she gulped air and gripped the bedpost. Leaping from bed had been a mistake.

Once her faintness receded, she dressed in a simple dress she could lace herself. She must get to the Westons at once. She'd finished dressing when Abby arrived with a breakfast tray. Her stomach quivering, she shuddered and shook her head. "I'm too late to eat all that. I'll take a roll for the ride."

Wren grabbed a roll from the laden tray and strode downstairs before Abby could reply. She nibbled on the roll during the carriage ride, and her stomach settled. Good.

When she entered the Westons' morning room, she almost winced. Lady Weston and Cassandra were sitting in opposite corners, and both were stiff as a gorgon's victims turned to stone. Relations between Cassandra and her grandparents hadn't improved.

Lady Weston frowned at Wren. "We'd begun to believe you'd forgotten your visit with Cassandra."

Wren did wince at that, and her chest tightened. Perhaps

their tension was due to her late arrival. "Sorry, I overslept. I rushed over as soon as I woke." She smiled at Cassandra. "Shall we go?"

Her mouth sulky, Cassandra rose without a word.

Wren swallowed. Her tardiness had wounded the younger girl. Damn her restless sleep. Would the magic lessons atone for her tardiness?

Lady Weston tilted her head. "Where are you headed?"

Suppressing her remorse, Wren smiled back. She'd devised the perfect excuse last night. "My former governess agreed to teach Cassandra deportment. I adored her growing up and thought Cassandra would too."

Although Cassandra stiffened, Lady Weston relaxed. "How wonderful." She reached to touch her granddaughter's shoulder but stopped short. "Have a good time, Cassandra."

Cassandra jerked a nod then left with Wren. Once they'd settled in the carriage, Cassandra glared at Wren and crossed her arms over her chest. "I don't need a deportment tutor. Mama taught me all that."

Not enough for court. However, Wren merely shook her head. "We're not visiting my former governess. We're visiting a witch for magic lessons." She narrowed her eyes at the younger girl. "You need those before you injure someone, or worse."

Cassandra winced but nodded. "I know. Papa had just begun teaching me when he died. But why did you lie to Lady Weston?"

Wren grimaced. "Because your grandparents wouldn't question deportment lessons, but they might magic lessons. Plus, the witch we're about to visit isn't fashionable, so they might not approve of her. But she's the only witch I know powerful enough to train you." Hopefully, the veiled witch would agree to do so.

Cassandra's eyes widened. "You found another Rhiannon descendant? Papa thought we were the only ones in Ormas, except for the royal witch."

Wren stilled, her heart quivering. So Lady Juliet was a

Rhiannon descendant too. Would she decipher the glamour spell? Shoving that aside, she handed Cassandra a leather tome. "Until we can explain your magic lessons to your grandparents, take this book about deportment."

Cassandra scowled and refused to accept it.

Wren pursed her lips. Stubborn girl. "I know your mother taught you, but I doubt she taught you enough for court. You'll need to study this, so your grandparents don't become suspicious about your deportment lessons."

Cassandra sighed but uncrossed her arms and accepted the book as the carriage slowed to a stop.

Wren glanced out the window at Rhiannon's Veils. A chill skittered across her skin. "We're here." Please let this go well.

Once they climbed from the carriage, Wren instructed her driver to return in an hour then led Cassandra inside the witch shop. The pervasive incense was stronger than before, causing her nausea to resurge. Oh no. She swallowed then called, "Madam witch, we require your assistance."

The veiled witch swept through the door of glass beads at the back, her exotically lined eyes darting between Wren and Cassandra. "Miss Keyes, who have you brought me?"

Wren rested her hand on Cassandra's shoulder and met the witch's gaze. "This is Miss Cassandra Weston, a friend of mine." She hesitated. How would the veiled witch react to this? "She's another Rhiannon descendant and requires a tutor."

Although the veiled witch didn't move, the sense of magic in the shop surged like the ocean during a hurricane. "*Another* Rhiannon descendant? What makes you think there's even one?"

Although Cassandra glared at the veiled witch, Wren suppressed a shiver. However, she lifted her chin and replied, "Because only a Rhiannon descendant could have created the spell I purchased here."

The veiled witch snorted, and the sense of magic waned to normal. "A spell that's still active, I see. You should have burned it as I said before."

Wren winced. Except if she did, Hawke would realize she'd been Rowan, and he'd never forgive her. But they weren't here about that. She nodded at Cassandra, who was eyeing her since the veiled witch had mentioned the glamour spell. "And Cassandra here has the same air of magic as you, madam witch."

The veiled witch tilted her head. "True enough." Her bracelets and tiny bells jingling, she beckoned to Cassandra. "Come here, child."

Cassandra crossed her arms and remained beside Wren. "I'm not a child."

A sigh undulated the older witch's black veils, and she glided across the room to grasp Cassandra's chin. "Who are your parents? I sense too much wildness in your magic for you to be gentry."

Cassandra jerked her chin free. "My mother was a lady, but my magic comes from my gypsy father. His name was Shandor."

As the veiled witch stilled, Wren sighed. So far, the meeting wasn't faring well. Perhaps they should visit Lady Juliet instead. Although then the Westons would find out, and the royal witch might see Wren's connection to the enchanted bird.

But then the veiled witch murmured, "I knew my apprentice would be from Ormas, but I didn't expect to discover her because I sold a reckless glamour spell."

Reckless? Wren opened her mouth to respond, but a wave of blackness swamped her. She staggered and threw her arms about Cassandra to remain upright.

"Miss Wren!" Cassandra clutched Wren.

As her vision cleared, Wren released Cassandra even though her knees still trembled. She flashed a wry smile to reassure the younger girl. "Sorry, I should have eaten more than a roll for breakfast."

The veiled witch snorted. "That was no lack of sustenance. 'Twas someone attempting to probe my spell. Not that they discovered anything."

Wren swallowed to wet her dry throat. The royal witch, no

doubt. But she straightened to her full height. "Never mind that. You and Cassandra must discuss her lessons. I'll wait by the door to watch for the carriage."

Wren stared out the window as Cassandra and the veiled witch talked. Perhaps the veiled witch was right about ending the glamour spell. Hawke had headaches because of it, she nearly fainted when witches probed it, and she still hadn't determined its cost. Yet could she bear to end the glamour spell? She'd lose Hawke if she did. Her throat thickened as tears burned her eyes.

After Wren took Cassandra home and arranged to fetch her next week, she had her driver take her straight to Hawke's parents' townhouse. She was late for the fete play rehearsal, so despite almost fainting before, she'd eat afterward. Hopefully, Hawke wouldn't notice. He'd scold if he did.

Kit swished into the entrance hall just as Perkins One ushered Wren inside. Her empty stomach clenched. She didn't need Kit's needling right now. Why was Kit always around at the worst times?

Kit smiled, although her eyes flashed. "Ah, Wren. Hawke and I were just speaking of you."

Wren blinked at her. What had Hawke said? Kit appeared angry rather than smug like usual. "Nothing negative, I trust."

Kit snickered. "From Hawke? Of course not. He's besotted with you."

Weight compressed Wren's chest. If only that were true. He'd not pursue Rowan or other lovers then. "Hawke's not besotted with me."

Kit tossed her head. "He is but doesn't realize it." She finally smirked at Wren. "So I can still beguile the fool into marrying me."

Wren paled and jerked back. "You'd marry Hawke believing he loves someone else?" Seducing him while disguised by a glamour spell was nothing compared to that.

Her mouth pinched, Kit arched a brow. "Why not? He possesses a fortune, and 'tisn't as if *I* love him."

Wren gaped at Kit. "But then neither of you could marry someone you love." Didn't Kit want that?

Kit snorted. "Naïve little Wren. You can't imagine not marrying for love. But love doesn't put food in your stomach, gowns on your back, or friends by your side. It just makes you vulnerable. Look at you—so in love with Hawke that you can't tell him or find another husband. I pity you."

As Kit swept outside, Wren whispered back, "I pity *you*." A creak drew her gaze to Perkins One rigid by the door. How embarrassing. She swallowed then smiled at the butler. "Have all my players arrived?"

Perkins One inclined a stiff bow. "Yes, Miss Keyes. Some time ago."

She nodded. Unsurprising considering how late she was. She trudged to the ballroom. Please let her make it through the fete play rehearsal without fainting.

CHAPTER 46

Sprawled in his usual seat, Hawke kept glancing at the ballroom door for Wren. *Where* was she? He tensed. Something must be wrong. He was about to leave to fetch her when she finally arrived.

He scrutinized Wren as she sat beside him. Was she well? She was wan, and her movements stiff. She looked worse than when she'd been writing the fete play. He must ask her what was wrong after rehearsal.

Wren smoothed her hair with a wry smile. "Afternoon, sorry I'm late. Shall we get started? Everyone take their places for the final scene. We'll start there and work backward."

Everyone darted into position, and the rehearsal began. However, Hawke performed the play by rote and eyed Wren the entire time. When she sank into a chair, he halted midway through the demon's rant about granting wishes for the pure of heart. Was Wren unwell? From lack of sleep again or something worse?

Wren glared and tapped her foot. "Hawke, what's wrong with you? You never botch that rant."

He flushed. Concern for her was what was wrong, but he

couldn't ask her with his family present, so he shrugged. "Sorry, I was distracted."

Wren pursed her lips. "Well, pay attention." She turned to Elise with a smile. "Start from where you curse the demon with the magical heirloom."

The rehearsal resumed, and Hawke managed his lines even though he still eyed Wren. Other than sitting instead of pacing as usual, she acted normal during the rest of rehearsal and still managed to exhaust everyone from her seat.

After rehearsal, he fetched Wren a heaped plate of sweet biscuits, which she devoured with more appetite than she'd shown for the past several weeks. Something was definitely going on, but what? His stomach clenched.

Hawke said nothing while his family discussed the new sirenic play then the foundering nightmara negotiations. When would they finally leave? He must talk with Wren. He darted glances at her during the interminable conversation. Like him, she remained silent. Eventually the others left, and he pounced. "Are you well?"

Wren wrinkled her nose. "Of course. My visit with Cassandra ran long, so I hadn't time for luncheon."

Fire flashed through him. Why did the ninny keep avoiding food lately? She must stop disregarding her health. He gritted a smile. "You'll make yourself ill if you don't quit skipping meals."

Wren scowled and set aside her empty plate. "I didn't intend to skip luncheon. But enough about that. Tell me about your visit to the royal witch."

Hawke eyed Wren for a long moment. If he continued admonishing her, she'd simply storm home. Besides, he ached to share his disappointing visit with her. He sighed. "There's not much to tell. Lady Juliet couldn't decipher more than we already knew, so I'm no closer to finding Rowan." Unfortunately.

Wren's hazel eyes flickered. "Oh dear. What shall you try now?"

He shrugged. "The witch shops again, but after the fete."

Wren couldn't help until then, and he must find his fete play accessory tomorrow anyway. The day after tomorrow was the fete play's dress rehearsal, and Wren would scold if he didn't find something suitable by then.

So after Hawke escorted Wren home and ordered her to eat and rest, he spent the evening attempting to find an accessory representing a demon. But he found nothing, so he must go shopping tomorrow to find one. Wonderful.

At breakfast the following morning, Hawke was steeling himself to visit the shops when he received a note from Buford requesting a meeting because the arachne silk had reached port. A reprieve! He chuckled and devoured the rest of his breakfast. He could go shopping before tomorrow's dress rehearsal. He might even know what to buy by then.

He rode to Buford's warehouse then sprawled in the chair before the merchant's desk. "The arachne silk arrived already? Why so early?"

Buford shrugged. "Favorable winds." A smile creased his weathered face. "Arachne silk, eh? Clever name."

Hawke grinned. Because Wren had named it. "I'll tell Wren you said so."

Buford chuckled and leaned back in his chair. "That Wren of yours is a treasure."

Hawke's heart squeezed. "I know." And the arachne silk might help other gentlemen see that. His stomach hardened. "She's wearing the sample bolt at Mother's fete the day after tomorrow. I decided her wearing it would sell the arachne silk better than Mother."

Buford blinked at him. "Why?"

Hawke shrugged. "Because Wren never wears extravagant gowns, so the arachne silk shall appear even more dramatic." No doubt its magic had aroused his bizarre hunger to kiss her at

Celeste's. He quelled the tingle echoing across his skin. Damned arachne silk.

Buford nodded, lacing his fingers. "Makes sense. Should I hold the arachne silk until after the Duchess of Childes's fete then?"

Hawke rubbed his chin. "No, send it out now. Court has been gossiping about it for weeks and knows Wren is wearing it at the fete, so as soon as they see it, they'll rush to purchase it." Exactly as he'd planned.

Buford grinned like a smug sphinx demanding travelers answer his obscure riddle. "I'll distribute the shipment to our usual suppliers today. Then we'll be prepared for the rush. And I'll dispatch a ship back to Mist Isle for another shipment."

As the merchant finished, his office door burst open, and a blonde girl sailed into the room. Once Buford and Hawke rose, she kissed Buford's cheek and slanted Hawke a coquettish glance. "Morning, Papa."

Buford beamed at her. "Morning, nymph. Hawke, I don't believe you've met my daughter Marianne. Marianne, this is Lord Beza."

Marianne fluttered her lashes at Hawke. "Papa's noble friend?" When Hawke nodded, she gushed, "Tell me, was the king's summer masquerade as magical as they say? Did a mermaid truly steal the king's heart? I wish we could have attended, but Papa said merchants, even wealthy ones, don't receive invitations to court dos."

Hawke almost laughed. Did the girl ever breathe? "I wouldn't call the masquerade magical, and I didn't meet Devon's mermaid. I'd already left before she arrived." Because he'd met Rowan. Tingling warmth suffused him.

Marianne pouted. "How dull." She inhaled, no doubt to prattle again.

Buford chuckled. "Why did you stop by, nymph?"

Marianne turned to her father and flashed a dulcet smile. "To ask if you'll take me to the Smith's party tonight. You left for the warehouse before I could ask."

A grimace flitting across his face, Buford nodded. "If you like."

Hawke almost laughed again. His merchant friend must despise parties almost as much as Wren.

Marianne bounced with a squeal. "Oh, lovely! I'll go get ready." She swirled from the office.

As they resumed their seats, Hawke coughed to disguise his laughter. "Loves parties, does she?"

Buford sighed. "Unfortunately. I should hire a chaperone to accompany her. My wife died three years ago, and I don't care for parties myself."

Clearly. Hawke shook his head. Poor Buford, raising a teenage daughter alone. Must be horrible. "Just make sure to hire someone reliable. Young people can get into trouble with a neglectful chaperone."

Buford nodded. "I'll have my people vet my chaperone. They hear everything." He leaned forward. "In fact, they've heard you've begun haunting witch shops all over Ormas. And you were never one to fancy magic. Made me concerned about my best investor."

Hawke stiffened, his neck burning. How much of Ormas knew about his visits to witch shops? Were those rumors why their parents had proposed he and Wren marry? He must find Rowan to end their meddling. He forced a shrug. "I found a spell and am attempting to locate its creator. To no avail. Even the royal witch couldn't help."

Buford frowned and tapped the desk. "Peculiar. I could have my people look for you. I'm sure you've only visited the best witch shops, and witches are sometimes... less than reputable."

Hawke nodded. "Yes, but only a fashionable witch shop sold this spell." Rowan was too genteel to visit a less than reputable shop.

Buford arched his brows. "Even so, my people would find a witch who'll tell you more about your spell."

Hawke's pulse surged. True, the merchant's people could learn things no one would ever tell the son of a wealthy duke. And he'd had no success hunting himself. He nodded again. "Very well, have your people start looking. But they must find an extraordinary witch. According to Lady Juliet, an incredibly powerful Rhiannon descendant created my spell."

Buford whistled, his eyes widening. "Impressive. I'll write when I have word of a witch who can help you."

His chest light for the first time since visiting Lady Juliet, Hawke shook the merchant's hand. "Thanks for your assistance." Would he find Rowan at last? Please, Goddess.

Buford grinned. "Not a problem. If you're distracted by your mysterious spell, you can't focus on important matters—like selling the arachne silk." He waggled his brows.

Hawke chuckled at the merchant's jest. Buford hadn't offered to earn a profit; he'd offered because he was a true friend. "I'll endeavor to remember those important matters. Until later."

Bursting with energy, he raced home as fast as the crowded streets of Ormas would allow. He'd tell Wren about Buford's offer after today's rehearsal. He halted at the corner of Mermaid Street and Mountainglass Lane. Or perhaps not. With the fete play the day after tomorrow, she didn't need any distractions. He'd tell her after the fete play instead. He nodded and urged his gelding back to a trot.

CHAPTER 47

*O*nce the fete play's dress rehearsal began, Wren checked everyone's accessory, but when she got to Hawke, his hands were empty. Her eyes narrowing, she pursed her lips. "Where's your accessory? You can't wear a black mask like you did at the masquerade."

She froze as her pulse quickened. Despite telling her about Rowan and their enchanted night, Hawke had never mentioned his lack of costume. Her annoyance had loosened her tongue. Had he noticed?

But Hawke merely winced and rubbed his temple. "I went shopping this morning but had no success. I swear I'll find something by tomorrow."

Her chest tightened. He'd another headache because of her slip. Perhaps 'twould fade if they settled his accessory. "Father has a horned mask I can lend you."

Hawke flashed a crooked grin. "Thanks. You're the best friend ever."

Wren almost winced. No, she wasn't. She'd seduced him using a glamour spell then continued deceiving him about it. Forcing a smile, she turned to the others. "Everyone else, please don your accessory, and we'll run the fete play from the beginning. And just like tomorrow, no stopping for mistakes."

Everyone darted into position and began the fete play. Unlike with the orphans, she didn't mouth their words but said them in her head as she paced before them. They finished the play with few errors. She sighed. They were ready. Thank the Goddess.

She beamed at everyone as they devoured tea. "Excellent rehearsal. Some advice for tomorrow. We've spent the last few weeks perfecting the fete play, but tomorrow, relax and enjoy it. No one at the fete knows our lines, so if we mess up, continue on, and they'll never know."

Edouard grinned over his teacup. "So if we mess up, do it with style?"

Wren nodded. "Exactly. Although I doubt any of you shall." But their performance didn't worry her—court's reaction did. Would her simple play satisfy censorious court ladies like Kit? Please, Goddess.

Wren echoed that prayer the following evening while Abby helped her into the arachne silk ballgown. Once the maid arranged her hair in a complicated coronet threaded with emeralds, she glided over to her mirror. Something was missing, so she asked for her emerald firegem necklace. Yet even with the necklace, something was still missing.

Wren narrowed her eyes at her reflection. Perhaps there was too much green. She pricked her finger and touched her ballgown. After a moment, gold wrens bursting into flight bloomed in the dark-green fabric, starting at her hem by her right ankle, swirling around her flowing skirt, and ending beneath her heart.

Her stomach quivering, she swallowed and smoothed her ballgown. She was as ready as she'd ever be. So she descended downstairs to meet her parents in the entrance hall.

Mother beamed at Wren. "Oh, my dear, you look lovely."

Wren blushed. Only because of Celeste's artistry and the arachne silk. "Thanks."

Father's eyes gleamed. "I'll have the two most beautiful ladies on my arm tonight. Although I doubt I'll keep one of them for long."

Mother threaded her arm through his. "And the other, you'll take with you to your grave."

Her parents' love momentarily calming her stomach, Wren grinned at them. "'Tis rude to suggest Father shall be burdened with me forever."

Mother and Father chuckled, then Mother tsked and said, "He shan't be. Hawke shall."

Wren's grin vanished. If only. But she'd not debate that with her parents tonight—she'd the fete play to worry about. "Shall we go?"

As they headed to Hawke's parents', her stomach began roiling again. Please let court enjoy the fete play. Please. She swallowed and feigned a smile when they entered the ballroom.

An impish glint flickered in the duchess's eyes. "You're exquisite, Wren. Just *wait* until Hawke sees you."

The duke winked and bowed over Wren's hand. "My son is a lucky gentleman."

Another blush burned Wren's cheeks. Except he didn't want her.

Selena dimpled. "You'll sell Hawke's entire shipment by the end of the first dance."

Aragon chuckled and shook his head. "No doubt as he intended, although I doubt he's prepared for that ballgown."

Really? Wren blushed harder. Perhaps Hawke *would* almost kiss her like he had at Celeste's. Tingling swept across her skin. She thanked his family then excused herself to glide to the back of the ballroom.

Her stomach quivered again as she approached the cerulean curtain beneath the musicians' balcony. Soon court would be watching her fete play before that curtain. Was everything ready? All her players, including Hawke, waited near the curtain, so probably.

Wren swallowed as she eyed him, her heart throbbing in her throat. Goddess, Hawke was so handsome in his evening clothes. Could she disguise her love and desire as mere friendship? She smoothed her ballgown then laid a hand on his arm. "Is everything ready?"

Hawke turned to face her with a crooked grin. His grin fading, he stilled, and his pale-blue eyes darkened.

Fire flashed through her. His gaze was hungry again, like at Celeste's and when she'd been Rowan. If she leaned toward him, would he kiss her? As herself this time?

After several long moments, Hawke ran his free hand through his inky-brown hair. "Wren, you look well."

Wren squeezed his arm, unable to resist a coy smile. His reaction proved she looked better than *well*. Light filled her chest. "Well enough to sell the arachne silk?"

His breathing erratic, Hawke swallowed and eyed her lips. "Yes."

Her pulse surged. He definitely burned to kiss her again. Without a glamour spell. How was that possible? The arachne silk ballgown was amazing.

Wren and Hawke were jolted from their daze when the duke and duchess glided to the front of the ballroom, and the duke boomed, "Thank you all for attending our fete celebrating our first grandchild and future heir." He nodded at Aragon and Selena, and the crowd burst into applause.

When that quieted, the duchess flashed a glittering grin. "And in honor of our grandchild, our dear Miss Keyes has penned a delightful play, which our grandchild's uncles and cousins shall perform." She gestured toward the curtain, and the crowd turned to face the players.

Wren's stomach roiled. Oh, Goddess. She and her players bowed then slipped behind the cerulean curtain. Swallowing to soothe her nausea, she glanced at the others and whispered, "Ready? Remember, mess up with style."

Her players grinned back, then Wren nodded at Mel to start, her pulse skittering. Please let this go well. The crowd murmured when Mel strode through the curtain wearing pointed ears and a white robe, but they hushed as he began his introduction. Her chest eased. So far, so good.

Soon Edouard and Pippa, wearing matching crowns, joined Mel and petitioned him for a child. The crowd chuckled when Elise swept onstage wearing a tiara. Wren sighed, and her stomach settled. Good, court was amused at least. Hopefully, 'twould last.

Mel left after describing Elise growing in wisdom and beauty, and her suitors, Dane with a broadsword and Xavier with a rapier, strode onstage. The crowd laughed as they bickered to impress Elise. Wren smiled—time for the demon.

A servant lowered a black curtain, and Hawke, wearing his horned mask, burst through. The crowd's laughter ceased when he cackled and threatened to abduct Elise. Then the crowd gasped as Xavier, Edouard, and Pippa distracted Hawke to allow Dane to escape with Elise. Warmth flooded Wren. Her simple play had engrossed court.

The crowd oohed when Elise and Dane unearthed a magical heirloom just before Hawke discovered them. Then Elise cursed Hawke to spend eternity granting wishes to those with a pure heart, and the crowd cheered. Wren grinned. Court was still enthused.

After Hawke ranted about his curse then stumbled behind the curtain, Dane begged Elise to marry him. The crowd cooed as she accepted him, and all the players but Hawke burst forth for their wedding. Wren drew a deep breath. Court enjoyed her romantic ending.

As Mel described Elise's happy life with Dane, the other players returned behind the curtain, and the crowd quieted. Then Mel exited as well, and the crowd remained eerily silent.

Wren tensed, and her stomach clenched. Had court not enjoyed her play after all?

Then the ballroom erupted into thundering applause. Her chest swelled. Court had simply been too entranced to applaud at first. She pushed Elise through the curtain to take a bow before shooing the others behind her. Her players deserved the attention.

On his way out, Hawke grasped her wrist and pulled her behind him. Her nausea resurged. She couldn't go out there. She attempted to jerk free, but he dragged her through the curtain.

Her entire body burned as she bowed. Please let the applause end soon. Although accolade, not scorn, this much attention was embarrassing.

At last, the duchess quieted the crowd and announced the first dance. Thank the Goddess.

His grip still firm about her wrist, Hawke arched his brows at Wren. "Shall we?"

She swallowed, her heart fluttering. She hungered to dance with Hawke again, but could she hide her love if she did? She peeked at him through her lashes. How could she resist one last dance?

Wren licked her lips then nodded, and Hawke drew her into his arms. Unable to glance up or speak without revealing her love, she trembled as tingling suffused her during their dance. If only she could act on her desire like she had as Rowan.

CHAPTER 48

s they twirled about the ballroom, Hawke kept his gaze on the emeralds gleaming in Wren's auburn hair. 'Twould be dangerous to look lower—she was more bewitching than a siren's song in her arachne silk ballgown. Why had he given her the magical fabric? All the gentlemen would mob her.

Her violet scent weaving about him, he forced himself to keep the proper dancing distance. What would Wren feel like nestled against him? Heat flashed across his skin, and his intimate dance with Rowan in the palace gardens echoed through him. Why had he thought about that while dancing with Wren? Agony pierced his head.

As Wren began trembling in his arms, Hawke glanced down and was ensnared. Her treacherous ballgown displayed most of her breasts, and her emerald firegem only accentuated that. Dear Goddess. His body hardening, he drew her closer until her dark-green skirt brushed his legs.

As the music faded, they stilled, but he couldn't release her. Why was he reacting to her like this again?

Wren raised her gaze, her hazel eyes dark, and she swayed toward him. Did she feel the same bizarre desire he did?

His heart surging, Hawke began lowering his head to kiss

her. Would she taste as sweet as Rowan? He froze. What was *wrong* with him? He couldn't kiss Wren in the middle of his parents' ballroom. Not only would Wren slap him, but Rowan would never court him once he found her.

He jerked back. He met Wren's dark gaze, and his body throbbed again. Damned arachne silk. He must escape before he destroyed their friendship. Unable to form words, even to apologize, he fled toward the refreshments table as if chased by hellhounds.

Hawke was guzzling a flute of sparkling wine and pretending not to notice Wren disappear onto the middle balcony when Kit caressed his arm. He twitched away and glared at her. "Kit, what are you about?"

Kit arched her brows. "Dispelling rumors about you and Wren. If you don't want everyone assuming you seduced her, you'd best dance with me."

He stiffened. Because of the fete play and arachne silk, the entire ballroom had been watching Wren, so they'd seen his bizarre reaction to her. Goddess, Kit was right. Everyone would assume he'd seduced Wren. He must protect her from such rumors. So he set his jaw and took Kit's arm.

As they began to dance, Kit's smoky eyes glinted. "If you want anyone to believe this, you must act like you mean it."

Except he didn't mean it. A flush burning his neck, Hawke gritted a smile. How long would this dance last?

Kit chuckled. "Better. Now tell me, what witch shop enchanted Wren's ballgown? Even Celeste couldn't sew such a bewitching ballgown."

He tensed but maintained his smile. How dare Kit disparage Wren? Spiteful harpy. "Wren's ballgown isn't enchanted. She'd never wear an enchanted gown. I could barely convince her to wear the arachne silk to help sell it, and 'tis merely woven by a magical creature and contains nothing but residual magic."

Kit smirked and tilted her head. "Ah, the arachne silk. *That's* why you held her after your dance. To heighten its allure."

Hawke hurled Kit in a complicated twirl. If only that were true, but selling the arachne silk hadn't occurred to him. He'd been too enthralled by Wren's allure. Tingling flashed across his skin again.

Still smirking, Kit tsked. "But 'tis really too bad of you to tease Wren like that, considering how she feels about you."

He stumbled as his stomach tensed. Wren merely felt friendship for him. Why would Kit smirk about friendship? He frowned at her. "What do you mean by that?"

Kit purred a chuckle. "Nothing."

Hawke eyed her. She meant *something*, but what? The music faded before he could reply, so he bowed instead. Thank the Goddess their dance was over. He could escape Kit now that Wren was safe from court gossip.

As he began walking away, Kit grasped his arm. "Another dance, I think."

His chest tightening, he extracted his arm. "No. One was enough." More than enough.

Kit fluttered her lashes. "I'll continue pursuing you until you submit."

Hawke shuddered. She would too. He never should have danced with her. She was too determined to trap him. How could he escape without drawing attention? He relaxed when Mother glided over with Mel. She'd rescue him, doubtless to match him with Wren. But he could handle that—probably.

Mother beamed at Kit. "I must steal Hawke for the next dance. If you wish another dance with one of my sons, you must settle for Mel instead."

Kit glowered at Mel. "I didn't think priests danced."

Mel straightened his white robe then offered Kit his arm. "They do if their mothers command them. 'Tisn't as if dancing were amoral."

Hawke almost chuckled. Mel's subtle insult would irk Kit. She deserved it after disparaging Wren.

Kit scowled but took Mel's arm. "How can I refuse such a flattering offer?" She slanted Hawke a coy glance. "Until later, Hawke."

Hawke winced. He'd be sure to hide later. Once Mel and Kit began dancing, Hawke turned to Mother with a crooked smile. "Thanks for the well-timed rescue." Her meddling had been welcome for once.

Mother nodded. "Of course, but you really should have Wren handle these matters. Now, where is she? I've not seen her since your dance."

Hadn't Wren returned from the balcony? He scanned the ball-room, but she wasn't there. He tensed. She must still be recovering from the fete play. Or had his almost kiss distressed her? He almost winced. Since Wren didn't need Mother pestering her, he shrugged with a bland smile. "I don't know. I'm not Wren's keeper."

Mother's eyes narrowed. "What did you do to her during your dance?"

Hawke forced himself to remain still. "Nothing." Except almost kiss her.

Mother muttered something too faint for him to hear.

His stomach tightened. What was she plotting now? He arched a brow. "What was that?"

Mother pursed her lips as she took his arm. "Never mind. Shall we greet some guests?"

As he and Mother spoke with various guests, Hawke kept eyeing the balcony, but Wren never emerged. Where was she? Even she didn't avoid dancing so much. Goddess, was she hiding from him? What had he done by almost kissing her?

When the music faded again, Mother glided over to Devon, who was escorting the beauteous Lady Annalise Greysnowe from the dance to the refreshments table. Mother beamed at Devon as he selected two flutes of sparkling wine. "Enjoying my fete so far?"

"As always." Devon handed a flute to Lady Annalise with a

smile. "'Tis nice to forget the nightmara and dance with a beautiful lady."

Sipping her sparkling wine, Lady Annalise coolly inclined her white-blonde head at the king before turning to Hawke. "I enjoyed Miss Keyes's play, almost as much as you seemed to enjoy playing the villain, Lord Beza."

Hawke suppressed a grimace at his given name. "Playacting is diverting." Although he'd barely remembered his lines after seeing Wren in her arachne silk ballgown.

Lady Annalise's cerulean eyes flickered. "I've not found it so, but I suppose it depends on your purpose."

Mother chuckled. "It depends on your temperament too, but Hawke always was a scampish child."

As Mother asked Lady Annalise about her ballgown, Hawke murmured to Devon, "Could you check on Wren for me? She slipped onto the middle balcony a while ago. I don't want to draw Mother's eye to her, but if I leave Mother, Kit shall attempt to trap me again." And who knew what his treacherous body might do if he encountered Wren alone?

Devon smiled. "Certainly. Although 'tis rare for a king to be asked to perform a discreet errand."

Mother and Lady Annalise finished discussing ballgowns, and Devon led Lady Annalise toward the balconies. As they left, the Westons joined Hawke and Mother.

After she and her husband greeted Mother, Lady Weston turned to Hawke, her eyes crinkling with laughter. "Fine performance."

Lord Weston grinned and nodded. "Your Miss Keyes is a marvelous writer. I enjoyed this play as much as the last."

Lady Weston added, "And so kind. Few would take our foundling granddaughter to her former governess for deportment lessons."

Hawke blinked. Wren's former governess was happily married to a gentleman near their parents' country estates, so wherever she was taking Cassandra, 'twasn't deportment lessons. But he only replied, "I'm glad everything is going well."

Lady Weston beamed. "Yes, Cassandra has been much improved since Miss Keyes visited."

Hawke managed a nod even though his neck prickled. What was Wren doing with Cassandra? And why hadn't she mentioned it? All she'd told him was that she was visiting Cassandra during his appointment with the royal witch.

As Lord Ravenstone replaced the Westons, Hawke glanced about the ballroom for Devon. Lady Annalise's parents had waylaid him and their daughter before the middle balcony. Hawke's chest clenched. How long would it take for Devon to escape the Greysnowes? Devon must check on Wren at once—something might be wrong.

Hawke swallowed. Perhaps he should risk Kit's pursuit and his unruly body to check on Wren himself. He'd go after Lord Ravenstone left.

CHAPTER 49

$\mathcal{W}$ren sighed and rubbed her forehead as she stared down at the inky garden. She'd been leaning against the parapet of the middle balcony for a while, but her limbs still trembled after the fete play and her dance with Hawke.

She licked her lips and inhaled the balmy summer air. Goddess, had Hawke really almost kissed her during their dance —in his parents' crowded ballroom with all of court watching? The arachne silk ballgown was even more potent than she'd realized. When he'd fled afterward, she'd escaped to the balcony to recover from the desire and exhaustion overwhelming her. But she'd return once her trembling ceased.

Suddenly, something rustled behind her and broke her reverie. Her heart surged. Had Hawke joined her? To sneak a kiss perhaps? She pivoted, and her smile faded. Not Hawke. "Mr. Winston, why are you here when the fete is inside?"

Backlit by the glow from the ballroom, Mr. Winston smirked. "Why are *you*, with the loveliest ballgown at the fete?"

A chill skittering her skin at the growl in his voice, Wren began edging past him to return inside. Mr. Winston wasn't safe company for a lady, especially one with a rich dowry.

Mr. Winston seized her wrist. "You can't leave yet, my dear, not when we've just begun to talk."

She struggled to free herself as Mr. Winston shoved her back against the parapet. Her chest froze. Oh, Goddess. She must escape.

When she attempted to kick his shin like she had at Aragon and Selena's marriage ball, Mr. Winston dodged with a snicker. "Such a feisty filly. But I'm wise to your tricks now."

Her head bent to avoid his mouth, Wren thrashed harder as Mr. Winston pressed against her. Her stomach roiled. He wrenched up her chin with his free hand. She shivered at his expression. Unlike his previous attempt to kiss her, his eyes were dark with wrath rather than lust. He'd not stop at a mere kiss. She thrashed again.

"Miss Keyes?"

At the king's voice, Mr. Winston stepped back and turned to stutter a bow but maintained his crushing grip on her wrist. "Your majesty, how nice to see you."

King Devon smiled at Wren as he escorted Lady Annalise onto the balcony. "Are you ready to rejoin the fete, Miss Keyes?"

Wren's chest lightened. Rescue, thank the Goddess. She yanked her wrist free as Mr. Winston ogled the beauteous Lady Annalise. "Yes, your majesty."

King Devon turned to Mr. Winston, his green eyes narrowing. "We shan't require your assistance, Winston. I believe you should retire for the evening."

Mr. Winston scowled but bowed and left without a word.

The last of her tension easing, Wren rubbed her aching wrist. "Thank you, your majesty." She'd not have escaped without his timely rescue.

King Devon released Lady Annalise to stride forward and inspect Wren's wrist. "What was that about?"

Wren grimaced. "Anger at Hawke, no doubt. Hawke pitched him over a balcony when he pestered me before, and they quarreled recently. So Mr. Winston had to prove he could defy

Hawke's threats." She shivered again. He'd almost succeeded too. Escaping to a secluded balcony hadn't been prudent despite her need to recover.

As Lady Annalise shook her white-blonde head, King Devon released Wren's wrist. "I see." He eyed Wren. "Are you well enough to return inside?"

She'd rather return home and go to bed, but Mother and the duchess wouldn't allow that. Wren suppressed a sigh but nodded. "Yes. I was about to return when Mr. Winston waylaid me."

King Devon escorted Wren and Lady Annalise inside then strode across the ballroom to fetch Wren some tea.

Wren's neck prickled as silence stretched between her and Lady Annalise. Like everyone except perhaps the king, she didn't know the icy beauty well. What could they discuss? Lady Annalise wouldn't be interested in the orphanage or plays, and Wren despised fashion and court.

After a moment, Lady Annalise drawled, "I suppose the Duchess of Childes *had* to invite Ravenstone."

Wren followed the other lady's gaze to where the genial count was speaking with Hawke and the duchess. Hawke met her eyes, and even from across the room, desire crackled between them. Doubtless due to the arachne silk. Her skin tingling, she wrenched her eyes from Hawke to answer Lady Annalise, "The duchess is powerful enough to disregard the Greysnowe-Ravenstone feud if she likes. And apparently, she does."

Lady Annalise pursed her lips. "I suppose, but I hate encountering the wretch."

Wren blinked. Had the inscrutable Lady Annalise revealed something personal? Surely not. Perhaps she didn't consider it personal, given the centuries-long feud.

Lady Annalise turned to Wren with a glittering smile. "Your ballgown is magnificent—even better than your dryad costume at the king's summer masquerade."

Wren's breath froze. Lady Annalise knew she'd been Rowan? Dear Goddess.

Lady Annalise continued, "The fabric is arachne silk, yes? The one Lord Beza just imported."

Wren gulped a ragged breath. Lady Annalise must be guessing. No one had followed her and Hawke into the gardens, and they'd avoided notice when they'd left. She lifted her chin. "Yes, 'tis arachne silk, but I didn't attend the masquerade."

Lady Annalise arched her brows. "If you count gracing the ballroom as attending, then yes, you didn't attend. But you were in the gardens dancing scandalously close to Lord Beza."

Wren paled as bile burned her throat. Lady Annalise had *seen* them? But how? She hadn't seen Lady Annalise. To brazen out her lie, she met Lady Annalise's gaze. "I'm afraid you're still mistaken, but gardens at night are too dark for clear sight, hence their affinity for dalliance. I'm surprised you ventured into one."

Lady Annalise's cerulean eyes flickered. "After the king met his mermaid, I required air."

Wren stared at Lady Annalise. King Devon had been escorting Lady Annalise for over three years—wasn't she upset he'd found another lady? Wren shook her head. But who cared about that? She must ensure Lady Annalise no longer believed she'd attended the masquerade. 'Twould be hideous if rumors started.

But before she could protest further, Lady Annalise flicked a graceful wave. "'Tis been pleasant talking with you, Miss Keyes, but I must go refresh myself. I look forward to your happy announcement with Lord Beza."

Wren winced as Lady Annalise glided away. Lady Annalise still knew she'd been Rowan. But perhaps that was fine. Lady Annalise was discreet as a sphinx entrusted with a secret riddle, and no rumors had started so far. It could be much worse—Kit could have been in the palace gardens instead.

She was shuddering at that when Hawke appeared beside her with a cup of tea. "Your tea."

Her heart fluttering, Wren tilted her head and accepted the steaming teacup. "I thought King Devon was fetching it."

Hawke shrugged, his jaw rigid. "I intercepted him at the refreshments table. He told me about Winston. Are you all right?"

She hid a shiver as she sipped her tea. She mustn't feed Hawke's outrage. "Yes, the king handled him."

Hawke grunted and clenched his hands. "I should kill Winston for pestering you."

Wren winced. Except Hawke would likely get caught. To soothe him, she flashed a grin. "Don't bother. 'Twould cause gossip and stain your clothes beyond repair."

Hawke snorted. "Now *that's* a reason not to commit murder."

She set aside her teacup to grasp his arm. "Hawke, please. Don't pursue Mr. Winston. I couldn't bear if harm befell you because of me." Her throat cramped. Like persistent headaches due to her glamour spell.

Hawke laid his hand over hers. "Very well. But I'll not relent if Winston pesters you again."

They stepped apart when their mothers strolled over. The duchess eyed her son with a faint smile and said, "A new dance is about to start. Take Wren out onto the floor."

Mother pursed her lips. "Yes, Wren has hardly danced tonight."

Wren almost winced. Of course, Mother had noticed that. But if Hawke held her again, she might act on her desire and kiss him before all of court. "I'm too fatigued to dance." Not exactly a lie.

The duchess tsked at Wren. "You must remember to rest before balls, else you'll never last."

'Twas impossible to rest while fretting over court's reaction to your play. Yet Wren inclined her head. "I promise to be livelier at the next one."

The duchess tsked again. "Escort Wren home instead, Hawke."

Mother shook her head at Wren. "And you go straight to bed. No writing." Then she and the duchess turned and sailed across the ballroom.

Hawke muttered, "You'd be more lively tonight if Mother hadn't coerced you into writing the fete play." He offered his arm. "Shall we?"

Wren nodded and threaded her arm through his, her limbs heavy. She truly was exhausted.

Hawke escorted her home, but unlike when she'd been Rowan, he held her at the proper distance on the short walk.

Yet tingling warmth suffused her at his touch, and she was trembling again as they climbed her front steps. She burned for another kiss. While they stared at each other without a word, she licked her lips.

His pale-blue eyes dark, Hawke began lowering his head. Goddess, he was about to kiss her again. Finally.

Her heart surged as she swayed toward him. But then her front door creaked open.

Like in the ballroom earlier, Hawke jerked away as if stung by a swarm of deadly melissae protecting their hive. He muttered a goodbye and fled down the steps.

Wren stared after him. Twice tonight Hawke had almost kissed her. The arachne silk ballgown must be irresistible. He'd not be so tempted otherwise.

CHAPTER 50

*H*is body hard and throbbing, Hawke bolted home. How could he have almost kissed Wren again? Was he *trying* to destroy their friendship?

He burst into his chambers and ripped off his cravat and evening coat. The arachne silk had bewitched him. He'd not be lusting after Wren otherwise. But 'twould cease once he found Rowan. He'd resume his hunt first thing tomorrow.

Yet resuming his hunt involved visiting Wren, so Hawke delayed until after luncheon. She needed the morning to recover from the fete, and he needed time to forget his bizarre reaction to her. But once he bolted several rolls stuffed with meat and cheese, he made himself head to Wren's. He joined her in the conservatory, only to halt inside the threshold.

Pallid with bloodless lips and bruise-like smudges under her eyes, Wren sat reading beneath a lymon tree. Somehow even her auburn hair seemed muted. Goddess, what was wrong? Had the arachne silk siphoned its allure from her? It shouldn't have done that, but it shouldn't have bewitched him either. He sat beside her, his chest clenching. "Wren?"

Wren sighed then met his gaze, her hazel eyes dull. "I suppose you're here to discuss your hunt for Rowan."

Hawke winced. He had been, but he couldn't discuss that with Wren so unwell. What could they discuss instead? "No, I'm here to discuss the fete. Everyone adored your play."

Wren shuddered, gripping her book. "Thank the Goddess, but I'm *never* writing another play for court."

He winked and flashed a crooked grin to tease her. "Too bad. I enjoyed playing the villain."

Wren snorted. "Of course you did. You'll have to content yourself with playing the rakehell instead."

Hawke stiffened, and his grin faded. "That no longer appeals. I just want Rowan." How had Wren forgotten that?

Wren's pallid skin turned translucent, and she pressed a trembling hand to her forehead. "I believe I need to lie down."

His chest clenching again, he leapt to help her stand. "I'll take you upstairs." She'd never make it otherwise.

As he half carried her to her chambers, Wren clutched his arm without a word of protest. Not at all like her. She *must* be ill.

Hawke pressed a kiss to her clammy forehead when they reached her door. "Get some rest. I'll visit tomorrow."

Wren wobbled a nod as she trudged inside her chambers.

He frowned after her for a moment then strode home. Whatever was ailing Wren, she'd need several days to fully recover. But he couldn't delay his hunt for Rowan any longer, so he must visit the remaining witch shops without Wren.

He retreated to his study and reread his list of witch shops. He'd eight more left, but they were spread across the fashionable areas of Ormas. Yet if he visited a couple this afternoon, he could manage the rest tomorrow. Which should he start with? Mirage, Esrever, or Bewitching Raiments? His head began to throb.

Before he could decide, Aragon and Mel sauntered into his study.

Hawke stuffed his lists beneath some invitations. His brothers would ask about them, and he couldn't explain without revealing Rowan. If they found out, Mother would too. He suppressed a shudder.

Aragon smiled at Hawke. "We're headed to The Gold Griffin."

Hawke's brows rose. Already? Until three weeks ago, Aragon hadn't visited the rowdy tavern since marrying Selena.

Mel tugged his priest robes. "Yes, I've been craving some fish pie since we didn't eat any last time."

Hawke stiffened, his neck prickling. Mel loved desserts and other sweets—'twas Aragon who adored The Gold Griffin's fish pie, not Mel.

Aragon arched a brow. "Care to join us?"

Hawke eyed his brothers. They were too casual. What were they about? He'd best delay his hunt for Rowan to find out. "Of course."

Hawke followed them into the waiting carriage then spent the ride probing for their true intent, but they evaded his questions. Suspicious. His stomach tightened as they strode into the teeming tavern and sat at a small table along the back wall again.

The plump barmaid slammed down three glowing tankards of gold ale then bustled away to fetch their fish pies.

Once they were alone, Mel studied Hawke over his tankard. "What's been going on with you lately?"

Hawke tensed. So it began. Of course they'd waited until they'd the gold ale to verify his responses. Perhaps 'twouldn't react to a silent answer. He shrugged, and his ale remained bright. Good.

Mel and Aragon exchanged a glance as the barmaid returned with their fish pies. Aragon waited until she'd left again to say, "You've avoided most court events for the past month."

Hawke relaxed with a crooked grin as he began his fish pie. This he could answer with the truth. "I decided to stop attending events that bore me. I told Mother as much."

Mel leaned forward, sipping his ale. "It's not just that. Deacon, a friend who works at Charmed Blessings, saw you and Wren there last week."

His eyes narrow, Aragon ate a bite of fish pie. "And Selena's friends have mentioned you two have visited witch shops all over Ormas. Why the sudden fascination with magic?"

Hawke tensed again and set down his fork. So this was about that. He couldn't explain those rumors without lying, so he repeated his earlier shrug.

Mel frowned. "Is something wrong with Wren? She detests magic and wouldn't enter so many witch shops otherwise."

Hawke shuddered as his chest tightened. Something was definitely wrong with Wren, but 'twasn't related to his hunt for Rowan. "She's been unwell lately, but I assumed 'twas due to the fete play. Mother *never* should have coerced her into writing it." Yet she'd been worse today, so perhaps the fete play wasn't to blame.

Aragon and Mel glanced at each other, then Aragon waved his tankard and asked, "Is that why you acted so peculiar at the fete?"

Hawke widened his eyes. "What do you mean?" His gold ale dimmed. He almost winced. So it reacted to misleading questions. Damnation.

Mel snorted. "Clearly you know. You only danced twice, once with Wren and once with Kit, then held both after their dance ended."

His neck burning, Hawke glared at his brothers. "I didn't hold Kit. She held me." His gold ale brightened again.

Aragon arched a brow. "But what about Wren?" When Hawke shrugged again, he chuckled. "So you *did* hold her. And you never returned after you escorted her home."

Hawke toyed with his tankard. His reaction to Wren's arachne silk had perturbed him too much to return. "I was weary of the fete by then." His ale dimmed at his half-truth.

Aragon and Mel exchanged another glance, longer this time.

To erase their knowing smiles, Hawke added, "And I only held Wren because the arachne silk bewitched me." His gold ale drained of light. He goggled at his tankard. "What? 'Twas the truth."

Mel's mouth twitched. "You must be lying, even to yourself."

While Hawke glared at Mel, Aragon tsked and finished his fish pie. "'Tis obvious to anyone with eyes that you and Wren have been in love for ages. Why do you think she never had suitors? She's pretty, well-bred, and wealthy. 'Twas because everyone knew she was already taken."

His head swirling, Hawke gaped at Aragon. He wasn't in love with Wren, and Wren certainly wasn't in love with him. Aragon couldn't be right, even though his gold ale still shone.

Mel chuckled. "And you've never had serious suitors either. Only lovers who rarely last longer than a week."

Hawke grimaced and gulped some ale. "Kit seems serious to me." Unfortunately.

Mel scowled at his glowing tankard. "Kit is remarkably blind when she wishes to be. Besides, she only pursues you to needle Wren."

Hawke stilled. Everyone truly assumed he and Wren were in love? He drew a ragged breath. Was *that* why Rowan had fled after the masquerade? His chest freezing, he drained his tankard. "Well, everyone is wrong. Wren and I aren't in love."

Aragon's brows rose as he waved for another round. "No? Then why did you ask us those questions about kissing her on Longnight years ago?"

A blush burned Hawke's ears. In the months before that disastrous kiss, he'd consulted his brothers, read books, and plotted every move, but he'd not anticipated her spurning him like she had. "Childish nonsense. Wren and I are merely friends."

Mel shook his head. "Really? I always thought all your lovers were to make Wren jealous. Why else would you have told her all about them?"

Hawke blinked. "Because we're *friends*." And friends shared secrets. And never noticed how kissable the other was. Tingling warmth suffused him.

Aragon and Mel burst into laughter. After a moment, Aragon murmured, "If she did the same, what would you do?"

Fire flashed through Hawke. Hunt down the bounders who seduced Wren and strangle them. He stiffened. What was the matter with him? He shut his eyes as agony seized his head. It meant nothing. As their fresh tankards arrived, he lurched to his feet and threw coins on the table. "I've some matters to attend. I'll see you later."

Hawke bolted from the rowdy tavern, ignoring his brothers' mocking grins. They were wrong. He and Wren were just friends. And he'd prove that once he found Rowan.

CHAPTER 51

After a night of dreamless sleep, Wren woke at her usual time for once. She rang for Abby then stretched like a firecat after a long nap inside a bonfire. She sighed. Too bad she now required utter exhaustion to get decent sleep. Damn Hawke's hunt for Rowan.

As she waited for Abby, her stomach began roiling and her mouth flooded. Not again. She slid from bed and paced on trembling legs to curb her nausea.

Then Abby bustled into her chambers with a laden tray. "Since soup was all I could get you to eat while sleeping yesterday, I brought a full breakfast."

Wren's nausea surged at the scent of eggs and bacon, and she dove for the chamberpot. As she retched with tears trickling down her cheeks, she croaked between heaves, "Take that away. Now!"

As Abby left, Wren vomited until only bile remained. Her sides aching, she collapsed on the floor and leaned against the bed with the chamberpot cradled in her lap. She'd been nauseous lately, but not like this. What was wrong with her?

Abby soon returned with another tray. The maid wiped Wren's face with a cool cloth and thrust out a glass of water.

"Rinse out your mouth, Miss Wren." Once she'd done so, Abby took the chamberpot then exchanged the glass for a steaming mug of mentha tea. "Now drink this." While Wren blew on the tea, Abby held out a plate of dry toast. "And eat this."

Wren shuddered. "I think not." She'd only vomit it, and she couldn't bear that again this morning.

Abby set the plate on the floor beside Wren. "It'll help. I promise."

Wren wrinkled her nose but nibbled the toast. Her stomach spasmed on the first bite, but soon settled. While Abby disposed of the chamberpot and laid out a simple dress, she finished her tea and two pieces of toast, and her nausea faded. Abby had been right. Thank the Goddess.

As Abby helped Wren dress, she murmured, "By my count, 'tis been seven weeks since your courses."

Wren blinked. Really? Her courses were always irregular, so she never tracked them. But doubtless Abby was right. "So?"

The maid coughed then continued, "I believe you're with child."

Wren's breath froze. Her gaze flew to the jewel box on her dressing table containing her contraceptive charm earrings. "Impossible."

Abby pursed her lips. "Is it? I recall your preparations for the king's summer masquerade. 'Twas clear you meant to seduce someone."

A blush burned Wren's cheeks. She definitely had. And it had been an enchanted night. She lifted her chin and met Abby's gaze. "We wore contraceptive charms."

Abby grimaced. "Magic's a chancy thing, even that from healers. Your nausea and exhaustion are both signs of a babe."

Wren collapsed on the corner of her bed, rubbing her forehead. She couldn't be pregnant, could she? Surely her exhaustion was simply due to stress and lack of sleep. And her nausea was due to that exhaustion.

Abby placed her hands on her hips. "If you aren't with child, then you're most unwell. You must see a healer."

Wren forced a nod despite her swirling head. "Check if Healer Althea is available, today if possible."

Abby relaxed then nodded and bustled out.

Wren began pacing about her chambers, her legs trembling again, although no longer due to nausea. Pregnant? Oh, Goddess. Abby must be wrong. But if Abby wasn't, what was she to do? Hawke would never believe she was pregnant with his child unless he burned the enchanted bird and the glamour spell ended. But once it did, would he ever forgive her deceitful seduction? Her stomach spasmed.

She continued pacing until Abby returned an hour later and said, "Healer Althea is able to see you now. I've arranged a carriage."

Wren swallowed and smoothed her dress, her heart skittering. Soon she'd learn what ailed her. Was she ready? She sighed. No, but she must go regardless. She began leaving but paused when Abby moved to follow. "Thanks, Abby, but I wish to visit my healer alone."

Abby's eyes narrowed. "Very well, Miss Wren."

Wren managed a faint smile as she strolled down to the carriage. Her parents and the servants couldn't realize anything might be amiss. Despite her feigned nonchalance, her stomach quivered the entire ride to her healer's. Once she arrived, she inhaled then opened the forest-green door. Time to learn the truth.

Her silver, melissa torc gleaming, Healer Althea's apprentice glanced up from the tome she was reading. She welcomed Wren then rose, waving at the right door. "Go on in. I'll fetch the healer."

Wren swallowed as she entered the consultation room and perched on the sofa along the back wall. Goddess, let her not be pregnant. She began tapping her fingers against her knee while she waited.

Healer Althea strode into the room, the melissae on her gold torc glinting. Although the magical bees marked her a witch healer, she never recklessly used magic and was one of the best healers in Ormas. So Wren had been her patient for years despite distrusting magic. Surely, the healer would swiftly discover whatever ailed her.

A beam brightening her plain features as she sat across from Wren, Healer Althea said, "Good morning, Miss Keyes. Your maid told me you've not been well."

Wren forced her fingers to settle. "Yes, I've been fatigued and nauseous for the past month, but I thought 'twas simply stress. When I vomited this morning, Abby insisted I see you." Please let Abby be wrong. Please.

Healer Althea nodded. "She was quite right to do so. Any other symptoms?"

Wren shrugged. Since they were so irregular, her tardy courses weren't worth mentioning despite Abby's suspicions.

Healer Althea hummed low in her throat. "I'll take a quick look then." Her fingers weaving a complicated pattern, she crooned the spell to invoke her healing sight. After a moment, the healer's brows furrowed.

Her heart pounding, Wren leaned forward. Dear Goddess. That frown wasn't reassuring. "What?"

Healer Althea flicked her fingers to drop her healing sight then smiled at Wren. "You're with child. Five weeks or so along."

Ice burgeoned in Wren's chest as she goggled at the healer. Abby had been right.

She was pregnant.

With Hawke's child.

Oh, Goddess.

She swallowed. Why hadn't the contraceptive charms worked? Was pregnancy the price for the glamour spell? "But we wore contraceptive charms."

Healer Althea eyed her. "Was that spell I sense draining you active when you were intimate?"

Wren stiffened as her neck prickled. The glamour spell was draining her? She managed a nod.

Healer Althea tsked. "You obviously weren't listening when I explained using contraceptive charms."

A blush warming her cheeks, Wren shifted in her seat. No, she'd been too focused on seducing Hawke to listen.

Healer Althea shook her head. "Standard contraceptive charms don't work when the wearer uses or is under the influence of strong magic."

Wren winced. The glamour spell was *definitely* strong magic. And since it influenced her and Hawke, both their contraceptive charms had failed. She licked her lips. "What do witches do?"

Healer Althea's brows flew upward at Wren's irrelevant question. "Witches get contraceptive charms meant to work around strong magic. And before you ask, no one proscribes those to anyone else because they make the wearer vilely ill if strong magic isn't used."

Wren twisted her hands in her skirt. So her pregnancy was due to the glamour spell, but only indirectly. What *was* its price then? She tensed. "You said a spell is draining me?"

Healer Althea frowned. "Yes, and that concerns me. The spell seems incredibly powerful. You said you've been unwell for the past month?" When Wren nodded, the healer's frown deepened. "Much too early for an ordinary pregnancy, so I suspect that spell is to blame."

Wren shivered. No wonder she'd been so exhausted since the masquerade. Not stress or lack of sleep, but the glamour spell had been draining her to continue deceiving Hawke. She gulped a ragged breath, her hands flying to cover her stomach. "Is the spell draining my child?"

Healer Althea's frown eased. "So far your child is faring better than you, but that could change considering the spell's power. I recommend you end it immediately."

Wren jerked a nod. Yes, she must. Even if the glamour spell never endangered their child, a child deserved both parents, and

Hawke would never believe he was the father otherwise. Although he probably wouldn't forgive her, he'd never blame their innocent child. She'd lose Hawke forever, but their child would have a father.

Her throat thickening, Wren set her jaw. "Could you tell me what to expect during pregnancy?" She only knew what little Selena had mentioned. Unlike with the contraceptive charm, she listened as Healer Althea explained pregnancy. She'd not make that mistake again. Once the healer finished, Wren thanked her then headed to Hawke's townhouse.

On the carriage ride, she rubbed her still-flat stomach. How should she approach Hawke? So far, he'd fought burning the enchanted bird because he was obsessed with finding Rowan. But he must end the glamour spell to see the truth. Could she withstand his fury when he did? Her heart quivered.

Yet Hawke was out when she arrived. She nibbled her lip. Should she wait for him? No, she was too rattled after learning she was pregnant to wait for Goddess knew how long. She'd return tomorrow first thing. And she'd bring a basket of nutbread to sweeten his reluctance, so she could convince him to burn the enchanted bird and end the glamour spell.

CHAPTER 52

Since he'd returned from The Gold Griffin too late to visit any witch shops, Hawke rode his gelding to the closest one on his list straight after breakfast the following morning. He'd continue until he visited all eight of the fashionable witch shops left, or found the enchanted bird's creator.

Mirage was sleek and bright with exhibits of decoy charms, invisibility cloaks, projected scenes, and other illusions. Yet the exotic clerk winced away from the enchanted bird, saying its power blinded her magical sight. Then she attempted to persuade him to buy an illusion of a favorite memory he could invoke at will. He declined—he'd find Rowan, not settle for a memory.

So Hawke rode on to the next closest witch shop on his list, Transmuted Metals, which brimmed with metal ores, enchanted horseshoes, magic elixirs, and other bits of alchemy. The burly clerk grunted at the enchanted bird and called it an impressive working far beyond his ken. He then showed Hawke horseshoes guaranteed to make the clumsiest horse light-footed. Hawke suppressed a snort. None of his horses, particularly his stallion, would tolerate enchanted horseshoes, so he passed.

He headed to the next witch shop, Black Moon, which resembled Toil and Trouble except more cluttered. Its hexed dolls, desiccated animals, charmed candles, and other folk magic were jumbled together on black tables. The wizened clerk's dark eyes brightened at the enchanted bird, and she offered to perform a divination on her favorite hen. He grimaced. How could the innards of a chicken help him find Rowan? So he refused and rode on.

But the fourth witch shop, Over the Walle, was unlike any he'd ever visited. Stocked with jars of ambrosia, sachets of faedust, bags of stardust grain, and other supernatural supplies, this shop obviously catered to Ormas's small population of magical creatures. And the clerk perched in the back of the shop was an elf, a wood elf by her brown hair and merlin garb.

His pulse surging, Hawke hesitated near the threshold. He'd never met an elf before. They were known for their wisdom, but they didn't always deign to share it with mere humans. Yet he'd lose nothing by asking. He set his jaw then strode forward and extracted the enchanted bird from his pocket. "What can you tell me about this spell, my lady?"

The elf cocked her head, the feathers braided behind her pointed ears brushing her face. She took the pearly carving from him and twirled it in her fingers. "An intriguing bit of magic."

His neck prickled. What did the elf see? Surely, she could tell him something, even though Rowan probably hadn't purchased her spell here. "Did you make it?"

The elf's lips quirked as she stroked the enchanted bird. "Oh no, this was *clearly* made by a human witch, albeit a powerful one."

Hawke nodded, his chest sinking. But perhaps the elf would reveal more if he asked. He flashed a beseeching smile. "Is that all you see, my lady?"

Her slitted eyes narrowing, the elf stilled. "Certainly not, but why should I tell you?"

He shifted beneath the weight of her dark-green gaze. Because he must find Rowan. But 'twouldn't convince a powerful elf, so he said, "Because a witch told me I was a focus of the spell."

The elf shrugged. "You are, but that may simply be due to proximity rather than intent."

Hawke blinked. Did that matter? Since being a focus hadn't convinced the elf, he'd only his need to find Rowan. Would that be enough? He tensed and leaned forward. "The spell belongs to a lady dear to me, and I intend to use it to find her again."

The elf relaxed, her merlin garb wafting about her. "An affair of the heart then." She arched a brow. "If this lady is so dear, why can you not find her?"

He winced. Of course, she'd ask that. He spread his hands with a wry smile. "Because I met her at the king's summer masquerade, and the enchanted bird is the only clue she left behind. But I must find her, so I can court and possibly marry her."

Her face softening, the elf shook her head. "You are fortunate I am a romantic. Otherwise, I would tell you nothing."

Warmth suffusing his chest, Hawke swept a deep bow. Thank the Goddess she'd decided to take pity on him. "My heartfelt thanks, my lady."

The elf launched the enchanted bird like a faebird, and it hovered in the air before her. She folded her hands in her lap and eyed the enchanted bird, and it began burning like the sun.

He squinted, his head throbbing. Would the enchanted bird explode like it had when human witches had probed it? He flinched and stepped back.

But then the elf clenched her hands, and the enchanted bird ceased burning and plummeted. Swifter than a real merlin, she seized the iridescent carving before it hit the floor. She caressed the enchanted bird. "Even more *intriguing* than I had thought."

Hawke tensed. Yes, but what had the elf learned? Please let it help him find Rowan at last. He narrowed his eyes. "What do you mean?"

The elf chuckled. "'Tis the most intricate human spell I have ever encountered." Her winged brows quirked. "The witch who created it was not only powerful but paranoid. She weaved a potent warding into her spell to prevent anyone from determining who created it, what it does, or how it does it."

His breath froze. Not even an *elf* could understand Rowan's spell? Then how was he to find her? He couldn't abandon his hunt now. If he did, their parents would force him and Wren to marry, which would destroy their friendship.

Stroking the enchanted bird, the elf continued, "Even if I broke the warding, since 'tis woven into the spell, I would shatter the spell along with it. And I would not recommend that, considering how the spell's energy is entwined with yours."

Hawke nodded. Because he was a focus of the spell. Yet he must find Rowan, and the witch who created the enchanted bird would know her. "So I must find the spell's creator then. But how?"

The elf shrugged. "Stumble upon her, I suppose. With that warding, 'tis the only way to find her." She stroked the enchanted bird a final time then returned it to him.

Heaviness filling his chest, he pocketed Rowan's spell with a small bow and handed the elf six gold coins. "Thank you, my lady. You've been most informative." Just not enough to find Rowan.

The elf pursed a faint smile. "The blessings of the Goddess upon your hunt."

Hawke inclined his head then strode from the elf's shop. Once outside, he sighed and withdrew his crumpled list of witch shops. He'd another four left, but visiting them seemed pointless.

His shoulders hunched, he hauled himself into the saddle then rode to Wren's to share luncheon. He must check if she was better than yesterday. Plus, he needed her after the elf's revelations. She'd cheer him and know how to salvage his hunt.

But when he arrived, Abby told him Wren was visiting her healer. His heart clenched. What was wrong with Wren? It must be serious if she actually visited her healer. Goddess, let her recover soon. He'd stop by tomorrow to check on her.

Hawke returned home but picked at his luncheon. What was he to do about Rowan? And what ailed Wren? To distract himself, he played his violin after luncheon, but he couldn't lose himself in the music like usual. So after a few songs, he cleaned his violin and put it away.

His head aching, he requested his stallion for a ride. Unlike his steady gelding, his stallion required a firm hand and unwavering attention to stay in the saddle. He couldn't fret about anything while riding him.

Once Hawke returned from his exhilarating yet exhausting ride, Hobb handed him a letter. "This just arrived for you, my lord."

'Twas from Buford, so Hawke thanked the butler then retreated to his study, tore open the letter, and began to read.

Hawke—

My people found a witch shop you should visit. 'Tis on Mountainglass Lane and called Rhiannon's Veils. The witch there has an extraordinary reputation—she can magic anything, no matter how difficult. Your spell may not have been purchased at her shop, but I've no doubt this witch can find out where it was.

Buford

Hawke sighed and tapped the letter against his thigh. Before visiting the elf today, he would have rushed to visit Rhiannon's Veils. But why bother? Only Rowan's witch could help him find her, and Rowan wouldn't have visited a witch shop near the docks.

Despite that, he reread Buford's letter, and his gaze lingered on the line about the witch's extraordinary reputation. Perhaps a witch with such a reputation could tell him *something* about the enchanted bird. He'd nothing to lose by visiting, so after checking on Wren tomorrow, he'd stop by Rhiannon's Veils.

CHAPTER 53

Chilled despite the balmy summer morning, Wren rapped on Hawke's front door. She gripped her basket of nutbread. Goddess, let this work. She *must* convince him to burn the enchanted bird and end the glamour spell for the sake of their unborn child.

When Hobb opened the door and said Hawke was in his study, she gulped a bracing breath. Time to reveal the truth about their enchanted night. Hopefully, Hawke would see past his fury to forgive her desperate deception. She requested a kahve tray then strode to the study.

Abandoning his correspondence, Hawke leapt to his feet and eyed her. "Wren, I was about to check on you. How was your visit to your healer? You look somewhat better today."

Wren shrugged. No doubt because now she knew to eat crackers first thing for her nausea. But she couldn't explain that until she revealed her pregnancy, and she couldn't reveal her pregnancy until he burned the enchanted bird. So she merely said, "Healer Althea said 'twas nothing to fret over. I'll recover soon." In eight months or so. She hoisted her basket. "I brought nutbread. Hobb should be bringing a kahve tray shortly."

Hawke flashed a crooked grin and stole the basket. "I just finished breakfast, but I can always eat nutbread."

She made herself smile as Hawke dragged a chair beside his desk for her. Please let the nutbread sweeten his reluctance. She avoided his gaze as she sat and smoothed her skirt. She'd wait to explain until he had his nutbread and kahve. Fortunately, Hobb soon arrived, so Hawke didn't notice her silence.

Once Hawke began devouring his nutbread, Wren swallowed and stirred sugar into her kahve. The glamour spell had caused a coughing fit when she'd almost mentioned it before, so she'd start by revealing why she'd seduced him. Her stomach knotting, she swallowed again. "The night of the king's summer masquerade I claimed I was writing, but in truth I attended to—"

"I met an elf yesterday," Hawke blurted. He rubbed his temple with a frown. "I apologize. Not sure why I said that. Please continue."

She tensed. The glamour spell had doubtless caused his outburst. But if she persisted, surely she could explain her desperation. "I attended the k—" Like last week, heaving coughs wracked her entire body.

Hawke leaned forward, his pale-blue eyes dark. "Are you certain you're well?"

Wren nodded and gulped some kahve, grimacing at the bitter brew. She would be if she could circumvent the glamour spell. She clenched her jaw. That wretched spell wouldn't defeat her. "I attended the king's m—" Blackness swamped her, and her cup crashed onto the desk.

When she revived, Hawke had carried her to the sofa and was wiping her face with a damp cloth. "You're not well. I'll escort you home to rest."

She sighed and tossed the cloth aside. "I'm fine. I promise." Except the glamour spell had overpowered her. She must convince him to burn the enchanted bird and withstand his fury before she could explain. Damnation.

Hawke grunted, his brows furrowed. "You've not been *fine* for the past month."

Wren winced. Because the glamour spell had been draining her. She must get him to end it. She lifted her chin. "Neither have you. You must burn that enchanted bird and forget about Rowan."

His frown darkening, Hawke crossed his arms over his chest. "I can't. You know that."

Her hands fisted in her lap. He had to, or she could never reveal the truth, and their child would never have a father. "Please, Hawke, please burn that wretched spell. For me?"

Hawke winced and grasped her hands. "I can't forget about Rowan. She might be my only chance at love, and without her... I've been suffering the most bizarre reactions."

Her throat cramping, Wren shifted in her seat. "Headaches, you mean?"

Hawke swallowed, eyeing her lips. "No."

Tingling warmth swept through her. Goddess, he meant their almost kisses. But if he burned the enchanted bird, he'd realize those weren't bizarre at all. She squeezed his hands. "Burn the enchanted bird."

Hawke dropped her hands as if scalded by a furious fire-lizard. "I'm sorry, Wren. I can't. 'Tis my only concrete clue to find Rowan."

Numbness filled Wren's chest. He didn't need to find her. She was right here, like she'd always been, but he couldn't see that due to the glamour spell. "You don't need Rowan. Plus, your obsession with her isn't healthy."

Hawke scowled. "I told you before that I'm not obsessed." He cocked a brow. "And what would you know about healthy relationships? You couldn't even accept a kiss without scolding."

Her body throbbed as their lovemaking echoed through her. She licked her lips. "I've accepted more than kisses without scolding."

Hawke stilled like a hungry tygris stalking a unicorn. "What? From who?"

Wren glanced at him from beneath her lashes and flashed a coy smile. Perhaps jealousy would convince him to forget Rowan. "I'll let you guess."

Hawke leaned forward, his eyes narrow. "Edouard? Dane? Xavier? *Mel*?"

Maintaining her coy smile, she shook her head after each guess. How could he not realize the obvious choice? Everyone else did.

Hawke seized her hands and growled, "Who?!"

Wren leaned forward until their lips almost touched. "I'll tell you if you burn the enchanted bird." Although 'twould no longer be necessary.

Hawke jerked back and dropped her hands again. "Never."

Her shoulders drooped. Why couldn't she convince him? 'Twas her he was hunting, after all. What was she to do? Fire flared beneath her skin, and she jabbed his chest. "Why aren't you listening to me? You claim to value my advice but refuse to heed it."

Hawke stiffened. "Because your advice is wrong. You didn't meet Rowan, so you didn't see how special our relationship was."

Her fury crumbling, Wren blinked back tears. She knew precisely how special their relationship was, and she'd destroyed it with her deceitful seduction. And now, she couldn't mend it because of that wretched spell she'd purchased. "You've spent every free moment the past month hunting Rowan with no success. You must cease hunting her if you ever want more than half a life."

Hawke glared at her. "My life is fine."

She arched her brows. Not when the mysterious lady he was so desperate to find was actually his best friend disguised by a glamour spell. "Really? I'm not sure either of ours are."

Hawke blinked. "What do you mean?" When she shook her

head, unable to explain, he ran a hand through his hair. "Wren, I can't cease hunting Rowan. If I never find her, our parents shall force you and I to marry."

A wild laugh bubbled in her chest. Fortunate, considering she was carrying his child. Only they must marry now rather than next year. "Perhaps we should."

Hawke gaped at her. "But what about marrying for love?"

Wren winced. She loved him enough for them both, but he must surrender marrying for love to protect their child. "Perhaps we'll be like your parents." When he snorted, she lifted her chin and said, "It'll be fine. Kiss me and see."

Hawke stilled, and his eyes darkened. "You don't want that."

Her heart surging, she tilted her head and licked her lips. She burned to kiss him again and had even before their enchanted night. "Don't I?"

Hawke swallowed and eyed her lips for a long moment. Finally, he drew her into his arms and lowered his head. His lips brushed against hers like fae wings.

Wren sighed into his kiss as tingling flooded her. More, she needed more. She threaded her fingers through his hair to pull his head closer then nipped his lower lip.

Hawke groaned as he crushed her against him and devoured her mouth. At last. After a too-brief moment, he wrenched his head back to stare at her.

Her body throbbing, she returned his stare. Goddess, why had he stopped? As she and Hawke remained intertwined, the enchanted bird gouged her breast. She tensed. If she stole it, she could take it home and burn it. She slid a hand beneath his coat and grasped the enchanted bird.

Hawke jerked back and seized her wrist. "*What* are you doing?"

Her throat tightened. He'd caught her. Damnation. She met his narrow gaze. Should she lie about it? No, she'd deceived him so much already. She set her jaw. "Burning this curse."

Hawke glared and wrested the enchanted bird from her grip. "'Tisn't yours to burn."

Wren scowled at him, fisting her hands on her hips. Actually, it was, but he'd not realize that until she burned it. "Someone has to."

Hawke strode to his desk then hurled the enchanted bird inside a drawer and locked it. "You should leave."

"Fine." She leapt to her feet, ice filling her chest. "I don't want to see you until you burn that thing."

Hawke paled. "You'd end our lifelong friendship over this?"

Tears welled in her eyes. "Our friendship ended the night you met Rowan. Farewell, Hawke."

Wren fled his study before he could see her tears. Unfortunately for them and their unborn child, she'd failed to convince Hawke to burn the enchanted bird and end the glamour spell. Goddess, what was she to do now?

CHAPTER 54

His head pounding yet again, Hawke collapsed in the chair behind his desk after Wren stormed from his study. Goddess, another headache? He requested his valet bring a tonic then closed his eyes and massaged his temples. John couldn't arrive too soon.

When the valet arrived, Hawke quaffed the tonic without opening his eyes. But he opened them when John began adjusting the fireplace. The valet was hanging a small pot on the chimney bar. He frowned. "What's that?"

John stilled, glancing over at Hawke. "Herb water to boil throughout the day. Since you've suffered so many headaches recently, I thought you'd want to try another headache remedy."

Hawke grimaced. A fire in the middle of summer would make his study stifling. But maybe 'twould help his head. At least Wren wasn't here to hurl the enchanted bird in it. "Very well."

After the valet lit a fire and departed, he leaned back in his chair and closed his eyes again. Goddess, his body still throbbed after that ravenous kiss with Wren. He'd only stopped when he'd imagined removing her dress so he could make love to her.

Hunger had almost consumed him like it had with Rowan. Why?

He groaned as his headache surged again. He must calm his body for his headache to ease. Slowing his breathing, he cleared his mind until his head no longer pounded. Then he extracted the enchanted bird from his desk drawer. Now that he'd recovered, he'd visit that witch shop Buford had recommended.

Hawke rode across Ormas and stopped for luncheon at The Gold Griffin since 'twas around the corner from the witch shop. He bolted his fish pie and gold ale then strode to Rhiannon's Veils, his pulse surging. Would the witch there reveal something new about the enchanted bird?

He blinked at the tiny witch shop's weathered red door. Unprepossessing for a witch able to magic anything. Perhaps her extraordinary reputation was nothing more than rumors. He ran his hand through his hair. He was here, so he might as well go ask about the enchanted bird.

Hawke strode inside, grimacing at the strong incense. The inside of Rhiannon's Veils was as unprepossessing as the outside. 'Twas empty except for a wooden table with two chairs and cabinets holding magical accoutrements. Not even a clerk was in the dim chamber.

Glass beads tinkled at the back, and a veiled woman sashayed into the shop. "How may I serve you today, my lord?"

He started. She was the witch he'd seen at The Gold Griffin. He should have realized. Like before, she seemed to sense he'd a spell in his pocket. He swallowed. "You make the Griffin's ale glow."

Her black veils fluttering, the witch inclined her head. An amused drawl shaded her voice as she replied, "I do. Is that what you're here to ask?"

Hawke extracted the enchanted bird from his pocket despite the chill prickling his neck. "No. What can you tell me about this spell?"

Unlike the other witches he'd shown the enchanted bird, the veiled witch only shrugged. "I can tell you I made it, but not much else."

He gaped at her. Rowan had visited *here*? How had she known about a witch shop near the docks? Light seized his chest. Yet who cared? The veiled witch could tell him Rowan's true name. He flashed a beseeching smile. "I can pay, if that's your objection. And I mean no harm to the lady who purchased it. I simply must find her. All I need is a name."

The veiled witch's exotically lined eyes narrowed. "You mistake me, my lord. I can't due to the spell itself." A sigh wafted her black veils. "I *can* tell you that you should burn that spell forthwith. It might cause irreparable harm unless you do."

His breath freezing, Hawke tensed and clutched the enchanted bird. Goddess, what had Rowan done? "What do you mean?"

The veiled witch shook her head. "As I told the lady who purchased it, magic demands equal payment. This spell is draining you both and shall continue to do so until 'tis ended."

He swallowed. The spell was draining him and Rowan? Was that why he'd never found her? She was too drained to attend court events? He drew the enchanted bird to his chest. "But if I burn the enchanted bird, I'll have nothing left of Rowan but memory."

The veiled witch flicked her fingers, jingling bracelets and tiny bells. "You might have more than you think." She paused before adding, "And *that*, Lord Beza, is definitely all I can tell you. Return home and burn the spell."

His jaw tensing at his given name, Hawke blinked as the veiled witch swept behind the glass beads. He'd found the witch who created the enchanted bird at last, but she couldn't tell him Rowan's true name. His heart clenched. How else could he find Rowan? He sighed and trudged from the witch shop.

Engrossed in his thoughts, he began riding home until a sultry voice called his name. He glanced about. Somehow he'd ridden to Broad Street rather than home. Kit was waving at him from in front of Celeste's. Wonderful. He nodded in return without dismounting.

Kit fluttered her lashes at him. "How fortunate I saw you. I'm unwell and would be grateful for an escort home."

Hawke almost snorted. Doubtful. She just wanted to pursue him again. But if he refused Kit's request before the most fashionable dress shop in Ormas, Mother would hear of it within an hour and would visit to scold him for neglecting family. And he must focus on finding Rowan rather than handling Mother. So he dismounted and offered Kit his arm. "Where's your carriage?"

Her sable hair gleaming the afternoon sun, Kit tilted her head and took his arm. "It should arrive at any moment." A flashy carriage halted before them. "And here it is."

He winced but handed Kit inside. No wonder Edouard bemoaned Kit's spending. He tied his gelding behind the lavish carriage then sat across from her.

Kit slanted him a coy glance. "I bought some of your arachne silk. Celeste is making a gown from it for me."

His body hardened as Wren in her arachne silk ballgown flashed before his eyes. Not again. He frowned, struggling to replace Wren with Rowan in her dryad costume, but she kept wavering back to Wren. Pain seized his head again, and sweat burst along his brow.

"Hawke?" Kit frowned at him. "Are you well?"

Hawke forced a crooked grin. "Of course." Except for his bizarre desire for his best friend and having lost all hope of finding Rowan.

Kit patted the seat beside her and purred, "Then sit beside me. I feel faint."

Since they were now alone, he snorted and crossed his arms. He'd attempt Wren's advice from the Westons' musical evening. Nothing else had worked. "Kit, stop pursuing me. I'm not interested."

Kit stiffened, her eyes narrowing. "Why not? 'Tisn't as if you're in love." She pursed her lips. "Or are you?"

Not exactly. Hawke shrugged and glanced out the window. He was interested in courting Rowan, but he wasn't in love with her—yet. But he could be, if he ever found her.

Kit snorted. "Well, *Wren* must be pleased." She snorted. "After all, she's loved you for ages but was too craven to admit it."

He swiveled to gape at Kit. Wren wasn't in love with him. If she was, she never would have spurned his Longnight kiss. And she wouldn't have welcomed another gentleman's attentions. The bounder. His stomach hardening, he almost growled.

Kit tossed her head as the carriage stopped before Blaine House. "Which I never understood because you were obviously besotted with her."

Hawke set his jaw. Yet another person assuming he was in love with Wren. Unlike his brothers, he'd not bother to explain to Kit. Even if she believed him, she'd simply use his explanation to needle Wren. He leapt from the carriage and escorted Kit inside then rode to his townhouse.

Back home, he strode straight to his study and began pacing. The enchanted bird had failed to lead him to Rowan. He glowered at the fire beneath the pot of headache remedy. Yet he couldn't burn the enchanted bird like Wren and the veiled witch had suggested. 'Twould feel like surrender to burn Rowan's spell.

Still pacing, Hawke rubbed his aching head. What could he try next? He still had the list of orphanages, but Wren had been certain they wouldn't help him find Rowan. He sighed, hollowness echoing inside his chest. Doubtless she was right.

Unable to bear pacing about his study any longer, he strode to the gamesroom and poured a large snifter of spiritwine. He tossed back his drink then extracted the enchanted bird from his pocket to place it in the center of the elementball table. How was he to find Rowan?

He eyed her spell and poured another drink. He idly spun the elementball wheel to activate the table. The black slate top dissolved into a scene of lava pools and volcanoes. He snorted. Now even a *game* was telling him to burn the enchanted bird. He drained his fresh drink and poured another.

CHAPTER 55

*W*ren didn't bother to emerge from her covers when Abby burst in shortly before dinner. She'd spent the entire afternoon sobbing over her disastrous quarrel with Hawke. She'd never cried so much in her life. Healer Althea had been right about pregnancy causing mercurial moods.

Abby ripped back the covers. "Your parents have requested your presence at dinner, Miss Wren."

Wren buried her ravaged face in her pillow. She couldn't handle choking down dinner with her parents. Although for her unborn child, she'd force herself to eat some soup and crackers like she had at luncheon. Just not with her parents. "Tell them I'm unwell." Not exactly a lie.

Abby set a tray on the bedside table with a clink. "Your parents were most insistent. I brought a cold compress for your eyes."

Wren sighed and accepted the cold compress. She couldn't allow her parents to see her distress. They'd want to help, but 'twas nothing they could do. And they mustn't find out she was pregnant—at least not until after she and Hawke had married.

She dressed for dinner then joined her parents. Yet when she entered the family dining room, their hushed conversation halted. She swallowed, her pulse skittering. What was going on? Their behavior was more suspicious than when they'd proposed she and Hawke marry. She forced a serene smile as she sat across from them.

Despite their probing looks throughout dinner, Mother and Father kept their conversation innocuous until dessert. Then Mother waved the servants out and turned to Wren with a faint frown. "Now that we've eaten, tell us what's distressing you."

A chill prickling her skin, Wren swallowed and crumbled her lymon cake rather than eating it. "Nothing is distressing me."

Mother and Father exchanged a glance, then Father asked, his eyes solemn for once, "Not even the news Abby shared with us?"

Wren stilled as her throat constricted. Abby had been her maid for years and couldn't have betrayed her. "What do you mean?"

Mother sighed and shook her head. "She told us you're pregnant, Wren."

Wren's stomach spasmed. Abby *had* betrayed her. She swallowed again. Goddess, how could she explain her unexpected pregnancy to her parents?

Father grimaced. "Although I'm not pleased Hawke anticipated your marriage vows, I remember the impetuous love of the young."

Wren winced and looked away. He might remember that, but he'd not understand purchasing a glamour spell to trick the one you loved into seducing you as someone else.

When Wren remained silent, Mother drew a sharp breath. "Hawke *is* the father, isn't he?"

Still looking away, Wren shrugged. Hawke deserved to hear he'd be a father from her. If she told her parents, they'd tell his parents, and the duchess would meddle before she could convince Hawke to burn the enchanted bird and reveal the truth. Setting her jaw, she faced her parents but said nothing.

Mother paled whiter than a grieving banshee. "He's *not* the father? Wren, how could you? We trusted you." She turned to Father. "How am I supposed to explain this to Caro?"

Father patted Mother's hand. "Wren, tell us the father."

Wren lifted her chin. "I can't." Not until Hawke knew.

Mother stiffened and shut her eyes. "Your betrothal to Hawke is definitely off."

Wren snorted. "'Twas never *on* as far as Hawke was concerned." Not that he'd a choice now. Nausea swamping her, she winced again.

Ignoring Wren, Mother said to Father, "We must return to the country at once. When we return to Ormas next year, we can claim the baby is the child of distant relatives who recently died."

Fire flaring in her chest, Wren leapt to her feet. "I'm not leaving Ormas."

Father's jaw clenched. "Unless you marry the father of your child at once, you must."

Wren glared at her parents. "I can't abandon the orphanage." Plus, she couldn't convince Hawke to burn the enchanted bird if she was buried in the country.

Mother's eyes slitted. "You should have thought of that before letting some unnamed gentleman seduce you. After your behavior, we can't allow visits to the orphanage."

Father crossed his arms. "You'll be confined here until you return to the country—we can no longer trust you."

Wren jerked back as if stung by a swarm of irate melissae. Her parents had never been so autocratic before. Blinking back tears, she nodded then dashed upstairs to her chambers and locked the door behind her. Who knew what other secrets Abby would betray if she allowed the maid inside?

Tears coursing down her cheeks again, she crawled into bed and curled beneath the covers. She never should have left. She sobbed until she slipped into a restless sleep plagued by nightmares where Hawke spent their lives hunting Rowan while she raised their child alone in a country hut.

. . .

WREN WOKE EARLY the following morning, but without crackers, she soon began retching. Perhaps she should have let Abby bring her some before locking the door. Her stomach roiling, she dressed and slipped down to the kitchen to beg Cook for porridge and tea. Fortunately, the simple breakfast settled her stomach.

After breakfast, she requested the carriage despite her parents' edicts. Thankfully, the servants prepared it without question—her parents mustn't have told them she was confined to the townhouse yet. As soon as the carriage was ready, she slipped out to visit the orphanage. She needed Kiera's advice about Hawke.

When Wren entered her study, Kiera frowned from behind her desk. "Wren, you look exhausted."

Not surprising. Wren dropped into the plush chair before Kiera's desk. "That's because I am." Damned glamour spell.

Her navy eyes darkening, Kiera arched her brows.

Wren shifted in her chair. How could she start? "Remember the witch shop beside the Bedsfords' old shop? Did you know the veiled witch is a Rhiannon descendant?"

Kiera blinked. "That explains her reputation. But what does that have to do with your exhaustion?"

Wren nibbled her lip. "Last month I purchased a strong spell there." She made herself meet her friend's gaze. "A glamour to prevent Hawke from recognizing me."

Kiera's mouth fell open. "*You* were the dryad at the king's summer masquerade. The one Hawke has been hunting."

Wren almost winced. Of course, her perceptive friend had instantly realized the truth. "Yes."

Kiera shook her head, her dark-blonde curls dancing. "Not surprising that Hawke has been hunting his mysterious dryad then." Her eyes widened. "But if he doesn't realize you're her, your glamour spell must be still active. Dear Goddess."

Wren grimaced. 'Twas worse than Kiera knew. "Yes, and Healer Althea said 'tis draining me."

Kiera paled, and her brow furrowed. "No wonder you're exhausted. You must end the glamour spell at once."

Wren nodded. "I know, but to do that, I must burn the enchanted bird containing it, and Hawke has it." She gulped a steadying breath before confessing the rest. "But the glamour spell isn't the only reason I'm exhausted—I'm pregnant."

Kiera gaped at her. "With Hawke's child. And he has *no idea*."

A blush burning her cheeks, Wren rubbed her chest. "Yes, and I failed to convince him to burn the enchanted bird, so I can't tell him. And Healer Althea warned the glamour spell might harm our child if it continues."

Kiera blinked. "I thought I'd tangled my life, but you've far surpassed me."

What did she mean by that? Wren shook her head. She'd ask her later. Right now she must resolve her tangled relationship with Hawke. "I need advice about how to get Hawke to burn the enchanted bird. I've tried everything I could imagine."

Kiera pursed her lips. "Since you failed as Wren, convince him as his dryad. Dress in your costume from the masquerade and tell him to burn the spell."

Wren sighed as her heart squeezed. She'd been too thorough for that. "I can't. I burned my costume the morning after the masquerade."

Kiera frowned and tapped her fingers on her desk. "Then seduce him as yourself. In a week or two, tell him you're pregnant, and he'll marry you straightaway. You can have him burn the spell once you're married."

Wren's throat thickened. If only she could. "I tried kissing him yesterday. He was enthralled at first, but soon jerked back. I doubt I could seduce him."

Kiera's fingers stilled. "Could you bribe one of his servants to burn it?"

Wren wrinkled her nose. "Hawke's servants would never

betray his trust." Unlike Abby. "Besides, I think he carries the enchanted bird during the day." Damn his obsession with Rowan.

Kiera hummed. "How about you visit Hawke and convince his butler not to announce you? That can't be unusual. But instead of finding Hawke, hide until he sleeps, then burn the spell yourself."

Wren cocked her head, light easing her chest. That plan might just work. She'd remain here through dinner then head to Hawke's. "Kiera, you're brilliant." She leapt to her feet. "Since that's settled, shall we visit with the orphans?"

Kiera stood as well, her eyes narrow. "As long as you take care not to tax yourself."

Wren grinned at her friend's mothering. Kiera had been an orphanage matron too long. "I swear to be careful." She'd never endanger her unborn child. Yet as she began toward the door, sudden blackness engulfed her, and she collapsed.

CHAPTER 56

*H*is head pounding and stomach roiling, Hawke scowled at the enchanted bird on his desk as he quaffed the headache tonic John had brought with breakfast. Goddess, why had he drunk the entire decanter of spiritwine last night? Never again—drinking so much solved nothing.

His head and stomach eased once he finished the bitter tonic, but he continued glaring at the pearly carving while devouring his breakfast. After a night pondering his quarrel with Wren and the veiled witch's revelations, the enchanted bird no longer appeared a clue to finding his only chance at love, but a curse like Wren had said. Rowan and her spell had done nothing but destroy his life—they had cost him Wren.

Hawke swallowed, his chest clenching. Obsessed with his hunt, he'd treated Wren horribly over the past month. He'd forced her to visit witch shop after witch shop despite her distrust of magic. And he'd almost made love to her yesterday because his unrequited desire for Rowan had overset him. Goddess, no wonder Wren had ended their lifelong friendship.

How could he have chosen a will-o'-the-wisp determined not to be found over the best friend he'd known forever? True, his night with Rowan had been extraordinary, and their visceral attraction could have burgeoned into love given time, but he'd only known her one night. And would she have vanished so completely if she'd truly wanted him?

Hawke's gaze drifted to the fireplace. Wren was right. He should burn the enchanted bird and forget about Rowan. Then perhaps he could repair his friendship with Wren. His stomach hardening, he stormed across the study and hurled the wretched spell into the crackling fire beneath the pot of headache remedy.

For a moment, the enchanted bird's pearly gleam flared until it shone like the sun before contracting to a pinpoint. Then Rowan's spell exploded with a blinding flash and thunderous boom. As smoke reeking of charred feathers flooded the study, agony pierced his head, and he collapsed to his knees, clutching his head and gulping air.

Rowan was *Wren*!

Wren slipping into the masquerade in her exquisite dryad costume flashed before him. Then her gentle teasing and tenderness shining in her hazel eyes during their enchanted night. Not surprising he'd desired her at once and felt like he'd known her forever.

Her velvet alto singing with his, "*Love me under the sky...*" echoed inside him. Naturally she'd known that Lantos waltz. 'Twas *her* lute tutor who had introduced them to the vastly unappreciated bard. And that waltz was one of her favorites.

Their ravenous kisses, her dainty body pressing against him, and her delicate violet scent surged through him. No wonder desire had tormented him during the past month. His body had recognized her even when her spell had baffled his mind.

Hawke croaked a laugh. Of course Wren had been Rowan. 'Twas the reason their night had been so perfect. And why he'd ached to cuddle with her after making love and been determined to find her when she'd vanished. Because everyone was right— he was in love with Wren, and always had been. He'd just been too craven to admit it after she'd spurned his Longnight kiss.

His head whirling, he rubbed his temples. So *why* had Wren

rejected him all those years ago? After learning Mother's plans to marry him off, she'd been desperate enough to purchase a strong spell to seduce him even though she distrusted magic. Surely she must love him as he loved her.

Hawke sighed. But Wren must have feared destroying their friendship. Disguised, their friendship would remain unscathed if her seduction went awry. No wonder she'd called the enchanted bird a spell for courage. He shook his head. If he were her, he might have disguised himself with a spell too.

Fire kindled in his chest. Yet *how* could Wren have continued deceiving him for the past month? She pretended to help his hunt, but she'd clearly meant to remain lost, considering how thorough her spell had been and how well she'd vanished.

Hawke frowned. After her efforts to remain lost, why had she attempted to burn the enchanted bird yesterday? 'Twas the way to end her spell, and she'd been determined to conceal the truth until then. What had changed her mind?

He set his jaw and staggered to his feet. He must see Wren—now. He sprinted to the stables, saddled his stallion, then thundered to her townhouse. After tossing the reins to a wide-eyed groom, he bounded up her front steps and pounded on the door.

When Perkins Two opened the door, Hawke shoved inside. "Where's Wren? I need her at once."

The butler paled. "Out, my lord. I'll fetch Lady Keyes."

As Perkins Two fled, Hawke paced about the entrance hall. Now that her spell had ended, what would Wren say?

Yet Wren's mother, not Wren, swept into the entrance hall. "I suppose Caro told you then. I apologize for my daughter's behavior, Hawke."

He scowled. "I haven't seen Mother since the fete." His breath froze. "Wait, *Mother* knows?" If their mothers knew about his enchanted night with Wren, so did their fathers. No wonder they'd proposed he and Wren marry.

Lady Keyes sighed and patted his shoulder. "Yes, of course. I informed her of Wren's pregnancy last night at the sirenic play.

We both thought it best to sever your betrothal at once. Although you must be angry with Wren, I'd be grateful if you persuaded her to tell us the father. 'Twould be best if they marry."

Pregnant?!

His heart stilling, Hawke stared at Lady Keyes without seeing her. Wren was pregnant? But he'd worn a contraceptive charm. Yet it must have failed because Wren couldn't have given herself to another. Not after their extraordinary night together.

He gulped a breath as his heart surged to resume its normal rhythm. Goddess, Wren was carrying his child. He was about to be a father. That changed everything, even more than their enchanted night had. Tingling flooded his chest. He and Wren must marry at once to protect their unborn child from scandal. Thank the Goddess.

Hawke licked his lips. No wonder Wren had attempted to burn the enchanted bird yesterday and convince him they should marry. Yet Lady Keyes didn't realize the child was his, so Wren must be concealing the truth from their mothers. How had they discovered she was pregnant?

Not that it mattered. Their mothers would forgive them once they married. But he must see Wren to do that. He grinned at Lady Keyes. "Where's Wren? I must speak with her."

Lady Keyes winced. "She slipped out early this morning. Visiting the orphanage, no doubt. She'll be unable to soon. We're retiring to the country until after the baby is born."

Hawke tensed, fire flaring in his veins. Wren wasn't slinking off to the country to bear his child in shame. He jerked a nod and left. He galloped across Ormas then leapt from the saddle and handed Peter the reins. "Be careful with this one. Is Wren in Kiera's study?"

Peter nodded as the stallion lunged for freedom.

His muscles tensing, Hawke strode to the matron's study and flung open the door. What would Wren have to say?

As the door banged against the wall, Wren and Kiera swung to face him. Wren's teacup clattered on the desk.

Warmth flooding him, Hawke eyed Wren and forced himself to remain by the door rather than yanking her into his arms. "Morning, Wren. Or should I say, *Rowan*?"

Her auburn hair tousled and skin wan, Wren swallowed with a tremulous smile. "So you burned the enchanted bird at last. Good." She sighed. "Rowan was only for that night. I told you she was a will-o'-the-wisp."

His pulse surging at her continued deception, he clenched his hands by his side. "That might have been the only truth you told me since you created Rowan."

Wren winced but said nothing.

Hawke inhaled and gritted a smile. How could he burn to kiss her and strangle her at the same time? "We must talk, but not here."

Wren nodded then rose. "Yes, we must." She turned to Kiera. "I'll see you later."

Kiera stood and embraced Wren, whispering in her ear. Then she bustled to Hawke and hugged him as well, murmuring, "Try not to be too harsh. Wren loves you so, and love causes all of us to be foolish on occasion."

His pulse slowed as he met Kiera's eyes. If he'd not been foolish enough to deny his love for years, Wren wouldn't have needed to deceive him. He nodded then grasped Wren's arm and led her outside.

When they reached his stallion, Wren broke her silence to whimper. "You rode that brute?"

Hawke almost chuckled at her dismay. His stallion wasn't that bad. He took the reins from Peter then leapt into the saddle. "He's merely spirited, and an exhilarating ride." Plus, he'd burned to see Wren, and the stallion was fast.

Wren wrinkled her nose as she accepted his hand up and settled behind him. "Or a terrifying one."

Like before, his body tightened as her violet scent weaved around him. Yet now he knew exactly what was the matter with him. Tingling filled his chest. He urged his stallion forward but kept him to a walk. Wild gallops weren't safe when carrying a lady, especially a pregnant one. However, that meant Wren was pressed against him for longer.

His body was painfully hard when they finally reached his townhouse, so Hawke helped Wren alight but didn't release her hand. He *must* kiss her again. After leaping down and flinging his reins at the nearest groom, he hauled her into his arms then grasped her hips and seized her mouth.

CHAPTER 57

$\mathcal{A}$lthough her stomach quivered after their tense ride, Wren couldn't resist returning Hawke's ravenous kiss. Why was he kissing her? Doubtless he was furious over her deceitful seduction—he'd been rigid and abrupt at the orphanage, and he'd not spoken on the ride to his townhouse. So was his kiss retribution for her deceit or because he wanted her despite his fury? Either way, 'twas as addictive as ever and might be the last time he kissed her. Her pulse surging, she twined her arms about his neck and pressed her body closer.

After a timeless moment, Hawke wrenched their mouths apart and raised his head. "Enough, Wren. A public street is no place for our discussion."

She licked her swollen lips and nodded, a blush burning her neck. He was right. Several of his neighbors were gaping at them and tittering. No doubt the inevitable gossip would be worse after that public kiss.

Hawke shuddered and eyed her lips like an insatiable manticore eyeing a nightmara herd. Then he stiffened and dragged her up the steps of his townhouse and into his study. He jerked a chair before his desk before dropping into his own seat. His jaw tight, he cocked a brow and crossed his arms before his chest. "So tell me, Wren, why did you disguise yourself with a spell to seduce me?"

Still breathless from their kiss, Wren swallowed and studied him. How could she explain without further rousing his fury? Somehow she must for their unborn child.

She swallowed again, her heart skittering. And she must reveal she was pregnant too. Dear Goddess. She needed sustenance for this. "Could you ring for tea before we start? We shan't wish to be disturbed later."

Hawke nodded and uncrossed his arms to ring the bellpull. When Hobb arrived, he said, "A tea tray, please."

The butler left, and Wren licked her lips and dropped her gaze to her clenched hands. She'd wait until they had tea to explain. Perhaps food would sweeten Hawke's sternness. Hobb soon returned with a tea tray then left, and she served their tea and sweet biscuits.

Ignoring his food for once, Hawke narrowed his eyes at her. "Now that we've tea, explain why you disguised yourself to seduce me. Using a spell, no less. After the charmed pen, you always swore you'd never use another spell."

So she had. She winced and finished stirring sugar in her tea. "Because after learning your mother meant to see you married, I was desperate for one night in your arms. 'Twould be too late once you married." She croaked a laugh. "I never dreamt your parents would choose *me* as your betrothed."

Hawke grunted and ate his first sweet biscuit. "Neither did I. But *why* were you so desperate you risked a strong spell?"

Wren forced herself to sip her tea. Because she loved him, but she couldn't admit that with him so stern. "If disguised by a glamour spell, I assumed our friendship wouldn't change. And it had to be strong for you never to realize the truth. Plus, without a glamour spell, I'd no chance of attracting you."

Hawke's pale-blue eyes darkened as he leaned toward her. "No chance of attracting me? Wren, I've always wanted you.

Why else would I have kissed you on Longnight when we were fifteen?"

She stiffened, her head swirling. Impossible. If he'd truly wanted her, he wouldn't have only attempted one kiss eight years ago. And he wouldn't have kissed Kit first. "You were just testing your budding prowess."

Hawke ran a hand through his hair. "Testing my budding prowess? Where did you get that *ridiculous* idea?"

Wren glared at him and devoured a sweet biscuit. "Don't bother to lie. I know you kissed Kit the day before you kissed me. She told me *all* about it." Her heart had shattered that day.

Hawke recoiled with a shudder. "I've never kissed Kit nor wanted to. Goddess, 'twould be like kissing a harpy."

She stilled. He'd never kissed Kit? "But how did she know you meant to kiss me?"

A blush darkening his cheeks, Hawke shifted in his chair then gulped his tea. "She must have overhead me consulting my brothers."

Wren gaped at him. Why would he have done that? Everyone could see she loved Hawke, so he couldn't have believed she would reject him. "You consulted your brothers about *kissing me*?"

Hawke glanced away with a cough. "I was nervous about our first kiss. After Harvestfete, I read books, consulted my brothers, and plotted every move."

She clenched her teacup, her fingers whitening. He couldn't have spent three months planning that kiss. "You did not."

Hawke shrugged and met her gaze. "I did. Everything had to be perfect because I meant to marry you. But when you spurned my Longnight kiss, I assumed you didn't want *me*. So I buried my feelings, even from myself, and treated you as just a friend."

Her heart fluttered. His feelings? Did that mean he loved her as she loved him? "So if I'd accepted your kiss all those years ago, you truly would have married me?"

Hawke licked his lips with a nod. "I'd even planned our

wedding—a romantic affair on Longnight when we were eighteen."

Her stomach clenching, Wren rubbed her forehead. Goddess, he'd planned their wedding too? "If only I hadn't believed Kit's lies."

Hawke frowned at her. "Why did you?"

She shrugged and crumbled a sweet biscuit. "Kit is gorgeous, so any gentleman would want her." When Hawke snorted, she added, "Plus, I could tell you were hiding something—you'd been secretive and tense that entire Longnight season. So when Kit claimed you'd kissed her, I assumed that was why."

Hawke blushed. "No, I was simply nervous about kissing *you*."

Wren blinked at him. She'd never considered kissing her would make him nervous, but of course it would have, especially if he felt as she did. "If only I'd recognized that, we'd be married by now."

Hawke nodded. "And no doubt hip-deep in children." His eyes gleamed. "Especially considering how well we did without trying."

She winced as her stomach lurched. "You heard about the baby?" Oh, Goddess.

Hawke flashed a crooked grin. "Your mother mentioned your pregnancy when I went to see you after burning the enchanted bird."

Wren winced again. Hawke should have heard about their child from her. "Of course she did. I attempted to tell you yesterday, but the glamour spell thwarted me."

Hawke sighed and nodded. "I suspected as much."

Her mouth drying, she gulped a bracing breath. Now that the glamour spell had ended, she must explain. "When I disguised myself to seduce you, I never meant to become pregnant, but the child is yours, Hawke."

Hawke arched a brow. "Of course the child is mine."

Warmth filled her chest. He instantly believed that after all her lies? He *must* love her as she loved him.

Hawke shook his head. "But why did my contraceptive charm fail? It never has before."

Wren shifted in her chair and forced herself to meet his gaze. "Because regular contraceptive charms don't work around strong magic, so my glamour spell negated *both* of our contraceptive charms."

Hawke blinked, his fingers tapping the desk. "That's right, I remember my healer mentioning that."

She sighed. "I was so intent on seducing you I didn't listen when Healer Althea told me the same." She reached across the desk to grasp his hand. "I'm sorry, Hawke."

Hawke stared down at their joined hands. "'Tis fortunate your glamour spell negated our contraceptive charms. Otherwise, you never would have sought to confess the truth. I'd have hunted a will-o'-the-wisp forever."

Her throat tightened. Yes, she probably wouldn't have risked revealing she'd been Rowan and destroying their friendship. "I felt awful for deceiving you, but what else was I to do?"

Hawke narrowed his eyes at her. "Yet you still pretended to help by directing me to witch shops you knew would lead nowhere."

Wren swallowed and gnawed her lip. "I didn't *know*. I only hoped they would."

Hawke jerked his hand free. "Your continued deception hurts the most in all this. Why didn't you just tell me the truth when I began hunting you?"

Tears burned her eyes. "Because I thought you'd despise me for my deceitful seduction, and I couldn't bear to lose you. Friendship was better than nothing." She averted her face as her tears spilled down her cheeks.

Hawke leapt from his chair to wrap her in his arms. Kissing her hair, he led her to the sofa. "Please don't cry."

Wren buried her face in his neck, her tears flowing harder.

Goddess, she didn't deserve his tenderness after her lies. "I can't help it. Healer Althea said mercurial moods and crying are symptoms of pregnancy. And she was right—I've never cried so much in my life."

Hawke crooned and rubbed her back until her tears slowed to nothing. Then he drew back and kissed her forehead. "What other symptoms should I watch for?" He waggled his brows. "I hope they're less alarming than this one."

She chuckled as she wiped her face. Of course he would tease away her tears. "Right now, fatigue and nausea."

Hawke tucked hair behind her ear. "I suppose that's why you've been unwell the last month."

Wren grimaced, her chest squeezing. "Not entirely. Healer Althea said the glamour spell was draining me."

Hawke paled. "Thank the Goddess I burned it then." He shuddered then swallowed and smiled at her. "So when shall you begin to show? I know little about pregnancy."

She wrinkled her nose. Neither had she until her visit to Healer Althea two days ago. "I shouldn't show for a few months yet."

Hawke set his jaw. "Even so, we must marry soon. Then an early birth shan't be too obvious."

A lump clogging her throat, Wren caressed his face. "Hawke, I'm so sorry. I never meant to entrap you."

CHAPTER 58

*H*awke arched a brow, his heart softening at her remorse. She wouldn't have vanished so thoroughly if she'd meant to entrap him. "No, you meant to seduce me then vanish."

Wren winced and lowered her hand. "I didn't think you'd care. Your lovers never lasted long, so I assumed you'd simply find another. Meanwhile, I'd have memories to cherish when you wed another."

And what memories they were. He captured her hand and kissed her palm. "One night was impossible for us. Although your glamour spell prevented my conscious mind from realizing you were Rowan, my deepest self *knew* you were her. If you hadn't been Rowan, I wouldn't have been determined to find her."

A blush darkening her cheeks, Wren blinked at him. "I didn't anticipate that."

Hawke almost smiled. Likely not. His hunt had spoiled her meticulous plan for their lives to return to normal. No wonder she'd kept attempting to dissuade him.

Wren's blush deepened. "I also didn't anticipate sensual

memories intruding so often. At the most inappropriate moments too."

Tingling warmth flooded him. Like when meeting at Celeste's or helping her mount or dancing at the fete. "Once roused, our desire was impossible to repress. Although my inappropriate reactions confused me and made my head ache."

Her gaze dropping, Wren tugged her hand free. "I suspect the headaches were the glamour spell. I'm sorry again. No matter how desperate, I *never* should have bought that wretched spell."

Thank the Goddess she had. Hawke captured her chin and tilted her face to meet his. "I probably shouldn't admit it, since it shall encourage you to use spells to deceive me, but I'm glad you did."

Wren gaped at him. "You are?"

His pulse quickening, he nodded and caressed her lower lip with his thumb. "You called yourself a fool, but I was one too. I pursued any lady except you because I feared you'd reject me again. I never would have possessed the courage to kiss you without the enchanted bird. It freed me—us—to act without fear."

Wren kissed his thumb. "What a pair of fools we were."

His chest swelled. He released her chin to recapture her hand then flashed a crooked grin as he kissed her palm again. "Ideally suited, I suspect."

Wren curved her fingers against his jaw, her hazel eyes softening to a tender green. "Oh, Hawke, I do love you so. I always have."

Hawke kissed her fingers, his heart surging. She admitted her true reason for seducing him at last. "That's good because I love you too."

His body aching, he drew Wren into his arms and kissed her. Now that they'd talked, he could make love to her again. He devoured her mouth, her violet scent filling his lungs. Goddess, she was delectable. And his now. When she mewed and fisted her hands in his hair, he chuckled and lifted his head. "I should have realized love was the reason behind a shy virgin's seduction and a bored rakehell's obsession."

Wren licked her lips. "Yes, now more kisses." She yanked down his head and seized his mouth.

Heat flashing across his skin, Hawke rumbled as he returned her fierce kiss. He began tugging down her dress but halted at the creak of ripping fabric. No matter his hunger, he couldn't ravage her like a lusty satyr. She was pregnant, after all.

Her skin flushed, Wren giggled and began unlacing her dress. "Try not to ruin my dress. 'Tis the only one I possess at the moment."

He captured her hands. How was he to resist her? Yet he must restrain himself. He closed his eyes, resting his forehead against hers. "I want you, but perhaps we'd better stop. I don't want to hurt you or the baby."

Wren chuckled and nipped his lip. "Healer Althea said making love was perfectly safe."

His pulse surging, Hawke opened his eyes and raised his head. "Really?" Please, Goddess.

Wren nodded, eyeing him beneath her lashes. "And that pregnant ladies must rest often." She kissed the corner of his mouth. "I believe I require some now. Escort me upstairs?"

He swallowed. She required rest? He sighed and forced himself to release her. "You'd better go alone. If I joined you, we'd not rest."

Wren grinned at him. "I'm sure we'll rest *some*." She tilted her head. "Come on, or must I purchase another spell to convince you?"

"You'd better not." His body throbbing, Hawke swept her from the study. When they reached his chambers, he locked the door and waggled his brows at her. "If you don't want me ruining your only dress, you'd best remove it."

Wren arched a brow then hummed and pulled the pins from her hair. As her auburn hair tumbled down her back, she slanted him a coy smile. "Only if you do the same."

Heat flared in his chest. "Gladly." He ripped off his clothes and tossed them on the floor. He grinned and echoed her arched brow. "Well?"

Unlacing her dress and undergarments, Wren ran her gaze down his naked body. "Impatient, are we?"

Hawke shuddered, hunger coursing through his veins. Their night together *had* been over a month ago. "Immensely."

Wren giggled then slipped off her garments and draped them over a chair.

When she began removing her stockings, he hardened further. She was close enough to naked, and he needed her now. He gathered her in his arms and tossed her on the bed.

As he leapt after her, Wren attempted to slide away. "Wait, my stockings."

His body painfully hard, Hawke rolled Wren beneath him. At last. "Leave them." He seized her mouth then began making love to her, and she soon returned his caresses with equal passion.

After they both sobbed each other's names in explosive release, he cradled Wren against him with her head on his chest. He twined his fingers in her vibrant hair, warmth suffusing him. She was finally where she belonged.

Wren nuzzled him like an angelkitten greeting her pride. "May I remove my stockings now?"

Hawke chuckled as light expanded his chest. "If you like." When she didn't stir, he tweaked her hair. "Was that hypo-thetical?"

Wren sighed. "No, I'm just tired after our vigorous lovemak-ing." She poked him. "I require sustenance to restore my energy."

His heart squeezing, he slid from bed and donned his dressing gown. "Then I'll fetch some." When she began to follow, he scowled at her. "Don't leave that bed. I intend to keep you there some time yet—three days might be enough to start."

Wren arched her brows yet flopped back onto the bed. "Very well, but hurry back with that food."

After a narrow glance, Hawke strode downstairs. He found

Hobb and requested enough food for luncheon and dinner to be left at his door. He also instructed they weren't to be disturbed short of a fire. Then he hurried back to Wren.

Now stockingless but wearing one of his shirts, Wren smiled from the center of the bed. "I couldn't dine naked."

Tingling swamping him, he sat beside her and pulled her into his lap. She was adorable in his shirt. "I could."

Wren purred a chuckle. "That's because you're a rakehell."

A zing darted through him. Only because he'd thought he couldn't have her. "Not anymore." He kissed her neck.

Wren shivered, leaning into his kiss. "But wicked habits are the hardest to reform."

Trailing kisses up her neck, Hawke sighed at the knock on his door. Their food, no doubt. Kissing would have to wait until after they'd eaten. He released Wren to fetch the food. His servants had outdone themselves, and the food alone covered the tea table, so he set the drinks on the dressing table. Since she'd avoided sparkling wine recently, he poured them lymonade instead.

Wren accepted her glass then eyed the food and filled a small plate.

He scowled at her meager selection. She was eating for two, and that wasn't enough for even one. "Is that all you intend to eat?"

Wren met his gaze, her eyes narrow. "Healer Althea said small yet frequent meals shall ease my nausea."

His chest loosened. Her healer would know. He nodded then devoured his own meal. Once Wren finished eating, he carried her back to bed to make love again. They spent the rest of the day eating, talking, and making love until they collapsed into a dreamless slumber.

Late the following morning, Hawke started awake. Had yesterday been a dream? He glanced beside him and relaxed. Wren was still sleeping on her side of the bed. Unlike after the masquerade, she hadn't vanished.

He slid from bed and dressed in silence. He mustn't wake Wren—she needed extra rest after last night. He'd attend to correspondence until she woke. Over breakfast, they must discuss their marriage and informing their parents. He grimaced.

Hawke strode down to his study. When Hobb brought a kahve tray, he asked for dry toast to be sent up to Wren. Aragon had mentioned that helped Selena's nausea, so it should for Wren too. He began his correspondence, humming the Lantos tune he'd sung to Wren at the masquerade. Hopefully, she'd wake soon.

He'd finished half his correspondence when Hobb coughed and said, "The Countess of Blaine, my lord."

Hawke stiffened, his neck prickling. What was Kit doing here? Even though she was pursuing him, she'd never visited his home before. Did she mean to engender a compromising situation? He glared at her without rising. "Why are you here, Kit?"

CHAPTER 59

Wren awoke full of energy for the first time since before the masquerade. She stretched and wrinkled her nose. Doubtless because the glamour spell was no longer draining her. She glanced out the window and smiled. Although 'twas nearly luncheon, so she *should* be refreshed, even after her vigorous night with Hawke.

A blush burning her cheeks, she caressed his side of the bed. What a night it had been—even better than their first. Last night she'd been herself, and Hawke loved her as she loved him. Tingling flooded her. And as a former rakehell, he was adroit at physically expressing his love.

What plans would he have for today? She must find him. Wren bounced from bed, and her stomach quivered. Unfortunately, her nausea was still here. But a plate of dry toast sat on the bedside table. Hawke must have requested it—yet how had he known toast would help? She shrugged. No matter. She devoured the toast, and her stomach settled.

She grimaced as she slipped on yesterday's dress. 'Twasn't too creased since she'd draped in on a chair, but she'd prefer a fresh dress. She sighed. At some point, she must write her parents to request her things. Wonderful.

Wren strolled down to Hawke's study but halted at Kit's voice. What was *she* doing here? Fire flashed through her.

Then Hawke snapped, "Will you stop flirting with me and admit why you're here? If it's to engender a compromising situation, you might as well go. As I told you before, I'm not interested, so I'd never marry you."

"How rude." Kit sighed then replied, "I heard about Wren's most unfortunate pregnancy the other day. I imagine you're as shocked as I by her *scandalous* behavior. I wanted to come comfort you yesterday, but I'd previous engagements."

Of course Kit had come to needle Hawke about Wren's unexpected pregnancy. Wren lifted her chin and swept into the study. "Eavesdropping again?"

Standing before Hawke's desk, Kit swirled around to gawk at Wren. "What are *you* doing here? Shouldn't you be hiding in the country?"

Suppressing a giggle at Kit's shock, Wren glided to Hawke behind the desk. "Why would I do that?" She beamed at Hawke. "I'm *famished*. Are you ready for luncheon?"

An impish glint flickered in Hawke's eyes. "I'm famished too, but not for food." He pulled her into his arms.

Heat flaring in her veins, Wren returned his hungry kiss. She purred and threaded her fingers in his inky-brown hair. She could kiss him forever.

Kit interjected, "What's going on here?"

Wren giggled as Hawke grumbled and raised his head. He'd forgotten about their audience too. If only Kit had noticed that and left.

His arm remaining about Wren, Hawke turned to Kit with arched brows. "I'm kissing my betrothed."

At his satisfied drawl, Wren's heart fluttered. Yes, she was. She beamed and caressed his face.

Kit's gaze darted between Hawke and Wren, her eyes wide. "But what about the baby?"

Hawke flashed a crooked grin. "I'm elated Wren is carrying my child already. It took Aragon a year to get Selena pregnant."

As Kit gaped at them, Wren tsked and poked his chest. "'Tisn't a contest." She turned to Kit, her eyes narrowing. "How did you hear about my pregnancy?"

Kit tossed her head. "Your mothers discussed it at the sirenic play the day before yesterday."

Wren and Hawke exchanged a glance. Her neck prickled. So Kit had all of yesterday to gossip about it. "And who did you reveal my pregnancy to during your engagements yesterday?"

Kit moued. "Just people who I felt could help you through your difficult time."

Hawke's lips tightened. "Who *exactly*, Kit?"

Kit shrugged. "Elise and Edouard at breakfast. Aragon and Selena when I attempted to visit Hawke's parents, who were out. The Westons and their granddaughters at Lady Winston's picnic. Then Mr. Winston accompanied me to court, where I spoke to King Devon, who was escorting Lady Annalise."

Wren almost snorted. How thorough. No doubt the rumors of her pregnancy had reached the hermits of court by now.

Kit examined her nails. "Everyone was most scandalized— except Lady Annalise. She only chuckled and said she expected a wedding announcement between you and Hawke within a fortnight."

When Hawke frowned at that, Wren shrugged. "At the fete, Lady Annalise mentioned she'd seen us together at the masquerade, but *she* never gossips."

Hawke muttered in her ear, "How fortunate 'twas her rather than Kit."

Very. Wren wrinkled her nose. The past month would have been even more fraught if court had known she was Rowan. She leaned into his embrace.

Kit glanced between them, and her mouth crimped. "I feel as if I'm intruding. I should leave you to—whatever."

Hawke jerked a nod. "We'd appreciate that." His lips flat, he glared at Kit. "But before you leave, explain why you lied to Wren about kissing me when we were fifteen."

Wren tilted her head. Why had he bothered to ask that? Kit had obviously been jealous of his interest in her.

Kit stilled then fluttered her lashes at him. "'Twas so long ago, I'm afraid I don't recall."

When Hawke stiffened, Wren laid a hand over his heart to soothe him. Then she arched her brows at Kit. "Somehow I doubt that. Your memory is better than a dragon's." And dragons never forgot anything.

Her jaw tightening, Kit glanced away. "Fine. You possessed everything I didn't—adoring parents, a fortune, and a boy who loved you above all else. And after a disappointment, I couldn't resist making you as miserable as I." Kit snickered. "Although I never expected you two to take *eight years* to resolve matters."

Wren softened. For all her sultry beauty, Kit had never enjoyed the love Wren had. And she'd been trapped with her drunkard father back then, so of course she'd been miserable. "We were all very young." She paused and smiled at Kit. "I forgive you."

Kit glared. "Of course you do. You're *perfect*, after all." She swirled and swept from the study.

His arm still about Wren, Hawke glowered after Kit. "You're more magnanimous than I. If she were a gentleman, I'd challenge her to a duel."

Wren shuddered. Thank the Goddess Kit was a lady then. She caressed his face to calm him. "I can afford to be. I've everything I ever wanted, while she has nothing." She nudged him with her hip and winked. "The only thing to complete my life would be luncheon."

Hawke relaxed and kissed her nose before ringing the bellpull. "I'll see to that then." Once Hobb arrived, he said to the butler, "We'd like luncheon."

Hobb inclined his head. "Cook has a full luncheon prepared and waiting in the family dining room. She thought you'd need it after last night, especially Miss Keyes. Pregnant ladies require extra sustenance."

She blushed while Hawke chuckled and asked, "So word has spread to the servants' quarters already?"

"Of course." Hobb bowed and strode from the study.

Wren sighed as Hawke escorted her to the family dining room. "Thanks to Kit, I doubt a soul in Ormas doesn't know about my pregnancy. Even the nightmara delegation must be gossiping." How embarrassing.

Hawke grimaced while he served her watercress soup. "Our parents must be in a dither."

She shuddered as her stomach tensed. Yes, they had been. She swallowed and sipped her soup. "They'll settle once they realize you're the father." Hopefully.

Hawke shook his head while he served her braised rabbit with green cucurbit. "Mother shan't settle until we're married."

Wren eyed him and nibbled on a roll. "But it shall be a scandal for months." Her skin tightened. A scandal that was entirely her fault. "Do you mind?"

Hawke shrugged while devouring his braised rabbit. "Not particularly. Besides, you carrying my child proves to other gentlemen you're *mine*."

Blushing at his growl, she began her braised rabbit to hide her smile. "So primitive. I should be annoyed."

Hawke winked then waggled his brows. "Yet I see you aren't."

Wren blushed harder. Because she felt the same possessiveness about him. She echoed him, "Not particularly."

His pale-blue eyes darkening, Hawke leaned over and kissed her.

Her fork clattered on the table as she kissed him back and her pulse surged. Goddess, how she loved his addictive kisses.

Hawke wrenched their mouths apart. "Enough. We've another course and dessert to eat. Can't have Cook scolding me for depriving a pregnant lady."

Wren giggled and finished her braised rabbit so Hawke wouldn't get scolded.

As he served her krab-stuffed chicken and mashed tubers, Hawke arched a brow. "I assume you'd prefer a small wedding."

She grimaced, nibbling on her mashed tubers. Definitely. "Yes, so we mustn't allow our mothers to plan it." They'd end up with a grandiose affair.

Hawke glanced at her as he toyed with his chicken. "How about a bloodbinding? I'd like one."

Her heart leapt. Only the most devoted sought bloodbindings. With their life forces irrevocably bound, they could only have children with each other and would likely die together. And Hawke wanted one. She beamed. "Me too."

Hawke relaxed then flashed a crooked grin. "Now we simply must decide how to tell our mothers."

Wren winced and finished her chicken. "I say we write them letters then lock the door until we've arranged the wedding."

Hawke chuckled as he served her shokolat mousse. "A sensible plan. Sounds like everything is settled."

She cocked her head, warmth blooming in her chest. "Not quite." When his brow furrowed, she grinned and devoured her mousse. "You never actually *asked* me to marry you. All ladies, even pregnant ones, deserve a proposal."

CHAPTER 60

*H*awke set down his spoon without tasting his shokolat mousse, his chest squeezing. He hadn't proposed, had he? He leapt and pulled Wren into his arms. Warmth flooded him. "Marry me, Wren. I've loved you since before I knew what love was and can't imagine living without you."

Wren beamed and cradled his face in her palms. "I'd be delighted to marry you, Hawke, for I've loved you just as long."

His heart surging, he captured her mouth in a ravenous kiss. After her shokolat mousse, she tasted even more delectable than usual. His body tightened. After a moment, he raised his head with a crooked grin. "*Now* that everything is settled, how about a game?"

Wren giggled and arched a brow. "A wicked game, I suppose."

"Of course." Hawke winked and whisked her to the games-room. He'd his reputation as a former rakehell to maintain, after all. "I thought we could play elementball."

Wren pursed her lips. "*Elementball*, really?"

He waggled his brows as heat flared in his veins. "A version with special rules. Wicked ones."

Wren's hazel eyes darkened, and she waved a hand. "Go on."

Hawke smiled. Just like when they were children, she couldn't resist his ideas. He spun the elementball wheel to activate the table. "For each point lost, you remove a piece of clothes."

Wren purred a laugh as the black slate top dissolved into a tangled forest. "A wicked game, indeed. Lovely." She cocked her head then grasped the brown elementball. "I'll take earth."

He grinned. How perfect. His former dryad playing earth in a forest scene. He seized the red elementball. "I'll take fire." Since he burned for her. He chuckled and offered her the white goalball. "And because I'm a gentleman, I'll allow you to roll first, even though you've the strongest element in this scene."

Wren's mouth twitched as she placed the goalball in the center of the table. "Only because you're eager to strip. Lusty satyr."

His pulse quickening, Hawke licked his lips as he strolled to the south goal. "I recall you saying dryads loved satyrs."

Wren fluttered her lashes at him while gliding to the north goal. "They do."

His body hardened as she bent to roll her elementball into the goalball. This game would be thrilling and torturous at once. When the goalball sailed toward his goal, he didn't move to block it. "Oops."

Wren giggled as he tossed aside his morning coat. "This game shan't take long if you don't defend your goal."

Exactly. Hawke winked at her, hunger throbbing beneath his skin. He placed the goalball in the center of the table and rolled his elementball to continue their game.

Midway through, he was only wearing trousers and Wren her shift when the door burst open after a scuffle. Although she squeaked and dove behind a chair, he turned to face the intruders, his jaw clenching. Damnation, he was a few rolls away from making love to Wren again.

Mother swept into the gamesroom with Lady Keyes trailing

behind her. Mother's gaze ran over his half-clothed state, her lips flattening. "I'm sorry to interrupt your game with your ladylove, but 'tis urgent."

Hawke sighed. And about Wren, no doubt. He glanced past their mothers to Hobb, who hovered by the door. The earlier scuffle must have been his attempt to block their mothers. "You may go, Hobb."

The butler relaxed with a sigh then shut the door and fled.

He sprawled in the chair concealing Wren. How could he convince their mothers to leave without revealing her? He arched a brow at Mother. "What's so urgent?"

Mother grimaced and sighed. "Wren—"

Tears shining in her eyes, Lady Keyes interjected, "Never returned home last night and sent no word. Have you heard from her?"

Hawke forced himself to remain relaxed. He must protect Wren from their mothers. "No."

Lady Keyes paled, her tears sliding down her cheeks. "Where can she be? I already checked the orphanage, but Kiera said she'd left before luncheon yesterday. Goddess, what if Wren has been kidnapped—or worse?"

He tensed at Lady Keyes's distress. But he couldn't reveal Wren if she chose to remain hidden.

Wren sighed behind him, her shift rustling as she rose. "Here I am, Mother."

Her tears halting, Lady Keyes gaped at her daughter over his head. "Wren, come out from behind that chair."

Hawke almost laughed when Wren coughed and replied, "I'd rather not. I'm not dressed."

While Lady Keyes sputtered, Mother glared at him. "Why didn't you admit she was here?"

He shrugged. Because his first loyalty was to Wren. "Lady Keyes asked if I'd heard from her, not if I'd seen her."

Mother's eyes narrowed. "A specious distinction. Explain. Now."

His mouth twitching at her scold, Hawke arched a brow. "This conversation would fare better in the morning room after Wren and I repair our appearance."

Mother sighed. "Very well, but if you two don't appear shortly, we'll return to fetch you. Come, Diana." She grasped Lady Keyes's elbow and dragged the older lady from the gamesroom.

He glanced up at Wren, whose scarlet face was just visible above the chair. His throat clenched. Their mother's intrusion had embarrassed her. To hearten her, he waggled his brows and drawled, "Not *quite* how we planned telling them."

Wren shuddered then straightened from her half-crouch. "Unfortunately not. Come on, I don't want your mother to fulfill her threat." After they'd dressed, she smoothed her hair and shook her skirt. "These wrinkles shan't come out without pressing. I should have been more careful during our game."

Hawke eyed her and took her arm, tingling suffusing him. "You look fine." Better than fine—deliciously rumpled.

Wren grimaced as he escorted her from the gamesroom. "For our fathers, yes, but not our mothers."

He halted and kissed Wren in the middle of the hall. Who cared what their mothers thought? Once she sighed and returned his kiss, he swept her into the morning room. He sat on the sofa with Wren in his lap. "Well?"

Their mothers blinked at them, then Mother pursed her lips and said, "Intimate for a couple refusing to marry."

Hawke shrugged and pulled Wren against his chest. He smiled when she cuddled against him. His kiss had heartened her. "A misunderstanding. We've since discussed it and decided to marry. We love each other, and my child deserves a father."

Lady Keyes gaped at them. "Your child? But Wren said you weren't the father."

He tensed. Why had Wren deceived her mother about that?

He relaxed when Wren took his hand and replied, "No,

Mother, I merely refused to name him. I hadn't told Hawke yet, so I couldn't discuss it with others."

Mother and Lady Keyes exchanged a glance, then Mother grinned and said, "We must plan the wedding at once."

Wren blanched, so Hawke squeezed her hand and forced a smile. He'd protect her from their meddling. "No, Wren and I shall handle that."

Mother began, "But—"

He glared at her. He'd not allow her to usurp their plans. "No, Mother. We'll send you an invitation in a few days."

Mother and Lady Keyes exchanged another glance, then Mother pursed her lips and replied, "Fine."

Their mothers rose, and Lady Keyes beckoned Wren. "We must return home now."

Hawke suppressed a sigh. No doubt their mothers would keep them apart until their wedding day. 'Twas only proper, and to avoid upsetting her elderly parents, Wren would return to their townhouse. Perhaps he could seize a kiss before she did.

However, Wren shook her head and didn't rise from his lap. "I'll remain here."

Lady Keyes began, "But—"

Wren wrinkled her nose. "Thanks to Kit, all of Ormas knows I'm pregnant, so living with Hawke for a few days before our wedding shan't cause much more gossip."

Light expanding his chest, he chuckled and hugged her closer. "And once we marry, gossip shall fade if we remain suitably dull."

Mother coughed, her lips twitching. "Are you sure you can manage that?"

Hawke flashed a crooked grin. "I daresay Wren shall curb me." Not that she'd need to.

Wren giggled and poked his chest. "An onerous task, to be sure."

Lady Keyes laughed as she shook her head. "Since you aren't returning home, I'll send you Abby and some fresh gowns."

Wren stilled. "I'd appreciate the gowns, but I'll find a new maid." She shrugged. "Abby was a suitable maid for a young girl, and her loyalty shall always be to you and Father."

He eyed Wren. *Abby* must have told Wren's parents about her pregnancy. She'd not refuse her longtime maid otherwise.

Lady Keyes nodded. "Very well. We'll wait to receive your invitation."

Mother sighed. "'Tis odd to no longer have your wedding to arrange."

As Wren embraced her mother, Hawke embraced his and waggled his brows to tease her. "You could always arrange Mel's instead. All you require is a dispensation from the Goddess."

Mother glanced away and shrugged. "Hmm, yes."

He blinked. Clearly she was already attempting to match Mel. Amazing.

After their mothers swept from the morning room, Wren turned to him, her eyes wide. "Do you suppose your mother means to match Mel with Kit?"

Hawke grimaced. Probably, knowing Mother. He shook his head then drew Wren into his arms. "Fortunately, her meddling no longer concerns us. Shall we return to our game?"

Wren chuckled and threaded her arms about his neck. "You simply want to seduce me."

His body tightening, he feathered a kiss against her lips. "Always."

Wren nipped his lip. "Fortunate for you, I love when you seduce me."

Warmth filling his chest, Hawke swept her back to the gamesroom. "I love you, Wren."

Wren squeezed his arm. "Took you long enough to realize that." She pulled down his head for a lingering kiss. "But I love you too. I don't sing Lantos for just anyone." She began humming the waltz from the masquerade.

His heart quickened. Goddess, how he loved her. He joined her on the chorus,

"Love me under the sky,
Sparkling with stars and the moon so high,
And I'll be able to fly."

WANT MORE?

Sign up for my newsletter for a bonus epilogue about the Longnight Wren and Hawke's family gets unexpected magical gifts as well as other exclusive stories and book extras, new book announcements, give-aways, and more.

And order the next book The Nightmara Affair about Kiera and Devon today! Keep reading to learn more about the next book in the Calatini Tales.

LIKE THE ENCHANTED BIRD?

Please consider writing a review. Reviews truly help spread the word about the titles you love.

THE NIGHTMARA AFFAIR

*I*n the kingdom of Calatini, an enchanted ballgown *and a magical evening can change everything.*

Orphanage matron Kiera didn't expect that sneaking into a masquerade wearing a bespelled ballgown would lead to a magical evening with the king, but for King Devon, it couldn't be more perfect. Kiera is intelligent, compassionate, and strong, everything he longs to find in a wife... and a queen.

And Devon needs a queen now: a generations-old treaty with the nightmara herds is due for renewal, and the matriarchal nightmara deal only with women. Yet when he asks Kiera to marry him, she can't believe he's serious—he's the king and far above her station. So to prove his love and win her heart, Devon convinces Kiera to act as his betrothed to negotiate with the nightmara for the good of the kingdom.

But once the treaty is signed, Kiera is certain their love affair will come to an end. She'll return to her life at the orphanage, and Devon will find a suitable noblewoman to marry. Because surely a king couldn't really marry a poor commoner like Kiera... right?

THE NIGHTMARA AFFAIR is a warm-hearted Cinderella romance with a steel-willed heroine and a noble, kind hero. This rags-to-riches love story is part of the Calatini Tales series of Regency-inspired historical fantasy romance novels and is perfect for T. Kingfisher fans.

*WANT MORE? Order **The Nightmara Affair** today!*

CALATINI TALES

The enchanting Calatini Tales includes...

The Spellbinding Courtship (Book 0.5)
The Enchanted Bird (Book 1)
The Nightmara Affair (Book 2)
The Secret Soulbond (Book 3)
The Goddess's Illusion (Book 4)
The Sun-Nymph Bride (Book 5)
The Beast Curse (Book 6)
The Lethe Elixir (Book 7)

ABOUT KATHERINE

A lifelong creator of her own bedtime stories, **Katherine Dotterer** writes cozy tales of fantasy romance inspired by Regency England. Born and raised in Maryland, she still lives there in an almost cottage surrounded by trees. When not writing, she enjoys reading anything she can find, singing in local choruses, hiking in nearby parks, watching the wildlife outside her windows, and cuddling with her cats. Visit her at Katherine-Dotterer.com to learn about her book releases, read her many book extras, and sign up for her newsletter.